"YOU'VE NEVER KNOWN A MAN," he said in a tone that told me I had touched a nerve.

"Ha! So *you* believe."

He pulled me into his arms. "Shall I show you?" His face above mine was hard with anger.

"No—I don't . . ."

His mouth came down on mine, covering it, stifling the protest in my throat. I beat at him, making incoherent sounds, but he held me fast, his strong thin lips moving back and forth, bruising, hurtful.

Suddenly he released me, pulling my arms away. For a moment I swayed, but he made no attempt to steady me, standing a little apart, breathing heavily.

"You vixen!" he accused bitterly. Then he turned and strode away.

Fiona Harrowe

PASSION'S CHILD

FAWCETT GOLD MEDAL • NEW YORK

A Fawcett Gold Medal Book
Published by Ballantine Books

Library of Congress Catalog Card Number: 82-90887

ISBN 0-449-12392-8

Manufactured in the United States of America

First Ballantine Books Edition: April 1983

CHAPTER

ONE

I STOOD on the cobblestoned walk and looked up at Number 25 with a speculative eye. A two-story house, it had a gabled attic and an openworked, iron-grilled gallery, nothing grand or extraordinary, a dwelling much like many commonly found in the middle-class districts of New Orleans in the 1850's.

Hesitating, undecided, I wondered if I should ascend the stone steps, knock on the door, and make inquiries. But what if it was the wrong house? The people inside might resent my intrusion, might think my request a little odd.

I was still debating when an open phaeton carrying two women pulled up to the curb. Both wore plumed riding hats and satin gowns, one of rainbow-shot blue, the other a dazzling orange with black velvet bows up the front. As they were handed down by the Negro driver, the one in blue glanced in my direction.

"Pardon, ladies," I said, approaching, "but I am trying to find a woman by the name of Angélica O'Neil. Could you tell me if she lives at Number Twenty-five?"

They exchanged a look. The woman in the shot blue shrugged. "Never heard of her."

Both were young and though not particularly attractive blooming with health, each having rosy cheeks and red lips.

1

Paint, of course. But in those days I was ignorant of such fakery and thought their lovely complexions a gift of nature.

The orange-gowned woman turned to her companion. "Do you think Kate might know?"

"Probably. She's on to everyone in the neighborhood."

"Come inside," the woman in orange said. "I'll see if Kate's at home."

I followed the two up the stone steps. The woman in blue unlocked the door and ushered me into a vestibule.

"Wait here," she said. Then the pair of them trailed up a staircase, disappearing into the shadowed upper reaches, leaving behind the echo of rustling skirts and the strong, sweet scent of frangipani.

I peered around with curiosity. The vestibule, though windowless and dim, glowed with color. A thick ruby-red carpet covered the floor; ruby-red portieres hung along one wall; and on the other, ruby-red roses ran riot over flocked white wallpaper. Across the vestibule the bronze statue of a naked woman holding a lamp aloft guarded the flight of red-carpeted stairs.

The statue fascinated me. I had never seen one like it. At home a marble bust of Shakespeare graced our piano in the parlor, and I had once observed a Winged Victory in a French Quarter garden—fully clothed, however. I longed to get closer and examine this nude bronze female, but the thought of being found at it constrained me.

I stood where I had been left, waiting for one or the other of the brightly gowned women to return. The quiet house ticked and creaked with small noises, but none sounded like approaching footsteps. Had the two women forgotten me? Where were they? Should I shout? (Unladylike.) Call? (But what?)

I had just decided to rap on the oaken door when a light, tinkling laugh floated down from above. I went to the foot of the stairs and, craning my neck, looked up into a host of shifting shadows. Suddenly a voice called, "Come on, then!" Thinking the words were meant for me, I threw the naked lamp-woman one last furtive glance and began to ascend. When I reached the first landing I hesitated, peering down a short carpeted corridor with closed doors on either side. No voices greeted me, only a baffling, hushed quiet.

Should I go on? Wait?

Sunlight fell in dust-moted shafts from a high window upon the opposite wall, which was hung with a large oil painting. Moving closer on tiptoe I examined it. One of the figures in the picture was bizarre, half man, half beast, and between legs that resembled the hind ones of a goat, grew a fleshy, rodlike protuberance. At the feet (or hooves) of this creature reclined a naked woman, her arms outstretched as if reaching to embrace or grasp this peculiar appendage. There was something about the picture that I found faintly repellent, yet fascinating.

I have to smile now when I think of my naïveté. At sixteen I knew little of the real world, of what went on between men and women behind closed doors. At home any discussion remotely relating to sex, lovemaking, reproduction, whether human or animal, was strictly forbidden. My novels, of which I was an omnivorous reader, spoke only of embraces and kisses with the implication that such pastimes frequently resulted in babies. The more lurid tales—strictly forbidden and smuggled home—told of women who sold their bodies, but exactly *how* they sold them was never made clear. I hadn't the foggiest notion of what a man looked like with his clothes off and quite truthfully had never even thought of imagining it.

The musical laugh came again, this time closer. I turned toward the sound and saw a door slightly ajar. Behind it voices murmured, then fell silent.

I had my hand poised to knock when a woman said, "Oh, stop...!" I don't know why that should have stayed me, but instead of knocking I gave the door a little shove and it swung open on oiled hinges.

The scene I confronted froze me. A large man puffing on a cigar stood looking down at a man and woman on the silk-hung bed. All three wore nothing, not a *shred* of clothing. And to my astonishment both men sported the same rodlike growths between their legs as the goat-man in the picture.

"God Almighty, are you going to get on with it or aren't you?" the cigar-smoker grumbled.

"Oh, hush up," the man on the bed said as he hoisted himself atop the woman.

She giggled and spread her legs. I couldn't see her face, just the legs and the pink soles of her feet.

"Give us a kiss," she coaxed.

The man stretched out and I heard a loud smacking sound.

"Wheeee!" she exclaimed after a moment. "But you've got a crackin' big one, haven't you?"

"The better to please you with, my dear."

The man with the cigar guffawed. "Wait till you feel mine. It'll tickle your tonsils."

The man on the bed was moving up and down now, his buttocks rising and falling. The woman moaned and whimpered.

My stomach twisted sharply. I felt hot, excited, prickly skinned and dry tongued. Suddenly a hand clamped down on my shoulder and another whipped across my mouth, stifling the exclamation that rose to my lips.

Dragged back into the corridor and whirled around, I found myself looking into the angry eyes of a grossly fat woman. Her hair, a nimbus of orange frizz, rose around a dead-white face daubed on each cheek with a spot of red the size of a dollar. She was dressed in a dark purple velvet gown, cut low in the bodice to reveal the upper halves of pillowy breasts. As she gazed at me, the look in her eyes turned from anger to astonishment.

"Angelica! Angelica O'Neil! My God!"

It gave me such a queer turn to be called by my mother's name, I could not utter a single word to deny it.

I never knew my mother.

My father, a reticent man, taciturn by long habit on most any subject, became positively mute whenever I questioned him about her. I could learn nothing beyond her name, Angelica O'Neil, that she was a lady, a native of New Orleans, and that she had died giving birth to me. Naturally I was curious. But there was no one to ask. Apparently she had been an orphan with no living relatives, and the people who might have known her before my time were either as mum as Papa or were not speaking to us at all.

I was living with Aunt Maude when I found out about my mother's past. Maude was not really my aunt or related to me in any way, at least as far as she would admit, but she preferred me calling her "Aunt," so I did. She was a small woman, almost tiny, with a handspan waist, a plain face, and graying reddish hair worn in an uncompromising, unfashionable knob atop her head. For all her diminutive size, however, Maude Briscoe carried herself with the sort of staunch authority that made strong men and women (or willful girls like myself) think twice before crossing her.

I had been left in Aunt Maude's care some eight years earlier, in 1848, shortly after gold was discovered at Sutter's Mill in California and Papa decided to try his luck there. That in itself was a contradiction, for Papa was anything but an impulsive man. Reserved, a creature of habit, always dressed impeccably in tailored clothes of somber hue, he led a well-ordered life as predictable as sunrise and sunset. Nevertheless, off he had gone to join the stampeding gold-hungry mob in its rush to the Far West. I suppose the treasure-trove madness then sweeping the country caught him unaware, or perhaps he was simply unhappy—he had the look of a sad man—and wanted a change.

He did not discover gold, and instead of lingering in the various primitive mining camps, hoping to make a strike, he had settled in San Francisco and set up the business that he knew best, a brokerage firm, this one dealing in flour and foodstuffs. He wrote to me over the years, reminding me that his intention was to send for me eventually. But somehow the time had never been right. Always there was some reason for the delay: the lawlessness of the city; the lack of proper society, reputable schools, or decent houses. I missed him, but distance had tempered the pain of our parting and the years had dimmed the first wild longing to join him.

One day in Mr. Popkin's dancing class I met Victoria Bridewell. Rumor had it that she had spent a short time at the Ursuline convent school before being asked to leave and that she had also been booted out of a female academy in Georgia. The reasons for her expulsions were a mystery which Victoria herself did not choose to dispel.

She was not a pretty girl. Her mouth was too wide, her blue-gray eyes too prominent, her figure flat-chested and thin. Only her hair, a lovely honey color, thick and silky, worn in a cascade of curls down past her shoulders, saved her from plainness. Victoria was an incessant chatterer. She knew everyone in the city and everything about them. Her stories of the

outer world from which I had been sheltered all my life, first
in my father's house, then at Aunt Maude's, fascinated me.
Victoria brought into my dull life the excitement of forbidden
knowledge; and I listened to her tales of scandal with something
close to awe. We soon became fast friends.

One Saturday afternoon, Mr. Popkin gave a tea dance to
which he invited boys. "Real *boys*," Victoria said derisively.
"Imagine! Those children from Brigg's Academy—boys!"

They were all younger than we, not much to look at, but
they were *males* and a few were fairly good dancers.

It was after this dance that Victoria and I had a falling out.
She had offered me a ride in her carriage, and we had no sooner
started for home when she turned to me in anger and accused
me of taking her partner away from her. I had a hard time
remembering whom she meant, since I had danced with so
many.

"You *do* know. The tall one, the one with the cowlick!"

"Him? Victoria—how can you say I took him away when
I did nothing of the sort!"

"You did! And don't you dare shout at me!"

"You're the one who's shouting!"

She brought her face close to mine in an ugly grimace. "You
are exactly like your mother."

I drew back. "My mother is dead. How could you know
anything about her?"

"I know plenty. She was a whore."

"What?" I was so naïve I did not know the meaning of the
word.

"A lady of the evening, stupid. A scarlet woman."

My face burned. I knew what "scarlet woman" meant. It
had been explained to me by Victoria herself (although not the
how of it) one morning on our way to church when we had
been passed by an open barouche carrying three garishly dressed
women.

"You're wrong, dead wrong," I retorted. "My mother was
a lady. She died when I was born."

"Your mother was a whore—everyone knows it. Why do
you think you and your father have never been invited to the
houses in the Garden District? And what about your father's
people? Do you ever hear from *them*? No. I didn't think so.

It's because your father jilted my mother and married a whore."

"My father was engaged to your mother?"

"Yes. They were supposed to be married, but then he went back on his word and left Mama in the lurch, almost on the church steps."

"Who told you that?" I whispered.

"I keep my ears open," she said. "People talk. They're still talking about it. Your mother was a whore—and she isn't dead. She's alive and, what's more, working at her profession."

"I don't believe it! You're lying! You're jealous and you made up the lie."

"Call me a liar again and I'll tear your hair out!"

At this point the carriage halted at my door. But I could not get out. Trembling with anger and shock, I was unprepared to go in and face eagle-eyed Aunt Maude. She would guess something was wrong, and I knew I could not bring myself to tell her what it was.

Victoria had sunk back on the cushions, and was chewing her lip, watching me.

"You are sure?" I asked after a long silence

"Cross my heart and hope to die."

"You're not saying this because you are mad?"

"No. I crossed my heart, didn't I? Your mother is alive. I heard someone say she's at a house on St. John Street."

When I went to bed that night my mind was swarming with a host of mysteries. My mother a scarlet woman, a Jezebel, a fallen angel? Had my father known? Aunt Maude? Why hadn't anyone told me before this? Victoria said my mother was still alive. How could it be? Perhaps long ago, after I was born, my mother and father had quarreled and she had run away. Perhaps he believed her dead, her death falsely reported. Perhaps, perhaps. All sorts of stories danced in my head, but when dawn came I was certain of only one thing.

I had to find her.

I told no one of my plan, not Aunt Maude and not Victoria.

So it was I came to be on St. John Street, confronted now by a rotund woman with frizzy orange hair, who had called me by mother's name.

CHAPTER

TWO

"*BUT NO*," *the fat woman said, pulling me away* from the door. "You can't be Angelica. Too young." Her eyes narrowed. "Who *are* you? How did you get in?" She jerked my arm. "Well, *say* something! Who sent you?"

"No—no one. I came—you see—I'm Angelica's daughter, Carmella Hastings. And I'm looking for my mother. I thought perhaps—someone said she might be here."

The fat woman gave me another squint-eyed look. "Angelica's daughter..." She studied me again. "Hmmm. Could be. Come below."

I followed her down to the vestibule. She opened the oaken door and led me into a small dining room where a burly man in shirt-sleeves sat at the table polishing silver.

He looked up at us, an ugly individual with black spiky whiskers and a patch over one eye, the other eye glowering in bloodshot moroseness. "New girl?" he sneered.

"Indeed not! This is a visitor—Miss Hastings."

He did not rise to acknowledge the introduction, but sat there scowling. "Ain't we gettin' hoity-toity. 'Visitor,'" he mimicked.

"Hold your tongue, Sam Halstead!" the stout woman ordered. "You may be my husband, but this is *my* house. Come along, Miss. Pay him no mind."

At the other end of the dining room she opened another

door, the upper half paned in tinted glass, and ushered me into a bedroom—a boudoir, I suppose one would call it.

"Might as well have a little light," said the woman I presumed to be Mrs. Halstead, pushing aside a heavy purple portiere.

Every inch of wallpaper had been hung with either a painting or a gilt-edged mirror. The pictures were much the same as the one upstairs: nude, pink-fleshed women gamboling with goatlike men.

With a groan Mrs. Halstead sank down on a high-backed wing chair and put her feet up on a stool. They were surprisingly small feet for such a large person and each was encased in a mauve slipper atwinkle with gold braid and crystal beads.

"That man's a thorn in my side," she said. "I took him in like I've done before when he's come out of the clink—prison, my dear, yes, prison. You'd think he'd be grateful, wouldn't you?"

"Why—yes." I wondered what Sam Halstead had done to have gone to prison.

"Not him. But it's no use going on about it."

She eased her body to a more comfortable position. "So you are Angelica's daughter. Be a dear and pour me a drink—over there on the sideboard. A finger of whiskey."

I found her request as extraordinary as her appearance. At Aunt Maude's, women might toy with a small glass of sherry or sip a little Madeira but they would never dream of asking for whiskey.

I poured the amber liquor from a cut-glass decanter, guessing how much a finger might be. When she took it, she scanned my face.

"The likeness gives me goose pimples. The same dark, almost black, shiny hair and the widow's peak! The skin, too, smooth as cat's cream with just a smidgen of pink in the cheeks. Angelica never had to use paint, you know. And the eyes—my God I didn't think two people could be blessed with such black lashes and such deep blue eyes. Spooky, I'd say. Sit down, my dear." She indicated a brown upholstered chair.

I sat while she gulped the whiskey, downing all of it with a single draught.

"Kate's my Christian name. Kate Halstead. Your mama knew me as Katie Dow. I heard that she had died."

"Oh, no," I corrected. "I've been told that my mother is alive—that she had come to St. John Street..." My voice trailed off.

"Come back *here?*" she asked in astonishment.

I linked my hands, squeezing them tightly together. "I think—I think she quarreled with my father and—and ran away."

"But my dear child, I haven't seen Angelica since she left with Mr. Hastings."

"Oh." I looked down, trying to hide my disappointment.

After a few moments Mrs. Halstead asked in a kindly voice, "How old were you, Miss Carmella, when you think your mother—er—was supposed to have run away?"

"They told me she died when I was born. That was sixteen years ago. You see, I know nothing of her. My father—well, he never spoke about Mama, but then I found out.... And I want so much to find her. Did you know her well?"

"Indeedy. I knew your grandmother too. She was a Spanish lady."

"Spanish?"

Immediately my mind took off, picturing an arched-nosed aristocrat wearing a black lace mantilla and languidly waving a fan.

"Yes, Spanish. Marguerita." She rolled her *r*'s. "Your grandpapa, however, was an Irishman, a man of the sea."

"A captain?"

"I don't rightly know. But his ship went down off Portugal and he was drowned. Angelica was a tiny baby then. Poor Marguerita, forced to hire herself out as a laundress. My dear—would you kindly pour me another finger of whiskey?"

Glass in hand, she continued. "Yes, I remember Marguerita. Worked herself into an early grave. A pity. And there was the tyke Angelica all alone in the world. Such a sweet little thing. We couldn't allow her to go into an orphanage, could we? Of course not. She was a good child and so grateful. When she turned fifteen she offered to take the place of one of the girls who had left. But Mrs. Stock—she owned the house in those days—would not have it. She thought of Angelica as her own daughter."

Mrs. Halstead tapped her glass with a thumbnail. "My dear, would you move the decanter closer? Here, on this table." She indicated the round marble-topped table at her elbow. "That way you won't have to be jumping up and down. Thank you. So obliging. Where was I?"

"Angelica was fifteen," I prodded, setting the decanter within easy reach.

"Yes, fifteen—that was when she took service with a wealthy American family. I won't tell you their name." She poured herself another drink, then leaned back with a sigh and closed her eyes. In repose her face looked older, more wrinkled, suffused now with a dusky flush.

I waited for her to resume her story. From somewhere came a loud guffaw, a man's hearty laugh. Then the thump and tinkle of piano keys.

"Mrs. Halstead? Mrs. Halstead!"

"Eh? Oh!" Her eyes flew open and she gave me a blank look.

"Mrs. Halstead—you were telling me that my mother— Anglica—went into service..."

"Oh, yes, yes. Indeed. My dear, it was the old sad tale, one thing leading to another. To make a long story short, Angelica was seduced by the young son, seduced and ruined."

I nodded. It was very close to what I had expected.

"Ruined and thrown out on the street by the ungrateful bitch—pardon—woman who had hired her. Well, my dear, Angelica had nowhere to go but here. After that—since, unfortunately, she was no longer what you might call 'pure'— she went to work for Mrs. Stock. She was a sweet thing— lovely, a good friend of mine, the best a girl could have." She withdrew a lace-edged handkerchief from her ample bosom and dabbed at her eyes. "And then she met your father."

"Here? She met my father here?"

"He was not a regular patron. He was with a group of friends. They were all a little worse for drink and his friends had dared him—"

"My father," I interrupted stiffly, "takes a whiskey now and then, but I have never seen him the worse for drink."

"Now, Miss Carmella, don't be offended. I wasn't putting your father in the same class as his friends. He was an upright man. Very upright." She hiccoughed loudly. "Why, I remember him in the parlor, sitting on a petit-point chair, hands folded. We were having champagne, three of us girls and that crowd of young bloods. Oh, what a merry bunch they were!" A faint smile curled her lips. "Your father refused the champagne. 'Sunday-school lad,' they teased him. Everyone laughed but Angelica. She said she fell in love with him the moment she set eyes on him. And he with her."

She sighed heavily. "Romantic, ain't it?"

A Negro maid came into the room and unobtrusively began to tidy up.

"Mrs. Halstead," I ventured, "if my mother isn't here, perhaps you could tell me where to find her."

She fluttered her handkerchief. "My dear, don't you think such a search should be conducted by someone else? Your father, for instance."

"He's in San Francisco."

"Ah—and left you . . ."

"With Aunt Maude."

"She doesn't know you're here? You came on the sly?"

"Yes." (Aunt Maude believed me to be spending the day with Victoria Bridewell.) "Mrs. Halstead. I simply *must* find my mother. It's terribly important to me."

"Of course, my dear. But I have no idea where Angelica O'Neil could be. Do you, Tess?" she asked, turning to the maid.

"There's an Angie at Willa's Palace," she offered.

"Willa's?" Kate Halstead's nose wrinkled in distaste. "That cheap bordello!"

"Where is Willa's?" I asked the maid.

"Thirty-two Chartres Street."

I was on my feet.

"Now wait, Miss Carmella," Kate Halstead protested. "A nicely brought-up young girl like yourself shouldn't go wandering about in such a neighborhood."

I thought quickly. She might prevent me. She might even insist on sending me home under escort.

"I won't go myself. I'll—I'll have our servant take a note." It was a lie. Our only servant, Hortense, a bunion-footed, gap-toothed ancient who cooked for us, would be affronted if asked to carry messages, especially to a house of ill repute.

"Well..." Kate gave me a long suspicious look, which I managed to meet with wide-eyed innocence. "You shouldn't be here either, you know. All right—run along then."

"Thank you, Mrs. Halstead. Thank you so much for your hospitality. And such an elegant house!" I added, sudden gratitude eliciting the compliment.

"D'you think so? But this isn't the best room. Have you seen the front room?"

"No..."

"You can't leave without seeing our famous parlor. You won't find the likes of it anywhere. I'm very proud of my parlor." She hoisted herself up out of the chair. "It won't take a minute."

In the dining room Sam Halstead's malevolent eye stopped me. "Say, ain't you Arthur Hastens's brat?"

"Don't talk to him," Kate Halstead warned.

But I was curious. "Yes, I am. Do you know my father?"

"He don't," Mrs. Halstead said, forestalling her husband's reply. "He's just being scabby. Come along." And, taking my elbow, she hurried me into the vestibule.

She parted the ruby portieres and I looked into a large room furnished with pier mirrors, gilt-backed sofas, hand-painted china lamps, and looped velvet hangings at the windows. At the far end of the room a woman sat at the piano idly running her fingers over the keys. A man in a black coat was leaning with one elbow on the piano cover, watching her.

Mrs. Halstead cleared her throat and the man looked up. He was dressed like a gentleman, and his age was somewhere in the thirties, I would guess. Dark haired, heavy browed, tall, wide shouldered and narrow waisted, he had about him an air of assured masculinity I found oddly threatening.

"Mrs. Halstead, I presume?"

"Indeed."

"And this..." He paused, his eyes running over me from head to toe, undressing me to the skin in a bold, unabashed appraisal that was rude and yet, in a curious way, flattering. "This is the new girl I've been told about?"

"I should say not!" Kate Halstead retorted. "This is the daughter of an acquaintance of mine who's come to call. Miss Carmella Hastings."

I thought I saw a look of surprise flit across his face, but I must have been mistaken for the next moment he said, "Very pretty."

I lifted my chin and turned away from his stare.

Mrs. Halstead took my arm. "See the chandelier?" She pointed to a cascade of prismed glass that hung from the ceiling. "Imported. Every one of them little doodads Czech glass. Cost me a fortune."

"Beautiful."

"And that table—an es . . . escri . . . Well, never mind, I can't think of the word. It's inlaid with rosewood, and them knobs are real gold."

"Lovely," I murmured, stealing a glance at the dark-haired man, who had gone back to the woman at the piano. He turned suddenly and caught my interested look. Putting his hand on his frilled shirt front, he gave me an exaggerated bow.

"Mrs. Halstead, are you sure your visitor . . . ?"

"Of course, I'm sure."

She ushered me out. When I said good-bye to her in the vestibule, she leaned over to kiss me, her whiskey breath dueling with the strong scent of jasmine.

From behind the curtained door of the parlor the black-coated man cheerfully called, "Good-bye, Miss Hastings!"

Ignoring his mocking farewell, I swept through the front door with a dignified, ladylike flourish I regretted he could not witness.

CHAPTER

THREE

ONCE ON the street, I hurried along. I had spent a great deal of time at Kate Halstead's, but I had come away with more information than I hoped for. On the corner I stopped at a little greengrocer shop to ask directions.

"Chartres? It's quite a way, Miss," the proprietor said. "I should hire a hackney if I were you. There's a livery just two blocks from here."

Kept on short rations by Aunt Maude, I had walked to St. John Street. If I hired a hackney, it would take the last of my monthly allowance and the next was not due for another three weeks. Still, if it meant finding my mother, what did the cost matter?

I found the livery stable without difficulty. Helped into the carriage by the driver, a frock-coated black man, I gave him my destination.

"Are you sho, Miss?" he asked in surprise.

"Yes, and please hurry."

Number 32 was a narrow wooden two-story house with a sagging porch and broken shutters. A dusty pink-blossomed oleander grew to one side, an empty rusting bird cage hanging precariously from one of its tired branches.

"Please wait," I instructed.

My knock was answered by a stern-faced woman wearing a brown sack apron over a faded blue dress.

"Pardon—I hate to disturb you—but I'm looking for—"

"If it's yer husband," she interrupted, eyeing me with hostility, "he ain't here."

"I'm not married, ma'am. I am looking for a woman who goes by the name of Angelica O'Neil."

"Don't know anyone like that."

"Angie, perhaps?"

She turned her head and shouted, "Clara! Clara, where's Angie these days?"

A voice replied, "God—I think she's down to the cribs."

"The cribs," the woman in the sack apron said. "On Canal Street."

And before I could ask her where—which one—she slammed the door in my face.

"Let me off on Canal Street," I said to the driver.

"Miss, it's bad, no place fo—"

"Please don't argue. I shall be perfectly all right."

He shook his head as he clucked up the horse.

The neighborhood became more derelict, the gutters littered with refuse, the houses more shabby and weatherworn, the gardens trampled or gone to weed.

Finally we turned a corner and I knew I was there without being told. Canal Street reeked; it stank of open drains and untended privies, of greasy, smoking fires—the stench of poverty, disease, and depravity. The overwhelming odor warred with my senses, and I drew a handkerchief from my reticule and covered my nose.

The street itself was unpaved, rutted, and lined on either side with a jumble of ramshackle buildings. Dreary two-story houses, their brick chimneys broken, their gables missing, homes obviously left over from more affluent days, crowded together with storefront dance halls, beer parlors, and lean-to shacks.

Females dressed in dirty Mother Hubbards sat in doorways smoking pipes or cigars, their skirts pulled up to their thighs, calling out to the men who passed. "Hey, Mister, you wanna jig with me?"

One puzzling sight was the women we passed carrying a

roll of carpet on their backs. Later I was to learn that these were prostitutes who, unable to afford the rental of a bed, used their carpets to accomodate their customers, unrolling them behind buildings or in alleyways or shadowed entrances.

We came to a long, low edifice that seemed a likely place and I asked the driver to stop.

"You doan wanna git down, Miss?" he asked in disbelief.

I hesitated. The neighborhood frightened me, yet I had come too far to turn back. What if my mother was somewhere beyond those battered, peeling walls, held prisoner, in pain, needing me?

"I shan't be a minute."

He mumbled a protest as he helped me from the hackney.

The outer door was ajar and I stepped through, pausing in the dim, low-ceilinged passage. Before me was a double row of cagelike cubicles alive with rustlings, thumpings, and voices. Again the peculiar stale-sweet greasy odor assailed me.

"Whatcha want for twenty-five cents, you bastard!" I heard a woman shout.

One of the crib doors opened and a man reeled out. I shrank against the wall as he staggered past me, glassy eyed, stumbling across the threshold to the street.

From down the passage came voices. "Hurry up, I ain't got all day," a woman complained.

"Hold your horses. I ain't ready."

Clutching my reticule in both hands, I forced myself to approach the first barred alcove and peered in. A lone woman sat slumped on the floor, her hand on the neck of a bottle. She was thin to the point of emaciation, her arms like sticks.

"Miss . . .," I began.

She looked up, red eyed, a little dazed.

"I am trying to find someone by the name of Angie."

She lifted the bottle and her skinny throat worked as she swallowed. "Fifth . . ." She coughed, then drank again. "Fifth one down."

My heart began to thump. My hands felt cold. Did I want to see her, did I want to go on? But of course. I had to.

I counted five and stopped. She was alone, leaning across the sill of a narrow window. "Want to have a good time, Papa?"

she called to some unseen passerby. "Oh—go to Hell!"

Her voice was husky, but it had a more genteel accent than the others. Or so I wanted to believe.

"Miss . . . ?" I cleared my throat. "Miss!"

She turned. She had a ravaged face. I can think of no other term. Deep purple circles underlined each eye, her brow was furrowed, her skin an unhealthy pallor. An ugly bruise swelled her upper lip. Her hair, of an indeterminate color, hung in lank strands around her shoulders. I stared at her, my heart filled with loathing and pity.

"What d'you want?" she asked, eyeing me with animosity.

"Are you . . . ?" It was difficult to speak. "Are you Angelica O'Neil?"

"My name's Angie. Angie Riley."

Was she lying? Was she too ashamed to admit her real name?

"Can I come in and talk to you?"

She opened the cagelike door.

I looked at her more closely. Kate Halstead had said I was the image of my mother, in fact had mistaken me for her, but I could discern no resemblance between this Angie and myself. Even if she were younger and her face less worn, it would have stretched credulity to believe we were in any way related, and yet . . .

"Are you sure? Are you sure your last name's not O'Neil?"

Her eyes narrowed. "What's this? Why all the questions? Who are you, my fine lass? Sent out by the magistrate to spy on us?"

"No, no, why should I spy?"

"Because it's against the law to drum up trade from the windows, that's why. As if you didn't know."

"I don't know—I swear. I'm looking for Angelica O'Neil. She's my mother."

"What? Tell me another."

"I'm sorry. I had thought . . ."

She couldn't possibly be my mother. I turned to leave.

"Where ya goin'?" Swift as a cat she brushed past me and barred the way. "Not so fast. I wanna know who sent you."

"No one sent me. Please—please, let me by."

"Like hell. Not until you answer my question. The police? Are they lookin' for me?"

At that moment a man in a battered top hat appeared outside the bars. "What's goin' on? Who you got there, Angie?"

"Somebody with a long nose, Jack, askin' questions."

"About what? She want to come on the turf?"

"I dunno." She turned to me, repeating Jack's question. I gave her a blank look.

"Do you wanna become a whore?" she shouted.

"Oh, no, no! You don't understand."

"Bloody well, I do. You're a spy."

"If she's a spy," Jack said, leering at me, "we gotta take care of that, eh?"

"No, no! My name is—"

"Oh, shut up!" Angie ordered. "What's that?" She tore the reticule from my hands.

"You can't!" I protested, reaching for it.

Her hand came across my face in a stinging slap. "Told you to shut up."

Jack moved around and peered over her shoulder as she rummaged through the small, bead-fringed bag. "She got any money?" he queried.

"Yeh."

"Share and share alike."

"Not me—I found it."

"Aw, c'mon, Angie."

Both of them had forgotten me. I had a searing instant of regret over the reticule (crocheted and beaded so laboriously by me) and its contents before fear whirled me about. Wrenching the door open, I ran down the corridor, tripping over my skirts in my haste. As I fled past one of the cubicles, a dirt-grimed claw reached out from behind the bars and grabbed my arm, holding it in a steely grip that heightened my fright to panic. I beat at the skeletal hand, hammering blindly with clenched fists until the viselike fingers released me. And then I was running again, stumbling over the threshold into the dusty street, my heart pounding, my knees threatening to give way under me. Grasping the ring of a hitching post, I tried to steady myself, hanging on to it as my breath came in ragged gasps.

Presently I was vaguely conscious that someone had stopped to watch me.

"Miss? Had a bit too much red-eye Miss?"

"No," I breathed. "No, I . . ." Still clutching the iron ring, I looked up to find a man in a plug hat and claw-tailed frock coat grinning down at me. Beside him stood a mongrel dog, a large, mangy animal held on a leash made of twine. The dog suddenly growled, showing yellow fangs.

"He won't hurt you, Miss. Mutt likes purty ladies too."

Ignoring man and dog, I straightened up and looked around. My hackney! Where was it and the concerned driver who had promised to wait? I craned my neck. Not a sign of a conveyance of any kind. Oh, God, the darkie must have taken fright and gone off, leaving me in this horrible nightmare street. What was I to do?

"I'll give you a dollar, Miss," the man said, lifting his hat, winking lasciviously. He was dirty and ugly, his unshaven face covered with pockmarks. "A dollar for a bit o' fun. How does that suit you?"

"Please be on your way, sir," I said, trying to sound as imperious as Aunt Maude, my voice, however, cracking on the "sir."

"A dollar and a half?"

I took a tentative step, meaning to edge around him, but the dog growled again and lunged, forcing me to shrink back against the post.

"Two dollars?"

A few stragglers had begun to gather: a runty little man with long, greasy locks; a thin, beak-nosed woman eyeing me with hard, flinty hostility; an inebriated, leather-shirted river man; and an evil-smelling urchin of indeterminate age clothed in layers of filthy rags. As I stood there, hemmed in, at bay, others began to join them. There was something about those onlookers, an aura of menace, that made my skin prickle.

"Get out of my way!" I ordered, desperation giving my voice a ring it had lacked earlier.

But no one moved.

"Two dollars is my top offer," the man in the plug hat said, grabbing the edge of my skirt.

I swung at him. The dog barked viciously, reared back on his haunches to spring, and I screamed. But the mongrel never got off the ground, its intended leap stopped by a whip that seemed to come out of thin air, slashing it across the muzzle with a smart, cracking sound. The injured animal howled like a banshee and sank down, cowering at its master's feet.

"Whoever wants the same, come and get it!" a male voice shouted as its owner pushed past the urchin.

It was the man from Kate Halstead's parlor!

He stood next to me, whip in hand, his eyes going around the circled crowd. There was a tense moment or two, and then the man with the greasy locks slunk away followed by the beak-nosed woman. Gradually the others, some with lowering looks, dispersed.

The man from Kate Halstead's parlor took me by the arm. "Come quickly."

"But—how did you find me?"

"I'll tell you all about it later. Here's my buggy," he said, as he bundled me into it.

He laid his whip over the horse's rump and we rattled down the street at a good clip. An overripe tomato thrown from a shadowed doorway hit the side of the buggy with a splattering thump.

"Keep your head in, Miss Hastings."

We careened around a corner, leaving the stench of Canal Street behind. Soon the horse was slowed to a walk, finally stopping under a leafy plane tree at the edge of a small park.

"Well, Miss Hastings," he said, leaning back and turning to me. "You've led me a merry chase this morning."

"I've . . . ? Have you been following me?"

"Trying to. But before I explain, let me introduce myself. Does the name Miles Falconer mean anything to you?"

"Falconer—Miles Falconer," I considered. "Oh, yes! I remember now! Papa's mentioned you in his letters."

"In a flattering context, I hope."

"He said you were a friend—that he dined with you frequently." Papa's letters were always brief, rather dull, with few interesting details. His accounts of Miles Falconer had never aroused my curiosity. I had pictured Papa's friend as much like himself, sober faced, middle-aged, a reserved individual of few words. That image, as I saw now, had been somewhat incorrect.

"But, Mr Falconer, why didn't you let me know who you were earlier?"

"I wasn't quite sure you were Arthur Hastings's daughter until I spoke to Mrs. Halstead. And even if I had been I don't think her parlor—with herself and one of her—ah—ladies looking on—was the proper place for introductions or the conversations that was apt to follow. Originally my plan was to call on you and Miss Briscoe in a day or two—I'm in New Orleans on business—but when I was told that it was you this morning . . . Well! you can imagine my astonishment."

"Yes, but you see I went there—"

"Mrs. Halstead told me the purpose of your call."

"You discussed me with her?"

"Among other things. Mrs. Halstead has investments in a dredging company I own, but that's beside the point. It's you I'm concerned with at the moment, you and some silly notion of finding a mother that's been long dead."

"I would hardly call it 'silly,'" I retorted, bristling. "I've been informed she's still alive."

"I must confess a continuing bafflement," he said after a short pause. "Mrs. Halstead said she understood your mother had died, and it seemed to me that your father would have confirmed it."

"My father was only trying to protect my mother's reputation."

"I see. On the other hand, he might have been telling the truth. Haven't you visited her grave?"

"No."

It had never occurred to me. Of course I should have gone right off, not accepted Victoria's story at face value.

"Your mother's maiden name was O'Neil, I believe. Then it would be the Catholic cemetery, St. Louis."

"If she were at St. Louis, Papa would have taken me there."

Which was not entirely true, for Papa had once told me he hated funerals and graveyards and thought people who made a habit of going to one and haunting the other ghoulish. Still, if my mother had not really died, how could he possibly have shown me her grave?"

"I suppose you won't accept *my* word for it, Miss Hastings?"

"I hardly think—"

"Very well." He snapped the reins, bringing the horse's

head up from an impromptu meal. "We shall pay a visit to St. Louis and see."

We rode in silence. I had the feeling that Mr. Falconer found me childishly obstinate and was going out of his way to prove it. And though he was my father's friend and had rescued me from an ugly situation, his superior air did not endear him to me.

I kept my head turned, staring out at the passing scene, the iron-fretted galleries and the bay-fronted shops with their green jalousies pulled up. On the steps of a church a flock of noisy pinafored schoolgirls were being herded together by a stern-faced nun in gray. It seemed an age since I had been that small, my hair in ribboned braids, chatting and giggling with my contemporaries about nothing in particular. I had accepted the world as it was without question then; but ever since Victoria had told me about my mother, that world had become an uncertain place.

To be sure, what I had seen today had shaken me. My face still stung from harlot Angie's slap and that claw! Ugh! The ugly sordidness of it all!

I must have shuddered, for Mr. Falconer said, "Are you all right? Cold? Hungry, perhaps? We could stop for a bite at Antoine's."

"No, thank you." I couldn't think of eating.

Crossing the Place d'Armes, or Jackson Square as it was now called, we passed under the shadow of the many-arched Spanish Cabildo with the funny little railed dome atop it and the soaring spires of the cathedral next door. In the center of the square, pigeons fluttered and perched on the huge statue of Andrew Jackson as he sat his rearing horse.

"Is my father well?" I asked, breaking another long silence.

"In excellent health. He sends his best to you. Ah—here we are."

Hitching the buggy outside, we walked through the iron gates and stopped at the caretaker's small cottage, where Mr. Falconer gave my mother's name. The caretaker, an elderly, stoop-shouldered individual with crinkle-lidded pale blue eyes, browsed through a large ledger while I hoped against hope his search would be unsuccessful.

"Angelica O'Neil Hastings," I heard the old man murmur. "Now, let me see . . ."

I moved away. She wasn't here, she *couldn't* be! Victoria had been so sure she was alive. I wanted my mother that way— I wanted to touch her, to hear her voice, to see her smile— not entombed in this crowded place with the dead.

And crowded it was. Because New Orleans had been built on a swamp, the dead were buried aboveground, those whose families could afford it in tombs or vaults, the poor in brick "ovens" along the walls. Over the grim stone edifices, brooding marble angels, and kneeling penitents hung an air of gloom. No wonder my father eschewed graveyards.

"This way, Miss Hastings." Miles Falconer's voice coming from behind startled me.

"She isn't . . . ?"

"Yes, I'm afraid so."

It was a mistake, I told myself. The old man could have misread the ledger, or perhaps it was another woman with the same name.

"The caretaker tells me the grave is two rows over and five down," Miles Falconer said. He took my arm, but then he must have felt the rigidity with which I reacted to his touch, because he quickly released it. "It's not far," he commented.

I followed him through a hedge and along the grass verge, a feeling of resentment growing in my breast. How I would love to prove him wrong!

But when he stopped before an eye-level, oblong vault and stepped aside to let me read the epitaph chiseled in stone, I knew that I never would.

ANGELICA O'NEIL HASTINGS
BELOVED WIFE OF ARTHUR
MOTHER OF CARMELLA
BORN 1820 DIED 1839

No mistake, no misreading, no coincidence. She was dead— dead and buried here in this tomb. Grief rose to my throat in a burning lump. I had never known her, but through the years I had thought and wondered about her. Then for a little while she had come alive, her image, however tempered by an unfortunate background, offering hope of a reunion. Now that hope was gone.

I bent my head as the tears welled and spilled down my cheeks. Death was so final. It was as if my mother had breathed her last only yesterday and I, who had never in my sixteen years come face to face with the loss of a loved one, now wept for her passing.

As I stood there with lowered chin, the tears still flowing, I felt a tap on the wrist and looked down to see Mr. Falconer silently offering a handkerchief. I took it, having lost mine on Canal Street, along with my reticule. But Mr. Falconer's handkerchief only seemed to remind me that he had brought me here, and in some illogical way I blamed him for my anguish. It was Victoria I should have blamed—Victoria who had misled me, whether deliberately out of pique or unintentionally out of ignorance. Yet my grieving mind refused to accept such reasoning.

"I'm sorry," he said.

Indeed, he should be.

"I didn't mean to make you cry, Miss Hastings. But I thought it best to have you know for certain now, so that you won't go on searching for someone who is not there."

"She wasn't *someone*. She was my *mother!*"

"I know that. And as beautiful a mother as any girl could wish."

I dabbed my eyes, blew my nose, and then in a small, tremulous voice asked, "You knew her?"

"Yes, briefly."

I turned to him. "Was she—do I . . . ?"

"Look like her? The spitting image."

"She was an orphan, you know."

"Yes, she had no one except Mrs. Stock, who took her in."

"Mrs. Halstead said she was a good girl."

"I'm sure of it. Unhappy circumstances put her on St. John Street. You don't believe your father would have fallen in love with her if she wasn't pure of heart?"

I shook my head. I felt better, the ache in my heart eased. Perhaps Mr. Falconer was a kinder, more sensitive man than I had thought.

I continued to feel friendly toward him as we sat at the Cafe Royale over steaming cups of hot chocolate and *begnets,* those crisp fritters akin to doughnuts but far more delicious. He asked me about myself—where I had gone to school, what I liked to read, if I got along with Aunt Maude; did I have any beaux? The last query I thought rather presumptuous, especially since he turned most of the personal questions I asked *him* adroitly aside. He was free in his praise of my father (promising to convey my messages of love and my wish to join him), saying that no man could be more loyal or generous.

"He helped me when no one else would. I hadn't a sou in my pocket when I came to him in this city, but he loaned me the money to go west without any collateral, simply on the strength of a handshake and my word."

"Had you known him beforehand?"

"Only slightly, though we both come from the same part of Virginia."

"Papa never talked much about Virginia. When he was young, his father sent him to New Orleans to open a tobacco brokerage. That was before I was born, but since then—" I broke off, not wanting to dwell on Papa's marriage being the obvious reason for his rupture with his family. "And you," I added brightly to cover my embarrassment, "have you been back to Virginia lately?"

"No."

"Have you no wish to return, Mr. Falconer?"

"I don't think the story of my life would interest you."

Nothing he could have said could have put me in my place so aptly. He was the adult; I was the child. From the lofty height of maturity he could ask me whatever he liked and expect an answer; but *I* must not presume. The friendly feeling I had harbored toward him for the past hour left me like air from a punctured balloon. I thought him cold and arrogant.

It got worse on the drive home.

"Now that you seem to have recovered from your ordeal, Miss Hastings," he began, raising his voice above the ringing clamor from Lafitte's blacksmith shop as we trotted past, "there is something I must say. You had no business going to a place like Kate Halstead's."

"Under the circumstances—"

"Under *no* circumstances. If you had had the sense of a goose you would have thought twice before venturing on such a quest. An intelligent person—if he or she thought it necessary—would have made inquiries by letter."

Earlier I had resented him, but now I was beginning to dislike him. Very much. I didn't want to admit to myself that perhaps he was right, that I should take his scolding meekly. But I did not have it in me to be meek. His haughty superiority rankled.

We rounded a corner, passing a heavy wagon loaded with timber. A small pickaninny hawking sweets from a tray stood on the banquette. "Prahhleens! Tahfeee! Two fer a picayooon!"

"Are you listening, Miss Hastings?"

"Of course," I said, shifting my attention from the candy-seller. "But I thought you had finished."

"Not quite." He bit the words in two. "There's more. You lied to Mrs. Halstead. You told her you were going home. When I learned from Mrs. Halstead's maid that she had mentioned Willa's to you, I suspected differently. Thank goodness the woman at Willa's remembered she had directed you to Canal Street. Do you realize what would have happened if I hadn't come along?"

"Yes, and I thank you for—"

"I'm not asking for thanks," he said, sweeping them aside. "I want your promise that you will never try anything like that again."

"I don't know why I have to promise you anything," I said in sudden defiance.

"By God, if I were your father I'd give you a sound thrashing."

"Well, you're not my father—*sir!*"

A muscle twitched in his jaw as he stared at me for a long moment. Then he gave his attention to the horse. We had gone several blocks without speaking when he said, "I believe Miss Briscoe lives on Pleasant Street?"

"Yes. At Number Twelve."

We drove the rest of the way in silence.

Aunt Maude's house looked deserted behind its white picket fence. It was her afternoon to have tea with the Lowery sisters and apparently she had not yet returned.

"I'd invite you in, Mr. Falconer," I said with chill courtesy, "but no one is at home."

"It's quite all right. In any case, I'm late for an appointment as it is. I may be gone from the city for two or three weeks on business before I have the opportunity to call as I had originally planned. However, I shall send Miss Briscoe a note apprising her of my presence and setting the date for a visit."

He must have seen the flash of alarm in my eyes, for he added, "Never fear, I won't breathe a word of your escapade to her—or to your father, for that matter—and unlike you, I do not hesitate to make that a promise."

It was the mocking tone of his voice in that last little reference to "a promise" that overrode any gratefulness I might have felt and prompted me to say tartly, "You should have been a preacher, Mr. Falconer."

"Why do you say that?"

"You have such a splendid, holier-than-thou attitude."

He laughed—the ultimate humiliation. I bunched up my skirts, preparing to get out of the buggy.

"Wait," he said, "let me help you."

"I don't need your help." I jumped down and turned to him.

"Thank you, sir. Thank you for *everything*, including the sermon."

He lifted his hat, and I thought he smiled when he said, "The pleasure was all mine."

CHAPTER

FOUR

AUNT MAUDE returned an hour later.

"You're earlier than I had expected," she said, removing her gloves. "Did you enjoy your visit with Victoria?"

"Yes, I had a very good time."

As always, curiosity where it concerned the habits and habitat of the aristocracy prompted Aunt Maude to ask me a number of questions: How was Mrs. Bridewell dressed? Did we take dinner or luncheon and what were we served? Did they have other guests? I was able to fob her off with bits and pieces of information I had gathered on my previous visits to the Bridewells. What I had to do now was to get Victoria to corroborate my story.

When she came by the following afternoon, I ran out to meet her at the garden gate, detaining her with quickly whispered instructions.

She rose to the occasion with a talent that would have done credit to a Madame Lalaurie.

Aunt Maude said, "I hope Carmella did not make a nuisance of herself."

"Not at all, Miss Briscoe. We loved having her."

A few minutes later, seated in my room, we had a good laugh over it.

"Well, now, Carmella," Victoria said, settling herself comfortably on the bed. "What happened yesterday? What did you do?"

"I went to look for my mother, Victoria. She's dead."

"Oh, but I heard—"

"She's dead, Victoria. I saw her grave."

"Oh." She shrugged. "I suppose it was just gossip. I'm sory. How did you find out she was in the cemetery?"

"It's a long story." I told her everything, beginning with my visit to St. John Street.

"You mean you actually saw a man and a woman . . . ? Oh, Carmella—how wonderful!" She clapped her hands. "And a Mr. Falconer saved you from a fate worse than death! How romantic!"

"Oh, tish. He isn't the least bit romantic. He scolded me like an old schoolmaster all the way home."

"You should have flirted with him, Carmella, batted your eyes and teased."

"It's not funny," I said. "I still have to explain my missing purse."

"Tell your aunt you gave it to charity."

"A good reticule and a half-dollar piece? Oh, I can't! Aunt Maude will be furious."

"Goodness," Victoria said, adjusting a pillow behind her neck. "I can't see what the fuss is all about. It's only a purse. Are you that poor?"

"Noooo . . . It's just that—well, Aunt Maude has her little peculiarities."

"You mean she's stingy. I wonder what makes her so odd," Victoria said, examining her nails. "Do you think it's because she's an old maid?"

"Oh, I'm sure of it."

Maude was the last of the Briscoes, an old New Orleans family that had once known financial comfort, if not moderate wealth. What had happened to bring her to reduced circumstances, a single-story pedimented cottage, and a pittance for income, or why she had not married, were subjects she never discussed. She had lived for so many years in genteel poverty that it became ingrained, a part of her, like her skin, so that even after I came along and Papa gave her a substantial sum (how much I did not learn until years later) for my keep, she found it impossible to change her habits.

"Tell her someone stole your reticule," Victoria said.

"I suppose I'll have to. Though she'll insist on reporting it to the authorities and making an embarrassing to-do if they don't find it."

"Let her. Anyway, it's just too boring to go on talking about. I came to tell you my sister, Dorothea, is getting married next month and you and your aunt are invited to the wedding."

"A wedding!" I exclaimed, instantly forgetting the lost purse. "How lovely!"

"Lyon, especially, wants you to come. He's quite taken with you, Carmella."

"Is he?" Lyon was Victoria's brother, older than she by a year or two, a slender young man closely resembling his sister—boiled blue-gray eyes, large mouth, and abundant honey-colored hair. He had always been unerringly polite to me, but this was the first I had heard of an interest beyond common courtesy.

"Oh, yes, he told me so."

Even though Lyon was not my idea of a dashing beau, I felt flattered. "I'd love to come. Oh...but wait! Victoria, I have nothing to wear. I *can't* go in my old dancing-school brown."

"I'll lend you a gown," she offered with uncharacteristic generosity.

"Would you?"

It was a pink ball gown frothing with gauze at the capped sleeves and at the hem. Aunt Maude said the basque was too tight and the neck cut too low and she did not approve of my borrowing a gown in the first place. "We have our pride," she reminded, a favorite motto that had been drilled into me over the years.

But because the Bridewell wedding was the social event of the season, an occasion Aunt Maude would not have missed for the world, her protest lacked the usual force and I went in the pink gown.

The Bridewells lived in imposing elegance in the Garden

District, a neighborhood peopled by affluent Americans who thought well of themselves but whom the aristocratic French Creoles, after a century, still looked upon as Johnny-come-latelies. The Bridewell house, painted white and set back in a vast garden of clipped hedges and leaping fountains, had fluted columns, a wide iron-latticed porch, and an upper gallery.

We entered through a green beveled glass door into a tiled foyer where a Negro butler took our wraps. Though I had been there before, the house, so different from ours, still awed me. The staircase, gracefully going up and up in a sweeping curve, fairly took my breath away—the staircase the bride later descended to her waiting groom.

As the couple stood together before the pastor I cried, sobbing silently into my handkerchief because it was all so wonderfully romantic. Afterwards there were congratulations and hugs and kisses and excited voices and the passing of champagne to toast the newly married pair while the fiddles warmed up and the furniture in the dining room was pushed back for dancing.

I did not lack for partners. Lyon was especially attentive, scribbling his name in my dance programme, reserving three waltzes and two reels. "I should like to have every dance," he said, "but that would be selfish and several gentlemen present would never forgive me."

He danced exquisitely, had polished manners, and paid me the most outrageous compliments. At one point I noticed one of my earlier partners, Tom Deventer, a blond, burly, rather awkward young man, standing on the sidelines following us with his eyes, a sullen expression on his face.

"Is he a friend of yours?" I asked Lyon.

"Tom? Very much so. But now I think he would crack my skull if he could. He's a bit jealous."

Champagne punch was served at a damask-covered table festooned with garlands of white lilies. As Lyon and I stood cooling ourselves and sipping from daintily handled cups, he said, "I believe you are the most beautiful girl here tonight. I had no idea you'd even noticed me until Victoria mentioned it last week. Fancy your telling her I'm a fine picture of a man."

I did not deny having said anything of the sort, though I did wonder why Victoria should make it up. But then the next man on my card claimed his dance, waltzing me into the vortex of swirling crinolined skirts and flying black swallowtails, and I forgot all about it.

For a girl who had never danced before except with old Mr. Popkin and a few adolescent boys, it was all very heady—the champagne, the music, the attention—and I almost made a scene when Aunt Maude came to collect me. The party had hours to go—all night someone said—and I wanted so very much to stay. But Maude took my arm with a taloned grip, her face set in grim lines.

"I have something to discuss with you."

I hated her for spoiling my fun, but more than that I was filled with a queasy foreboding. I had seen that grim face before, and it did not augur well.

Maude did not speak until we got home. As soon as the door closed behind us, she turned on me.

"You lied," she accused, her thin lips white with anger. "You lied! And you know what God does to liars."

"Aunt Maude, I don't know what—"

"You told me you spent the day with the Bridewells, that someone stole your purse. A falsehood, a despicable falsehood!" Her voice and outrage mounted. "How could you! Sit down. *Sit* down! Now tell me where you were all that day and what really happened to your reticule."

"I—"

"Mrs. Bridewell denied the whole story. You were never there, not for luncheon or for tea. And she was most upset because you got Victoria to back you up."

"I—"

"Have you any idea how you embarrassed me? After all I have done for you, the sacrifices I've made. Well—I'm waiting. And it had better be the truth."

How could I tell her about the bawdy house, my visit to the cribs on Canal Street? It would be like confessing a mortal sin. I couldn't. "I—I went out in the morning—down to the French Market for a cup of chocolate."

"With whom?"

"Tabby Smith."

Tabby was one of her cronies' daughters. In desperation I had plucked the name out of the air, a poor choice.

"Tabby would no more go to the French Market without a proper escort than she would fly. Are you going to tell me where you really were? Was it a man—have you been seeing a man?"

"Oh, no, Aunt Maude. I swear it. No."

"Am I supposed to believe you? After the lies you have already told? Do you think . . . Why you're just like your—" She caught herself.

I waited, poised on the brink of a revelation. In all the years I had been with Aunt Maude, never once had she mentioned my mother. But now, resentful yet curiously expectant, I wondered if she would breach the promise she must have made to my father to keep me in ignorance.

"I don't know where I've gone wrong," she went on, apparently thinking better of it. "I've tried my best to instill in you the high moral principals every gentlewoman claims as her birthright. And now this."

"I'm sorry, Aunt Maude."

"Is that all you can say? You're sorry? I want more than an apology. I want an explanation."

I looked her straight in the eye, that little woman with the knobbed head, a flush of indignation on her face, and something inside me hardened. I saw her suddenly as a hypocrite and a snob. She could toady to Mrs. Bridewell, who had money and power; but she could bully me, who had neither. I wasn't going to tell her about my mother. I wasn't going to expose myself to her snide ridicule. I wasn't going to tell her anything.

"So—you choose to remain silent, do you? Well, I have a cure for that. You will be confined to your room on bread and tea until you change your mind."

"You—you can't! I'll write my father—"

"I can. Your father has instructed me to bring you up the way I see fit. He trusted me to make a lady of you, and I shall not break that trust."

By the third day I had begun to think seriously of running away. It would be a simple matter to break open the padlocked window and decamp; but once out, where would I go? The Bridewells? Even if they took me in, that was the first place Aunt Maude would look. And I could think of no other refuge in the city. If only I could let Papa know that Maude Briscoe had become my jailer. If only I could make my way to him in San Francisco. But for that I needed money, and I had none.

On the morning of the fourth day I heard a carriage stop at the door. A few moments later Victoria's voice came to me.

"I'm so sorry that Carmella is indisposed, Miss Briscoe," she said. "Perhaps I'd best call tomorrow."

"I'm afraid she won't be able to see you tomorrow either," Aunt Maude replied.

"Oh . . . ?"

Aunt Maude did not elucidate, so Victoria said, "I'm sorry to hear that." Another pause. "I see you are ready to go out. May I give you a lift in my carriage?"

I wanted to shout to her, to say I was being held prisoner. But how could she help me? Victoria had already tarnished herself in Maude's eyes even if Maude believed Victoria had acted under duress.

I was lying on my bed, despondent and full of black thoughts when I heard the carriage return. Aunt Maude? Back from her whist party? Straining my ears I made out the sound of someone fumbling at the lock, and then Victoria's voice—never sweeter—called, "Carmella?"

"Here! In here, Victoria!"

A key was thrust into the lock and the door opened. I threw myself into Victoria's arms. "Oh, Victoria! I was never so glad to see anyone in my life. But how did you open the front door?"

"A hat pin," she said smugly. "And don't ask me where I learned the trick. The key to your room was on a peg in the hall. Now, what's this all about?"

"Aunt Maude discovered I lied about spending the day with you. And I wouldn't tell her where I had been."

Victoria wrinkled her nose. "Phew! It's stuffy in here. Can't we go into the parlor?"

The parlor looked cool and strangely unfamiliar. We seated ourselves on the sofa, Victoria propping her feet on a stool in a very unladylike fashion.

"Didn't your mother punish you at all?" I asked.

"No. Why should she? I didn't do anything but back up a friend. The whole thing amused her. She said what could one expect of a tart's daughter."

"That was unkind."

"You can't blame Mama. After all, your father did jilt her. I suppose it still hurts."

"She doesn't have to take it out on me."

"I don't see why you have to get huffy about it."

"I'm not getting huffy."

Victoria wound a long silky curl around her finger. "Whatever Mama thinks, there's one person in the family who dotes on you. My brother."

"Does he?"

I began to wonder why Victoria had come back. She never did anything unless it benefited her. Boredom, perhaps. Victoria avoided boredom like the plague. Apparently outwitting Maude, even for an hour, provided diversion.

"Dotes is mild for it," Victoria went on. "Lyon is head over heels in love with you."

"Is he?"

I was thinking again about my father, about San Francisco. If I could only get to him, see him face to face, explain in a way I could never do in a letter, he would understand.

"Victoria," I said abruptly, "would you lend me some money?"

Her hand paused on the curl. "How much?"

"Enough to go to San Francisco?"

"California? What do you think I am? I haven't got it." She paused the twisted curl back over her shoulder. "Why don't you marry Lyon?"

"Lyon?"

"My brother. I think he'd marry you in a minute if you would have him."

"That's just talk."

"He says you are the sweetest, most beautiful girl he's ever known. You make him feel manly."

"Really?" I tried to recall what I had said to him at the wedding, words that might have pleased him. Was it my complimenting him on his dancing, saying I admired the way he didn't puff or snort, telling him I enjoyed waltzing with him more than the others? Or was it the way I clung to him after one prolonged, dizzying whirl, my head spinning with excitement and champagne?

"Cross my heart and hope to die, Carmella."

"But we hardly know one another!"

"Does it matter when it comes to true love? Wouldn't you *like* to be Mrs. Bridewell? It would be such fun—you and I sisters-in-law."

Marry Lyon? "Are you serious?"

"Never more. He's in love with you, Carmella."

Marry Lyon? I turned the thought over in my mind. I would be Mrs. Lyon Bridewell—rich, respected, a person to be reckoned with. I would be free of Maude, her sharp tongue telling me what to do, what to wear, how to eat, free of her harping and criticism.

"Do you think you could care for Lyon?"

He was not handsome—those protruding eyes!—but he had a nice figure, slender, of middle height, and he had looked quite elegant in his black formal coat and white stock.

"I—I think I might." Why not? I had everything to gain and nothing to lose. "But wouldn't your parents object?"

"Of course they would. They have a bride picked out for him. Marie Le Jeunne. Very rich—very plain." She made a wry face. "He hates her. He says he'll never marry—unless it's with you. Naturally, you'd have to run away together."

"You mean *elope?*" The very word opened exciting vistas, putting Lyon in a far more dashing light.

"Lyon is quite a catch, you know," Victoria continued. "Have you decided? What shall I tell him? Oh, come on, Carmella. Once you are Mrs. Bridewell, Papa and Mama will have to accept you."

"Well . . . You are *sure* Lyon wants me?"

"He'd come himself and ask you, but because of your Aunt Maude I don't think it's wise."

"Yes." I leaned back and closed my eyes for an instant, then opened them wide. "All right, I'll do it! But how?"

"Leave everything to me."

She left, carefully locking the door of my bedroom behind her. I listened to the receding rustle of her delaine skirts, the creak of hinges. There was a small silence, then voices on the front porch. Aunt Maude! Had she caught Victoria on the threshold or had Victoria made it safely out? And why was my aunt back so soon? I put my ear to the door but, except for a subdued murmuring in which my name figured once or twice, was unable to make out a word of their conversation. As they stood and spoke, I heard a carriage rumble to a halt and a moment later a man's voice.

I pressed closer to the door. Now they were inside, not Victoria, just the man and Aunt Maude.

"Miss Hastings . . . I'm sorry . . . could she . . . ?"

It was Miles Falconer.

Again it was difficult for me to understand what was being said. How maddening!

Aunt Maude was talking now, then Mr. Falconer. Wasn't she going to let me out? What was he telling her? He didn't stay very long, perhaps twenty minutes, a half hour. After he had gone, the sound of Aunt Maude's sensible high-buttoned shoes approached down the hall. The key turned in the lock. She had that grim look again.

"Did your whist game break up early, Aunt Maude?" I inquired.

"Miss Belloc took ill."

"I'm sorry to hear that."

"It was just as well. I'd forgotten that Mr. Falconer meant to call."

"Mr. Falconer?" I asked innocently. "The same Mr. Falconer that is a friend of Papa's?"

"Yes. Victoria was here too, as you probably know, since I'm sure you had your ear to the keyhole. She drove me to the whist party and came back later to look for a comb she had apparently lost on our front porch. I met her outside. A lovely, courteous girl. A real gentlewoman. I don't know why you can't be more like her."

"Yes, Aunt Maude," I said in a subdued voice. What an actress Victoria would make!

"Did Mr. Falconer bring greetings from Papa?" I asked with just the right touch of polite interest.

"Carmella—I'm not here to discuss either Victoria Bridewell or Mr. Falconer." She fixed me with her gimlet eyes. "I know now where you were. Please! I don't want any denials or falsehoods. How *could* you? How could you demean yourself as to go . . ." She blushed, her face turning a splotchy red. "Young ladies in my day did not even know such places existed. And you, bold as brass, behind my back—"

"Who told you?" I burst out. "Who? Was it Mr. Falconer?"

"Does it matter who told me?" She knotted her liverish hands. "I'm ashamed to write to your father. I don't know what he'd say. All the years I've tried..."

She went on in the old vein, enumerating her sacrifices, but I wasn't listening. Furious, beside myself with anger, I could only think of Miles Falconer. It must have been he. He had betrayed me, broken his word, and after making such a to-do about promises! The hypocrite!

"I want to speak to Mr. Falconer," I demanded.

"You shall do nothing of the sort. In any case, he's gone on to St. Louis."

Lucky for him. I hated him and there was murder in my heart.

"I can see no sign of true remorse," Aunt Maude was saying. "You shall stay here in this room, on bread and tea, until I feel you have realized the enormity of your transgression."

"Oh...!"

"What?"

"Nothing, Aunt Maude."

Several days later, Victoria came while Aunt Maude was out, gaining entrance with her hat pin and bringing a box of chocolate bonbons, a gift from Lyon. When she had closed the door behind her and given me the box I said, "Victoria, did you say anything to Aunt Maude about my going to Kate Halstead's place?"

"Me? Why in the world would I want to do that? Of course not."

"She knows. Mr. Falconer must have told her. He was here."

"Yes, I met him on the doorstep. But let's not worry about him. I've such good news!" She sank into a chair and reached for the box of bonbons in my lap. "May I? Mmmmm—have one."

"No, thanks. What's your news?"

"Lyon is thrilled that you've said yes. And it's all arranged. Tonight."

"Tonight? So soon? I can't tonight. I haven't my clothes— my hair needs washing..."

"It's tonight or never, Carmella."

"Why?"

"Mama and Papa have gone to Houmas for a few days, and Lyon is afraid if he doesn't go tonight he might not have another chance.

Should I? It wasn't too late to change my mind.

"Don't make him wait, Carmella. You know how men are. He might have second thoughts."

If I said no, then I would have to stay on with Aunt Maude. Papa would keep promising to send for me but never would. I could see myself as I grew older, tamed on bread and tea, becoming an old maid like Aunt Maude, my hair fixed in a knob, wearing gray bombazine dresses with crocheted collars and cuffs. The years stretched ahead, years and years, all dismally dull. Lyon offered honorable escape. And he loved me; Victoria had assured me of that.

"Yes. Yes, I'll do it! I'll be ready and waiting."

CHAPTER

FIVE

SHORTLY AFTER midnight, a dark shadow tapped at the window. Hours of suspense had drawn my nerves to a quivering tautness, and as Lyon fumbled with the lock—apparently he did not have his sister's talent for lock-picking—I clenched my fists in a sweat, sure that his tinkering would awaken Aunt Maude.

At last he had the window open. "My darling," he whispered, brushing my cheek hurriedly with his lips.

"Oh, Lyon, let's be quick," I said anxiously.

He wrapped the cape he had brought for me around my shoulders and took my arm. "I left the buggy down the street."

The carriage lamp cast an eerie glow on the cobbles, a halo of light in the blackness. Thunder grumbled in the distance. A flash of lightning suddenly illuminated the street, the jalousied shutters of the sleeping houses, the dusty trees and hedges.

Lyon helped me into the buggy, then jumped in beside me. I turned my cheek to be kissed, but he was intent with untangling the reins and didn't see my gesture.

"I have arranged for a parish priest in the French Quarter to marry us," he said after we had gotten under way. "Do you mind? Or perhaps you are a Catholic."

"High Church."

"Same thing."

"Isn't this fun?" I asked brightly as we clattered along.

"Ummmm."

Lyon lashed at the horse and it quickened its pace to a brisk trot. We squealed around a corner as thunder cracked and boomed, the dark sky throbbing with blue-white lightning. The wind rattled the leather buggy top, whooped and gusted, thrashing the trees as we passed. I took a deep breath. Was this really *me*, Carmella Hastings, barreling through the tempest with a lover who had just rescued her from a wicked aunt? My hero. I only wished he would be more articulate, vow his undying love, put his arm around me, kiss me, tell me that I had made him the happiest man in New Orleans. Perhaps all of that would come later.

It began to rain, not a pitter-patter of drops, but suddenly great sweeping sheets. The carriage lamp went out and we had only the sporadic flashes of lightning to see by. The horse slowed to a plodding walk, clip-clopping blindly through the downpour. After some time Lyon, leaning forward, said, "We should have been there by now. I don't quite recognize these houses."

"Are we lost?"

"I—I don't know."

I shivered, hugging my arms against the wet chill. The roof of the carriage began to leak, the water plunking on my forehead. My toes had gone numb and I tried curling and uncurling them in my thin slippers.

"I'll have a look," Lyon said, halting the horse, handing me the reins.

He got out and disappeared behind a curtain of solid rain. I waited, huddled in the damp cape, peering out at the wet, inky night.

By the time he came back my teeth were chattering like castanets.

"It's on the next street," he said, water dripping from his hat and nose.

My spirits rose a bit when we halted before a small house with a pitched roof and lights glimmering behind the blinds. Lyon lifted me out and carried me in his arms, wading through puddles as we crossed the muddy banquette. An old woman opened the door.

"Monsieur Bridewell? *Entrez! Entrez!*"

We must have made a sorry-looking pair, Lyon streaming with water, his coat drenched, I wearing a sodden cape and my hair half out of its pins.

At my apology the old woman said, "Father Étienne will not notice. He is half blind."

She led us into a small parlor crammed with ancient dusty furniture and heated by a large potbellied stove. Father Étienne, asleep in a chair, had to be prodded awake by his housekeeper. An old man with a head like a pink waxed egg, he peered at us through rheumy eyes.

"*Qui? Qui?*"

"The bridal pair," the old woman explained loudly in French. "Monsieur Bridewell *et* Mademoiselle Hastings."

"Ah—Lyon!"

I remember little of the ceremony. Father Étienne conducted it in mumbling Latin sprinkled here and there with a French phrase or two. The old woman and a Negro kitchen wench were our only witnesses. I wondered briefly about the kitchen wench, whether she could be counted as a bona-fide witness and whether Father Étienne was a bona-fida priest. Defrocked? But no, he would not be wearing the collar. Retired, set out to pasture most likely.

These thoughts, however, were soon replaced by another more important one. The afterwards. The *Wedding Night,* the source of so much whispered speculation among my contemporaries. The bedroom scene at Kate Halstead's rose before me, the man's heaving body, the woman's moans and sighs. I stole a look at Lyon. He was listening to Father Étienne, his mouth slightly open, his wet hair hanging lankly about his ears. I could not imagine him naked no matter how I tried.

But there was to be no wedding night, not then. Lyon, afraid to venture out again in the lashing downpour, asked Father Étienne if we might stay until morning. Making an early start, we were to ride some ten miles upriver to Willowfoxe, a plantation belonging to Tom Deventer, the friend of Lyon's I had met at the Bridewell wedding.

"He's just come into his inheritance," Lyon explained, "and has gone to Boston on business. He plans to remain there for a month or two. By then I'm sure Papa and Mama will have come around and invited us home. In the meanwhile we shall have Willowfoxe to ourselves, servants and all."

So I spent my first night as Mrs. Bridewell on a narrow cot belonging to the housekeeper, wearing a tentlike gown kindly lent by her in order that my clothes might dry on a chair placed before the potbellied stove. I slept little, plagued by unpleasant dreams and long stretches of wakefulness during which I tossed restlessly. My hasty marriage, the elopement, my new husband, the house, the priest, the bed in which I lay all seemed part of a crazy, fragmented dream.

Lyon, bedded down in the overcrowded parlor amidst my petticoats, spent a poor night also.

"I kept sliding off that damned sofa," he complained later.

We left at dawn of a chill, sunless morning, taking the river road north. The rain had muddied the way, leaving morasslike stretches that threatened to mire the carriage and at one point actually did. Poor Lyon had to descend and, sloshing and thrashing about knee-deep in water, hoist us out. After that we spoke little. Lyon looked somewhat morose. I wanted to ask him if he regretted our elopement, but did not have the courage to do so. As Willowfoxe hove into view above the olive-colored trees, it began to rain again.

We turned from the road, jolting and splashing down the willow-shaded drive, the trees opening up to clipped, green, rolling lawns crested by the house itself, a two-storied mansion with a high, hipped roof, triple dormer windows, and wide galleries surrounded by turned-wood colonnettes. The moment we drew up to the front steps, two darkies came running out. Unfurling umbrellas, they escorted us up to the verandah. A black butler at the door gave Lyon a hearty welcome. He seemed quite pleased to learn that Lyon had taken a bride and kept pumping his hand, his face split in a wide grin.

"It'll make a man uv yo, Mr. Lyon—sho will."

"Thank you, Noah. And now I would like a brandy. I need it. My—my wife, I believe, would appreciate a bath and fresh clothes. You don't mind, Carmella, if I stay down here and have my drink? Tante Berthe will show you to your— our—," he corrected with a flush, "room."

A woman had emerged from a door beneath the stairs, a

mulatto, thin, with graying kinky hair and a long, sad face. Lyon turned to her. "Can my wife have Miss Mary's old room?"

Mary, Lyon explained, was Tom's sister, married and gone from home. "And perhaps Miss Mary would not mind if she borrows some of her clothes."

"No, Mr. Lyon."

I followed her up the stairs and into a large many-windowed room. A small black boy hurried in to light the fire, and when the flames sprang up I moved to the hearth. I don't think I had ever felt so cold and miserable in my life. I was hungry too. I hadn't had a decent meal in almost a week.

"I would like a cup of cocoa while I'm waiting for my bath, please," I said.

"Yes, Mrs. Bridewell."

Mrs. Bridewell. I hugged myself. It would take getting used to.

After I had toasted myself back and front at the hearth, I went over to the wardrobe and saw that Mary had indeed left several gowns. And at the bottom of the wardrobe I found a box, smelling of lavender, that contained chemisettes and petticoats.

I chose a violet velvet gown, the skirt trimmed with bands of black velvet edged in black lace. The form-fitting bodice culminated in a low neck and off-the-shoulder sleeves.

Two hours later, bathed, my dark hair dressed with combs and wearing Mary Deventer's violet velvet, I inspected myself in the gilt-framed oval mirror that hung on the wall. Enchanting, I thought, my pink cheeks glowing with daring immodesty, my eyes sparkling with anticipation. And how well Mary's gown fitted my figure, showing off my small waist and the white curving tops of my bosoms. Would Lyon be impressed? I came downstairs to find him waiting for me in the salon. He, in the meantime, had also changed and looked quite handsome in buff-colored trousers and a yellow waistcoat.

We had an early dinner *a deux;* court boullon, oysters, chicken breasts en papillote, pecan cake—a remarkable meal when one considered that the Deventer cook had received instructions only a few hours earlier. But I didn't consider the cook; I didn't think of anything but that wonderful food so different from Aunt Maude's stark fare, mine to eat, quantities of it, if I chose. I chose. Lyon kept filling my glass with champagne. "Drink up, Carmella." I needed no urging for that either.

Looking over at his plate, I said, "Aren't you hungry?" with a full mouth, breaking one of Aunt Maude's rules. How wicked, how brash, how delightful! I was Mrs. Bridewell now, a married woman. Fie on Aunt Maude's rules! "You haven't touched your chicken."

"I'd rather feast on the sight of you."

"Oh, Lyon, that was sweet," I said, reaching for another biscuit.

A bright flush stained his cheeks. I noticed he drank whiskey along with his champagne, but he had the right to celebrate as well as I. And whiskey was so masculine.

It wasn't long before we were both giggling and laughing foolishly. The champagne, lack of sleep, and an underlying uneasiness which neither of us would admit openly, had combined to make us silly. Except for the peck on the cheek at Aunt Maude's and the chaste kiss that had united us, there had been nothing between us to indicate we were newlyweds.

"We bamboozled them, didn't we?" Lyon said, repeating himself for perhaps the tenth time, sending us both into another fit of laughter.

"Yes—didn't we?" He filled my glass again.

Finally I reached the point where I could not eat another mouthful or sip another drop. The stays of my tightly laced corset digging my ribs had become an instrument of torture. I was tipsy, unpleasantly so, and my head ached.

"I—I'm very tired, Lyon." I brought the napkin to my lips, stifling a belch. "If you will excuse me, kindly? I will go up to bed."

Did he blanch, or was it my imagination?

"Of course, of course, go right ahead, angel. I shall join you sh-shortly."

"Yes, well, then . . . ," I murmured, glancing at him through demurely lowered lashes, trying again to imagine Lyon without the buff trousers and yellow waistcoat, then hastily putting the thought aside.

Upstairs Tante Berthe was waiting to help me undress and I gave myself over to her willingly. What a relief to get out of the gown, the stiff crinoline petticoats, what a blessing to have the corset unlaced and removed. Since I could not find a nightdress and had none of my own, I kept on the chemisette, a silk creation trimmed in delicate lace.

Tante Berthe left a small lamp burning on the bedside table. After she had gone I climbed gratefully into bed, sinking down on the soft goosefeather mattress with a sigh. The pillows and linen sheets edged in lace smelled of lavender and soap, and I snugged deeply, closing my eyes, then hastily opening them again. Was it proper to go to sleep before the groom arrived? A little thrill tingled down my spine and I turned on my side, my eyes glued to the door.

I must have dozed off, for when I awoke the lamp had burned low, its flickering wick throwing large shadows on the wall. I turned my head at a slight sound and saw Lyon standing in the middle of the room peering at me. Wearing a nightshirt that hit his thin, sticklike legs just below the knees, he looked disappointing if not a bit comical.

"Are you awake?" he whispered.

"Yes, Lyon."

Gazing at him, I felt a sudden small stab of doubt. Had I done the right thing? At the supper table, full of champagne and good food, everything had seemed so romantic. But now— I was alone with my husband, a man I hardly knew, a boy I had promised to love, honor, and obey for the rest of my days.

"I've brought us a good-night toast," he said, holding a bottle with one hand and two glasses with the other.

"I've already had so much. Oh—very well." I sat up while he poured, the bottle chattering against the glasses.

"God—but you are beautiful. Your hair." He put a hand out tentatively, touching my hair as it fell over my shoulders and down my back. "I've never seen anything like it."

I smiled. We drank to our future. I put the glass down; the champagne had gone flat.

"More?"

"No, I—uh—aren't you going to kiss me?" I asked at last.

He sat down on the bed and leaned over. Our lips met, his surprisingly warm. My arms went up around his neck and I drew him closer. The pressure of his mouth sent hot and cold ripples up my spine. My first lover's kiss, my first. But I wanted

more, and my lips parted as I pressed even closer to him, my
breasts pushing into his chest.

Suddenly he drew away.

"Don't you like that?" I asked.

"Yes, yes, but—you surprise me. I always thought that new
brides were—well, modest, if not a little afraid."

"I'm sorry if I am not as modest as you think I should be.
And I am not afraid. Really, Lyon. We are man and wife now,
aren't we?"

"Yes." He put his hand on my knee and began to stroke it.
Again the little thrills chased one another up my spine. He
grew somewhat bolder and his hands went under my chemisette
as he outlined my thigh and hip. I saw that his nightshirt was
beginning to bulge in the area of his crotch. My nipples burned.
I longed to have him touch them, but was afraid to suggest it
for fear he might think me more immodest than he already did.

Suddenly he said in a low, growly voice, "Lie down on
your stomach, and I'll rub your back."

I thought it rather odd to suggest a back rub at a moment
like this, but I did as he said.

He lifted my chemisette and began to stroke my back, his
hands going lower and lower until he reached my buttocks.
Then he lowered his head and kissed me there, his tongue
running up the cleft. I felt a surge of fire sere my loins and I
unconsciously arched my hips. He began to knead my buttocks,
squeezing, kissing them in turn, giving little bites, using his
tongue in quick, urgent strokes. My face flamed, perspiration
broke out on my forehead. I longed to turn over, to clasp him
to me, to beg him to ease the torment that gripped my loins.
But he had me pinioned between his knees and he went on,
breathing heavily, moaning low in his throat as his mouth and
hands became more frantic. Finally he separated my buttocks
and my body arched with the feel of his sudden thrust. "Not
there! Not there!" I wanted to scream, instinctively feeling it
was the wrong place. But once the first shock of pain had
passed, the sensaion was not unpleasant and as he moved back
and forth, waves of excitement began to pulse through me. His
hands clutched my arms, his nails digging into them, his hoarse
panting egging on my own rising passion. His arm went under

my stomach raising my hips against his kneeling body, his
strokes stronger, more excruciating now. God in heaven! And
then with a sharp cry, he collapsed on top of me, shuddering
convulsively.

After a few moments, he rose on his elbows, kissed the
back of my head, patted my naked rump, then pulled my chemisette down. "Thank you, my sweet."

I turned over and raised my arms to him. He kissed me
lightly on the lips. "Go to sleep now, Carmella. My wife." He
looked happy, content.

He crawled in beside me, pulling the covers up over us both,
and in another minute I could hear his even breathing as he
slept. But I lay for a long time staring up into the satin-lined
tester, bewildered, vaguely unhappy. Was this the consum-
mation? It had not been anything like the act of love I had seen
at Kate Halstead's. Perhaps only whores did it that way. Perhaps the first night was different. But no, something was wrong.
I instinctively felt that Lyon had not really changed me: I was
still a virgin.

As the days passed I found that Lyon preferred bedding me
in his own peculiar fashion and though in my naïveté I assumed
it was what all men did with their brides, it left me with a
feeling of confusion, a vague unrest I could not clearly define.
He enjoyed kissing me, to a point. He did not like parted lips,
and if my mouth inadvertently happened to open, he would
draw away. Neither did he like my breasts. That puzzled me,
because I thought men loved breasts in women, but Lyon did
not share this fondness. Never had I appeared naked before
him. He thought it immodest.

Otherwise he seemed a perfect husband—kind, affectionate, attentive, and fun to be with. At nineteen he was still as
much a child as I, and we played like children, literally—cat
and mouse; beggar, beggar; blind man's buff—laughing and
romping about Willowfoxe without a care in the world. In the
mornings we rode, sometimes following the curve of the brown
river, sometimes exploring the Deventer acres that reached for
miles and miles into the bayou, guiding our horses along animal
paths that skirted the humped knees of twisted mangroves growing up from the murky, algae-choked waters. We took long

naps in the afternoon, played patience, read to one another, and at night we slept the sleep of the innocent in each other's arms.

Was I happy? I thought so. Certainly Lyon was. I did not love him. I knew something was missing then. There was that vague dissatisfaction, those clouded nights. Still I wonder if we could have remained at Willowfoxe the rest of our lives, just as we were, the two of us, alone in the big house, cut off from the rest of society, if I might not have grown to love Lyon and put faith in my own happiness.

But I never had the chance to find out. Our idyll lasted all of three weeks, three brief lighthearted weeks that ended tragically, horrendously, a nightmare that was to haunt me for years to come.

We had gone up to the bedroom a little worse for after-dinner brandy, and Lyon, donning one of Mary Deventer's gowns, began cavorting about, sending me into gales of laughter.

"Put on my boots!" he cried. "We'll change places. My breeches too."

I thought it a capital idea—great fun. I drew his breeches on over my chemisette, then pulled on his boots. They were far too big for me and I clumped about in them like a clown until he caught my hand, swinging me into a formal minuet. We sang as we danced, our voices raised in boisterous disharmony, bowing elaborately, pirouetting, knocking our heads together. Lyon, holding me at arm's length, whirled me about in a dizzy circle, catching me as I stumbled, and I clung to him, weak with hysterical merriment.

Suddenly the door slammed open. I turned my head, the laughter dying on my lips.

Tom Deventer stood on the threshold, an angry scowl on his face, a dueling pistol in his hand.

Lyon and I gaped at him.

Tom took a step closer. "You goddamned bastard!" he cried, his voice shaking with rage.

"Tom!" Lyon exclaimed. "I thought—you were supposed to be in Boston!"

"I was and I've come back as you can damn well see. Why are you here with this bitch?"

"She's my wife, Tom. Carmella is my wife."

"Your wife?" He laughed, an ugly sound, a blood-chilling, mirthless laugh.

I backed away, tucking my breasts inside the low-cut chemisette, feeling exposed, shamed, ridiculous in Lyon's overlarge boots and tight, half-buttoned breeches.

"Mr. Deventer," I began.

"Shut up!" he commanded, his contemptuous eyes raking me from head to foot. "Hold your tongue, you little slut."

"Don't!" Lyon cried, his face flushed. "Don't speak to Carmella that way."

"And why not? Look at her in that disgusting getup, half naked."

"She's Mrs. Bridewell. I *told* you. My wife. We were married by Father Étienne.

"I don't give a damn who married you. You sneak, you dirty low-down rotten sneak. The minute my back is turned you betray me—and in *my* house."

"You said Willowfoxe was mine, any time—"

"Not to bed a woman, not to bed anyone but me. And you swore it, on your word of honor, that there would never be anyone but me."

I stared at him, then at Lyon in bewilderment. I did not understand—I couldn't. My mind refused to take it in. Nothing, not my reading, not Victoria, not even the brothel on St. John Street, the cribs on Canal, had prepared me for this. A man bedding a man?

"But that's in the past," Lyon protested. "I have a wife now. I love her, Tom."

"You love her," he sneered. "Did you tell her that she meant all the world to you—just as you did me?"

My stomach cringed. A clammy chill prickled my bare arms and I began to inch toward my dressing gown.

"Stay where you are!" Tom Deventer ordered, swinging the pistol around. "I want you to stand right there, bitch, do you hear?"

I froze, my limbs stiffening, only my eyes daring to move,

glancing at Lyon who stood clenching and unclenching his fists at his side.

"Well, Lyon, you haven't answered my question."

"That's all in the past," Lyon replied.

"Is it? We'll see about that. And in the meantime show your precious Carmella what love is really all about."

"No," Lyon said.

"Yes." Tom tucked the pistol under his arm and began to undo his breeches. They were coffee-colored breeches with pearl buttons. I shan't ever forget the way the light glinted on those milky buttons, nor the way the ring on Tom Deventer's finger sparked as he moved his hand.

"Get down on your knees, Lyon."

"No! I won't! I won't!"

Tom, his face an angry blotched red, his lips quivering, pointed the pistol at Lyon. "Down on your knees!"

"No! No! I hate you, Tom Deventer, I hate you! You are vile, evil. I h—"

The detonating shot shattered the air, jerking a scream from my throat. Lyon tottered for an eternal moment, his wide eyes darkening to a slate gray, before he crumpled to the floor. He lay very still, on his side, one arm flung out as if he were sleeping, except that his eyes were open in a blind stare.

I ran to him.

"Stay!" Tom barked. He pointed the smoking pistol at me. "Bitch! I told you not to move. You're the one I should have killed. You!"

I shrank back.

"See what you've made me do? Damn you to Hell!"

I tried to speak but my tongue refused to utter a sound. I gazed at the muzzle of the gun, a black hole, gazed at death and couldn't believe it. None of this was happening. I was caught up in some nightmare from which I would surely awaken.

But there was the pistol and Tom Deventer's eyes mad with cold fury. His finger twitched and I heard a click as he drew the hammer back. I couldn't die, I was too young, God wouldn't permit me to die; it went against all the laws of creation! *No!*

"What made you think you could take him away from me?"

My heart was knocking so loudly and painfully I could not utter a word.

The muzzle moved a fraction of an inch. I watched it, fascinated, the hole at the end seeming to grow larger and larger, blacker and blacker.

"You don't deserve a quick death. Something slow, very slow, to make you suffer. Garroting. Would you like to be strangled?"

I tried to wet my lips. The gun twitched and steadied. I saw his finger on the trigger, a stubby finger attached to a large hand wrapped about the pistol's handle.

I wanted to close my eyes, but I couldn't, I daren't. I kept on staring.

Then from the doorway a soft, slurred voice said, "Tom—Tom, son, give me the gun."

"Go away!"

"Give me the gun, son. Give your old Tante Berthe the gun." She spoke calmly, soothingly. "Be a good lad and give me the gun."

She was behind him now, reaching up. I didn't move. I wanted to scream, *Give it to her!* but the words only rang in my head. A swirling mist seemed to have come up between me and the two fingers and the gun, a mist growing darker and darker. I fought it with clenched fists and a heart pounding unevenly, because I believed with an unshakable conviction that if I took my eyes off that gun, even for an infinitesimal second, an explosion would rip the air and I would fall as Lyon had. So I stood there with burning eyes, staring through the gathering murkiness at the muzzle while Berthe in her even, gentle voice said, "Give me the gun, Tom."

Her hand came up slowly, and then with a sob Tom dropped it into her waiting palm.

CHAPTER

SIX

*M*Y RECOLLECTION *of what happened afterwards* is faulty. But I do remember being put to bed. I think it was Tante Berthe who made me drink a spoonful of bitter liquid and drew the covers over me. I remember the feel of wool blankets, the hot brick wrapped in a towel at my feet, the shadows on the ceiling before my eyes closed in merciful sleep.

What ocurred after I awoke in that bed, who dressed me, who brought be back to Aunt Maude's, and how we made the short journey is lost. But I recall Aunt Maude, her face livid with anger, what she said, what she called me—a slut like my mother.

"You've ruined my reputation," he said in a voice full of malice. "What a fool I was to take you in."

Her hands spasmodically gripped her handkerchief as she spoke,th knuckles whitening each time her fingers clenched it. I think she would have preferred having my throat between her tensed fingers instead of that scrap of linen, would have gladly strangled me if she could have gotten away with it. The thought did not disturb me. It was trivial. And that were a few trivialities? The real nightmare was so much worse. Through every waking moment, I lived and relived Lyon's death. And I had no one to speak to, no one to exorcise the ugly, recurring picture, the evil dream.

"I should have realized bad blood always shows."

I wondered how different she would have spoken had the Bridewells accepted me as Lyon's wife. She must have known where I was these past three weeks, known and waited for a happy outcome.

"I will write to your father and have him send for you at once."

I looked at her and said nothing. The muscles of my face felt numb. Should I smile, nod, say Thank you? My father did not matter. He was such a distant memory. I could not even recall his face.

"God will punish you," I heard her say. But I was already being punished, for what I did not know.

Aunt Maude locked me in my room again. No one came to see me. Victoria did not even try. There was only Aunt Maude.

"Now it's in the papers." She shoved a copy of *The Picayune* at me. "I hope you're satisfied. Never, *never* has anything like this happened to a Briscoe! In the tabloids—the whole sordid elopement and murder. Mrs. Bridewell cut me dead on the street yesterday. The papers say the family knew nothing of the marriage. Victoria claims it was a shock to her."

Of course they knew. Lyon had written them a letter. And Victoria, who had either wanted the excitement of playing puppeteer or had genuinely wished for her brother to prove his manhood, had arranged it. But now she had neatly separated herself from the affair. Her betrayal infuriated, hurt, bewildered, and finally embittered me.

The trial of Tom Deventer was held within two weeks of the murder—uncommonly soon, but the influential Bridewells and Deventers had demanded that it come to court quickly. Neither family wanted the proceedings to linger on, providing a stirred-up public with more gossip from the word mills already grinding at full tilt.

I took the stand as star witness, but I may as well have been the accused. The circumstances of my father's disreputable marriage were unearthed from the past and published in the newspapers. Characterized as the man who had jilted a socially prominent young woman (now by coincidence the mother of the dead victim) and taken the inmate of a St. John Street brothel as wife, my father was made to seem an unprincipled rake.

And I was his daughter. What could one expect?

The same papers hinted that I had lured the innocent Lyon Bridewell into marriage, that it was I who had planned our elopement, bribing a messenger to deliver passionate notes to him in secret.

The newspapers' lies did not bother me, however, half as much as the position the defense decided to take with the full cooperation of the prosecution.

Lawyer Helm, the prosecutor, informed me of it a day before the trial opened.

"They are going to plead that Tom Deventer shot Lyon, mistaking him for a thief."

"How can they?" I retorted. "It's not true."

"My dear child, the truth can sometimes be unnecessarily cruel. What good would it do to bring up Lyon's and Tom Deventer's—er—ah, sexual aberrations? And we would have to do that if we insisted on a charge of murder."

"But it *was* murder."

"We cannot prove it. There is no way we *can* prove it. So, my dear, my advice is to answer questions put to you with a yes or no, and offer no other information, none of what you have told me. Innocent people would suffer."

"But the law—"

"Why dont you leave the law to me? We men are quite capable of taking care of such matters. Don't bother your pretty head about the rights or wrongs. There is a higher justice, you know."

In the courtroom itself a higher justice looked blindly down while the farce played itself out.

"Mrs. Bridewell," the lawyer defending Tom Deventer began, "is it true that on the night of August 16, 1856, you and the deceased, Lyon Bridewell, eloped?"

"Yes, sir—at his request." I couldn't help adding those three words.

"Just answer yes or no, Mrs. Bridewell. You went to Willowfoxe without Mr. Deventer's knowledge?"

"I thought—"

"Just yes or no."

"Yes."

"So when he returned home late at night and saw a light in his sister's room, it was quite possible for him to believe the house was being robbed?"

"The servants—"

"Just answer yes or no, Mrs. Bridewell."

That is the way my interrogation went. None of the Deventer servants were called to testify. A Negro's testimony in a court of law held no legal weight, a fortunate circumstance especially in this case, that prevented any embarrassing cross-examination. However, no objection was made when their depositions were read. They all swore they had no knowledge of Tom's sudden arrival at Willowfoxe. They were asleep and so could not inform him that he had guests.

I sat there in the midst of those falsehoods, my heart hardening. I think the Deventers' lawyer would have been happy to repudiate my marriage. He may even have tried to bribe Father Étienne, but the old priest proved incorruptible—he had little to lose by being honest at his age. I wonder sometimes what they all would have thought if they'd known the marriage had never been properly consummated. But then that might have raised the sort of embarrassing questions the Deventers had sought to avoid. Not that I cared for *them*, but poor Lyon deserved better than to have his cold-blooded murderer pictured as a man simply defending his home.

After a short deliberation the jury found Tom Deventer guilty of manslaughter and the judge gave him a suspended sentence.

Two days later Aunt Maude heard from my father.

"Speaking of ingratitude!" she exclaimed, scanning the letter in her hand. "Why—I never . . . ! Here," she said, thrusting the pages at me, "read for yourself."

My dear Miss Briscoe:

Your communinqué was waiting for me when I returned from a six-month business trip to Sacramento and Fresno. I must say I would have cut my stay short had I know of the events described. Shocking! I thought my daughter would be safe with you and now it seems she was nothing of the kind. I hold you directly responsible. Our agreement bound by a substantial fee, was that Carmella should receive care, *protection*, and an education. You have breached that pact . . .

Aunt Maude, twisting her hands, murmured in the background, "To think I gave the best years of my life . . . ruined . . . ruined!"

I read on:

. . . therefore as soon as it can be arranged I am sending for her . . .

I read the passage again. Yes, it was *true!* After all these years it had happened. I was going *home*. Strange to think of a place I had never seen as home. But Papa would be there and that made the difference.

There was more:

". . . I am writing to a friend whom you might have already met, a Mr. Falconer now in St. Louis. He is planning to return shortly to San Francisco and I shall ask him to go by way of New Orleans and bring Carmella with him. He is apprised of her situation . . .

My joy collapsed to dismay. Mr. Falconer! My father, unwittingly, had made the worst possible choice of an escort. We had a long, and from what I understood, hazardous way to go. To travel that distance with someone as disagreeably superior as this man filled me with mortification. Papa had apparently informed him of my marriage and the subsequent scandal and I could expect to hear his views on the matter. But what could I do? Write Papa and ask him to replace Miles Falconer? It might take weeks, perhaps months to receive a reply. And what if Papa could not find a replacement? He would not permit me to make the journey alone. It seemed I had no alternative.

The first week in April, I received a letter from Mr. Falconer telling me he would arrive in ten days. "In the event I am delayed or am unable to communicate with you before hand," he wrote, "please be packed and ready to leave on the morning of the 12th. Take very little. We shall be traveling across the Panamanian Isthmus and up the West Coast of California. Space will be quite limited."

What Mr. Falconer meant by "very little" I interpreted broadly, going through my things, discarding what I could do without; old schoolbooks, back issues of fashion magazines, a shabby gown beyond repair, worn riding boots, a faded, much-mended cloak. The rest went into a steamer trunk crammed so full the lid had to be jammed shut and secured with a rope. It was a surprising accumulation for one who had lived with austerity, but like Aunt Maude I had never thrown anything away and what I had now represented eight years of my life. I was determined not to leave behind anything I cherished.

However, when Miles Falconer came to fetch me early in the morning on the appointed day, he took one look at the trunk and said, "Did you not understand me correctly, Mrs. Bridewell? We can only take bare essentials."

"These *are* essentials, Mr. Falconer." He made me uncomfortable. His broad-shouldered figure filled Aunt Maude's prim, old-maidish parlor with an air of male virility that bordered on the indecent.

"I doubt it, Mrs. Bridewell. Please remove what items you will need and put them in a portmanteau no larger than this." He indicated the luggage he carried, a fair-sized bag but small when compared to the trunk.

"You must be jesting. Why I couldn't pack as much as one gown and a petticoat in something like that."

"Try."

"No!" I cried. "I have no intention of embarking on a journey without clothes!"

"You hardly seem naked to me," he remarked, his eyes taking me in from the tips of my shoes to the top of my chignon-netted hair.

I made a great effort to swallow my rage. "Whatever you say, Mr. Falconer, the trunk *goes.*"

His face became bland, the hazel eyes expressionless. Only a slight twitch at the corners of his lips gave a hint that some emotion might be percolating beneath the unruffled exterior. It was a play of features I was later to term "the calm before the storm." But I had not yet learned to read the signs and so I went on.

"You can carry my trunk out, sir; that is, if you are able to manage without help."

He set his hat carefully down on a chair. "You seem to have difficulty with your hearing, Mrs. Bridewell. No trunk. *Please.*" Every syllable was uttered with an exaggerated courtesy. "It would be an encumberance we both would later regret."

I drew myself up. "I am sure my father is paying for this journey, and I shall take the trunk if I like."

Something unpleasant flickered behind his eyes. I had the strong feeling that in another moment he would strike me. But instead he reached into his coat pocket and pulled out a small knife, which he deftly unsheathed.

The knife startled me.

"Are—are you threatening me, Mr. Falconer? Because if you are . . ."

He reached over and with several quick slashes, cut the rope binding the trunk. Slamming the lid open, he reached in, grabbed a handful of petticoats and tossed them over his shoulder.

"Don't!"I shouted, clutching his arm. By now the clothes had become secondary to what I felt was a contest of wills. I resented his peremptory attitude with a passion that boiled at white heat. "I won't have you tossing my belongings about!"

"Have a tantrum if you wish." He pried my fingers from his coat sleeve. "But I'm afraid it does not change a thing."

"How dare you!"

Aunt Maude appeared in the parlor. "What have we here?"

Miles Falconer said nothing. He did not seem the least discomposed to have Aunt Maude find him with his arms full of petticoats and furbelows. But I poured out my resentment in a torrent of words.

"That's enough, Carmella," Aunt Maude interrupted in a crushing tone I obeyed automatically out of long habit.

"Do as Mr. Falconer says."

He had won. The small bag was packed while I gritted my teeth, my mind whirling with black thoughts of revenge.

We left immediately in a hackney, rumbling through the early morning streets past silent shuttered houses and shops.

A country wagon loaded with green cabbages, heading for the French Market, was the only vehicle we passed. When we reached the wharves, however, the day had apparently long since commenced, for the place was alive with bustle.

When Miles Falconer pointed out our ship, the *Northampton*, I could only stare at it in dismay. I knew little of vessels, only having been aboard the *Belle Creole*, an elegant river craft with polished mahogany decks and freshly whitewashed sidings. This ship by contrast was a tramp—shabby, streaked with coal soot and rust, and small, very small.

"Hurry," Mr. Falconer urged, taking my elbow, making for the gangplank. "We are late as it is."

"But it seems—it seems so *unseaworthy*," I protested, dredging the word up from one of my innumerable novels.

"Nonsense. Do you think I'd put us aboard a ship that wasn't safe? The *Northampton's* seen glorious service on the Atlantic run, still sound. Both sail and steam. Watch that step."

My cabin had a narrow bunk, a cracked mirror, a tiny chest, a tin basin, an enamel pitcher, and fittings that once must have been gilt but were now tarnished to a lusterless green. Space was at a minimum. I and my portmanteau were an intrusion, and once the wooden slatted door closed behind me I had to fight the sensation that I had been thrust into a broom closet. The stale air, the strong odor of bilge and damp, did not help. Removing my bonnet, I leaned over the bunk and struggled with the porthole, yanking and pulling until it finally flew open. Through it I could see the ship tied up alongside us, a sleek clipper, *The Swallow* painted in red on its white hull. She was all masts and rigging now, but I could imagine her at sea, sails unfurled, billowed by wind, cutting swiftly through the water like some huge, many-winged bird. I wondered why Falconer had not chosen such a vessel, which surely must offer superior passenger quarters, rather than this old scow he seemed to prefer.

Later, when I went up on deck, I asked him.

"Because, my dear Mrs. Bridewell, clippers do not make the Panama run. They sail by way of the Horn, most setting out from New York, going round South America and thence up the coast to San Francisco. We are taking the shorter route— it will save time."

"Are you in such a hurry that you would sacrifice comfort, if not safety?"

"To answer the last first: I've already told you this ship is as safe as any; comfort is secondary; and yes, I am in a hurry. The sooner I get you to your father, the happier I will be."

"In that I heartily agree, Mr. Falconer. You don't imagine I relish the prospect of a prolonged voyage with you?"

"Certainly not." His mouth twisted into a smile. "But this is not a pleasure trip, is it?"

"Not in the least." And turning on my heel, I went back to my cabin, resolved to have as little to do with Miles Falconer as the ship's confinement would permit.

I watched from the porthole as we got under way, moving slowly, the wharves with their cluster of masted ships growing smaller as we stood out in midchannel. A sidewheeler passed, belching gray smoke from its twin stacks, the water churning white beneath its great wheels. Then with a lurch and throbbing of engines, the *Northampton* swung around, heading toward the Gulf some 107 miles distant.

The ships horn blasted twice, raising goosebumps along my arms, gripping me with sudden excitement. I was leaving New Orleans for good. Behind were Aunt Maude, Lyon, the trial, and all the nastiness of the past. Ahead waited a great adventure, a new life, a new city, new faces—and Papa to welcome me to it all!

CHAPTER

SEVEN

THE SHIP'S passengers, twenty-five in all, took their meals, a late breakfast and early dinner, in two shifts. Miles and I were on the first shift. I suppose I could have arranged to eat later and thus avoid him, but I did not want to make an issue of it.

As I entered the dining room salon that first afternoon, I saw Miles already seated at one of the tables. He was talking to a man who had his back to me.

"Ah—here is my charge," Miles said, getting to his feet.

The man turned and slowly rose. He was young, he was handsome: square chin, a classic nose, and a tanned face framed by blond sideburns and sun-streaked hair. His eyes, a deep blue, were frankly admiring.

"Miles, you old reprobate, you didn't tell me your so-called charge was a beautiful woman." He smiled at me, showing white even teeth.

In a rather stiff, offhand way, Miles said, "Mrs. Bridewell, this is a fellow Virginian, Mr. Derry Wakefield."

"How do you do?" I said, giving Mr. Wakefield my hand.

"Charming," he murmured as bent to kiss it. His lips brushed my skin with a touch that tingled my nerve ends. "Indeed the most charming creature I have met in a long, long while."

I liked him at once. I liked the way he looked in his gray

peg-leg trousers and his finely tailored worsted coat. I liked
the way he smiled, the blue of his dancing eyes, the feeling
he gave me of being important, noticed, alive.

"How fortunate to be making this trip together," Mr. Wakefield said as we seated ourselves at the table. "I was just telling
Miles that I was looking forward to weeks of tedium—and
then you appeared."

It was a compliment—exaggerated perhaps—but one that
warmed me.

Miles cleared his throat. "Mrs. Bridewell has been fretting
about the ship's ability to reach its destination."

Fretting. Why did Falconer have to describe my legitimate
concern in such childish terms?

But Wakefield did not seem to notice. "You needn't be
anxious, Mrs. Bridewell, not with two strong men to protect
you."

The food was surprisingly good: a thick gumbo followed
by crayfish in piquant sauce. But I suppose anything would
have tasted delicious with Derry Wakefield sitting next to me,
attentive and amusing.

"I made an Isthmus crossing in '49," he said. "At the height
of the Gold Rush. I was only eighteen then."

I did a hasty calculation in my head. Eighteen—what?—
six, seven years ago—that would make him twenty-five—a
marvelous age! Was he promised, engaged, married?

"An older cousin had persuaded my parents to let me go.
They thought..." He paused to chuckle. "They thought it
would make a man of me." He leaned forward and spoke to
Falconer. "Did you by any chance ever make that trip before
Aspinwall put his railroad across the Isthmus?"

"Yes."

"Formidable, wasn't it?"

"Yes, it was," Miles Falconer said tonelessly.

"I, for one, will never forget it." Wakefield turned to me.
"Impenetrable, fever-ridden jungle, hostile Indians, bands of
renegade cutthroats, and hordes of gold-seekers bartering for
canoes—bungoes, they called them—to take us up the Chagres
River. Am I boring you, Mrs. Bridewell?"

"No, not at all. Please continue."

I was aware of Miles's patient ennui. Perhaps he had heard

similar stories. But why should I care if he found Derry Wake-field's account uninteresting?

"My cousin John, an amateur botanist, became quite ecstatic about the plant life and was forever wanting to stop to collect specimens, a practice that nearly proved our undoing." He paused while the waiter filled his cup with coffee.

"What happened?" I asked.

"We got separated from the others, and as we rounded a bend we were set upon by an ugly mob of Indians and white ruffians."

"How terrible!"

"We carried guns, primed and ready, of course. John and I managed to kill three of them before the others took fright and disappeared into the trees."

Miles said, "Strange, those brigands must have mistaken you for men returning from the gold fields. They rarely attack those going."

"Yes, isn't it?" Derry Wakefield commented, not the least disconcerted by Falconer's rude interruption.

"When we reached Gorgona we had to leave the river and continue on to Panama by mule. I won't dwell on *that* except to say that it rained every step of the way. Then, once we reached port, we had to wait three weeks before we could find a steamer to take us on. The voyage itself was humdrum and would be too tedious to recount."

Did you find gold?" I asked.

"No," he said, shaking his head ruefully. "A few ounces of worthless dust. That was all."

"But it made a man of you," I teased.

"It most certainly did." He laughed, his eyes sparking pin-points of amusement as they went over me.

On our first night out to sea I stayed up to watch the moon rise after most of the other passengers had retired. Behind me, in the salon, a group of men, Miles Falconer and Derry Wake-field among them, had gathered to play cards. I found a slatted chair and sat down to enjoy the evening, throwing my head back to gaze at the diamondlike stars glittering in the dark sky above. The voices of the men at their gaming came to me in the intermittent snatches.

"Mrs. Bridewell?"

I turned, a little startled, but smiled when I saw who it was.

"What a pleasant surprise!" Derry Wakefield stood in the light thrown on deck by the salon's chandelier.

"I—I wasn't tired enough to go to bed."

"Your first sea voyage?"

"Yes. But from what I understand, the Caribbean is not considered a proper sea."

"Don't let anybody tell you that. If you'd ever been caught in one of its fierce hurricanes, you'd think differently."

"It seems so peaceful now. I don't feel in the least seasick."

"Perhaps you won't ever be. Come to the rail. I'll show you something."

I got up and he gave me his arm. I liked the strong, solid feel of it as we strolled to the ship's side.

"Look," he said, pointing.

There, cutting the water in a phosphorescent glow, were several large fishlike creatures. As I watched, one leapt out of the water in a graceful arc, then another and another, a whole school cavorting alongside us.

"Dolphins," Wakefield said.

"Why! I never . . . ! They're absolutely the most astonishing things."

"Aren't they? For some reason they love to follow ships. Good luck, sailors say."

We watched for some time until the dolphins disappeared.

"Have you known Miles for long?" Derry Wakefield asked.

"No. I met him only a few months ago. He's a friend of my father's."

"So he said. You're Arthur Hasting's daughter."

"Yes. Do you know my father?"

"Slightly. We—that is our families—are from the same county in Virginia."

"Along the Pamunkey River?"

"Yes. Beautiful country. Have you ever seen it?"

I shook my head. "No. Well, I suppose your father never went back. Emigrés rarely do."

"Emigrés? I don't understand."

"Perhaps your father can't be put in that category. But emigrés are sons who have been sent off into the world and invited not to return: Miles, because of a duel; I, more recently—well, the gossip wouldn't interest you."

It did, but I felt it would be unladylike to admit that.

"Miles is still dueling, you know," Wakefield went on, "I heard he called some man out in New Orleans, Mariette, I believe is his name. But then you probably know all about it."

"I'm afraid not."

"How surprising. He fought the duel because the man had insulted you."

"What! Are you sure?"

"A friend of mine was Mariette's second. It seems the scoundrel read something in the papers which he repeated in a public place."

I was glad the darkness hid the sudden heat that rose to my cheeks. I had also read the tabloids that had so incensed Aunt Maude during the trial.

"But when was this?"

"I believe around the tenth or eleventh of April."

So that was why Mr. Falconer had not arrived at Aunt Maude's until the day the ship sailed.

"Did—did he kill Mariette?"

"Wounded him—in the right arm, they say."

But he could have killed him, or been killed. For me. And he had said nothing about it.

"What a strange man," I murmured.

"Yes. Doesn't say much. Plays his cards close to the chest. In fact, rumor has it that he has won and lost a fortune at cards."

"He's a professional gambler?"

"No, I wouldn't call him that. His income is derived from various properties in New Orleans and San Francisco. He told me once he owned a small mine near Hangtown but claimed the gold in it was all played out. He believes all the mines in that area are finished. I think he's wrong. Mark my word, there is still plenty of glitter to be found in those mountains."

"You are going to try your luck again?"

"Why not?" He gave me a wide grin. "But then we've spent enough time on unimportant matters. I want to hear about you."

The moon had come up and it shone on his fair hair, turning it to silver. He looked slender, urbane, and very much at ease as he lounged against the rail, smiling at me.

"There isn't much to tell, Mr. Wakefield. I—I lived with Miss Briscoe—Aunt Maude—for eight years, went as a day student to Peebles Female Academy, and I married—no doubt you heard of *that*."

"Most unfortunate, most unfortunate," he murmured sympathetically. "To lose your husband in such a wretched accident. And you had been married only a—a what . . . ?"

"Not quite a month."

"Sad. But I see you are not wearing widow's weeds. I wonder—"

"Oh," I interrupted hurriedly, "Mr. Falconer advised against it. On account of the warmer climate. He says the Isthmus is quite tropical. It's not that I did not love Lyon—my husband—I did. And were I to remain in New Orleans, I would not think of being seen except in black crêpe."

"My dear, there's no need to apologize. You are much too young to be in mourning. What you wear is irrelevant, for I have no doubt you carry your husband's image in your heart."

"Yes," I said, twisting my hands, gazing out at the luminous night. The truth was that Lyon's face, his voice and laughter were beginning to fade from my memory. Our morning rides, daytime frolics, and nightly lovemaking seemed to have happened a long time ago. Only the picture of him lying crumpled in death remained hauntingly clear.

"There now," Derry Wakefield said comfortingly. "I have made you feel sad. I am a boor to have brought the unhappy situation back to you. Please forgive me."

He lifted my hand and pressed his lips to it, banishing the morbid image of poor Lyon from my mind.

"You are very beautiful," he said in a low voice, my hands still in his. "The most beautiful woman I have ever seen."

It was the sort of compliment that called for a flirtatious rebuttal, I suppose, but I didn't feel at all coquettish. I felt strangely moved.

"I was drawn to you the minute I laid eyes on you. Do you think me impertinent to say it?"

"Oh, no, no!" I protested, touching my free hand to his waistcoat.

He grasped it and held both my hands against his chest. "Can you feel how my heart is beating?"

"Yes," I whispered, "like mine."

He leaned down, his lips resting lightly on mine. "You are trembling, my dear." He drew back. "Have I frightened you?"

"No—oh, no!" Perhaps I *was* afraid of this man whose touch had aroused a disquieting excitement inside me.

"If I kiss you . . ."

Oh, please do! I wanted to urge. But mightn't he then think me bold, wanton?

"I shan't mind," I murmured.

He pulled me slowly into his arms, circling my waist, drawing me close until my breasts were pressed against the buttons of his waistcoat. He ran his finger down my face, following the curve of my neck. I couldn't see his eyes as he bent toward me, his mouth trailing across my cheek, finding my lips, tasting them. I stood on tiptoe, head tilted back, breathless, trembling again. Suddenly his arm tightened, his mouth moved from side to side, hungrily, as if to devour me. His kisses became more passionate, more frantic. The very bones in my body were dissolving into sweet fire. My lips parted and his tongue flicked in, touching, exploring. Never had I been kissed like this, never felt such tremulous sensations. I leaned into him.

He lifted his head. "Carmella . . ."

My arms went up around his neck, pulling him back, quelling the hesitancy in his voice. I wanted his mouth on mine again. I wanted the feeling of my bones melting, and the hot blood rushing to my face, and my tongue on his, and his hard body, his urgency now swollen, pressed against me.

He nuzzled my ear and bent his head to kiss the pulse in my throat, his mouth burning my flesh. My hands passed over the back of his golden head and slowly down between his shoulder blades. How would he look naked, I wondered—a wicked, wicked thought which nevertheless sent a shudder of pure delight through me.

"Carmella, you are driving me mad," he murmured, his lips resting on my cheek.

"Kiss me, don't stop . . ."

A burst of laughter, voices, drew us suddenly apart. Someone was coming up from the salon.

"Straighten your hair," he whispered.

I ran my hands over my hair and jerked my bodice into place. Then, standing some feet apart, we studied the sea in silence.

"So—there you are," Miles Falconer said.

"Through with your game?" Derry asked. "Mrs. Bridewell and I were enjoying the evening air."

"We saw some dolphins," I added, my voice a little unsteady.

"Most instructive," Miles said. Was he peering at me? Did I look guilty, sinful?

"Mr. Wakefield tells me that you recently fought a duel," I said, seeking a topic to divert him. "Because of me."

Miles Falconer did not answer at once, but extracted a cigar from a gold case, then lit it, the match flame throwing a cone of yellow light across his strong nose and frowning black brows.

"Yes, I fought a duel I am sorry to say, sorry because I think duels, for the most part, are errant nonsense."

"But you—"

"I had no choice. The man made a scurrilous remark about you, Mrs. Bridewell, and you happen to be the daughter of a dear friend. I called Mariette a liar, and the next thing I knew he had slapped me. I would have broken his jaw and settled it there, but others restrained me. This was New Orleans, they said; disputes among gentlemen were resolved differently there."

"So it was my father's honor, not mine—"

"My dear Mrs. Bridewell," he said with biting irony. "I hold your honor in great respect."

Mr. Falconer, as always, had a way of taking the wind out of me, of making me feel small and petty.

Derry Wakefield moved closer. "I shouldn't hesitate to fight a duel for your honor, Mrs. Bridewell," he said quietly. "I think Mariette deserved to die."

A stray puff of wind had ruffled his hair, and his eyes as he gazed at me were filled with a soft, tender light. He seemed to me at that moment like a knight-errant standing gallantly between me and a barbarous world.

"Thank you, Mr. Wakefield," I said with heartfelt sincerity.

Miles Falconer turned to look at him, then at me.

Let him stare, I thought, let him think what he likes. I don't care. I have found something I have always wanted, something I have always dreamed about. For the first time in my life I am truly in love.

CHAPTER

EIGHT

A WEEK later I stood at the rail of the Northampton with Miles Falconer and Derry Wakefield and watched the Panamanian coastline take shape. It was an awesome sight. Blue-green mountains rose abruptly on the horizon, their peaks swathed in towering thunderheads, the valleys misted with vapor. Through wispy streamers of fog, there glimmered a verdant green, a blanket of lush foliage which clothed the landscape down to the very water's edge. Even out at sea I could feel the steamy heat of the jungle, smell its sweetly rotting odor on the faint shore breeze.

An Indian in a dugout darted out from one of the inlets, the boat's ragged sail billowing in the wind. The native stood before the crude mast, a solitary figure, dark and stocky, giving the forbidding scene behind him an added air of mystery.

"Slippery, sly devils, those savages," Derry commented.

"Savages," Miles Falconer repeated, irony edging his voice. "Those savages are slippery and sly because we have made them so. It's the only way they can survive our treachery."

Derry's brows went up. "That's rather strong, isn't it?"

"Not at all. Read your history. Remember Columbus? Here, in the Caribbean, searching for a route to fabled gold, he massacred whole tribes; and those he spared, he took prisoner. The people hanged themselves rather than submit to slavery. Almost a half century after Columbus there was Drake, on the same

quest for gold, treating the Indians no better than his prede-
cessor. And more recently, ourselves, still looking for El Dor-
ado, this time in California, tramping across their forests in
great swarms, treating those 'savages' worse than we treat our
dogs. Is it any wonder the natives who wish to survive learn
cunning?"

"You see it from a narrow view, Miles. Very narrow."

Falconer shrugged, turning his gaze once more to the horizon. Derry caught my eye and winked.

Ever since that starlit night when he had kissed me, we'd
had few opportunities to be alone. Miles Falconer suspected
something, for he watched me more closely after that, rarely
playing cards in the evening, strolling the deck by my side like
a tenacious chaperone if I claimed I needed air or exercise.
One night he was detained in conversation by the captain for
over an hour and Derry and I managed to get together, ex-
changing hurried words and endearments as I nestled in his
arms. Falconer narrowly missed catching us.

Later he took it upon himself to give me advice I found
spiteful and mean-minded. "I wouldn't get tangled up with
Wakefield," he said. "He won't marry you."

"Why not?" I retorted. By now I felt that Derry loved me
as I did him, that it would only be a matter of time—a decent
interval respecting my mourning—before he declared himself.

"Derry is not the marrying kind. He has loved and left
dozens of silly young women like yourself from Virginia to
San Francisco."

"Really?" I said haughtily to hide a pang of jealousy. "Perhaps he never found the right girl."

"And you, of course, are the right girl. Yet suppose, for
argument's sake, he should decide to marry you. He would be
hard put to support a wife. Derry himself will be the first to
admit his pockets are virtually empty. And he can't go back
to Virginia."

"Is his family that much against him?"

"I thought he had already told you."

Derry had hinted at it when he called himself an emigré,
but had not explained why he had become one. Men of good
family usually left home, or were disowned by their kin, for

three reasons; making a vastly unsuitable marriage as my father had done; killing a man in a duel; or cheating at cards. Derry was not married, and if he had participated in a duel with a fatal ending he would surely have mentioned it when he spoke of Miles Falconer's affair of honor.

"He was accused of cheating at cards?" I hazarded.

"It's not for me to say."

"But such accusations are often untrue."

Falconer made no comment. He was not going to explain. It went against his code, I suppose, to speak of another man's disgrace. But I somehow did not think a little slight of hand (if that is what it was) at monte or faro *was* a disgrace. Cards had always seemed rather silly to me; the importance men attached to them absurd.

"In any case," I said defiantly, "I don't care. I'm in love with him."

"In love, are you? And what of Lyon, Mrs. Bridewell, did you love him too?"

"Of course. But one can't mourn forever."

"You are perfectly right, if one considers two months 'forever.' Well—it's not my affair. What *is* my concern, however, is delivering you safely to your father. In the meanwhile I expect you to conduct yourself with a modicum of propriety."

Propriety. What good had it ever done me? I looked back on my dull years with Aunt Maude, the bleak Sundays at church, the boring Tuesday teas, the routine Saturday calls.

And now?

How could I possibly be proper when it came to Derry? Or he with me. We were meant to love each other, and I was not going to spoil my happiness by keeping him at a distance simply because it wasn't "proper."

The ship's engines throbbed and we moved forward, slowly rounding a spit of land.

"Limon Bay," Miles Falconer said. "And there's Aspinwall. The Spanish call it Colón."

Beyond the docks where several ships were tied up, I saw clusters of frame buildings standing under the tattered shade of fronded palms.

An hour later we debarked and were taken by a mule-drawn

hackney to the City Hotel; where we would spend the night prior to boarding the train for Panama City in the morning. It wasn't long before I was perspiring copiously in the oppressive heat. I could understand now why Miles Falconer had advised against heavy clothing. Even in my muslin gown, I felt sticky, uncomfortable, wilted. We had hardly reached the hotel when it began to rain, a heavy downpour that brought no cooling breeze but only increased the humidity.

The hotel itself had the look of a third-or fourth-rate hostelry. But Miles Falconer said we were lucky to get any accommodations. Many people coming off the boat had to sleep on cots set up on the balcony.

We had our dinner in a narrow dining room, eating at one long table, much as we had done on shipboard.

Miles said, "I'm afraid we'll have to stay another day or two. The man I was supposed to meet here has not arrived yet. They are expecting his ship to dock tomorrow, a day after at the latest."

I looked at Derry and he gave me a quick reassuring smile. "Miles, I hope you won't think it presumptuous if I wait too?" he asked. "I've enjoyed your company, and yours also, Mrs. Bridewell, that I hate to think of going on alone."

"Suit yourself," Miles said, in what I thought was an abrupt manner.

Miles Falconer's man arrived the following noon and he went off to meet him, first, however, giving me another lecture on "behaving like a lady."

"If it's Derry you are worried about," I said spitefully, "he's gone to a cockfight."

I sat in the hotel lounge with a Mrs. McNutt from Passaic. She and her husband were going to settle in San Francisco where Mr. McNutt's brother had opened a bake shop. She described the entire process of bread-making in endless detail. I was looking for a polite way to escape her company when Derry suddenly appeared.

"Ah—there you are!" he exclaimed, coming toward me, smiling and extending his hand. "Mrs. Bridewell!"

I introduced him to Mrs. McNutt. He acknowledged the introduction in a charming manner, sending a pleased flush to her face.

"I hope you won't think me impolite to snatch Mrs. Bridewell from you," he said. "The desk clerk has informed me that he has a message for her. I believe from your father, Mrs. Bridewell."

"I hope it isn't bad news," Mrs. McNutt said.

We crossed the lounge and went out the door. Derry drew me aside, making sure that Mrs. McNutt could not see us. "How was that?"

"You mean—"

"It was a ruse."

"Oh, Derry!" We both laughed. "You are so clever! How could you guess?"

"I saw your face. Bored, bored, bored."

"But I thought you had gone to a cockfight."

"I did, but I kept thinking of you. Carmella . . ." He lifted my hand, kissed each of my fingers and the palm. "Let's walk," he said.

Away from the hotel's shadow the sun was blinding. We rounded a corner of the building where several large willow trees shaded the tin roof. He drew me under their branches.

"Carmella . . ."

His arms linked about my waist and he bent his head, resting his mouth against my cheek. I shifted my face slightly and we kissed chastely. He laughed in his throat, a laugh more like a growl, and with a convulsive movement pulled me to his chest, his lips claiming mine in a long, passionate kiss. My arms went up about his neck and I felt his heartbeat, a thud against my breasts.

"Carmella, I'm mad about you. If only . . ." He broke away, looking deeply into my eyes. "If only I could hold you and not have to be afraid of prying eyes."

"Oh, Derry, I feel the same."

"I'm afraid it's not what a gentleman should say to a lady."

"Oh, Derry!" I flung my arms about him, covering his face with small nibbling kisses.

"I have no money, Carmella. I can't marry you. I can't marry anyone. And yet you are the only woman I could possibly love. I feel—you may think it strange—I feel you are already my wife."

"It isn't strange, Derry. There isn't anything I wouldn't do for you. Derry, please kiss me again."

But he took hold of my wrists and held me away.

"We can't—not here in public. If someone sees us...My dear, I wouldn't risk ruining your reputation."

"I don't care, I—"

"No—hush." He touched my lips with a finger. "I can't have you speaking like that."

"I mean it, Derry."

He lifted both my hands and kissed them. "If we could be alone, for an hour, a half hour..."

"Yes, Derry, yes. Where?"

"My room. Tonight, after everyone's gone to bed." Then, looking at me, he shook his head. "No, you mustn't. No."

"Yes, yes! I'll be there."

There was doubt in his eyes, and pain. "I am a dastard."

I pressed my fingers to his lips. "Don't. I love you. God smiles on lovers."

I had no idea what time it was. It seemed hours since the sun had set in a red, angry flush, bringing sudden darkness. I sat on the edge of the bed wearing my wrapper with nothing beneath but my chemisette. My hair was still up in a chigon and ear curls, and I kept twisting one and then the other around my finger. I could hear a man and woman talking in the corridor, footsteps, the sound of a slamming door. Someone close by laughed shrilly. The noise outside seemed to increase rather than diminish as time dragged on. Did people in this hotel never go to sleep?

I went to the window and peered out into the night, but I could see nothing except a dim light winking far out to sea. It began to rain again, thrumming on the tin roof with a hollow, echoing sound.

Was I doing the right thing? Yes, *yes!* I mustn't think about right and wrong. But a girl who valued her reputation did not go to a man's room alone, at night, especially if she felt as sinfully drawn to that man as I did. Would Derry think the less of me?

I got to my feet and began to pace the room. Why should

he? He had only to look into my eyes to know that what I felt for him went beyond the touch of lips, the pressure of an embrace. I loved him. From the moment he had turned to me on the *Northampton* my life had become inextricably bound with his. And Derry loved me too. He would marry me once his prospects improved. "I feel you are already my wife" he had said. What better proof of a man's intentions could a woman have?

Presently the sounds of activity outside abated and then ceased. Only the rain continued, a steady monotonous downpour. I inched the door open and putting my eye to the crack saw Miles Falconer coming along the passageway. I shut the door quickly, leaning against it and listening as he unlocked his own door, opened and shut it. I stood there counting my heartbeats, sixty to the minute. When I had reached what I thought was the equivalent of ten minutes, I cautiously peeked out again. No one was in sight.

A lamp down the hall cast a feeble light on the worn floorboards. A cricket rapsed somewhere, loud and shrill. I closed the door softly and started tiptoeing, wincing at the loud creak of a wooden slat. Just as I came abreast of Falconer's room, the door opened and he stood there like a menacing ogre, his hulk outlined by the light behind him.

"And where do you think you are going?" He spoke in a low, intimidating voice.

"To—to the lavatory."

"Oh?" His tone told me exactly how he felt about the verity of my answer.

I drew myself up. "Are you accusing me of lying?"

"Now that you mention it—yes."

"Why you—you cad!"

"I may be a cad, Mrs. Bridewell," he said smoothly, "but that doesn't make *you* any less a fabricator."

"I don't wish to discuss it with you. Good night!" I started to walk away but he reached out and grasped my wrist.

"Not so fast, Mrs. Bridewell."

"Let go of me this instant!"

Something about the man brought out the perverse in me. It would have been wiser to retreat and postpone my visit to

Derry's room, but once Miles Falconer had challenged me I found it impossible to give in.

"I resent your high-handed manner, Mr. Falconer. I resent your playing God the Father. I resent—"

"Hush! Do you want to wake the entire hotel? If we must argue, come inside." He pulled me into his room and closed the door behind us.

"If this isn't the height of sheer audacity!" I spluttered, trying to free myself. "Let me out!"

He released my arm but ignored my command, and leaning against the door, studied me. "Mrs. Bridewell, you seem to forget that you more or less promised to behave until we reached San Francisco.

"Are you insinuating that I am not?"

"You were no more going to the lavatory than I was preparing to dance a jig."

"Well, dance your jig, because I *was* on my way to the lavatory."

He was in shirt-sleeves, his open collar revealing a patch of dark hair, and I found the sight of him in such partial undress disturbing.

"May I make an educated guess as to where you were going?" he asked.

"Please do," I challenged.

"Not to the lavatory, but to a certain gentleman's room."

"How presumptuous!"

"I beg of you!" He held up his hand in a mock gesture of self-defense. "Forgo the maidenly protest. I just happened to catch a glimpse of you and the—ah—let us call him the 'unnamed gentleman' in a passionate embrace."

"Spy!" I shot at him. "Not only are you a tattler but you are also a spy."

"Tattler?"

"You told Aunt Maude about my going to St. John Street— though you gave your solemn word you would say nothing."

By then I had come to realize Victoria Bridewell's deceptive nature and as a consequence wasn't really sure whether it was she or Miles Falconer who had informed on me. But I was in no mood now to give Miles Falconer the benefit of my doubt.

"I won't dignify that statement by a denial," he said.

"Because you are unable to. Spying and tattling are hardly gentlemanly occupations, are they?"

His facial expression did not change, but behind his eyes flickered a small naked flame that leapt up for a split second and vanished.

"Do you really believe you can put me off by calling me names?" He grabbed my wrist again.

"You have no right—let go!" I struggled but he held on, his fingers tightening cruelly.

"Look at you." His eyes swept my belted dressing gown. "And you were going to him just like any paid doxie."

The insult jabbed a raw nerve. I struck him. It happened so quickly, so unexpectedly, it surprised even me.

He put his hand to his cheek where the imprint of my blow had left a red blotch. His face had gone stiff, white, his eyes hard. I sensed a powerful emotion working behind that white mask, a raging fury held barely in check, and a little shiver worked itself up my spine. I did not know what sort of violence I had triggered, but it—he—frightened me. Why, then, did I persist in baiting him? I don't know.

"I'll do that again," I said, "unless you open that door."

"You'll not do it again, not to me. You are a spoiled, willful child. What you need is a good thrashing."

"If you try—just try, I'll scream."

"I don't doubt it. But I'm not going to be threatened by you—or anyone. Go ahead, scream. Suffer the embarrassment of being found by the hotel guests, including your erstwhile lover, wearing nothing but a wrapper in my room."

I suddenly realized he had whiskey on his breath, and for some reason it fueled my anger.

"You call me a doxie?" I hurled at him. "Why you are nothing better than a drunken black sheep!"

His eyes flamed. I made to move back but he caught my shoulders and began to shake me so violently that my hair tumbled loose from its pins. Flailing out I struck him blindly, muttering between gritted teeth, "Black sheep! Black sheep!"

With a quick, catlike movement, he stooped and lifted me over his shoulder. I gave a strangled cry, "Stop!" beating futilely on his back with my fists.

He carried me across the room and threw me roughly on the bed. "We shall see who is who," he said, removing his belt.

I tried to rise, but he pushed me back. Tears of rage brimmed my eyes. "You can't! I shall tell my father!"

"Tell him. He'll thank me."

I lifted myself once more and he bunched up the front of my dressing gown in his fist. I could hear my chemisette tearing underneath. "For once in your life you are going to learn you can't have your way."

I spat at him. He threw me back on the bed and my wrapper fell open but I didn't care. At that moment I was not thinking of him as a man, only as a tyrant on a par with Aunt Maude, but worse, much worse. He had gotten his belt free and he paused suddenly, looking down at me with the same sort of look he had given me in Mrs. Halstead's parlor before he learned my name. There was something oddly exciting in the way his eyes took in my exposed breasts, my hips, and the dark patch of hair under my transparent chemisette.

"You can't!" I cried, ashamed to be feeling anything but disgust and anger toward this man. "I am not a child."

"God—no!"

I kicked out, catching him in the midriff.

I should not have done that. Almost before my foot connected with his body, I knew it was a mistake. He would take my slaps and futile punches, but not a kick. Dogs were kicked, not men.

His wrath broke and he cracked the belt across my stomach. The pain seared me like a brand and before I could collect the scream in my throat, he had straddled me, his hand over my mouth.

"Shut up!" he ordered through his teeth, his eyes slitted with fury.

And now I was really afraid.

"You seem to have a fondness for callow boys. First your husband, then that"—his head jerked in the direction of the door—"milk sop. You've never had a real man, have you?"

"If you mean—"

He brought his mouth down on mine in a savage kiss, painful, brutal, as if to punish. I beat at his back, raking his shirt with my nails, feeling the stuff tear. When he let me go I rolled to the edge of the bed and tried to scramble free but he brought me back, ripping the chemisette completely from my body. He tossed it aside and pinned me between his knees. His dark hair had fallen over his forehead; he was like a madman, and for one flashing moment I had a vision of the Indian in the masted dugout, a dark stocky savage Miles had defended, a figure of the terrifying unknown.

"No!"

But my denial was lost—a weak, futile cry in a tumultuous storm.

With a sharp jab of his elbow, he separated my legs. Holding me down with one hand clamped on my shoulder, he quickly shed his trousers and lowered his weight, his hand running up my inner thighs. I struggled under him, writhing from side to side, but I succeeded only in pressing my naked breasts against the unrelenting hardness of his chest. His arm went under me, a band of steel, imprisoning me while his lips claimed mine, twisting and turning, ravaging my swollen mouth.

When he entered me I arched my hips in shock at the pain. The stabbing jolt was so unexpected, so unlike anything I had been led to expect that it launched me into a new frenzy of terror. I plunged my hands into his thick dark hair trying to pull him away, but he sank his teeth into my shoulder and began moving inside me, going deep, deeper with each thrust. I wanted to scream, "Stop!" but I seemed unable to gather the strength. And as he moved, my hands fell limply to my sides, my mind divorced from the affront upon my body, thinking only of revenge, of hate.

He finished with a shudder, sprawling over me. I felt wet and sticky between my legs.

He lifted himself and looked down at me. I couldn't see his eyes—my own were full of tears. He moved from me, resting his hands on the bed, drawing his trousers on. Then he paused and said:

"My God!"

I saw his face now, pale; his eyes reflecting perplexed astonishment.

"You're a virgin!" His brow creased. "I never dreamed . . . Why didn't you tell me?"

"I didn't think you would rape me."

He leaned over and pulled the wrapper from out of the tumbled bedclothes and tossed it over me.

"What kind of husband did you have? My God—a virgin!"

He went to the table and lifted the whiskey bottle, then put it down. "I never imagined . . ."

I watched him closely. Until tonight I had never seen him other than cool, poised, collected. The breach of that calm exterior, the savage eruption of temper, was surprising but hardly more so than his present distracted air. He was upset and showing it. Gazing at him as he reached again for the whiskey bottle and poured himself a drink, I momentarily forgot my aching limbs, the whiplash across my belly, the puffed lip where he had bruised it. My pain faded as a feeling of sweet revenge surged through my blood. He had wronged me and I would make him pay. I had the upper hand now.

But I was mistaken, as I had been before and would be again. No one ever got the upper hand with Miles Falconer.

CHAPTER

NINE

"*I* WAITED *for you last night,*" Derry said. "Waited until long past midnight."

"I'm sorry, Derry. Miles—Mr. Falconer—caught me just outside the door."

"Does he—did he suspect?"

"I think not." I had decided not to tell Derry what had happened, although it had been my original intention. I had even pictured Derry challenging Miles Falconer to a duel, the two of them standing at ten paces under Aspinwall's palms. But if Derry should kill or wound Falconer, the subsequent scandal might throw a shadow over our future. Or suppose the reverse should happen, suppose Falconer should kill Derry? I couldn't risk that. I wanted Derry alive, unhurt, wanted him to reach California, find his gold, marry me. And no affair of honor should stand in the way.

I would plan my own revenge. I was not quite sure what it would be, but my heart swelled when I thought of the possibilities. Retribution must come in the form of a slow, painful ordeal, something that would humiliate him as he had humiliated me.

"I should never have asked you to come to my room," Derry said.

"Please, please, I *wanted* to. I put my hand over his. "My darling, we'll find a way to be together. Be patient."

We were sitting in the hotel lounge while Miles went to make sure our tickets were in order. Except for a terse apology, he had not spoken to me since the night before, and when he looked at me his eyes were veiled.

"Carmella, of what are you thinking?" Derry asked.

"Of you," I said quickly, returning his smile, relegating Falconer to the back of my mind. "Just you, darling."

"You're beautiful and sweet. I adore the way your eyes sparkle, that saucy little grin of yours."

I wanted him to go on saying things like that, making me feel admired and loved. I yearned for intimacy between Derry and myself, for shared secrets and dreams.

But Miles Falconer was walking toward us, a slight frown between his eyes.

"The train leaves in fifteen minutes," he said brusquely. "We'd best get over to the depot—a short walk, or would you prefer riding, Mrs. Bridewell?"

It does not matter to me. Derry?"

"We can walk. I assume our luggage will be put aboard?"

"Yes," Miles answered. His manner toward Derry, as usual, was polite, rather chill, but Derry did not seem to notice. He had told me that Miles Falconer was known for the distance he kept between himself and others. "A cool sort," was the way he put it.

The parlor car into which we were shown had plush and cane seats, a velvet rug running down the narrow middle aisle, large rain-streaked and sooty windows set in bright brass frames. We took our seats, and the train, tooting a funny little whistle, drew out of the station.

The journey covered a distance of forty-five miles in a world of eerie jungle, gloomy, sunless, and drenched with intermittent showers. Huge red blossoms like bloody gashes sprouted from tree trunks leaning over the Chagres River, its muddy waters reflecting the funneled engine and the long string of cars behind.

Within long stretches of forest nothing at all grew under the trees. "Lack of light," Derry said. So the trees struggled with one another, rising tall and slender, fighting to reach the sun. Except for a multitude of birds, I saw no animals at all. And no Indians.

"Hunted out," Derry said.

Miles did not speak but sat with his head buried in the *Aspinwall Courier*, rustling the pages at intervals. I found the sound vastly annoying.

It was five in the afternoon when we chugged our way into Panama City. Above the clay-tiled rooftops the mother-of-pearl towers and dome of a cathedral scintillated in the angled sunlight. The upturned faces in front of the station and along the tracks were swarthy for the most part, but here and there the white visage of a gentleman or lady could be seen.

We descended to heat that seemed less oppressive to me than Aspinwall's. The shops, too, appeared fairly decent in contrast to the scruffy ones on the Caribbean side of the Isthmus.

"It's changed since '49," Derry remarked as we sat in a hansom waiting for our luggage to be loaded. "I remember the heaps of refuse, the foraging dogs, and the fallen drunks cluttering the puddled streets. The city fathers must have cleaned it up."

"Yes," Miles said. "Rubbish discourages commerce."

On our way to the hotel we passed several villas surrounded by high adobe walls, the palms and flowering trees peeping over them suggesting gardens behind. But these apparently affluent residences were few in comparison to the smaller baked-clay warrens, the tin-roofed shacks, and the palm-thatched lean-tos. The hotel itself coul have been a replica of the City Hotel, with the same enclosed verandahs, the same wooden stairs, and the same dusty lounge that smelled of cooking oil and damp rot.

"Our steamer will be ready to board in the morning," Miles said as we sat wedged among a hundred other diners an hour later. "I advise an early to-bed."

I did not look at Derry. Again Miles had been too vigilant for us to snatch even a moment alone. His zealousness in keeping us apart seemed laughable in view of his own breach, and I wondered if deep inside he did not feel a bit hypocritical in his role of policeman.

The next morning we were taken out on lighters to the *San Mateo*, a black-hulled steamship with crisscross rigging and an ugly smokestack at either end. From the deck I had a view of the Panamanian coastline curving out into a spit dotted with clumps of palms against a backdrop of lurid jungle green. Far to the west the gray Pacific, smooth as a lake, stretched to a luminous horizon.

The ship carried about 150 passengers, mostly men. Those in first class, like Miles, Derry, and myself, were well dressed, but the steerage passengers, with their rope-tied rucksacks and cheap cardboard cases, wore cracked, muddy boots and patched coats. They were crowded together, sleeping in hammocklike beds, one slung over the other in tier after tier, their cramped quarters affording little privacy, much less room to move about in, though I was told the women and children were separated from the others in a curtained-off area. It must have been unbearably hot in the hold with the ship's engines pumping away, for I could feel the fetid heat like a blow each time I passed the narrow hatchway that led below.

I thought such conditions inhumane and said so to Miles. He agreed. "As bad as they are, there's been a great improvement over the old days when the Gold Rush was on and men were packed together aboard these ships like herrings in a barrel. By comparison they are traveling in luxury."

It wasn't my idea of luxury. But truthfully, for the most part, I paid little attention to my fellow passengers. Derry filled my thoughts. During the day when I could see and talk to him, when we could stroll the deck together (with Miles shadowing us like some oppressive nanny), I felt happy enough. It was the long dark nights, when I lay in a bunk rolling to the gentle sea swell, listening to the snores of my female companions (we were four to a stateroom) that were a torment. Tossing and turning as much as my narrow bed would allow, I would wonder if Derry was lying awake too, restless, longing for me as I did for him. I would have given anything to be possessed by him, to be his wife in fact if not in name, to have had him as my first. Damn Miles Falconer for robbing my lover of his due! What right had he to pretend he was a man of honor?

One night, after having spent hours in the usual feverish seesaw between Derry and Miles, I fell asleep and had a strange dream. Curiously my mother played a large role in it, and though I had never seen her I recognized her because she looked so like me, except for the hair, which instead of my own dark color was inexplicably a flaming auburn.

She smiled at me seductively, red full lips parting over white teeth, but the next moment Miles Falconer appeared and I realized her smile was meant for him, not me. He came up to her and she put her hand on his arm, tilting her chin, smiling up into his eyes. He embraced her, bent his head, and kissed her. I could see the line of my mother's white throat straining as she met his lips, saw her hands creep up to his broad shoulders and clasp his neck. He began to unbutton her bodice and she, impatient, helped him. She wore nothing underneath (and a little thought pinged in my dreaming brain, *Whores go naked under their gowns).* Her milky breasts shone, smooth and firm, their coral ruchings peaked like tiny buds. His hands went over the twin globes, cupping and stroking, before he bent down to kiss each. I heard myself gasp with pleasure as if they were my breasts, feeling the warmth of his lips. His mouth opened and his tongue began to lick the nipples and my gasps turned into a low moan.

Then I awoke.

The dream left an unpleasant taste of guilt in my mouth. I felt disoriented, puzzled, deceived. My mother and Miles? How obscene! Could Miles have been Angelica's lover? He would have been eighteen at the time she married my father, close to her age. The idea shocked and disturbed me. I didn't want to think about it, yet the dream haunted me all the next day.

I remembered it again vividly one wet rainy night when at long last Derry and I managed to find ourselves alone. The captain had arranged a social in the salon and an entertainment below for the steerage. Those of us who had not cared to attend either event, stood on deck huddled under a tarpaulin to avoid the intermittent showers that swept the ship in gusts. I don't recall what had taken Miles from my side, but Derry and I unmindful of the rain had sought refuse in the lee of a lifeboat. We wasted little time in conversation, but locked in an embrace exchanged hungry, passionate kisses, our tongues touching and tangling, plunging me into feverish turmoil. My heart beat like a wild thing at the closeness of his body, its muscled hardness.

"Carmella—I do love you."

His hands moved down my bodice, undoing the buttons slowly. "If—would you—could you . . . ? I simply want to see them, even in the dark."

"Yes, Derry, oh, yes."

He brushed the chemisette aside and I felt the heat of his hand as he held my breast, just as I had seen Miles do in the dream, just where I had always yearned for Lyon to touch me. I wondered at the thrill that ran through me, the way the blood rushed to my face. When Derry caressed the nipple with his lips I gasped, the same way I had gasped in my dream.

I drew back. "You—you mustn't," I said, but my voice was weak, tremulous.

"You are so beautiful, every part of you, and every part dear." There was worship in his voice, tenderness. "I won't kiss you there, if you say no." He began to close my chemisette. "I thought you loved me."

"Oh—I do, I do!" I pressed my lips to his mouth, found his hand, and brought it back to my breast.

He pushed the cloth aside and began to stroke me again, his thumb going slowly over the nipple, while his mouth found the hollow at the base of my throat. I could feel the pulse there throbbing under his lips.

He bared the other breast and, holding both, bent to kiss the cleft between. "Beautiful," he murmured, "so beautiful." He trailed tantalizing kisses over them, took a nipple once more in his mouth, this time sucking on it, not letting it go. I touched his bent head, wanting to press him into my body, yearning for him to take me, to ease the mounting tension in my loins.

"Carmella . . ."He rested his cheek against one breast. "I can't bear it. We should be together, not here, like two furtive lovers in the rain."

"I know, darling. It's not the rain I mind, but—"

"Mrs. Bridewell?" Miles's voice reached me through the misted darkness. "Mrs. Bridewell?"

God in heaven! My first impulse was to remain silent, but Derry must have thought better of it. Quickly he rearranged my clothing, buttoning me up with nimble fingers.

"He would guess, and it might go ill for you," Derry said.

How ill I chose not to speculate.

* * *

We had been at sea for a week when some two dozen passengers, including one of my cabinmates, came down with yellow fever. The highly contagious, often fatal disease was no stranger to me, for my nurse, Cecilia, had died of it in a New Orleans epidemic when I was a child.

As the news leaked out on board ship, near panic ensued. Miles immediately raised a fuss to have me moved.

"Mrs. Bridewell is under my care," he told the captain. "I want her placed in another cabin."

"We are hard up for space, Mr. Falconer." The captain was a heavy-set man with full sidewhiskers and a harried look in his crow's-footed gray eyes. "We are doing our best to cope with matters."

"The best is not enough. I cannot risk Mrs. Bridewell catching the illness."

The captain studied the chart on his desk. "I am trying to isolate the sick from the well. Some are too ill to be moved."

"They shall die in any case," Miles said with what I thought was cold heartlessness.

"True," the captain murmured. "Very well. I will see what can be done."

We waited on deck while the captain made the necessary arrangements.

"I suppose I should thank you for your concern," I said, unable to hide the sarcasm in my voice.

"You needn't," Miles replied shortly. "My concern is for your father, and were it not for him, I wouldn't give a tinker's damn what happened to you."

"My, my," I mocked. "How direct you've become. Swearing, using such unbecoming language."

He gave me a look that would have nailed a lesser soul to the mast. I pretended to ignore it. "You weren't too concerned for my welfare," I went on in the same mocking tone, "at the City Hotel, were you?"

"I've already tendered my deepest apologies. Once, I believe is enough. What happened cannot be undone, though I would give my right arm to have it so. You can be certain the incident will not be repeated."

"Can I? Suppose you get drunk as you were then, suppose that—that . . ."

"You appear before me in little more than your wrapper?" he supplied. His lip curled. "My dear, you overestimate your charms. Drunk or sober, if I am inclined to bed a woman, I can find at least three or four aboard this ship that would be equally appealing, perhaps more so since they would not have your waspish temper."

"And I suppose yours is as sweet as honey."

"Not if I am goaded, and for *that* you have quite a talent."

And before I could think of a suitable reply, he turned away.

All but eight of the yellow-fever victims died. I had hardly known them, but their passing depressed me and when their shrouded bodies catapulted into the sea, I wept.

The funeral delayed us further, but then the *San Mateo* picked up steam, plowing through the waves, bearing northward. We had four ports of call, Acapulco, San Blas, San Diego, and Monterey, before we reached San Francisco, and the captain was thinking of eliminating San Blas. As Derry explained it, the owners of our ship, the Pacific Mail Steamship Company, had the reputation of running the fastest line on the West Coast, a reputation the captain and crew had been ordered to preserve at all costs.

"The captain will probably hug the shoreline to shorten our route," Derry said.

I had noticed that we were frequently in sight of land, the tawny, tree-dotted hills and curving beaches always to our right.

"But it seems that it would be more expedient to sail in a straight line instead of following the ins and outs of the shore."

"Ordinarily, yes. But if you look at a continental map of the United States and Mexico, you will see that the coastline bulges outward. To put to sea would add leagues to the voyage."

"Well—yes, I suppose you are right. As a matter of fact," I added, "it's rather comforting to be so close to land."

"I suppose most passengers feel the same. Actually it takes extraordinary seamanship and a thorough knowledge of the charts to keep the ship from striking tidal reefs."

"Reefs?" I echoed, looking at the cream-crested combers, one following the other as they broke on shore. "In these waters?"

"My dear, I did not mean to frighten you. I'm sorry. There is no cause for alarm, I assure you. The Pacific Mail prides itself on its officers. They are all well-trained, skilled, and seasoned men."

But what Derry did not tell me was that even the most expert mariners proceeded along the coastal route under a handicap. Existing charts were incomplete and sometimes misleading, lighthouses and buoys marking dangerous submerged promontories practically nonexistent. So we steamed on, the passengers in ignorance, the engines sending thick billows of black smoke from the stacks. We ate, we slept, we strolled the deck, played cards, read, conversed, Derry and I holding hands whenever we could manage to evade Mile's disapproving scowl.

Then two days out of Acapulco at four o'clock in the morning on a calm sea the ship hit an underwater ridge.

CHAPTER

TEN

THE SHUDDERING jolt nearly knocked me from the bunk. It awakened my cabinmates, and one of the ladies began to shriek, "My God! My God!" as a mirror fell with a tinkling crash.

"What is happening?" an alarmed voice passing outside the door queried. Our lamp had gone out and nothing could be seen in the inky blackness.

"We're sinking!" the hysterical lady sobbed. "I know it! We're sinking—oh God!"

I heard running footsteps, shouts, and the ship's horn bleating in distress. The eerie sound brought a sick lump of fear to my throat. I searched blindly for a match, found and struck it. The single flame threw a macabre yellow light on two pale, frightened faces and the figure of the lady who "knew it" hastily getting into her clothes.

"Are you certain?" I began. "The captain—"

A knock on the louvered door cut me short. "Everyone out! Hurry! Don't dress, ladies, come as you are. Everyone out!

Habitual modesty being stronger than the peril of a watery grave, we all drew our petticoats over our nightgowns and flung wrappers around us before hurrying out on deck.

The ship's crew acted with remarkable discipline. Though there was panic and pandemonium, they managed to herd the passengers into some semblance of order, separating the men

93

from the women and children. Standing on the bridge, the captain spoke through a bullhorn.

"Please—please—all of you remain calm. We have plenty of time. The ship has sustained only minor damage. But for safety's sake, we'll disembark. No pushing! *No pushing!* Everyone will be taken care of—we're only a few yards from shore. Behave like civilized men and women, *please.*"

People were in all states of undress, women in petticoats and shawls with blankets thrown about their shoulders, some of the men in their long johns but wearing shoes and hats.

"Women and children first," the captain ordered. "The odd-numbered lifeboats. No pushing, please!"

The ship had begun to rock on the incoming tide.

Miles was at my side. Except for his waistcoat and jacket he was fully dressed. "Come along, Carmella." He got hold of my elbow and started to direct me toward the Number 1 lifeboat.

"Where's Derry?" I asked, hanging back. "I won't go unless I know Derry is safe."

"Damn you!" Miles cursed between his teeth. "Forget Derry. He can take care of himself."

A whiskered man ran past, shouting, "Hurry, you fools! The ship's stove in! She's filling up with water."

An officer caught him by the sleeve. "Hold your tongue!"

The whiskered man yelled, "We won't last, we won't—"

The officer hit him in the jaw with his balled fist.

"D'you want a stampede?"

I pulled at Miles, trying to free myself. "Where's Derry? I must find Derry!"

Cursing, he scooped me up in his arms.

"Let me down! Derry! Derry!" I pummeled his chest, my legs kicking in a flurry of petticoats.

Holding me tightly, he pushed his way across the crowded deck and dumped me unceremoniously into the lap of an indignant matron already seated in the lifeboat with a score of others. Before I could apologize, the boat began to move on its davits, swinging into the sea where the waves slapped at the sides. The men in our boat leaned on the oars, pulling us around, heading toward the invisible shore. All I could think of was Derry. Had he been injured? Why hadn't I seen him?

If something happened to Derry I couldn't go on. He was the core, the center of my soul. Nothing else mattered.

In my agitation I rose to my feet, looking back at the ship. Someone hissed, "Sit down!" but I continued to stand, peering through the darkness though I could see nothing. The wind had grown stronger, sweeping the waves into huge combers and I staggered as we slid into a watery trough. When we began to climb out again, a huge wave caught me before I could regain my balance and I was swept overboard.

My first reaction was one of total disbelief as tons of water dragged me down into choking, lung-bursting darkness. I swallowed quantities of salt water before I had sense enough to shut my mouth against the screams of terrified protest rising from my chest. After what seemed an eternity of thrashing about, I broke the surface long enough to take a deep breath before another huge wave washed over me.

I did not know how to swim, or even how to stay afloat. Ladies, and for that matter most men, never thought it expedient to learn. But instinct and fear kept me paddling and kicking. My sodden, clinging garments impeded my movements and threatened to drag me under until I wriggled free of my wrapper and one of my petticoats. The water, to my surprise, was beastly cold. In the darkness I could see nothing except the foamy, phosphorescent crest of the next wave.

"Help!" The wind tore the weak sound from my mouth, less than a whisper in the roaring turbulence. Gasping and bobbing, I rode under another mountain of water.

A sudden horrible feeling of helplessness, the feeling that I was but a speck in the vast, hungry, fathomless sea, engulfed me. But it lasted only a moment. For despite my earlier wish to die if Derry did, a strong, bulldog sense of survival I never realized I possessed took hold of me like a pair of hands, giving me the strength to raise my voice in a shriek.

"Help!"

The sea was *not* going to claim me! I wouldn't let it!

"Help!"

A ray of light cut through the water, a beam so faint I thought I imagined it. But then I heard a voice shout, "Grab hold!" and an oar was thrust at me.

They dragged me into the boat, gasping and sobbing, water

streaming from my petticoats. A blanket was wound around my shoulders. The same voice that had ordered me to sit down now trumpeted, "Serves you right!" But the woman sitting next to me murmured kind words as she mopped my face, brushing the damp hair from my brow. I was stunned to hear that I had been in the sea only a matter of minutes.

By the time we reached shore the sky was beginning to pale. Helped from the boat, I stood on unsteady legs as the ground under me seemed to heave and pitch like the *San Mateo's* deck. We were in a small bay where the waves broke in lacy foam along a sandy beach strewn with driftwood and decaying seaweed. Behind it rose the green jungle, a mass of dark trees whispering and rustling in the predawn breeze.

We woman huddled together while the other boats arrived, discharging their passengers. Some of the children having recovered from their initial fright began to complain of being hungry. A babe in its mother's arms wailed incessantly, refusing to be quieted, until the mother sat down away from us and gave it her breast. Out in the bay the ship, though leaning to one side, gave no sign of sinking beneath the waves.

I shivered under the blanket, chilled by my clammy petticoats. The woman who had sat next to me on the small boat said, "Why don't we gather wood and build a fire?"

"Oh, yes," I agreed. "A wonderful idea!"

Now that the light was stronger I recognized her. A plump, short individual, she was traveling with her daughter, a little girl of seven, and a companion, a thin woman with abundant red hair worn in an untidy bun. Neither of them was attractive; both, gossip claimed, were prostitutes. Though they kept to themselves and behaved decorously, I did not doubt it. They had a certain air, a particular camaraderie between them I had sensed between the two women in the open barouche on St. John Street. The other female passengers avoided them like the plague, taking care to keep their distance, no small feat on shipboard. However, I felt no compunction to snub them, and were it not for my absorption with Derry I might have befriended the pair. They aroused my sympathy, for when I looked at them, I thought of my mother and wondered if she too had been so scorned by her more fortunate sisters. But it was the little girl toward whom I felt most compassionate. Was it because I believed, there but for the grace of God and Arthur Hastings go I? Perhaps. At any rate, the child, unlike her mother, was lovely. She had golden ringlets that bobbed when she walked, large blue eyes, and a pert nose. Her mother called her Sarah.

She, the two prostitutes, and I set about picking up chunks of driftwood and setting them in a pile. We managed to get a sailor to light the fire, although he said he didn't see the point to it. By that time the sun was peeping over the trees and the sea wind had died. "In a half hour, you'll be wishing it was cold again," he told us.

"Is the ship badly damaged?" I asked the sailor.

"I don't know, Miss. Here's another small boat comin' in. Mebbe they could tell us."

The boat contained a single passenger—Derry. I ran to the water's edge as he jumped out.

"Carmella!"

His arms went around me and I nestled close to him for a few moments, conscious of the shocked looks from the women who had drawn away from me and my wood-gathering friends.

"Oh, Derry, I'm so ashamed. I fell overboard and had to be rescued. But don't tell Miles Falconer. He'll find something nasty to say."

"So it was you. We'd heard that somebody got a ducking."

"A ducking! I thought I was drowning." I could laugh about it now.

"I should hope not." He linked his arm in mine as we walked up on the beach. "Are you sure you weren't hurt?"

"I'm sure, Derry. Can't we go back to the ship?"

"Not yet. The captain feels it would simplify his problem if the women and children remained here for a while. There doesn't seem to be anything wrong with the *San Mateo* except that she's stuck on a sandbar. Miles and the men passengers are helping the crew shift the cargo so that she'll float on the incoming tide. I should be there now giving them a hand, but I took the opportunity of coming ashore with the sailors sent to recall the others. I had to see if you were all right first."

"You're sweet, Derry."

"Sweets to the sweet." He smiled down at me. "Is there anything I can do for you?"

"I'd like my clothes."

Little Sarah nudged me, tugging at the edge of my blanket. "Could he bring a biscuit?" she whispered.

"I'll try," Derry said.

We waved good-bye as Derry and the sailors shoved the boats back into the water and rowed toward the ship.

Meanwhile the sun climbed higher. We moved back into the shade, the properly bred females seating themselves apart from us. The plump little prostitute introduced herself as Mrs. Porter, the thin one as Miss Mason. We discussed the ship, speculating on how long we might be stranded ashore, Miss Mason giving us an account of a "gentleman friend" who had been shipwrecked off the coast of Peru and had spent a year there waiting for rescue. I, of course, had to put in that my grandfather, a ship's captain, had drowned at sea in a storm near Portugal. We had been conversing for perhaps fifteen minutes, meanwhile watching the *San Mateo*, when Mrs. Porter turned her head and said:

"Where's Sarah?"

She had been playing in the sand beside us only moments earlier it seemed, and now she was nowhere in sight.

"Where's Sarah?" Mrs. Porter repeated, her voice rising with fear.

"She's around somewhere, I'm sure," Miss Mason tried to assure her.

"Where—I don't see—the water . . . !" The plump woman struggled to her feet. "Sarah! Sarah!"

Miss Mason touched her hand. "She didn't go anywhere *near* the water, Daisy; we'd have noticed."

"Sarah! I'll box her ears! Oh, God, where is she? Saraaaah!"

I hurried over to the other woman. "Mrs. Porter seems to have lost her little girl. Did she come this way?"

They looked at me with blank eyes. Not only did I consort with prostitutes, but I had openly embraced a man who was neither my husband nor close kin.

"Surely one of you must have seen her."

A small boy in a striped jersey said, "I did. She went in

among them trees." He pointed to a banana thicket on the edge of the jungle.

I turned quickly to go when a woman said, "You can't rush in there alone."

It was Mrs. Ransome, who had the cabin next to mine. She was a robust matron whose husband had been a consular agent in Mexico for many years.

"That's jungle," she said. "I've seen people swallowed up in that kind of forest and never found."

"But this is a little girl," I protested. "And her mother— whatever you may think of her—is frantic."

Mrs. Ransome hoisted herself to her feet. "I can appreciate that. I'm a mother too. I'll help. At least we can go in pairs."

No one else volunteered.

"Keep the sun's position in mind," Mrs. Ransome cautioned before we separated from Mrs. Porter and her friend.

It was steamy under the trees. The smell of rotting vegetation hung like a tangible aura in the cathedral gloom. Because sunlight filtered in only at odd intervals, I wondered how any of us would be able to follow Mrs. Ransome's advice.

Meanwhile we kept calling Sarah's name, parting giant ferns, looking under bushes and vines. I could hear Mrs. Porter shouting too, her voice getting fainter in the distance. "Sarah? Sarah, where are you?"

Gnats and mosquitoes rose in clouds as we moved through the undergrowth. The blanket I still wore, though cumbersome and hot, protected me in some measure from their onslaught, but my shoeless feet gave me trouble. Decaying matter, skeletal leaves, spongy twigs, and an occasional unseen insect tortured my tender soles. Bird cries of alarm echoed from treetop to treetop, but we rarely saw one of these tropically plumed creatures, and I wondered what other denizens lurked in the shadows around us.

I thought of the child Sarah in this dangerous, claustrophobic wilderness, alone and by now probably frightened. I could picture her weeping as she stumbled, tripped up by a trailing vine, calling to her mother and getting no answer but the mocking shriek of a watching, beady-eyed bird of prey. Was her small heart beating frantically even now? Poor child, poor little darling.

"Sarah!" I yelled at the top of my lungs.

I stopped and held up my hand. "Wait! I think I hear something."

Mrs. Ransome cocked her head. "I don't. But then you have younger ears."

"It sounds like someone crying. Over there. I shan't be a minute."

"Mrs. Bridewell..."

"It's just beyond that tree."

I stepped over a log alive with ants, and walked quickly to the tree. But there was no one there. I hesitated, listening. Yes, that whimpering sound again. Farther on. I threw Mrs. Ransome a glance over my shoulder and then hurried forward, coming out into a small clearing bathed in tropical sunlight.

"Sarah! Sarah, are you here?"

Only the sound of a thousand insects, a humming shrillness, answered me.

I turned to retrace my steps, or thought I was retracing my steps, going back through the trees, even stepping over a log. But Mrs. Ransome was not waiting for me when I got to the place where it seemed I had left her. I called out and when I received no reply, hurried on.

In a matter of minutes I realized that either Mrs. Ransome had not waited for me—which was unlikely—or I was lost. I stood very still, my heart beating as I imagined little Sarah's might beat.

"The jungle swallows you up," Mrs. Ransome had said.

If I could catch a glimpse of the sun I could tell which was east or west, and taking a westerly direction come out on the beach. However, here in this part of the rain forest bathed in perpetual emerald shadow such a sighting was impossile. I turned back again in order to find the clearing I had just left.

It wasn't there.

And now I was really lost. Momentary self-castigation gave way to a rising panic. Everything looked so *alike!* Oh, God, which way?

For a few moments I experienced the same feeling of utter helplessness that had washed over me in the sea. It had almost undone me then as it would surely do now, if I let it. I must *not* give in to it.

I shifted the blanket on my shoulders, clasping it around me with quivering hands. Then I began to walk. Sooner or later I had to come to another clearing.

The blanket grew heavier, its weight drenching me in sweat. But I was afraid to discard it, not so much because of the insects but because in some obscure way, I felt it offered protection against fright. As I walked, I called out to Mrs. Ransome or to Sarah every now and again, my voice gradually taking on the tones of weary futility.

Presently I came to a stream, a sluggish, leaf-choked rivulet, the sight of which cheered me considerably. Streams ran down to the sea, I told myself. I had only to follow it and eventually I must emerge from this rank, verdurous nightmare.

I had been walking for some time when the stream was joined by another, a more swiftly moving one. Along it ran— could it be?—yes, a path! Buoyed by hope, forgetting a growing thirst and painful feet, I went on. Soon the stream became wider, now running over a bed of gray rocks and pebbles. I heard the sound of tumbling water and in another moment came into a small clearing where the stream pouring over an outcrop of rocks fell into a circular pool.

I got down on my knees beside it and drank, taking long grateful draughts. The water tasted brackish but eased my parched throat. The pond was shallow; I could see the bottom and the undersides of the floating lily pads that grew around the edges. I sat down and dangled my lacerated feet in the water, thinking how wonderful it would feel to bathe all over. My earlier immersion in the sea had left a residue of salt on my underclothes, which together with perspiration made them feel like an itchy hairshirt next to my tender skin.

I debated for a few moment, torn by the need to reach safety and the pull of the cooling water. I felt I shouldn't tarry, but on the other hand a quick wash would refresh me, thus enabling me to continue on at a faster pace. Throwing the blanket aside, I got out of my petticoats and chemisette. When I stepped into the water it came up to my waist and felt heavenly. Crouching, going under, I rinsed my hair, throwing its long wet heaviness back from my face. Plucking a trailing branch of vine, I stripped it of leaves and used it to tie my hair. Then wading farther in I stood under the rocks and let the water fall on me, closing

my eyes, opening my mouth, enjoying the feel of the refreshing
splash on my back, between my breasts.

Suddenly, over the sound of falling water, I heard a whistle,
the kind of piercing catcall the toughs on Canal Street had once
directed at me. I whirled about. There, standing on the rim of
the pool, were three men, one in a frayed, old-fashioned cutaway coat, the two others naked to the waist except for sweat-
stained kerchiefs knotted about their throats. All three wore
battered palmetto hats. With them were two Indian women,
dark skinned with beaked noses, high cheekbones, and narrow
eyes. They were decked out in long, bedraggled skirts, one
with a low-cut, stained satin bodice, the other with no bodice
at all but a necklace of brightly colored feathers. A trio of laden
mules lapped at the water's edge.

The man wearing the cutaway coat whistled again, showing
tobacco-stained teeth through a bushlike tangled beard. "I say—
lookeeee! A neked gal. Do my eyes tell me right?"

"Seems so," one of the others replied, removing his hat and
swatting the insects from a lean, bony face. "A purty one too.
And look at them tits? Oh, my, oh, *my!*" He licked his lips
and tugged at his stubbled jaw.

I ducked my shoulders, fear rising like acid in my throat.
"I see you—you speak English," I ventured, eyeing my clothes
which now lay beneath the careless boot of the third man, an
ugly scar-faced brute with an iron claw for a hand. "If you
gentlemen—"

All three broke into coarse laughter, slapping one another,
repeating, "gentlemen, gentlemen," until the forest rang.

"Ha, ha, hoho! Gentlemen! Did yuh hear that, Bowie?"

"I been called everything—pig, bastard, guttersnipe—
everything but gentlemen," Bowie, the lean man, chortled.

I waited until their laughter subsided. Then I said with as
much dignity as my nudity and awkward position could muster,
"I am Mrs. Lyon Bridewell. I and a friend were searching for
a lost little girl and we got separated. If you would escort me
back to the beach where our ship lies—"

"Escort, escort," the iron-clawed man broke in, mocking
me. The bony-faced one commenced hee-hawing again.

But the man in the cutaway held up his hand. "Wait—wait,

you damn bastards, wait!" He looked at me through puffy, slitted eyes. "You from a ship?"

"Yes, the *San Mateo*."

"That muss be the steamer we seen in the bay," the claw-handed man observed.

"Yes," I interjected. The ship couldn't be too far away, then. "And they'll be searching for me."

Or so I hoped, crossing my fingers under the water. Surely Mrs. Ransome had found her way back and given the alarm? Two of us. Little Sarah and me.

"They ain't goin' to find you," Bowie said. "Cause we did. And finders is keepers. Ain't that right, Dipper?"

"Yeh, yeh!" the claw-handed man agreed. "And what goddamned pissin' luck. A woman—all white meat too. Well, 'gentlemen,' what do you say? Since I'm the oldest, I go first."

"Who says?" The cutaway man drew back a fist.

"Now, Zeke, age before beauty."

"Oh, yeh?"

While they were arguing, I edged toward the farther side of the pool, hunched over, moving silently through the water. As I started to climb out, the cutaway man, Zeke, yelled, "There she goes—damn you!"

They caught me before I had taken a step. I struggled, fought, screamed, while they laughed, each pulling at me until I thought I would fly apart.

"Wait—wait, comrades, now this ain't the way," Zeke protested. "There's plenty to go round and we'll all take our turn. But not here. Too close to that ship. If what she says is right, them people'll be lookin' for her."

I stood between the men, hands crossed over my bare breasts, shivering despite the torpid heat.

"Where'll we take her?" the claw-handed man, Dipper, asked. "Can't wait too long. I'm hard as a bung starter now."

More ribald laughter. I glanced at the women who had remained silently in the shadows, watching with impassive faces. Were they wives, mistresses, servants to these ruffians? Could they, would they help me?

"Less go up to the fort," Zeke said. "It ain't but a half hour from here and no trail leadin' to it from this side. C'mon, get a leg on, round up them mules."

Bowie leaned over and squeezed my breast. "You juss wait, honey."

"I want my clothes," I said in a cracked voice.

Zeke bent down and threw them at me. I got into my chemisette and petticoats, fumbling with the ribbons, close to tears. *Were* people looking for me? They had to be. I did not want to think of what would happen if I was not found. The blanket lay trampled in the mud. No one seemed to notice it, and I said nothing. Perhaps, if a search party from the *San Mateo* came this way, they would see it. A clue.

"Don't try anythin' funny," Zeke said, tapping the butt of a pistol stuck in the belt of his trousers, "or I'll put a bullet through one of your purty little kneecaps."

"You'll pay for this," I said, shaking with fear and anger. "My father is an influential man in San Francisco."

"Well, he ain't here now, is he, honey?"

He hoisted me atop a mule and we started off. I had no idea what cargo I sat upon. Covered by canvas, it felt lumpy. That the men were renegades, possibly thieves, seemed obvious. How they had gotten to this Mexican jungle was another matter, but I did not dwell on it. All I could think of was rescue, but as we got farther and farther from the falls, hope faded.

When we came to a sunless stretch devoid of undergrowth, one of the mules balked suddenly and its covered load slipped to one side, spilling several burlap sacks with a clank and a clatter. The men gathered about to set it right, and for a fleeting moment I thought of making a run for the distant trees. But the thought died. How far could I hope to get without help?

The Indian women standing next to my mule were conversing in low tones. They used a language that was strange to me, not Spanish, for most natives of New Orleans can recognize, if not speak or understand, the tongue. Still, I reasoned, one of them may have picked up a few words that would be familiar to her.

"Senorita," I began, addressing the woman with the feather boa. "If you could—would—*ayudar* me. I would pay."

She gave me a blank look, her brown face smooth and impassive.

"Socorro!" I pleaded. "Help!"

I believed she understood, for I saw contempt fill her dark eyes, along with a flicker of hate that stung.

I felt aggrieved, insulted. What had I ever done to her? We were both females; we shared that in common. Then I remembered Miles saying, It's the only way the Indians survive our treachery.

Had she lumped me in with the others, her oppressors, the white-skinned exploiters? Had she sensed even in my impassioned plea a haughty patronage? But why shouldn't I feel superior? Perhaps Derry was right. They were sly. I looked at the women more closely. They didn't in any way look sly. They looked—well, sad. The one with the feather boa had a bruised welt under her eye where someone had hit her, probably Zeke Bowler or Dipper. It occurred to me then that these women had not come willingly, that they must have been abducted as I had been.

"Senorita," I tried again. *"No quierre escapar?"* Her expression did not change. I tried again in English.

"Senorita, have you no wish to escape?"

She said nothing, did not make any sign that she understood. If she did it was obvious she wanted nothing to do with me.

We started off again, the jungle giving way to flat, grassy swamp. After skirting it, we began to climb a steep slippery hill, the men pulling the heavily laden mules up the incline. The Indian women panted behind us. Zeke urged my mule on with cries of "Hup! Hup—hup!" Each time he lifted his arm to slap the mule's side I had a glimpse of the pistol tucked in his belt. I began to think of how I might get at it. My thoughts did not go as far as pulling the trigger, but I saw myself waving it in a threatening manner, forcing these cutthroats to release me and the two women who would act as my guides. It was pure fantasy, of course, but it kept me from thinking about what lay at the end of this fearful journey.

An old ruin with crumbling walls and a windowless tower crowned the top of the hill. It had an eerie, desolate stillness about it, and the wind soughing through the stony jagged gaps sounded like some tormented creature moaning in distress. I did not like the place even before Zeke led us through a broken archway into a rubbled courtyard where vines and bushes grew amid the fallen masonry. Though there were signs of recent occupation—blackened campfire ashes, broken bottles rotting orange peelings, chicken feathers—the air of mysterious, forbidding antiquity persisted. The Indian women refused to enter. They hung back, silent and morose, rubbing their bare arms, a shuttered look on their dark faces.

"Superstitious bitches!" Zeke mumbled and went back, cracking his whip at them. "Git! Git!"

They cringed, throwing up their arms to ward off the stinging blows. But they would not move. Angry, infuriated, Zeke shouted, "Dipper! Bowie! Give me a hand!"

The two men hurried over, whips snaking, whistling, snapping on the shoulders of the women. The sight of those poor creatures being punished in such a way sickened me. I slid from the mule's back and stood for a moment asking myself what I could do—when I suddenly realized that no one was taking any notice of me. This time I did not stop to think or debate. The cruelty of these men offered a far worse alternative than the jungle. Quickly, I stole behind the mules; crept forward to a low place on the ruined wall and leapt over it, all in the space of seconds. Then, regaining my feet, I ran toward a copse of trees on the leeward side of the hill.

Slipping on patches of mud, I fled, holding tight to my dragging petticoats, urging every nerve and muscle on to greater and greater speed. The copse seemed much farther away than I had thought. I stubbed my toe on a rock and went to my knees, the pain shooting up through my leg, but I scrabbled to my feet again, raspingly short of breath, sweat blinding my eyes, hobbling now, limping at a fast pace with only one thought in my head—Get away, *getawaygetaway!* Down I went, down and down, the incline less steep but still slippery. Now at last the trees were drawing closer: I could see the limbs, the palm fronds, the rough bark, a spiky bush.

Behind me a shout went up. They had discovered my absence. I heard running footsteps behind me and I lunged forward, my heart near to bursting, but a hand grasped my shoulder, halting me, flinging me around. Zeke reached out and hit me across the face, a glancing blow but one that made me reel.

He caught me before I fell, bunching up the front of my chemisette so tightly that the cloth tore.

"You bitch! I told you not to try anythin'! Now, you're really gonna pay!"

I didn't say anything—I couldn't; I was sobbing. Freedom had seemed so close.

"Git along now." He pushed me forward and again I fell to my knees. This time I couldn't get up; my muscles simply refused to work. Zeke reached down, grasped my hair, and pulled me to my feet, nearly lifting the scalp from my head.

"Stubborn, ain't you?"

"Oh, God!"

"Git along—git along!" And I was dragged, stumbling, falling, slithering in the mud and grass, my arm nearly pulled from its socket. He lifted and threw me over the wall. I lay on the ground on my elbows, my hair fanning forward, tears mingled with sweat.

"I told you we should have taken her at the falls," Bowie said. "Should have hunkered the daylights out of her."

Zeke tore the chemisette from my back, then dragged me over to the center of the overgrown courtyard. I tasted grass and dirt and the bitter tears of shame as I lay there gasping and staring glassy-eyed at the booted feet of the men and the bare callused ones of the Indian women. So *they* had been beaten into submission, made to enter the stone archway. I squinted up between swollen lids. The boa-feathered woman looked down at me, contempt written in her eyes. I gathered spittle in my mouth and let it fly at her feet. Exactly why I had done that, my confused, tortured brain did not know. I hated them all!

"Take off her petticoats," Zeke ordered.

I felt a hot, heavy hand on my back, the fingers scrabbling at the ribbons, the tearing wrench, the cooling air on my naked buttocks. A pinch, a lingering pat with the same hand.

"Keep your paws off!" Zeke bellowed.

"Ya goin' to let me have a go at her?" Bowie whined.

"Wait your turn."

The whip cracked over my head, once, twice. I screwed my eyes shut, biting my underlip, determined not to utter a

sound. But when the whip came whistling across my back like
a running, searing flame, turning my insides to molten fire, I
heard myself scream.

"Ha!" Zeke exclaimed. "Don't like that, do you? Well, I
got something here that'll please you better."

I dug my fingers into the black dirt, trembling, shaking from
head to foot, trying to suppress the whimpering sound that
shook my body, my mind tensing for his assault.

I waited, waited . . .

I did not hear the shot, only a piercing cry before Zeke fell
heavily across my legs. I turned my head, sweeping the hair
from my eyes. A puff of smoke drifted lazily past Zeke's inert
body. The other men, crouched low, pistols in hand, were
staring at the tumbled wall.

"Drop your weapons!" a man's voice ordered.

Who . . . ? Someone from the ship?

Dipper's and Bowie's pistols went off in a scattered explosion as they ran to take cover behind the mules. The women,
without a murmur, sank to the ground, covering their heads
with their arms.

"Don't get up, Carmella!" another voice shouted, one I
recognized. Miles!

"You're outnumbered!" a third voice called from beyond
the far side of the enclosure. Derry!

They had come to rescue me. Bless them, bless Derry, bless
them all!

But it wasn't over. The smell of gunpowder hung pungent
and sharp in the hot afternoon air. In a short while it would
be dark, for twilight was brief in the tropics, day turning to
night with scarcely a pause. Dark, and the men out there (how
many?) unable to see my enemies.

Dipper and Bowie were arguing. "I tell you we gotta use
her as a shield. They'll never shoot—if we can grab her. It's
our only chance."

"If you think I'm goin' to stick my neck out . . ."

"All right, all right, *I'll* do it."

I watched, one eye fearfully cocked open, my heart bumping
against my ribs, digging my body into the grassy sod, wishing
I could pull it over my head. I saw Dipper peering out, saw

the firm set of his mouth, saw the gun in his hand, the barrel glinting in the rays of the westerly sun. I measured the distance between myself and Dipper and began to snake back, inch by inch, then halted. I was afraid to be caught moving, terrified I would be killed in the crossfire, and I pressed my face once again into the sour-tasting dirt.

"Give yourself up!" the man who had spoken first shouted. It sounded like Mr. Ransome.

"Let me get away!"

"No! We can't do that!"

The next volley of shots jarred my every nerve into jumping, screaming protest. Two of the mules kicked and brayed and with their loads slipping and falling galloped through the archway. Dipper had gone down and for a moment I thought he was dead, but then he began to slowly crawl forward, the gun in his hand. The gun was pointing at me.

Suddenly I was back at Willowfoxe, gazing into the small, black round hole of death. And terror swept through me, gripping me in heart-pounding paralysis.

"I'll kill her, I'll shoot her!" Dipper's voice echoed against those ghostly walls. "I'll kill her unless you let me go!"

The world exploded again and I buried my head in the ground, tensing my body to the swift, searing pain of a bullet, the richocheting sounds rebounding inside my skull.

When the last echo died, an unearthly silence descended. I let the breath out of my lungs and mentally went over my body—feet, legs, thighs, buttocks, back, head. Nothing seemed amiss. I lifted my head an infinitesimal fraction of an inch and saw Dipper lying face down two feet from me. His body twitched, then was still, the gun falling from his limp hand.

"There's one of you left," Miles called. "Come out. Might as well give up, or you'll go the same way!"

A single shot hit the wall and a spurt of flaky granite showered down. The mule with Bowie behind it began to move, but the animal suddenly took fright and commenced kicking and bucking. Bowie darted out and grabbed one of the Indian women, jerking her to her feet. He shoved her in front of him just as another shot caromed out of the dimness. The woman's look of infinite, unbearable tragedy contorted her features as blood gushed from the wound below her collarbone.

Still holding the sagging body of the woman, Bowie advanced toward the wall.

Then suddenly another of the Indians leaped up. She grabbed Dipper's gun and aimed it at Bowie's back. I heard the click of the hammer. It made an incredibly loud noise, the click of an empty barrel. Bowie heard it too. He wheeled about instinctively, leaving his back unprotected, a blunder that cost him his wretched life. A shot pierced him between the shoulder blades and another got him at the base of the skull.

Face down, I shut my eyes tightly, too frozen with shock to move or to weep, as I listen to the distant braying of the runaway mules, to the crunch of approaching boots.

Miles turned me over. "Are you hurt?"

"No—no . . ."

He drew me up. The dying sun had stained the sky crimson and gold and Miles's eyes were inscrutable in the reflected light. He put his coat about my shoulders, bringing the front together, buttoning it, and for a moment I had the odd sensation that he was going to kiss me.

But then someone exclaimed, "Carmella—are you all right?" and I turned to give Derry a happy, tear-brimming smile.

CHAPTER

ELEVEN

*M*R. RANSOME *was most apologetic.* "My *wife* should have had more sense than to allow you—or anyone— to go into the jungle without an experienced person." He himself knew the country well, having traversed much of Mexico on muleback in the course of past duties. "Worse yet, this particular locale crawls with smugglers and renegade thieves."

Mr. Ransome had led the search. Taking Miles, Derry, and two of the crew, he had traced my movements from bits of lint that had brushed off my blanket as I thrashed through the undergrowth. Once at the falls, where they had discovered the blanket and hoofprints, he had followed the mule droppings to the fort.

"Have they found the little girl?" I asked.

Mr. Ransome shook his head. "Not yet. The mother and the other woman were persuaded to return to the beach while another party went to look."

When I came aboard ship the captain shook my hand brusquely and said a few kind words, none of which hid the angry look in his eyes. Then, before I could question him about little Sarah, he hurried off to order the ship under way.

"I take it they've found the child," I said to Mrs. Ransome, who had been there to greet us.

She shook her head sadly.

"You can't mean we're leaving without her?" I asked, horrified.

"I'm afraid so," Mrs. Ransome said. "What's more, the two women, refusing to give up the search, disappeared into the jungle again."

"But we can't simply abandon them! Why that's—inhuman!"

"The captain claims the delays have already cost him his bonus, if not his job. As it was, my husband and your friends, Mr. Falconer and Mr. Wakefield, had a hard time persuading him to wait while they searched for you.

I turned to Miles and Derry. "Can't either of you induce the captain to change his mind?"

"I'll try," Miles said. "Although I've already had it out with him. These officers are a callous lot. Their first loyalty is to the steamship company, and everything else can go hang. The line that can establish the speediest run gets the bulk of the trade, and of course the captains of such ships stand to gain accordingly."

"If she were *his* daughter, I'll wager he'd spare no effort to track her down."

"I have my doubts there, too."

Derry said, "Don't upset yourself, Carmella. You know, the two women and the child could very well have died in the fever epidemic we had on board."

"But they didn't!"

It may have seemed that my reaction to the loss of these three people who were practically strangers to me was excessive. Aside from humanitarian reasons, I found it hard to explain that in some obscure way I identified with little Sarah and the thought of her dying alone and afraid appalled me.

Derry also promised to speak to the captain, but he doubted it would do any good.

The ship's doctor, an older man with a ruddy complexion, treated my lacerated feet and the festering whiplash welt on my back, murmuring all the while that the world was going to rack and ruin. It certainly seemed that way to me.

Everyone knew that I had been held captive by a band of rogues. I suppose the sailors who had been in the rescue party had passed the story around. Mr. Ransome tried to mitigate its more unsavory implications by giving out that I had been kidnapped for a price. Only Mrs. Ransome really believed it. Nothing I could have said, no denial on my part, would have stilled the wagging tongues. If the women had looked at me earlier with jaundiced eyes, they now shunned me. Only the men seemed friendly, showing a prurient interest that Miles quickly discouraged. Derry threatened to throw any man who insulted me into the sea, if I would but name him.

Derry was my one consolation during those trying days. He promenaded on deck with me, sat by my side at meals, told funny little stories in an attempt to cheer me. Of course, Miles was always close by. If only he had left us alone. I needed Derry's arms about me, his tenderness to heal my wounds, just as much as the doctor's unguent which was slowly healing my back. But I had to be content with a secret squeeze of the hand and a murmured, "I love you"—endearments I nevertheless cherished.

When we anchored in the roadstead at Mazatlán, Derry suggested the three of us go ashore with the other passengers. "It will be a diversion," he said to me. It would also be our last Mexican stop before we reached the coast of California at San Diego, our last opportunity to purchase native artifacts. Miles thought the acquisition of assorted clay pots, straw sandals, carved coconut shells, serapes, and rebozos, sheer foolishness. All were items, he claimed, that could be bought quite handily in the shops in California if anyone wanted them. Nevertheless, he gave me a fistful of dollars, saying I could buy whatever I liked as long as it could be packed in my portmanteau.

We landed on the beach in small boats and were immediately surrounded by Custom House officials in white shirts and pantaloons demanding to inspect our luggage. When we explained we were merely visitors they let us go on. Miles proposed we have an early lunch at the Fonda de Canton, a Chinese hotel kept by Luen-Sing, a man he had known at Bonanza Creek. The restaurant, a short hackney ride from the waterfront, was a blue-fronted adobe building with a rotuned Oriental at the door beating a gong to announce the noon meal. Inside, rooms filled with tables led out to a palm-shaded courtyard already crowded with diners. They were mostly Mexicans who sat nursing squat classes of tequila, smoking thin, long cigars, and eyeing a boisterous party of North Americans, men and women from another ship who apparently were celebrating someone's birthday.

Mr. Sing himself waited on us, resplendent in baggy black trousers and a buttercup yellow tunic trimmed with emerald green braid, his jowled face creased into a beaming smile.

"Mr. Miles! Good to see you. Stay maybe long time? We talk over old Gold Rush days."

"I'd like that. But we,"—he introduced us—"are here for just a few hours.

They spoke for several minutes in Chinese. Then Mr. Sing asked if we would prefer Mexican or Chinese food. I chose the Mexican and was served a tortilla wrapped about a filling of shredded chicken topped with a hot sauce that seemed to lift the top off my skull. While I sputtered and coughed, Miles looked on with amusement. But Derry leaned over and gave me his handkerchief, then called loudly for water.

As I dabbed at my tears, I became aware that the North Americans were staring at me. I looked across and the first person whose eye I met was Sam Halstead!

I couldn't be mistaken, for that single baleful orb set in a disgruntled face had made quite an impression on me. My gaze swept the table. Where was Mrs. Halstead? Was her husband going to San Francisco alone, and if so why?

I was on the point of calling Miles's attention to Mr. Halstead's presence when I thought better of it. I would have to give some sort of explanation to Derry and I felt reluctant to discuss my visit to St. John Street. It was not a subject I cared to dwell on. I wondered—not without some uneasiness—if Mr. Halstead might approach us, but apparently he had no wish to confront me. He as well as his companions went back to toasting the birthday celebrant amid guffaws and peals of laughter.

A half hour later I had forgotten all about him. Mazatlán was a charming city. Built at the foot of a hill on a rocky headland fronting the sea, it was cooled by a gentle breeze even during the hottest part of the day. Houses of white, pink, cream, and pale blue with arched entrances and tiled roofs nestled under the tops of shaggy coco palms. The principal streets were swept clean, the shops along them as large and showy as many on St. Charles Street at home. While the men prowled about in search of a good Panama hat, I bought a black lace mantilla and a white muslin blouse embroidered with a red and yellow Aztec design.

Derry, who had visited Mazatlán in '48 on his way to the gold diggings, thought I might like to see the old marketplace. After climbing a maze of steep, narrow alleyways, we reached the small square where the poorer natives did most of their buying and selling. Even this late in the day business went on at a brisk pace. Umbrellalike stands or canopies of palm leaves gave shelter to displays of vegetables, fruit, and grains spread out on beds of greenery. Here and there a table offered jars of refreshing drinks, orange juice, coconut milk, barley water.

I was eating a mango, a sweet, pulpy fruit, when I noticed Mr. Halstead again. He was trying on a broadbrimmed Guayaquil somberero, a hat that gave his whiskered face an even more sinister look. Miles must have seen him too, for he excused himself and went over to speak to Mr. Halstead. Their conversation did not last but a minute or two and then Miles was back with us.

"A friend of yours?" Derry asked.

"Hardly," Miles said, but did not elucidate.

When we got back to the ship, I managed to get Miles alone and question him.

"Halstead's on his way to San Francisco," Miles explained. "I presume his wife finally invited him to leave, no doubt giving him the money to get out of New Orleans. He claimes he's been offered employment in San Francisco, but you can be sure it won't be of an honest kind. I don't trust him."

"Did he know my father?" I explained how Sam Halstead had stopped and asked me if I was "Arthur Hasteins's brat."

"Indeed he did. Your father was responsible for sending him to jail many years ago. It was on an extortion charge, I believe."

"How could Mrs. Halstead ever have married such a rogue?"

"She was young, I suppose, and fell in love with him." He gave me a direct look. "Why does any woman fall in love with a rogue?"

"I'm sure I wouldn't know," I said sweetly, refusing to rise to the bait.

We disembarked again at San Diego, a city with a deep circular bay and yellow, sered hills rising behind it. While Miles attended to some business on the wharf, Derry and I, with Mrs. Ransome acting as chaperone, hired a guide and took a carriage ride into the interior to view the sights. It was a blue-skied, balmy day, delightfully cool, such a relief from the debilitating climate we had sailed through these past weeks. I was so happy to be with Derry without having Miles between us, so happy with the day, my love, my youth (how resilient one is at sixteen, how quick to push unpleasantness from one's mind!), I could have skipped and danced with joy. The guide, a little man with a bulbous nose, conscientious and eager, was glad to have paying customers. Most people who came into San Diego, he explained, were in a hurry, on their way to somewhere else, not interested in visiting the environs beyond the town proper. He talked incessantly, hardly drawing breath, pointing out each little frame house, narrating its history, and identifying its builder as well as its present occupants. At one point we got out of the carriage and climbed a hill to see the Presidio, a fort wrested from the Mexicans during the war in 1848 (or had it been '49?), a whitewashed building with a magnificent view of the bay.

From there we rode along a river through a valley of farmland to the old Spanish mission, San Diego de Alcala. It had been erected, our guide informed us, by Father Junipero Serra, a Franciscan, in the last century, one of the seven missions he founded in California. It was in ruinois disrepair, the sunbaked, adobe bricks crumbling in places, though the high flat tower with its five bells remained intact.

The padre himself, a Father Ornoco, came to greet us as we drove up. He insisted on taking us through the chapel, a dark, dim chamber with cracked and peeling walls and roughhewn benches instead of proper pews. We dropped some coins into the poor box and the padre blessed us for our charity.

"The gardens have been much neglected," he said, "but you

are welcome to stroll in them and spend as much time as you like. I am sorry I can offer no refreshments."

But we had our own. Derry, through the offices of a local cafe, had procured a picnic lunch which the guide now brought out. We spread the carriage rug under an ancient wide-limbed live oak and Mrs. Ransome and I did the honors, unpacking the large straw hamper which contained cold chicken, a crusty bread, a small round of cheese, and a bottle of wine. Derry opened the wine, a local product, tasting it, pronouncing it good. It was all very festive, but I could not help imagining how much more so it would have been had Derry and I come alone.

As the meal progressed, Derry kept refilling our glasses and I soon began to feel a little giddy. Mrs. Ransome yawned audibly.

"Shall we go back," the guide asked, "or would you like to catnap for a bit?" He himself had been unusually silent during the meal.

"Catnap," Derry said, stretching himself out on his back, placing his hat on his chest, and closing his eyes. "Forty winks and then we can leave."

No one argued with him. The guide mumbled something about lying down in the carriage, and Mrs. Ransome settled herself against the trunk of a tree. I seemed to be the only one wide awake. I felt miffed, slighted, deserted. The least Derry could have done was to keep me company. I sat there nibbling on a chicken leg while the garden drowsed in the lazy afternoon sun.

I threw the chicken bone aside, and getting to my feet began to walk aimlessly along a weed-choked graveled path, my skirt making swishing sounds as I moved. In the tall grass a cicada began to sing, hoarse and shrill. I turned from the path and entered a small, ragged orange grove, neglected and unpruned but still flowering with a heady perfume and here and there bearing a golden fruit. I picked a blossom and was tucking it in my hair when I heard a step behind me.

It was Derry, smiling, and very much awake.

"Derry!"

He held out a posey of wild flowers, blue lupine, golden poppies and magenta red-maids.

"For me?" I said, touched. "You gathered these. . . . ? But I thought you were asleep."

He laughed. "I'm wide awake."

"Derry Wakefield! Did you put anything in their wine?" I asked suspiciously.

"Just a few drops of laudanum. It won't hurt either of them. They'll have a good sleep, perhaps a little headache afterward, and in the meanwhile we'll have some time together."

"Oh, Derry!" I went into his arms, the long ache of waiting and wanting trembling on my lips, meeting his hot mouth with the urgency of a thirsty wanderer who has finally found water. We stood locked in a timeless embrace while the cicadas sang and the sweet summer-scented air blessed us.

"You don't know—how can I explain," Derry said, letting me go, his eyes searching my face, "how painful it was for me when you disappeared in that dreadful jungle? My dear, never, *never* do that again."

"I promise, my darling. I shan't—"

"Don't talk, don't say anything. Just kiss me again."

If I had harbored any doubt as to my ability to be roused by a man again after my ordeal in Mexico, the doubt vanished without a trace now. I wanted Derry, everything that was female in me wanted him. He kissed me tenderly, softly parting my lips, his tongue meeting mine. I pressed closer and his arms went down to my waist, my hips, then back again, finding one breast, caressing it. He released my mouth, trailing kisses along my cheeks, my chin, my throat, his head bending to kiss each breast. I hugged the top of his head closer and the heat of his mouth sent a wave of excitement through me. He found my lips again, kissing me hard, hungrily.

"Carmella . . ." He broke away. One lock of hair had fallen over his forehead, damp with desire and love. "I cannot—I can't bear it. You must know this is torture, exquisite torture, but to kiss you without—"

"I want you, Derry, I want you as much as I did in Panama."

"The others will be asleep for at least another half hour. Are you sure?"

"Yes."

He took my hand and led me under the trees. Looking about, we spied a small pergolalike building with part of its red-tiled roof gone. We went inside. Dim, the earthen floor littered with yellow leaves, it was not the white-curtained chamber furnished with the gilt-knobbed bed and flounced hangings I had often dreamed of as the setting for our lovemaking.

"You can change your mind," Derry said, kissing me lightly, tenderly on the forehead, putting his lips to my ear. "Carmelia?"

The blood sang in my veins. Change my mind? A fig for the white-curtained room, the gold-knobbed bed!

"Never." My arms went up around him and I lifted my face brimming with happiness. "Never, never, never, never!" each "never" punctuated with a quick, passionate kiss.

He removed his coat and spread it on the floor, then turned to me and began to undo my bodice, the buttons slipping through his fingers as I watched, my lips parted, holding my breath. He kissed my throat, baring my shoulders to his lips, the firm touch sending little shivers down my spine. The dress came away in a swirl, the petticoats next. He laughed softly as I stepped out of one and then another.

"No wonder I was half mad. I couldn't *feel* you, not with all those clothes."

I turned and he unlaced my corset, lifting it from me, grabbing me around the waist, his lips trailing fire down my bare back. Then he reversed me and brought his mouth to my naked breast, his lips sucking at my nipple until I felt it grow hard.

"Don't," I said, not meaning it; "don't." A tense yearning grew in my loins as he transferred his mouth to the other breast, and looking down I saw that the nipple he had just released had grown smooth and round. Desire, I thought, desire. I felt consumed by it. I ran my hand through his silky fair hair and he lifted his face, drawing me close, pressing my naked breast against his shirtfront, my thighs along his body, so that I could feel his burgeoning manhood.

And the thought flashed through my mind: *This is wrong, wicked, sinful.* But the idea only made it all the more thrilling. He moaned as he brought me down to the floor, kissing me all the while, his hands driving me wild, going up along my buttocks, between my legs, over my hips.

He mumbled something in my hair and I said, "What is it, love?"

"Help me out of my clothes."

I unbuttoned his shirt while he kissed my fingers; together we drew his trousers down, his undergarment. I looked at him, a golden god in a shaft of sunlight, the finely molded torso, my lover, my heart.

He did not have to nudge my legs apart. I took him eagerly, welcoming him to my body, giving it to him with joy. When he entered me I gasped, then raised my hips to feel the full warm thrust, the next and the next, each one sending quivers of delight through me. Soon we were moving in rhythmn, a rhythmn that seemed to come naturally, one that I had watched but never experienced with either Lyon or Miles (certainly not Miles). I hadn't loved Lyon, I knew that now, and I disliked Miles. This man I adored, and it made all the difference. He made my body move and respond in ways it had never done before. The mingled scent of orange blossoms, sweat, dust, and desire heightened my senses and I closed my eyes, clinging to the moment, grasping at it, greedy, not wanting to let go. A sudden wave of unbearable excitement radiating from my groin made me clutch and claw at Derry's moving shoulder blades. He gave one more savage thrust and a smothered scream rose to my lips as he shuddered to a climax.

We lay for some minutes in silence. The slant of the sun through the paneless arched window had changed only slightly, and I gazed at the dust-moted light, satisfied, sated, happiness passing a smooth, sleepy hand over my drooping eyelids.

"We mustn't tarry." My lover's voice roused me. "They'll be looking for us." He was pulling his trousers on.

"Oh, Derry. I could stay forever." Smiling, I held out my arms. He bent and kissed me.

"I love you," I said, rubbing his cheek with mine.

"And I love you." He drew away and removed a ring from his finger, a silver ring of heavy design set with an opal he had bought in the market at Mazatlán.

"This is for you, sweetheart, my darling. A small token of my esteem." He put it on my finger, where it dangled, much too large. Were we betrothed then? Did he mean to get me another ring later, one that would fit? Was this his way of saying, "Wait, my love, until I can afford better?"

I was too shy to ask.

"It's the only appropriate thing I can think of at the moment," he said, looking at it ruefully, dispelling my doubts. Of course he could not make a formal proposal. There was his poverty, my father.

I kissed him, his cheeks, his lips. "I can't wear your ring now, Derry, not on my hand where Miles could see it. He would make an unpleasant fuss. I'll put it around my neck on a ribbon, next to my heart where it belongs."

Where Derry belonged, for in the eyes of God we were truly man and wife now.

CHAPTER

TWELVE

THE LAST ten days of our voyage were the most tedious, the most aggravating, and the longest of all. Battling prevailing offshore winds, the vessel chugged and vibrated at a snaillike pace, crawling slowly northward up the coast, riding out one storm that threatened to send us crashing against jagged rocks, later becalmed by a thick fog that closed down on us like a shroud. The nearer we came to our destination, the more irritable the passengers grew. Quarrels sprang up at the slightest provocation, and more than once men on the brink of fisticuffs had to be pulled apart in the dining salon.

Through most of this upheaval I felt detached. I minded only that Derry and I could not be alone long enough to make plans for the future. Though nothing definite had been said, I knew that we would go on seeing each other after we reached San Francisco. We would have to contend with my father instead of Miles, but I felt sure that in some way, somehow, we would manage. In the meanwhile I tried to put a good face on matters, telling myself that soon this interminable journey would be over.

"You seem mighty cheerful," Miles accused one morning.

"Why—because I don't whine and find fault like the others?"

"It's not in your nature to lose an opportunity for protest."

"I'm in love now. Love makes a difference."

He cocked a cynical eye.

"But then," I added crushingly, "how would *you* know about love?"

"I gave up your sort of sentimental, cloying puppy love at an early age. But not you, I see. If I remember correctly, you tried to sneak into your lover's room. And I wouldn't be surprised if you haven't finally managed to climb into his bed."

My face turned scarlet and I looked away. Had he guessed? Did it show?

"Have you?" he asked, turning my chin. "Have you managed it?"

I looked him straight in the eye. "No. And you are a fine one to talk of bed."

He dropped his hand. "You are right," he said softly, an odd note of regret in his voice. "I'm a fine one."

"Don't think I won't tell my father," I said, wanting to hurt. "And if he kills you in a duel, he'll be in the right."

"I'm willing to take any punishment he deems fit."

"Drawing and quartering would be too good for you," I said spitefully. "Better than you merit."

The wharf was thronged with people. I looked down at the crowd, the frock-coated gentlemen in their top hats, the dandies in mustard-colored waistcoats and brimmed wideawakes, the red-shirted miners and beaver-hatted shopkeepers, wondering where among them was my father. Would I recognize him? Would he know me? Not that I had finally arrived, I began to feel nervous. Would he reprimand me for my hasty marriage to Lyon? For the subsequent scandal? Would he guess at my affair with Derry? And what of Miles taking me to bed? Rape, really, for I had been an unwilling victim. And suddenly I was not too sure I would tell him about Miles. It was a delicate subject, embarrassing, and I knew Papa would want to know the circumstances. He would ask if I had provoked Miles, and I didn't know how could I look him in the eye and say no.

Winches whined and the gangplank was thrown down. Miles said, "Come along," and took my arm.

"Derry?"

"I'm right behind you, Carmella."

I put a smile on my face, hoping that I looked like someone's daughter being reunited with a father she knew, not the shadowy stranger Papa had become to me.

I needn't have worried. I knew him at once. The brow was a little more furrowed than I recalled, but the light brown hair, the sculptured nose, the sidewhiskered cheeks, even the sober gray coat were the same, as if we had parted just yesterday instead of years ago.

"Papa!"

He, too, recognized me instantly, for his face broke into that rare but transforming smile that had been the joy of my childhood. "Carmella!"

I went into his arms, sobs clogging my throat.

He held me away. "Now—now, this is not an occasion for weeping, child." But there was a suspicious moistness in his own eyes. "Let me look at you. Ah—how you have grown! And so lovely, a beauty! Isn't she, Miles?"

"Indeed."

"It was a mistake not to have sent for you sooner," Papa continued. "I won't ever forgive myself. But we won't dwell on it. Now that you're here, I'm going to make up for it. Things will be different."

He wasn't going to reproach me. In gratitude I gave him another hug, a kiss.

"Well, well," said Papa, embarrassed. "Is this your luggage?"

"Yes, Papa—and oh, I want you to meet a friend."

Derry, who had been hanging back during our greeting, now came forward. "Papa, this is Derry Wakefield. He's from King William County too."

"Wakefield? Ahhh—yes. I seem to remember Peter Wakefield, your father, yes, he's—Gramfort Hall. How do you do." He pumped Derry's hand. "We are practically neighbors."

"Delighted to meet you, sir."

"You are on a visit to our fair city or here to stay?"

"To make my fortune, sir. If I'm lucky—in gold."

Papa smiled. "Gold has become elusive. But there is no harm in trying. I did the same. By the by, if you've nowhere to stay, you are welcome to put up with us."

I didn't look at Derry. It was all I could manage to keep from laughing out loud in delight. Stay with us! And I had wondered how we could be together after the voyage. Never in my wildest imagination had I pictured Papa inviting Derry to be our guest.

"And you, Miles. We'll want you to stay too."

I hoped he would refuse. He tried:

"But I . . ."

"Nonsense. I won't take no for an answer. A room has already been prepared for you."

Papa had leased a house on Gough Street, a spacious two-story frame building with a scrollworked railing on the porch, long narrow windows, and a round, rose window in the attic. On the inside a polished staircase led up from a tiled entryway, which divided a parlor, a small library, and a game room from the dining room. The second floor held four bedrooms and a bath, something of an innovation at the time. The furnishings were rather plain, but expensive and of good quality. The house belonged to a New England sea captain now engaged in the China trade. Wishing to transplant his wife to California he'd had it built for her, but she had died of fever en route and he had never moved in.

"If you like the house," Papa said, standing before the marble fireplace, rubbing his hands together, "I can buy it. I believe the captain will be ready to sell when he returns from his latest voyage."

For the time being we were alone in the parlor. I had washed and changed and come downstairs ahead of Derry and Miles.

"You mean you would buy it for me?"

"Of course," Papa said. "We are a family now."

I looked at the patterned carpet, a figurine of a coolie and rickshaw on a small table, the portrait of Mrs. Captain over the fireplace and tried to imagine this place as home. How long had it been since I'd had one? Certainly Aunt Maude's cottage had never felt like home; frayed, shabby, musty. And the house of my early childhood seemed so vague, so distant. My father was offering me a home of my choice, a house with four bedrooms and a polished staircase. But there was Derry . . .

"Papa," I said, "do you ever think of marrying again?"

"No," he answered at once. "The good ladies of the city are always trying to matchmake, but I have no desire to take a wife."

"You are still handsome."

"No," he answered firmly. "I want to make a home for both of us. That will suit my need for domesticity just fine."

I sat down on the horsehair sofa, feeling the slippery prickles through my crinoline. "Papa, *I* shall want to remarry some day."

"Remarry? My dear, you never were. The Bridewells, according to a communication I have received, annulled your marriage. Which is just as well. It cancels out that whole unpleasant business and will save you a great deal of embarrassment here in San Francisco. You don't mind?"

"Not at all." A final snub from the Bridewells. But, really, I *didn't* mind. My marriage had happened so long ago, it was a childish escapade. Lyon, the boy husband, and I, the girl wife, playing at house. But now with Derry . . .

"Papa, I shan't want to remain single."

"I don't expect you to. I'm not one of those unreasonable, possessive fathers. But, my dear, you are still so young."

"I'm nearly seventeen."

He smiled. "Seventeen *is* young. I want you to wait until you are at least twenty. Twenty-one would suit me even better."

"Twenty-one! Papa, I shall be an old maid then."

And what of Derry? How could I possibly wait?

"You, an old maid? Nonsense. No, my wish is to have you make a good match. I mean to have you wed to a fine man of excellent family, a respectable gentleman with substantial means."

"Not an old man, Papa."

"Certainly not a callow youth."

Would he—did he—consider Derry callow?

At this point Derry himself came into the parlor, greeting us, telling Papa again that he had not expected genuine Southern hospitality in this outpost of civilization, praising the house and his accommodations in his charming, courteous manner. I was so proud of him, so happy to see how he and Papa got along.

But it was Miles that Papa turned to during our meal, Miles

he queried about our voyage, Miles whose opinion he sought concerning the price of cotton and tobacco, and a possible railway line connecting New York with California. I could see by Papa's manner how much he thought of Miles, and I wondered how he would feel if he knew that his trusted friend had assaulted me at Aspinwall.

Derry contributed a comment here and there, but for the most part kept silent, even when Miles glossed over my mishap in the jungle. Miles simply said that a little girl had wandered off while we were ashore and that I, in going after her, had become lost too. I was grateful for his abbreviated account in which he left out the tale of my abduction. It would have upset Papa unnecessarily. What I did not like was the way in which Miles seemed to come out of the episode like a concerned and protective guardian.

"We had a few bad hours there," he said, "and so did Mrs. Bridewell."

"Miss Hastings," Papa corrected. "My daughter has resumed her maiden name."

Miles did not seem surprised (understandably, for my virginity had given proof of an unconsummated marriage—the basis for most annulments).

Derry said, "Indeed. I shall have to get accustomed to that."

And when no one was looking, he gave me a secret little smile.

The following day Papa was closeted in the study with Miles for the better part of the afternoon. When Miles left, Papa summoned me to the parlor.

"Sit down, Carmella." He himself remained standing, looking ill at ease, a slight flush straining his pale features.

"I don't know how to begin. . . . I've just spent an extraordinary two hours with Miles Falconer." He paused, looking at me from under his brows. "Can you not guess why?"

"No, Papa."

"He has offered to marry you."

"What?"

"That was precisely my first reaction. Not that he would make an unsuitable husband—as a matter of fact I would be very happy if. . . . But there was something about Miles's manner that didn't seem right. He did not act like a suitor smitten by love."

Papa paused again, as if expecting a comment, but I could think of nothing to say. Miles's proposal was the last thing I expected. Never once had he given the slightest hint that he had matrimony in mind. Was it because of Aspinwall?

Papa went on. "Miles gave his reasons, something about your charm, about his being a part of the family. They were reasons that seemed flimsy or contrived to me and I suspected a reluctance on his part to reveal his true motive. Naturally I asked him if he thought he had compromised you in any way. Finally, after much persuasion, I managed to worm the truth out of him."

So it *was* Aspinwall and Miles felt he ought to marry me. I remembered him saying, "I am willing to take any punishment . . ." Was he equating marriage with punishment? Or atonement, perhaps? Of course. Oh, damn him, damn him!

"A sorry business," Papa said. "And I don't hold Miles in the least blameless. But he must have had *some* provocation."

Just as I had feared. "I suppose Mr. Falconer made it seem as if I were the Devil's handmaiden in disguise."

"He did no such thing. On the contrary he said it was entirely his fault. But one has only to examine your past misconduct to realize that you were far from a sainted angel."

He brought out my behaviour at Aunt Maude's, my elopement, the scandal, everything that I believed he had chosen to sweep aside as best forgotten. "I spoiled you as a child. But at Miss Briscoe's I thought you might learn the etiquette and decorum of a gentlewoman. It seems I was mistaken."

He never raised his voice. He did not shout, stutter, or stumble. His tone was even, but it hurt.

"I am sorry I have been a disappointment to you, Papa."

"Sorry won't do, Carmella. I thought you could be trusted."

"That's not fair!" I cried, stung by the last accusation. "I'm willing to take responsibility for my behaviour, but not for Mr. Falconer's. You make it seem as though *I* had assaulted *him*."

"Do I? I've known Miles for many years. He is a level, cool-headed man. I have seen him come out of a fracas where everyone around him was boiling over with anger and ready to tear each other limb from limb, without raising an eyebrow.

He had a reputation for good judgment, for unruffled calm. But there is a point beyond which even the most amiable of men will not be pressured, and when Miles reaches that point his temper can become violent. You *must* have done something. Disobeyed, insulted him. He will give me no details; I want to hear them from you."

What could I say? Though Miles had not revealed that he had intercepted me on my way to Derry's room, I felt less than grateful. If he had not spied on me, none of this would be happening now.

"I was in my dressing gown, going down the corridor to the lady's lavatory when Mr. Falconer came out of his room. He was drunk. We had a few words, I can't recall what, and then he—he dragged me inside."

Papa did not believe me. I could see it in his eyes. The odd thing was that my story was true—as far as it went.

"You did not go to his room on your own. Entice him, perhaps out of some misbegotten vanity?"

"No, no, I swear it. Whatever gave you such an idea? I am not in the habit of 'enticing' men."

He studied me for a few moments. I lowered my eyes, squirming inwardly under his gaze. The subject matter, sexual assault, was not one a girl could discuss comfortably with her father.

"Then how is it that Lyon Bridewell asked you to run away and marry him without a proper courtship or engagement? You *must* have encouraged him, perhaps allowed him to take liberties, and as a gentleman he had no choice but to ask you to be his wife."

"I did not encourage him. I swear it. He fell in love with me. Can I help it if I am attractive, if men seem to notice? I am my mother's daughter."

The instant I said that I knew I had done a terrible thing. It was as if I had dealt him a mortal blow. The blood drained from his face and his lips trembled on the verge of speech. But he said nothing. By bringing my mother into the argument I had opened an old wound, torn away a scab that had taken years to grow. And I had done more. Without saying a single word, he knew that I knew. The small lies I had wrung from him in the past, his self-imposed reticence, the decade and a half of silence, the promises wrested from Aunt Maude and others, had been for nothing. It was no longer his secret. My mother had been a whore. Looking back I can see that my knowing was inevitable, that sooner or later I was bound to find out. The wonder was that I had not discovered her true identity sooner. My father should have realized it too. In some ways he was as obdurate and sentimentally blind as I.

Now, gazing at him, white and speechless, I felt stricken.

"Papa—forgive me. I did not mean to . . ."

To what? I could think of nothing to say. To confess that I knew was out of the question. To discuss it calmly, openly admitting the truth, would have helped me, but not him. His pain would be too much, too cruel, for he was not one to bare his feelings. The conversation we had been having was as far as he had ever gone (or would go) in discussing the intimate matters of our lives.

"I am sorry," I repeated.

The pretense would continue. And if I had entertained the notion of telling him I had seen my mother's grave, I dismissed it now.

"Well . . ." he murmured after a long, palpable silence. "I'm afraid I have belabored a point which apparently cannot be helped now." He sat down and drummed his fingers on the little inlaid table beside him. "The fact remains, that Miles wishes to make amends, Carmella. Under these—ah—unfortunate circumstances he is acting in the only way an honorable man can. He is quite willing to marry you."

Willing!

"I won't be any man's wife out of a—a misguided sense of—of charity."

"I would hardly call Miles Falconer a charitable man. Fair, but not one given to benevolence."

"Honor then," I said, heat flooding my face. When I thought of the insults Miles had thrown at me these past few months, my gorge rose. If he was punishing himself, he was punishing me doubly. "I am not going to be tied to a man I don't love for the rest of my life. Oh, Papa—I *can't!*"

"You are still so young. Do you think for a moment that what you call 'love' is the basis for a happy marriage?"

The ghost of bitterness underlaid his words, and in the midst of my indignation I wondered fleetingly if he had been terribly unhappy himself, whether his love for my mother had faded quickly. But I didn't dwell on it. I was too caught up in my own difficulties to think of his.

"Besides," my father went on, "real love often develops after a man and woman have been wed for a while. Family, like interests, similar backgrounds, trust—these are the things that make a lasting union between man and wife."

"All the more reason why I cannot marry Miles. Papa, we have *nothing* in common. We dislike each other. I—I, for one, cannot endure his company for more than ten minutes. Papa, I implore you, I don't want to marry Miles Falconer."

Again he studied me, his lips slightly compressed.

"You haven't got your eye on someone else, have you, Carmella—this Derry Wakefield fellow?"

The way he said "this Derry Wakefield fellow" warned me. Apparently he did not think Derry suitable. Not at present. Impeccable antecedents, but no money.

"He was most helpful on the voyage, Papa. That is all," I lied. Derry's ring, which I wore (as promised) on a ribbon beneath my bodice, seemed to burn my skin. "A pleasant young man, but I think at present his interest is taken up with finding gold."

"Yes," Papa said. "So he informed me."

"Papa . . ." I took a deep breath. "You yourself said you did not want me to marry until I was twenty-one."

"That was before Miles told me what happened at Aspinwall."

"But, Papa, it wasn't as if I were a—a virgin maid. I *was* married, you know. And . . ." I blushed. "Nothing—uh, you know what I mean—came of the incident." I was referring to a possible pregnancy. He understood.

"Thank God for that. If there had been anything of that sort, there would be no question about your marrying Miles."

"Then you won't insist?" I asked hopefully.

"You make me out an old ogre, Carmella. I'm only thinking of what is best for you. Of course I won't insist."

I jumped to my feet and, leaning over, hugged and kissed him. "Oh, Papa, I do love you."

"Now, now," he said, turning a little pink, "there's no need for that. But—I want you to remember, Carmella." He held up a warning finger. "You must do nothing that will excite talk. Society is no different in San Francisco than it is elsewhere. Good, decent society, that is. I have a small coterie of friends I want you to meet later. But in the meantime I have hired a housekeeper who will take charge here and give our home an air of respectability."

Had I gotten rid of Aunt Maude only to have her replaced by some stuffy, middle-aged matron?

"Papa—you are not thinking of using her as my chaperone?"

"The thought crossed my mind, but I understand such individuals are considered old-fashioned now."

"Oh, yes!"

"Perhaps she will only accompany you when she feels it necessary for appearance's sake. I can count on Miles to be discreet, of course, about what happened. So there is no worry in that quarter. But—well, San Francisco can be a rough place. There are some parts of it that are unsafe for decent women alone."

"I shall do my best to avoid them, Papa."

"Well, yes, I'm sure you will. But the woman I have employed will be more than a mentor. She will have the management of three servants—a cook, a butler, and a maid—in addition to performing other mundane domestic duties, chores you needn't worry your pretty head over."

I believe I might have enjoyed those chores. Furthermore, I should have preferred running Papa's house myself (though goodness knows I had no experience in such matters) and to be my own mistress. But I felt it unwise to protest.

"As you say, Papa."

It would make being alone with Derry difficult. But not impossible. My wish to be with him again had not changed.

CHAPTER

THIRTEEN

THE HOUSEKEEPER Papa hired looked as though she had been plucked directly from a caricature in *Black's Old Sketch Book*. The conventional bonneted widow of high moral fiber, she wore her weeds and the ivory cameo brooch pinned to her ample bosom with an air of assertive propriety. Mrs. Tibbets was her name, and when Papa introduced us I gave her my hand with a feeling of dismay. Was it to be Aunt Maude all over again? The tight lips, the caustic criticism the disapproving looks? I quailed at the thought.

But I soon found that Mrs. Tibbets's appearance was deceptive. In reality she had the character of a petty bully, a cream puff to those who showed strength, nasty hardtack to those who seemed weak. Self-centered, single-minded, she was also surprisingly qullible. Though she had lived in San Francisco for three years, she still could not find her way about, did not know east from west, muddled directions, and often became hopelessly lost. She was much happier staying at home directing the servants from an armchair in the parlor.

Derry had found accommodations at the Portsmouth Hotel. He thanked Papa for his offer of further hospitality, but felt he should be closer to the business section and to the outfitters from whom he would be buying supplies for his trek into the gold country. To me he said:

"I can't even kiss you here. Eyes all around. Perhaps you can manage to come to the hotel some afternoon?"

"Oh, Derry, I want to. I'll try my best."

Every other Thursday Mrs. Tibbets pried herself loose from her comfortable chair long enough to visit an elderly aunt who lived in a boardinghouse on Russian Hill. She looked upon those biweekly calls as a charitable duty, though from what I had observed she thoroughly enjoyed bullying the poor old lady. How the elderly aunt felt, I had no idea, but to me those visits were to prove a godsend.

Generally our butler drove Mrs. Tibbets and fetched her back some two and a half or three hours later. Sometimes I transported her. Unlike Mrs. Tibbets, I had quickly learned to find my way and employed the intervening hours to call at the dressmaker recommended by a friend of Papa's. Papa wanted me to have a whole new wardrobe from boots to bonnets. Bless him! I was particularly anxious to appear before Derry in a pretty gown, for he had only seen me in the same two dreary outfits I had worn throughout the voyage.

After my final fitting on the first of my gowns, which would be ready the following Thursday, I dropped a note to Derry arranging a meeting. It seemed an age before the day arrived, and when it did I could barely keep my temper in check. It was Mrs. Tibbets's afternoon with the aunt and she *would* dawdle! Once I deposited her at Mrs. Spaulding's Boarding-house—Good Cooking and Homey Atmosphere—I clucked up the horse and we trotted as fast as I could urge the beast to the home of my dressmaker.

The gown, a lovely jade green made of poplin, trimmed in black grosgrain ribbon with a looped overskirt, was finished.

"Yes—yes!" I murmured, turning and twisting before the mirror, my cheeks pink with excitement. "I'll wear it." My fingers trembled as I tied the matching narrow-brimmed bonnet with its gauzy green veil under my chin. "You can burn the old one."

I made the horse fly, and we rolled up to the ladies' side entrance of the Portsmouth Hotel in a cloud of dust. Derry was waiting for me. I gave him a dazzling smile before I twitched my bonnet's veil into place.

He helped me from the buggy and tossed a coin to a small

boy who had run up the moment I stopped. "Give the nag a slow walk around the corner," Derry said, "and see that she has a drink of water."

He took my arm. "You're trembling, my darling. You needn't fear, no one will notice. It's only a short flight up and most of the guests are out for the day."

"I'm not afraid, Derry. It's just the excitement."

He squeezed my arm.

We ascended a wooden staircase, dark and creaking, smelling of beeswax and tobacco. Not everyone had gone out for the day as Derry claimed. From behind closed doors came muffled sounds of movement; a cough, the clink of glass, the creak of bedsprings. A man in a heavy greatcoat and dusty leather boots descending the stairs paused on a landing to let us pass. His eyes swept me from head to toe, lingering on my veiled face, and even after we had gone by I could feel his gaze on my back. I blushed as I imagined what he must be thinking. Only harlots and women of loose morals came to hotels, veiled, leaning on the arms of men.

But a few moments later it did not matter. We were at the door to Derry's room. He unlocked it and, lifting me in his arms, carried me across the threshold, shutting the door with a backward shove of his foot.

"Darling," he said, flicking aside my veil and kissing me, slowly lowering me, his lips taking mine with a *mmmm* sound in the back of his throat. My arms crept up around his neck, my mouth parting under his. He had such a delicious, wonderful mouth, I could never, never get enough.

"Carmella." His smile made me glow. "You are so lovely."

I stepped away and turned, pirouetting before him. "Do you like my new gown?"

"Indeed I do!"

"And see..." I pulled his ribboned ring from my bodice. "I'm never without it, Derry."

"Come here and kiss me."

It was a longer kiss this time, more passionate, more urgent, his turning, twisting tongue seeking the moist inner recesses of my mouth, reminded me that he was *real*, that it was happening, that I was here with Derry and he was embracing, loving me. Then his lips were on mine again, drawing them into his own, pulling me into a pulsating vortex, leaving me dizzy and breathless.

"Derry!" I gasped, resting my head against his hot cheek.

Holding me away, he looked deeply into my eyes. "There is something you must know about me, sweet."

"What is it, Derry?" I whispered fearfully, moved by the passion in his voice.

"I'm a very jealous man. *And* possessive. *And* resentful of other men's attentions. I could have killed that brute on the stairs for looking at you the way he did."

I shuddered at the thought, and yet it secretly pleased me.

"You really *do* love me, darling, don't you?"

"You may think I haven't the right—"

"Oh, but I do, I do!"

He laughed. "Someday, when I've found my pot of gold, I'll make it all up to you." He took me into his arms again and kissed the crown of my head. After a few moments of silence, he said in a more sober vein, "You may consider me a little mad in my jealousy, but I cannot even bear to think that someone else had you first."

Thinking of Miles, my body stiffened. But then he went on:

"Your husband, what was he like?"

"Lyon?" I said, relieved. "He was a sweet boy. We were both so young, hardly past childhood. You needn't be jealous of him, darling."

I couldn't tell him about Lyon, any more than I was able to confess about Miles. My marriage had ended on such a sordid note, and my episode with Miles—well, I had gone through *that* with Papa. No good would come of repeating it.

"I belong to you," I said, lifting my head for his kiss. "I've never loved anyone but you."

He undressed me quickly, shedding my petticoats and skirts, touching and caressing my naked skin, pressing his lips to the sensitive secret places he seemed to know instinctively would make me shiver with delight.

"Cold?" he asked, enfolding my trembling body.

He lifted me up, carried me to the bed, and set me carefully down on the edge. "Don't go away, precious," he ordered, shrugging out of his coat.

Naked, he knelt at my feet and, bending his head, kissed my knees.

"Dimpled, so sweet, so sweet."

He had a little mole between his shoulder blades and for some reason the sight of that mole at the apex of his curved bare back excited me terribly. He stroked the insides of my thighs, his head still bent, his skillful fingers going higher and higher until they reached the dark patch of pubic hair.

"Derry!"

"Do you want me to stop?"

I tried to answer but could not. His fingers had slipped inside and he was gently teasing me there. My face grew warm, sweat beaded my forehead as a terrible sweet tenseness grew in the pit of my stomach.

"Please . . .!" I begged breathlessly.

He bent me back upon the bed, lowering his hard muscled nakedness over the full length of my body. "You have such beautiful white breasts," he whispered against my cheek.

When he penetrated me, my hips rose involuntarily to meet the thrust. Still inside and holding me, he rolled me over so that I was on top. I raised my head to look into his eyes and my hair suddenly came loose from its pins and fell in a silken curtain, enclosing us both in perfumed darkness. His hands grasped my buttocks and he moved, gyrating and rocking me, slowly at first, then faster and faster. His mouth grasped a nipple as he drew me to the edge of some cataclysmic discovery, and when the final sheet of flame flared up I cried out in astonishment.

He shifted me, so that I lay in his arms, my head tucked under his chin.

"You are like no other woman I've ever known, Carmella," he said, breaking a long silence.

"Why do you say that, darling?"

"Most girls in you place would act coy or indignant. You've given yourself to me without once making me feel like a rotter."

"It's because I love you, Derry."

"And why is that?" I could feel him smiling.

"I don't know," I said, pausing to reflect. "I suppose it's the little mole on your back."

We both laughed.

We didn't speak again and presently I was aware that he had fallen asleep. I lifted myself on an elbow and gazed down at him, at his chest rising and falling, the golden head lying on the pillow. Tenderly I brushed a damp lock back from his brow. How young he looked, how vulnerable. I loved him so much I wanted to weep. I loved his beautiful body, the texture of his skin, the strong arms, the slender hips. I would do anything he said, go anywhere, wait a thousand years for him if he wished. He filled the empty, lonely spaces of my soul with warmth and tenderness. How lucky I was to have found the one man in the world I could give myself to without shame, with pride and an overflowing heart.

A fly buzzed insistently, loudly, from behind the drawn curtains.

I lay back, my eyelids growing heavy.

I had to get up and leave. If I was long past the hour I had set with Mrs. Tibbets, she might wonder.

"Derry . . ."

He groaned and his mouth moved, pursing before he kissed my breast. Oh, I wanted to stay, never mind Mrs. Tibbets, the old frump. It was criminal to have to leave. But Derry awoke with a convulsive jerk, rolled over, and sat up.

"I must have fallen asleep," he said, running his hand through his hair. He smiled at me. "Is it late? What excuse did you give, darling?"

I told him I was supposed to be at the dressmaker's.

"Then you must hurry. We don't want Mrs. Tibbets running to Papa with some tale."

"Derry—couldn't we . . . ?"

"There is nothing I should want better." He leaned over and planted a kiss between my uppointed breasts. "But it wouldn't be wise."

I got into my clothes, all those burrons, ties, and hooks. Derry stood by the door, waiting with a small patient smile.

We were on the street and the boy was bringing the buggy around when Derry said, "Sweetheart, I must say good-bye for a while."

"Good-bye?" I echoed dumbly.

"I am joining a party that leaves early in the morning by

steamer for Sacramento. From there we ride up into the Sierra to a place called Hangman's Creek."

"Hangman's . . ." The ground beneath my feet opened. "But— but, Derry . . ." I couldn't comprehend. "Leaving . . . ?"

"Don't be upset, darling. The sooner I go and find my gold, the sooner I will return."

"But—why—why didn't you tell me earlier?"

"I didn't want to spoil our lovemaking. I *am* sorry, darling. I hate more than anything to leave you behind. You aren't going to cry, are you?"

"No," I said, swallowing hard.

Good-bye—oh, God! Tomorrow. And I had thought we would meet again in two weeks.

"It isn't as if you hadn't known, sweet," he said reasonably.

"Yes, yes, I knew, but—" I bit my lip. "I thought we could—I thought . . ."

"Be brave, darling Carmella. Remember I love you."

"Yes—yes, of course." The lump in my throat swelled.

He kissed me lightly on the cheek through the veil. Not even a proper good-bye kiss. "Derry . . ."

"Up you go," he said, helping me into the buggy. "I'll write, care of the Union Hotel. You can pick up my letters there. You'll answer them?"

"Yes—yes—of course."

"It won't be for long. Six months at the most. Good-bye, darling." He stood there, waving until I turned a corner.

I arrived at the Russian Hill boardinghouse late, but Mrs. Tibbets did not seem to notice. She and the aunt had partaken of Mrs. Tibbets's favorite sweet, apricot jam tarts at tea, and Mrs. Tibbets went on and on about them as we drove home, blissfully unaware of my dejection.

How could I possibly manage for six bleak months without Derry?

I tried to cheer myself with the thought that the time would go quickly, that I had the beautiful memory of our lovemaking to sustain me. Derry's words still echoed in my head: "You are like no woman I've ever known."

Yes, I should be thankful. Our rendezvous had gone without a hitch. No one had suspected, no one had seen us.

Or at least I thought so.

When I came into the parlor with Mrs. Tibbets, Miles Falconer rose from the horsehair sofa.

"Good afternoon, Miss Hastings, Mrs. Tibbets," he said in a cool, formal voice, inclining his head slightly.

"Is Papa not at home?" I asked, a little flustered, somewhat embarrassed. Ever since Papa had confronted me with Miles's proposal I had studiously avoided him. He occasionally came in the late evening to visit with Papa and I could hear their voices in the study. Though Papa never discussed his business affairs with me, I assumed this is what he and Miles Falconer talked about. Or perhaps it was merely a social visit. Miles, I surmised, had no burning desire to see me either.

"Your father was detained," he said. "I came along early because I wanted to speak to you about an urgent matter."

"Oh?" I said, glancing at Mrs. Tibbets, who was removing her gloves.

"Yes," Miles said. "Mrs. Tibbets, if you don't mind?"

"Not at all."

She was dying of curiosity, I could sense it, and for a moment I hoped she would say it wouldn't do to leave me alone with a man. But she didn't.

"Well, then," Mrs. Tibbets said, fluttering her gloves. "I do have to change for dinner."

When she had gone, Miles closed the double parlor doors behind him. "Sit down, Carmella."

"Must I?"

"Stand, if you prefer. I am having some whiskey." He indicated a glass on the table. "Would you like a sherry?"

"No. I'd rather not make this a social occasion. What is it you have to say?"

"I'll be brief. This afternoon, just by happenstance, I saw you going through the ladies entrance of the Portsmouth Hotel with Derry Wakefield."

God in Heaven! I might have known. Miles was absolutely uncanny. If anyone at all had seen us it would have been him.

"How dare you make such a statement?" I demanded, deciding to take the offensive. "I was nowhere near the Portsmouth Hotel this afternoon or any afternoon. You have no right to come to this house and make such a vile assertion."

"I saw you," he repeated, his eyes hard, uncompromising. "You were wearing that same jade-green gown and your bonnet was veiled."

"You always jump to nasty conclusions. I don't happen to have the only gown of jade green in the city," I flared at him. "Jade green is a very fashionable color just now."

"Is it? And do they all have rosettes of black velvet just so?" He came up to me and flicked the rosettes on the bodice.

"Take your hands off me. You forget you are no longer my watchdog."

"Do you admit it?"

"I admit nothing. Furthermore, I do not wish to continue this discussion." I turned my back and started for the parlor doors.

He was there before me, barring the way. "I can tolerate anything but a liar. A liar and a coward."

"I am not a coward!"

He studied my face for a long moment, his own a hard mask. "No. I was wrong there. I stand corrected."

"Or a liar."

"There I will quibble. You *were* at the Portsmouth Hotel with Derry Wakefield. I saw you. I shall not ask for how long or what you did."

"How gallant!" I sneered.

"I know you are daft, silly-schoolgirl-daft about him," he went on, "and I kept my promise by not telling your father how you behaved at Aspinwall or on the ship."

"And I suppose your behavior was better."

"I have already made amends. I offered to marry you."

"Out of a sense of duty, to save your own honor!" I jeered.

"Not at all. Because I have a high regard for your father. I don't want to see him hurt by scandal. That is why I'm talking to you now instead of going to him."

I turned from him and walked back to the fireplace, standing there looking down into the empty grate. Why did Miles have to spoil everything?

"Do you realize what it would mean if someone else had seen you?"

"I don't care," I said, wheeling about, cheeks hot with anger. "I love him, he loves me. When he comes back we're going to be married."

He leaned against the sideboard, hooking his thumbs in his waistcoat pockets. "The date has been set?" And when I did not answer, "Has he spoken to your father?"

"No—no, he wants to find gold first."

"I see." There was a world of meaning in that "I see," full of mockery and sarcasm.

"Think what you will in that mean, sordid little mind of yours," I taunted. And when he did not reply, I went on. "You needn't worry about Derry and me. He's leaving tomorrow. You won't have to creep about spying on me for at least six months or so, not until Derry returns."

He came up and stood over me, his eyes making a cool, unemotional appraisal.

"Just remember," he said, "if you find yourself pregnant, don't try to fob the child off as mine."

"Damn you!" I raised my arm and he caught it before I had the chance to hit him. He held it in a tight grip, his fingers bruising the flesh, looking down at me, seeming to probe the very marrow of my bones.

Then he released me and without a word picked up his whiskey glass, strode to the doors, opened them, and went through.

CHAPTER

FOURTEEN

DURING DERRY'S absence I had intended to spend the time in demure, domestic occupations. I would be a stay-at-home, I vowed, just as if I were already affianced. But San Francisco was a lively, youthful city full of gay, party-loving people. In a few short years it had grown spectacularly from a village of wooden shanties to a sohphisticated metropolis with luxury hotels, fine theaters, and a wealthy elite, and I could no more resist being drawn into the social whirl than Mrs. Tibbets could resist apricot jam tarts.

Shortly after Derry left for Hangman's Creek, Papa gave a dinner party to introduce me to his business friends, their wives, and their offspring, people of my own age. And it was then I met Dolly Hobart, daughter of Edgar Hobart, who had made a fortune in real estate.

I liked Dolly at once. Eighteen, perhaps nineteen, with blond hair, a pert nose, and a bell-like laugh, she had the sort of effervescent personality I found very appealing.

After dinner while the men lingered over port and cigars, the women retired to the parlor where Esther, our Negro maid, served coffee.

Dolly helped herself to a lump of sugar, then turned to me and asked, "Have you been to the city's shops?"

"No." I shook my head ruefully. "Except for my dress-maker's, I haven't been much of anywhere."

"Then we'll have to remedy that. I'm going on a shopping tour tomorrow. Would you like to come?"

"I should love to."

"Good. I'll pick you up in my carriage. Around ten."

"Perhaps I ought to ask Papa."

"Whatever for?"

"I don't know. I suppose shopping is respectable enough."

"I should hope so." She gave me an oblique look. "You must have done something very wicked to be so concerned with respectability and your Papa's permission. Well, never mind," she said with a laugh, "you can tell me all about it later."

The next morning we set off with light hearts and a flurry of laughter. Our first stop was Davidson's, where we bought frou-frou underclothes, dainty lawn camisoles, and lacy chemisettes. From there we went on to the City of Paris on Clay Street, a large store owned by Monsieur Verdier, a Gallic merchant who featured genuine French imports.

"Cage crinolines have just come into fashion," Dolly said, pausing before a counter that held what looked like enormous bird cages.

"They're not to be worn, surely?"

"Indeed. I have asked my dressmaker to have my next ball gown made to order for just such a contraption."

"Oh, Dolly!" I exclaimed, smothering a laugh.

"They look quite elegant covered by yards and yards of tulle. You should have one too. Who is your dressmaker?"

I told her.

"She's good, but rather conservative. However, I'm sure if you insist, she'll comply. You don't want to be out of fashion, do you? My parents are giving a ball to celebrate their anniversary on the fifth of the month, and you and your father are on the guest list."

"A ball! How nice. I wish . . ." I wish Derry could be my escort, I wanted to say, but Dolly had already gone on to the ribbon counter.

We had lunch at the Poule d'Or, or Poodle Dog as Dolly laughingly called it. "I thought you might like it," she said. "The place is owned by a man from New Orleans."

"Then I'm sure the meal will be excellent. But, Dolly—two women alone? I mean, will we be seated?"

"Certainly. You're such a worrywart. The first level is set aside for ladies and family groups."

We ordered green turtle soup and ragout of duck, and—Dolly insisted—a half bottle of wine. I felt very constrained. It did not occur to me until later that going to meet Derry at the Portsmouth Hotel was a far grosser breach of the moral code than dining in public without a male escort. But then where Derry was concerned, I became deaf, dumb, and blind to the ordinary rules of conduct.

"This is a rather large establishment," I said, looking around.

"Mmmmm. There's more. A second floor used for banquets and a third for special guests.

"Special quests?"

"Intimate suppers," she said. "Veiled women slipping upstairs to meet their lovers in private rooms furnished in voluptuous velvet and wide, wide beds."

"You sound as if you had first-hand knowledge."

The green turtle soup came and the waiter poured our wine then quietly retired.

"Do you?" I asked, leaning forward.

"Yes," she answered, sipping her wine. "He was very dashing, a young navy lieutenant from the gunboat *Cyane*. I met him at the Morrison ball. I was attracted to him—*very*." She rolled her eyes. "And when he invited me to a private dinner at the Poule, I knew what he wanted."

"Were you a virgin?" I asked, letting my soup grow cold.

"Well—not exactly." She tittered. "But I won't go into *that*."

"How was it?"

"Divine. Absolutely divine. We had champagne, oysters on the half shell—oh, I remember the whole menu—veal tartare, quail on toast, and ice cream. Too much, really. Afterwards, he kissed me and then—well, you can imagine. He was a marvelous lover. Marvelous."

My *affaire* was marvelous, too, I thought, except that I wished Derry had taken me to the Poule d'Or instead of the Portsmouth Hotel.

"Are you in love with your lieutenant?" I asked.

"Why, no. Not at all. You mean because I went to bed with him? My dear, that's all a lot of romantic twaddle. I'm going to fall in love and marry a rich man. Navy lieutenants earn very little. I daresay he spent a whole month's pay on me that afternoon. And you, what about you?"

"I'm not a virgin either." I didn't feel it necessary to go into the whole long story of my marriage or to tell her about Miles. "I'm in love with my—my beau, and I am going to marry him the first moment I can."

"No money, is that it?"

"He's gone up to the mines. I feel certain he will be rich one day. Really. He's—he's very clever. And a thrilling lover."

"I won't ask his name, though I'm dying to know. No. You'd better not tell me. I might let it slip." She reached across and squeezed my hand. "I wouldn't want to do that."

The ragout of duck was delicious and we finished it in silence. When Dolly ordered another half bottle of wine, I said, "Dolly, it's getting late. Shouldn't we go?"

"Piffle! What's the hurry? Don't fret so. Aren't you having a good time?"

"Oh, yes. I haven't had so much fun in years."

Her eyebrows went up. "Not even with Mr. Thrilling Lover?"

I blushed. "That was different."

"Hmmmm. Maybe so." She toyed with her glass, her eyes traveling over the room. "I say, there's a man on the far side who's staring at you. He just came in. Seated next to the staircase. Alone."

I looked over. Miles Falconer! My nemesis. I gave him a weak, watery smile.

"Do you know him?" Dolly asked.

"Unfortunately, yes."

To my chagrin, Miles rose and threaded his way through the diners to our table.

"Good afternoon, Miss Hastings. Enjoying your luncheon?"

"Very much. Oh, this is Miss Dolly Hobart. Miles Falconer."

"A pleasure." Miles bowed over her hand.

"Have you young ladies been shopping?" he asked in a tone that made shopping seem the most frivolous and useless of pastimes.

"We've made a few purchases," I answered coldly.

"Well, then, I won't keep you from your meal. Glad to have met you, Miss Hobart."

Dolly, watching his departing back, let out her breath. "Where did you ever meet *him?*"

"He's a friend of my father's. A skunk, if you want to know, a low-down skunk."

"Really?" Her face lit up with interest. "But such a handsome one."

I took a quick look across the room. "Handsome? I hadn't noticed."

"The best-looking man I've ever met. Not married? Oh, dear, oh, dear. I like dark men, tall—and such shoulders. Really, Carmella—he's not your secret lover?"

"Heavens no!"

"I can't understand why I haven't met him sooner," Dolly continued. "Is he received in good society?"

"I don't know. He says he doesn't care much for society."

"So well dressed. He has money, I take it."

"I've never asked." I wished she would not go on about Miles. His very presence, though out of earshot and at some distance, made me uncomfortable.

"I noticed his coat," Dolly continued. "Beautifully tailored and a discreet ruby stickpin. I shall have to ask Papa to put him on our guest list."

"Dolly, he's not the gentleman he seems. He can be rude and he has a violent temper."

Her eyes twinkled. "I like him more and more. I am sick unto death of mollycoddles and simpering fools."

"Have it your way. But my suitor is twice the man."

"I shall look forward to meeting him then," Dolly said.

We left the restaurant soon after, going out into the teeth of a strong wind which had come up during our meal, blowing dust and debris in whirling eddies along the street. Holding on to our bonnets, we crossed the plank sidewalk to our waiting carriage. I was about to climb in after Dolly when I felt a tap on my shoulder. Turning, I found myself looking up into the ugly, one-eyed visage of Mr. Halstead.

Showing tobacco-stained teeth, he gave me a grimace that passed for a smile. "Pardon, Miss Hastens, I'm Sam Halstead—from New Orleans, if you recall."

My first impulse was to deny any knowledge of him. But I didn't wish to prolong contact with this unsavory creature by starting an argument in front of the coachman, now standing by to help me up.

"What is it?"

"I wonder could you do me a favor, Miss?" he wheedled, clutching a dirty felt hat between his hands. "I been tryin' to see your pa these past few weeks, but his clerk says he's too busy. Could'nt you get in a word for me? I'm sure he'd listen, seein' as how you and I know'd each other."

Despite the whine there was an undercurrent of threat in his voice, one that angered yet frightened me.

"We didn't *know* each other," I said with controlled heat. "And I have nothing to do with my father's affairs."

He laid a hand on my sleeve. "Miss—"

"Don't touch me," I ordered, "or I shall have my coachman give you a taste of his whip."

As the man stepped forward, Sam Halstead threw me a look of pure venom from his one good eye. Then, hunching his shoulders, he slunk off.

"Who was that?" Dolly asked.

"Someone wanting the price of a drink."

"Are the riffraff accosting ladies now? My coachman could have dealt with him. Shall I have him fetch the police?"

"No, it's all right, Dolly. I sent him packing."

Once or twice that night at supper I was on the point of telling Papa about Sam Halstead. But the thought that I would have to explain how I had met him in the brothel on St. John Street deterred me.

Yet the encounter had left me with a lingering unease. Had Sam Halstead followed me or had he seen me by pure chance? Five days after he had stopped me in front of the Poule d'Or, Mrs. Tibbets sent me out to get her some headache powder from an apothecary on Montgomery Street. As I drove slowly along looking for the shop, I passed an iron-roofed building with a wooden sign that, read:

MILES FALCONER
LAND AGENT

On impulse I halted the buggy. Then I sat for a few minutes debating. Should I go in and speak to Miles about this rogue or let it pass? Heaven knew I did not relish confiding in Miles, but suppose Mr. Halstead was up to some mischief?

I got down from the buggy and tied the horse to a post. Inside I confronted a pale, thin young man who asked for my name. I had hardly gotten it out of my mouth when Miles came out from an inner room.

"Carmella! What a surprise!"

I thought for a moment he was pleased to see me until I realized he was merely puzzled.

"Come in," he invited. "We can talk more comfortably in the inner sanctum."

The room was furnished with leather chairs and a large teak desk littered with papers. Books lined one entire wall.

"Sherry?" he offered.

"No, thank you."

"I know this isn't a social call, Carmella . Something must be wrong."

"I'm not quite sure." And then I went on to tell him about my meeting with Mr. Halstead.

After I finished, Miles gazed thoughtfully at the top of his desk for a few moments. Then, lifting his eyes, he said, "I'm sorry this had to happen, Carmella. Both your father and I have had recent dealings with Mr. Halstead, and I've since seen to it that he's left the city."

"What did he want?"

Miles hesitated before he answered. "He was trying to extort money from your father. Blackmail, really. He threatened to go to the newspapers with an account of your mother's background unless your father gave him ten thousand dollars."

"How humiliating for Papa!"

"Of course your father refused to give him a penny. He was all for turning the culprit over to the authorities. But I persuaded him to let me handle Mr. Halstead. He agreed. The scandal would have ruined him socially—not that he cares for himself; it's you, he said, he worries about."

"That's so like Papa. But—if he would only *talk* to me! There's so much I would like to know about my mother."

"Well, yes, it's a painful topic."

"Can't *you* tell me anything?" I leaned forward in my chair. "I remember you saying you knew her briefly."

"That's true. I was passing through New Orleans when I met her. I went to tea at your father's house."

"She poured?"

"She did. Lovely manners. A lady."

I sighed, picturing my mother, her slender hands poised over the tea table.

"Did Papa love her?"

"Very much."

"And she—did she love my father?"

"Yes."

"Do you think—if she had lived—people would have come to accept her?"

"I'm sure of it. It's quite possible for someone like that to be a gentlewoman at heart. For instance, there is a beautiful courtesan in this city who could pass as an educated woman of refinement in society's most selected drawing rooms."

"You know her, this—this courtesan?"

He nodded.

"How well?" And then, unbidden, almost as if a devilish imp had prodded me, "Is she your mistress?"

The question, as I might have forseen, displeased him. "Miss Hastings, you must learn to control your curiosity. You are becoming quite a busybody."

"Mr. Falconer," I said, infusing his name with the same stiff formality he had given to mine, "may I point out that you seem to have trouble controlling your own Paul Pry inclinations?"

"Ah, but I am a—"

"A man," I interrupted angrily. "And older. And that gives you the right."

"Yes."

I glared at him, and suddenly the sober look fled from his eyes and he threw back his head and laughed.

"Why do you treat me like a schoolgirl?" I demanded, furious.

"In self-defense," he replied, his eyes dancing with amusement.

"Oh—go to—go to blazes!" And with that I stamped out of his precious inner sanctum, slamming the door so hard the glass window in it shivered.

The following Tuesday I received the Hobart invitation, engraved on cream paper in flowery script. It was to be among many such cordial bids. Until my arrival Papa had accepted few of these invitations, but now—as he put it—to make up for his neglect, he wanted me to have a good time. Poor Papa. I don't think he himself knew how to have "a good time."

At other people's parties he always seemed to be on the fringe, ill at ease, wearing a forced smile, and if cornered by some dowager making the sort of courteous small talk that I sensed pained him. Often I had the feeling he would have been far happier at home, alone with his newspaper and cigar. But he went to everything now, trotting me around, insisting that he was delighted to do so. I loved him for it, and because I did I suffered enormous guilt whenever I stole down to the Union Hotel to inquire about mail from Hangman's Creek. My covert behaviour betrayed Papa's kindness, but I could no more stop looking for Derry's letters than I could stop wanting him.

The Hobart ball made the Bridewells', which I had once thought so grand, seem little better than a country dance.

I wore a new gown that night, one that I had persuaded my dressmaker to do up using the crinoline cage. It was of pale blue tulle illusion with seven ruffles banding the wide billowing skirt, each ruffle edged by a narrow ruche of white lace. The neckline exposed my shoulders and dipped daringly in front where a large, white silk flower nestled provocatively. The same sort of white flower adorned my hair. I wore dainty satin slippers and carried a white ivory-handled fan. And as I fluttered the fan, examining the effect in the mirror, I could not help thinking how far I had come from Aunt Maude's serviceable gray gowns and stodgy button shoes. I only wished Derry was there to see me.

We were early because we were punctual, and in those days, as always, it was fashionable to be a little late. The house as we drove up was brightly lit, the white-pillared entrance glow-

ing like the facade of a Greek temple. Our carriage was taken
by a groom; a butler led us in to a huge, two-storied entryway,
and Papa gave him his cape, stick, hat, and card.

A double door was thrown open and the butler's voice very
English, announced us. Our hosts hurried to the door, shook
our hands, said how glad they were we had come. Dolly rushed
up to me and squeezed me as much as our hooped skirts would
allow.

"Don't you look scrumptious!"

"And you, Dolly . . .!" She wore white, flounced and swagged
and banded with black pearl-sewn ribbon.

Papa appeared uncomfortable. "I always am the first at these
things," he whispered as we strolled toward a bank of gilded
chairs. "I should know by now."

But it wasn't long before the others began to arrive, and the
room soon filled with women, their gowns a rainbow medley
of pinks, blues, lavenders, and yellows, and the men in black
and white evening attire. The fiddles tuned up and the waiters
appeared, threading through the crowd with trays of champagne.

I had no lack of partners, each coming up to Papa beforehand
to ask his permission. Papa, standing behind my gilt chair,
would speak the man's name by way of introduction, adding,
"Enjoy yourself, my dear."

When I try to remember who I danced with on that night I
am at a loss. Names and faces elude me. I can remember only
a series of frilled white shirtfronts. For all I knew it may have
been the same young man I waltzed with over and over again.
To me they were all Derry. It was his arm that encircled my
waist, his steps I followed, his voice that murmured in my ear,
his breath brushing my cheek. I was happy; I moved on winged
feet, floating from one pair of darksuited arms to another. The
quadrille, the reel, the waltz.

I was obliquely aware of Papa in the background smiling
his constrained, fixed smile of Dolly, in white, pearls twined
in her hair, winking at me over a pair of stalwart shoulders.

Only once during the evening did I emerge from my eu-
phoria. Apparently Dolly had induced her parents to extend
Miles Falconer an invitation despite my poor opinion of him.

He was talking to Papa as my latest partner returned me from a brisk and rather breathless reel.

"Oh, Carmella, there you are," said Papa, looking more cheerful than he had all evening. "Miles has just asked if he might have the next dance. You don't mind, do you?"

"I thought—"

But Miles did not give me the opportunity to think. The orchestra had already struck up a lilting waltz, and Miles swept me into his arms, whirling me off through the crowd.

He was an excellent dancer, I had to give him that. I closed my eyes as I had done with the others, and let the music carry me where it would.

"You aren't bored, are you?" Miles asked suddenly.

"No, why should I be?"

"You look it. Or perhaps you were merely dreaming of Derry Wakefield. Wishing you were in his arms instead of mine?"

"What if I do? It's no concern of yours."

"But it is. When I'm dancing I like to have my partner's full attention."

"I don't know why you asked me in the first place. Yes, yes, I do. Out of spite, out of pure spite."

"Nothing of the sort. You are easily the loveliest girl here and I like lovely girls."

Was he serious? Compliments from Miles were as rare as hen's teeth. I glanced quickly at his face, but his expression told me nothing.

We danced in silence for a few minutes; then he said, "And what do you hear from your devoted lover?"

"Really, Miles! And you were the one who accused *me* of being a busybody."

"So I did."

"But since you apparently must know, Derry is doing quite well."

It was a guess and I hoped a correct one. I had received no letter from Derry, though it had been several weeks since he had gone. However, I consoled myself with the fact that mail service between the mines and the city was erratic. In any case, I felt I would hear shortly.

"How fortunate," Miles was saying. "I've been told there's been a flood up toward Hangman's Creek, several bridges down and the place cut off from communication with the outside world."

Was he lying? Trying to catch me in a trap? "Funny," I said with a toss of my head, "Derry made no mention of a flood." And I looked him straight in the eye.

A roll of drums resounded through the room. "Supper will be served in the dining room!" the butler announced.

"Ah, supper," Miles said, taking my arm. "May I?"

"Sorry, but I have already promised Papa."

He gave me a curt bow as he handed me back to Papa, then disappeared in the crowd.

Later I saw him with Dolly. She was talking to him in an animated fashion over a plate heaped with food, smiling, laughing up into his face. He leaned toward her a little, as if to hear better, and I saw his eyes going over her bare shoulders and her partially exposed breasts. I felt a sudden stab under my heart. Not jealousy. For how could I be jealous of a man I disliked so? No, it was anger at Dolly. To my mind, by coltishly flirting with Miles she had betrayed our friendship and gone over to the enemy.

CHAPTER

FIFTEEN

IT WAS *impossible to remain angry with Dolly for* long. Generous, spirited, in love with life, she bubbled with a good humor that never failed to infect me.

"I really can't help it if I find Miles Falconer attractive, can I?" she asked. "Please forgive me, Carmella. But if he were your beau, if I had any idea—"

"Not in the least," I interrupted. "It's just that I think you deserve better."

Three days had gone by since the ball, and we were sitting in Papa's parlor in the late afternoon over a cup of tea. Mrs. Tibbets having excused herself and gone to her room for a nap, we were able to converse freely.

"Thank you for that, bless your heart, Carmella." She leaned over and gave me a swift hug. "But I might not want to do better. He's handsome, he comes from a good family—though a black sheep, I've heard. Still, he has money and is unmarried."

"You aren't thinking seriously about him?"

"I don't see why not. Although he does seem the type that would prefer a mistress to a wife."

I remembered Miles's praise for the beautiful courtesan. "He consorts with prostitutes."

Dolly gave a deep sigh. *"I* wouldn't mind going to bed with him."

155

"Don't be ridiculous."

"Why not? Those strong arms . . ." She closed her eyes for a moment. "Do you know *I* had to ask him to dance? Forward of me, but I didn't care."

"He has a terrible temper, Dolly."

"That's the second time you've said that. Why? Have you seen him give way to it?"

"Once . . ." I was on the verge of telling her about Aspinwall, but again found I could not. It was a memory that held not only shame (for I *had* goaded him) but something else. Whenever I thought of Miles Falconer crushing me to his chest, his brutal, bruising kiss, a strange little shiver would run up my spine. I could not understand why. He didn't attract me; in fact, the opposite was true.

"He slapped me," I fibbed. (*I* had slapped him.) "He called me a spoiled child and struck me."

"And—and . . . ?"

"Why, what do you mean by 'and'? I was very angry, of course, and he apologized. Well, anyway," I added, a little annoyed by now, "I don't choose to spend the afternoon talking about *him.*"

"Oh, Carmella, you're not put out with me, are you?" She gave me a winning smile. "Don't be. The real reason I came was to invite you to a theater party. Lotta Crabtree will be performing and she's supposed to be absolutely marvelous. I'm dying to see her, aren'y you?"

"The real Lotta Crabtree?" My mood took an immediate upward swing. "I'd love to! I'll ask Papa."

He was delighted, he said; relieved, I thought. I don't believe he enjoyed the theater any more than he did balls or dinner parties.

"I'm so glad to see you've made friends," he said. "Dolly is a little—well, a little skittish, but there's no harm to her. Are you happy here, Carmella?"

"Oh, yes."

I loved San Francisco. I found it exciting, fascinating, glamorous, fun, like an opened box of bonbons presented for my special pleasure. I loved its streets thronging with a mixed lot from the far reaches of the world. I loved the shops, the sidewalk displays, the raucous cries of the hawkers, the excitement of Steamer Day. I loved the smell of it, the sea wind that came up in the late afternoon, the early morning gusts redolent with chaparrel blowing down from the hills, the white fogs that would creep in of an evening, the mournful sound of the ships in the bay. I loved the air of naughtiness, of sin, when we rolled past the Bella Union in Portsmouth Square, catching a glimpse of the gambling inside, a barmaid's brightly colored skirt, a snatch of lusty music, the sound of uproarious laughter.

Two months passed and I still hadn't heard from Derry. I looked in at the Union Hotel almost every day now, steeling myself to meet the supercilious clerk's eye and his, "Sorry, nothing for you, Miss Hastings." Disappointment would be replaced by anger—why didn't he write as promised?—only to be followed by worry. What if something has happened? Mining camps had a notoriously high rate of violent deaths. Shootings and stabbings were commonplace, not to speak of rock slides, flash floods, and the ferocious grizzly known to attack without warning. How selfish of me to think of a letter when he might, even now, be lying somewhere alone, injured, and helpless. Yet I continued to go through the same round of hope, disappointment, annoyance, and concern.

In the meanwhile, life went on at Gough Street. Papa opened accounts for me at Davidson and Lane's and the City of Paris. From Shreve's he brought me a pearl necklace and a set of gold-backed combs studded with sapphires. I don't know how much Papa paid for my jewelry—he would never say—but those pieces must have been expensive, for he suggested I keep them in his small, study safe instead of my jewel box upstairs.

I grew fonder of him as I got to know him better. Not that he was more open with me than he had been before, but I had learned to read his moods from the quirk of an eyebrow, the set of his mouth, or the tone of his voice. His habits, his likes and dislikes, became familiar. He wanted his supper on time and conversation at the table to be light or amusing. He did not care to hear scandal or gossip but was always receptive to news of some enterprising individual's success whether in commerce or the arts. He preferred cigars to cherroots, port to whiskey.

* * *

One afternoon as I was preparing to set out for my usual inquiry at the Union Hotel, a boy came to the door with a note. He refused to give it to the butler but said his instructions were to put it in my hand. I thought at first it might be a communication from Derry, and after rewarding the urchin with a coin, I went into the study, shutting the doors behind me, to read it.

The envelope was grimy, the paper cheap, and it was not from Derry.

Dear Miss Hastings:

I am holden your Pa prisner. If you want to see him alive agin youd best bring $10,000 to the Bird-in-the-Hand on East Street nere old Sidney Town. COME ALONE. If I sees you with anyone or suspects someones folleren you I'll SLIT YOUR PAS throat. So I'm warnen you. No triks. The Bird-in-the-Hand by 3 oclock.

Sam Halstead.

I sank down on a chair and reread the note slowly, my stomach twisting into a sick knot. Sam Halstead! So he had managed to sneak back into the city. And abducted Papa. How? That very morning I had kissed Papa good-bye. He had been on his way to see a man at Fort Mason about a shipment of flour and said he might miss supper. Sam Halstead must have intercepted him somewhere along his route.

For the first time in my life I had to make an important decision concerning someone I loved. The self-debate over my hasty marriage had been a serious matter, but nothing like the difficult choice I must make now. My father's life depended on what I did or did not do. And the thought scared me.

Should I give in to this rogue, this extortionist? But Papa had refused to do so before and might not thank me for it now. Should I go to the police? But miscreants like Sam Halstead could smell a policeman a mile away. Perhaps I ought to ask Miles for help. But Halstead knew Miles, and the minute he saw his face he would carry out his threat against Papa.

I got up out of the chair on legs of straw and went to Papa's liquor cabinet. Brandy, whiskey, port, sherry. I chose the whiskey, and filling a shot glass drank it neat. It set my chest on fire but it cleared my head.

Of course I would bring the money. I had no alternative.

The combination to the safe was kept under the lid of Papa's cigar box. Twisting the dial, I opened it and brought out a bag of gold eagles and another of paper money, all there was. I counted twice; it came to $1,000 both times. I added my sapphire combs and pearl necklace to the coin bag. Sam Halstead would have to accept what I had. Then on impulse I removed Derry's ring from around my neck and tucked it under a folio lying in the safe. I might lose my expensive jewelry but I couldn't risk parting with Derry's ring.

In the pantry I found a small shopping basket and slipped the clinking bag and bundles of cash inside, covering them with a tea cloth.

As I passed the parlor on the way out, Mrs. Tibbets called, "Are you going into the city, Carmella? Be a dear and get me a sack of horehounds, would you?"

I hesitated before I answered. Should I? But no, I couldn't tell her, nor could I take her. She would be worse than useless.

"Yes, Mrs. Tibbets."

Once in the buggy with the reins in my hands, the nerve (or whiskey) that had carried me thus far deserted me. I began to tremble. What if I couldn't find the Bird-in-the-Hand? What if I were too late? Or worse, what if Sam Halstead would not accept my offering? But how foolish of me to anticipate. *Coward!* I jeered at myself; and smacking the horse smartly on the rump with the reins, I set off at a trot.

Doubt sat on my shoulder like a bald vulture. Perhaps I *should* borrow the rest of the money from Miles. I wouldn't have to tell him about Sam Halstead—just ask him for a loan, saying Papa needed it and would pay him back shortly. I turned down Montgomery Street and came to a halt at the door of Miles's building.

He wasn't in, the clerk said. "Mr. Falconer will be here tomorrow, however. Is there a message?"

"No." It was just as well, I reflected. The idea of requisitioning money from Miles without arousing his suspicion was idiotic. Even in my upset state I should have realized that Miles would want to know why Papa had sent me on such a mission. It was best that I tackle this alone.

"By the way," I said, "could you direct me to East Street?"

"East Street?" The clerk's pale brows rose in shock.

"Yes. My butler is new in the city and is—is wanting to meet a friend at the Bird-in-the-Hand."

"I don't know that particular tavern, Miss. But it's in a disreputable neighborhood if it's on East Street."

"Could you draw me a diagram?"

It was Canal all over again. The same stench hung in the air—the odor of open drains, frying food, stale liquor, and putrifying garbage.

A late afternoon lull predominated as I drove, an hour of respite during which I imagined the night crawlers were girding themselves for the evening's mischief. I kept looking from side to side, reading the names of saloons and dance halls under my breath. I passed the Grizzly Cafe, where a chained bear napped in the shade of the roof's overhang, its coat mangy and matted, its worn head cradled on its padded paws. A few doors from it a faded, scalloped board proclaimed in barely discernible letters: BIRD-IN-THE-HAND.

I hated to leave my rig unattended in such an unsavory neighborhood, but there were no small boys who, for a nickel, might watch my horse and turn-out. Gripping my basket firmly, I descended some steps to a door and went inside. There I stood for a moment, blinking, trying to adjust my eyes to the gloom. The place smelled of sawdust, urinals, and spilled liquor. A long bar on one side of the rectangular room was empty except for a man dozing behind it. Around a cleared space in the center of the room, a space presumably used for dancing, were several trestle tables nested with upturned chairs. A man in a leather apron with a gunny bag slung over his back was sweeping rubbish along the floor.

I said to him, "Is Mr. Halstead here?"

He lifted a slack-mouthed face. "Hey? Hey?"

"Never mind." I went over to the bar and shook the man awake, posing the same question to him.

"Halstead?" he asked drowsily.

"He has a patch over one eye."

"Oh—him. Sam. No, he ain't come in yet."

Suddenly the sound of loud voices on the stairs outside echoed through the quiet room, and a moment later the doors burst open. A motley group of men funneled in, laughing boisterously.

"Drink! Drinks!" they shouted, sweeping up to the bar, jostling me aside, banging their fists on the counter top.

"Beer! Steam beer!"

"Gin fer me!"

"Gimme some of yer rotgut whiskey!"

And one lone voice, "Pisco brandy!"

They pushed and shoved and cuffed each other good-naturedly, a clutch of ruddy-faced, windbeaten, bearded ruffians, tall, short, barrel chested, spike thin, dressed in assorted wrinkled and salt-stiffened jackets and breeches. Sailors, I assumed, and from their talk just off a ship.

I edged my way farther into the shadows, wondering if I ought to leave and wait outside. But I was afraid I would miss Halstead. Suppose he came in by another door—or down from the wooden staircase I now noticed at the deep end of the room. And where was he keeping Papa? Upstairs, perhaps. Earlier my mind had been too taken up with the money and my own fears to dwell on Papa himself. Had Sam Halstead tied him up, gagged him, perhaps knocked him unconscious? If he had hurt him. . . . Oh, God, where was the blackmailing scoundrel?

"Miss Hastings!"

The sailors had hidden his entrance. He wore a rusty-black coat and a battered stovepipe hat which he did not bother to remove.

"Have you the money, Miss Hastings?"

"As much as I could bring, but you shan't have a penny of it until I see my father."

"How much you got?"

"I'll tell you when I see my father. Where is he?"

"He ain't here. Well—you don't think I'd risk it, do you? How'd I know you wouldn't have the Vigilantes swarmin' all over the place?"

"I came alone. Where have you been keeping my father?"

"In my place. It ain't far from the Bird."

"Get him, Mr. Halstead."

"I can't."

"Why? Is he hurt? What have you done to him?"

He pushed the stovepipe back from his forehead. "A little knock on the head."

"A little knock . . . !" I paused. "You're lying. What proof can you give that you have him?"

From inside his coat he produced a battered top hat of gray felt, the kind Papa habitually wore. "It was just a tap—ain't much."

"If you've injured my father. . . . Take me to him at once!"

When we got outside, dusk was falling and the streets were beginning to fill with passersby. My horse and buggy still stood at the curb. I took a deep breath although the air here was hardly any better than it was inside. But it sobered me up enough to realize I would have to climb into that buggy with a scoundrel.

"I have a gun in my basket, Mr. Halstead," I lied. "And I shall watch you carefully."

He chuckled, a sound that sent shivers up my spine.

We set off, passing open doorways from which light and the sound of raised voices spilled. Creaking wooden signs swung over cellar stairs where men lounged in the shadows.

Sam Halstead spoke only to give me directions. "Turn here." "Go to the next block."

As night closed down, I became aware that we had left the East Street neighborhood (some called it the Barbary Coast) for Little China. Paper lanterns painted with strange caligraphy glowed like fireflies against a backdrop of Stygian darkness. From somewhere close by came a burst of clanging cymbals, shrill music, and a nasal singsong voice.

"Is it much farther?" I asked nervously.

"Up the next street."

We halted before a two-story tenement completely enveloped in darkness. Dimly I made out a shop and a staircase to one side climbing to a single windowed apartment above. From the building beside it a tiny light glimmered behind a drawn shade.

Sam Halstead led the way up the matchstick, ladderlike staircase which groaned and swayed at every step. He opened

a door and bade me enter. As I stumbled over the threshold
he snatched the basket from me, nearly taking my arm with it.
I lunged out blindly to retrieve it, but he laughed, evading me,
slamming the door and drawing a bolt.

The rasp of the bolt raised gooseflesh along my arms. "Mr.
Halstead!"

"Shut yer mouth!"

He struck a light and touched the small blue flame to a
candle. One look around the bare room furnished only with a
cot, a table, and a chipped wardrobe told me Papa was not
there. Mr. Halstead and I were alone.

"What is the meaning of this?" I cried. "What have you
done with my father?"

"Nothin'." He grinned. "I ain't seen him for a month."

"Then—then the hat...?"

"I stole it, Miss. I got me a better pigeon now."

It had been a hoax. He had lured me to this place using my
father and his hat as bait. No wonder he had not snatched the
basket from me on the way, something he could have done
easily despite my false threat of a gun.

"I didn't see as how you'd be able to put your hands on
real money," he said, "but your pa will."

"My father will see you hang!"

"Don't worry 'bout *my* neck, Miss Hastens. Have a care
for you own. If he tries anythin' foolish I'll wring it like a
chicken's. Now you be a good girl and sit down on that bed
and don't say a word. Sit!"

I backed away and sat down, my heart jumping like a scared
rabbit's. He put the basket on a table and removed the cloth.
Opening the money bag he began to count the coins, glancing
up at me now and again to see if I had moved.

"That's a good start," he said when he had finished. "And
them baubles ought to be worth something'. Now give me your
gown and bonnet—and them shoes."

"What?"

"You heard me. I don't want you runnin' off while I'm out
sendin' your papa a message. Your gown—"

"But I can't!"

"There's a blanket if you're modest. Now hurry up or I'll
rip them things from your back. Hurry!"

I got out of my gown quickly while he watched, a lascivious look in his one ugly eye. Wrapping the dirty, odorous blanket about me, I sat down on the bed and removed my shoes.

"That's better." Muttering something about "safekeepin'," he bundled the money bag and cash in my clothes and tucked the parcel under his arm. Then he went out and I heard a key turn in the lock.

I waited a minute or two, then ran to the door and tried it. When it wouldn't give, I called, "Help! Help! Someone help me!" Only a scampering sound, mice or rats, answered.

I sat down on the bed again, shivering under the blanket. By now Papa must be home—and worried. Neither Mrs. Tibbets nor the servants knew where I had gone. Miles, when he returned in the morning to his office, would not know either. How long would it take for Sam Halstead's note to reach Papa? It would ask for $10,000, the sum Halstead had wanted when he first tried to blackmail Papa. Ten thousand dollars! I had no doubt Papa would pay it, but how galling to hand over the money to such a scurvy renegade.

But in the meanwhile I would have to wait, and I did not like the look in Sam Halstead's eye. I would have done better to have armed myself with a sharp kitchen knife or even a pair of scissors. I got up and looked in the basket. Two stray coins lay at the bottom and I tucked them in my bodice. Then I moved to the wardrobe. It contained a pair of white baggy pants, an embroidered Mexican shirt, a serape, and the Guayaquil sombrero I had seen Sam Halstead trying on at the marketplace in Mazatlán. Had he worn these clothes as a disguise to sneak back into the city after Miles ordered him to leave? I searched the bottom of the wardrobe, under the mattress of the cot, beneath the table, every corner of the room, but could find nothing I might use as a weapon.

It was a long, ghastly night. Sitting cross-legged on the cot, afraid to lie down, my eyes glued to the door in apprehension, I catnapped, my head jerking up at every untoward sound, expecting Sam Halstead's momentary return. At some time during those endless hours the candle guttered out. I remember going to the window and drawing the dingy curtain aside. I tried to lift the window, but it was nailed shut. Pressing my nose against the dusty glass I peered out into the darkness, but except for the inky outline of the building across the way could see nothing.

Back I went to my vigil. I must have dozed off again, for the sound of heavy feet on the stairs jolted me upright. The light in the room had changed, gray fingers of dawn from the window probing the cobwebbed shadows. The footsteps stumbled, and an oath was muttered as the key rattled in the lock.

Sam Halstead stood swaying on the threshold, reeking of whiskey. His hat and my bundled clothes were gone.

"What you say?" he queried drunkenly, wagging a dirty finger at me. "You bitch—what you say?"

"Nothing," I answered through dry lips.

"So high and mighty. Think you can beat Sam Halstead at his own game, d'you? Well—I'll show you."

He slammed the door and came lurching across the room toward me. I shrank back against the wall. "Mr. Halstead—"

"Shud up, shud up, you tart!"

He grasped the blanket and tore it from me. I dove after it and he slammed me back on the mattress, his patch awry, the good eye red and gleaming with lust.

"I'm gonna have you, then feed you to the ducks!"

"My father—"

He threw himself on me, his hands scrabbling, pulling and yanking at the ribbons of my camisole, furious at the cloth that kept him from my bare skin. His loathsome, swollen passion kept butting my thighs, while his slobbering lips groped for my mouth. White-hot anger surging through me brought my balled fist slamming against the side of his head. He grunted, then suddenly collapsed across me. I shoved his torso aside and he rolled over, falling to the floor with a thump. His heavy alcoholic snores told me that it wasn't the vigor of my blow that had felled him but his own sotted state. But it didn't matter. I was free; I could go.

Hesitating a moment, I thought—clothes? Quickly stepping over Halstead, I went to the wardrobe and with nerveless fingers slipped on the baggy pants, tying them at my waist with the drawstring. The shirt, the serape, and the hat. No shoes. I scrabbled along the bottom of the wardrobe and found a pair of backless straw slippers jammed up against a side wall. Slippers in hand, I tiptoed to the door, eased through, and was down the stairs in seconds.

My rig was gone. I could have wept with disappointment, I had so counted on getting away in it. Had it been stolen? And what about my clothes and the money? Had Halstead spent it on gambling and liquor? And the message to my father? But I couldn't think about those things now. I had to put distance between me and the horrible man upstairs.

Stuffing my feet into the slippers and tucking my hair under the sombrero, I set off at a hasty clip, the open straw sandals slapping at my heels. The street I followed made a bend, running into a thoroughfare (and, by the Oriental faces I saw, still in Little China), busy even at this early hour. The earth-packed road was lined with pyramided packing cases and boxes. Across a narrow sidewalk from them were the shops, false storefronts, angled-roofed huts, and shanties bearing Chinese legends on the doors, windows, and board signs in a bold, thick script. I stopped a small Chinese woman carrying a basket heaped with white-bellied fish and asked directions. She shrugged, muttered a few unintelligible words, and hurried on.

Thinking that perhaps one of the merchants might possess a knowledge of English, I went into a shop, a tiny doll's cubicle partitioned off from its neighbors by paper-thin walls. On its single counter covered with a yellow cloth lay fans, ivory chessmen, combs, jade figurines, and delicately painted china cups. Over this display of craftsmanship hovered a thin, brooding Chinese dressed in a white embroidered smock.

"I'm looking for Montgomery Street," I enunciated slowly and loudly, thinking that once I got on Montgomery I could find my way home.

"Mungumeree? Ahhh." He tapped his temple. "Mungumeree. You go, you go to corner, turn . . ." He waved his right hand, then held up two fingers. "Two blocks."

I followed the shopkeeper's directions but became hopelessly lost in a maze of dark alleys. Somewhere, somehow I found myself hemmed in by dark walls behind which could be heard voices and movement, a curious high-pitched chirping, the rattle of what sounded like crockery, thumps, and the thin wail of a child. Garbage lay underfoot, discarded and rotted

leavings giving off a foul putrefying odor which mingled with
the spicy cooking smells of the kitchens inside. A rat darted
out and paused to stare at me with beady eyes.

I screamed, consumed with the nighmarish sensation that
these loathsome creatures were all around me. But no one came
to see; not one face appeared at a doorway.

Panic gripped me and I ran blindly, turning sharp-angled
corners, racing under wooden porticos and ladderlike stairs,
fleeing down one alley into another, a series of dark, dank
tunnels without light or air.

At last I came to a wider, somewhat uncluttered, though by
no means cleaner, alley. Here the doors had wickets or barred
windows like a row of jail cells. As I stood there, trying to
decide which way to go, a plaintive voice called, "China girl
nice. You come inside, please?"

I turned. A face the color of old ivory was pressed to one
of the wickets. While I stared at her, the door opened. The
girl, beckoning, spoke again: "Come inside, please?"

She was wearing a short, black silk blouse with a narrow
band of embroidered turquoise down the front and nothing else.
Her pubic area was shaved and her feet were bare.

She coyly twitched her blouse open, revealing a glimpse of
slight breasts. "Two bittee, lookee; flo bittee, feelee; six bittee
doee," she chanted.

Because of my clothes she had mistaken me for a man. "No
thank you, not today."

"Please," she begged, her eyes suddenly desperate.

Pity stirred in me. "I'll give you the money. You won't
have to 'doee' anything."

Dolly had once told me that these girls were slaves, some
of them bought as mere children from impoverished parents in
China by dealers who scoured the Chinese countryside for
unwanted female children.

Apparently this girl found it difficult to understand that I
was offering her money without wanting anything in return.
She took a step past the threshold. "Charlie—you come inside?"

I took one of the coins from my bosom and pressed it into
her hand. "Keep it for yourself."

No sooner were the words out of my mouth than an old

Chinese harridan, her features contorted in rage, came flying through the door and snatched the coin from the girl. Then she began to beat her with a stick, screaming and carrying on all the while. The girl howled at each blow, cringing, throwing up her arms to protect herself. At the doorway, three women appeared, watching the scene, but made no move to go to the girl's rescue. One, in fact, lifted a lip in scorn.

I did not want to get mixed up with these people, and yet the theft of my money as well as the beating angered me. I tried to grab hold of the harridan's arm, but she brushed me off as one would brush off an irksome fly, sending me reeling with a whack of her stick. The scornful crib girl snickered.

"Stop it! Stop it at once!" I shouted.

Two Chinese men who had been sauntering by, paused to watch. "Can't you stop her?" I pleaded with them.

But they did not understand. Finally the harridan dragged the girl inside and the crib prostitute who had snickered spoke to the men in Chinese, beckoning, showing her breasts, pointing to her genitals in a suggestive manner.

Disgusted, filled with loathing, I turned from the scene. As I commenced to walk away, a woman entered the alley, the first white face I had seen since I had lost myself in this hellhole. She was an odd-looking creature, middle-aged, I guessed, dressed in a wide, sweeping black skirt and a man's pilot coat edged with tarnished silver braid. The face under a soiled mob cap had a stern, almost forbidding expression, but the moment she noticed me the tight mouth relaxed into a smile.

"Madam—I beg your pardon." I touched the edge of my sombrero. "But I seem to have lost my way."

"Easy to do in these parts," she said.

"I'm so glad to find someone who speaks English." Glad was hardly the word. Despite her strange appearance, the woman, at the moment, seemed like an angel from Heaven.

"Going round in circles, is that it?"

She had discolored but strong-looking, even teeth.

"Yes, and I am trying to find Montgomery Street."

She pursed thin, grayish lips. "By golly, you're miles from it. Tell you what. I'm on my way to the Spiggot—I own it— and I'll have one of my boys give you a ride in the cart. No trouble. I have an errand he can busy himself with."

"That's kind of you, but if you could just direct me." I didn't trust her.

She shrugged. "Suit yourself. See that building? Go round the corner, another right, and that will bring you out on Jackson Street. From there you . . ."

I listened closely, repeating after her, trying to memorize streets and turnings.

"Got that?" she concluded.

"Yes—and thank you."

When I reached Jackson Street the first thing I noticed was a hack parked in front of a Chinese silk shop. A little man in an oversized greatcoat sat dozing on the box.

I reached up and tapped his knee. "My good man, I wish to engage you."

He looked me up and down in astonishment. "I'm already engaged by them ladies." He jerked his thumb toward the shop.

Through the door I saw a pair of hatted and gloved women examining a bolt of cloth. I had a momentary twinge of conscience before I turned back to the little man.

"I'll give you a gold eagle to take me home," I said.

He bent down to inspect the coin as I held it in my hand.

"Well . . . I—"

"A gold eagle," I repeated. "The ladies can find another conveyance."

I got home to find that Papa was gone and Mrs. Tibbets was lying down with one of her headaches. When she heard my voice she emerged from her bedroom and descended the stairs holding a vinegar-soaked cloth to her head.

"Carmella! Where *have* you been? And what are you doing in those clothes?"

"Where's Papa?" I asked, ignoring her questions.

"Where would he be? Out looking for you. He and Mr. Miles. Do you realize what trouble you've caused? Going off without a word, staying the night, God knows where. Everyone sick with worry, everything in a turmoil. Your father—"

It was precisely at that moment that Papa came in the door with Miles at his heels. I fell into my father's arms and promptly burst into tears, an outpouring of wrenching sobs that finally silenced Mrs. Tibbets.

CHAPTER

SIXTEEN

*S*AM HALSTEAD *had never delivered his message* to Papa. "Cold feet," Miles said. "He was afraid."

When Papa arrived home well past supper that night and found I had not returned from the city, he turned around immediately and went down to police headquarters. With their help, he had scoured the shops, inquired of all my friends, servants, passersby, anyone at all, giving my description, asking if I had been seen. He spent the balance of the night at Wilson's Exchange waiting for Miles's return.

It wasn't until Miles's clerk repeated my request for directions to the Bird-in-the-Hand that they got their first clue. At the Bird they learned that I had been there and had left with Sam Halstead. Further interrogation among the regulars revealed his place of residence.

Sam Halstead at first tried to deny he had seen me. But— as Miles put it—"a little shaking up" convinced him he had. As I suspected, he had gambled away the money and my clothes. The rig too. But he swore through a mouth of loose bloody teeth that I had run off, he had no idea where.

It was then that Papa and Miles had started their door-to-door search through the Barbary Coast and Little China.

"You can be sure we aren't popular there," Papa said, "though we did grease a few palms."

After I told them my story, Papa shook his head. "I must say you make me proud. Any other girl in your place would have lain down and died right at the start in that scoundrel's miserable lodgings. Isn't that right, Miles?"

"Indeed, sir."

Did I detect a hint of admiration in his eyes? Perhaps.

But the next day as we were having tea in the parlor Miles said: "I do think it was unwise of you to have gone alone, Carmella. I said as much to your father. If—"

"*If . . . ,*" I broke in, needled by his tone of reproof. "I *did* look for you, Miles. And you weren't there."

"You might have waited, been less hasty."

"You speak as though I had engineered my own abduction," I said. "I daresay—"

"Now, now," Papa calmed. "Miles was only suggesting, Carmella."

I stirred my tea with a vigor that sent the cup rattling.

"May I have another slice of that cake, Carmella?" Papa asked, casting me a mild "tsk-tsk" look.

With a sigh I cut the cake, then settled back in my chair. We drank in silence. A gust of wind hooted down the chimney and whispered along the eaves.

Papa said, "Will Carmella be required to testify at Halstead's trial?"

"I'm looking into it," Miles said. "I'm going to see if we can't get the blackguard shipped out—an indefinite voyage around the world on a slave master's vessel. Hopefully he won't survive the sea air."

At last Miles had said something I could wholeheartedly approve of.

When I emerged from our house on Gough Street after three days of recuperative seclusion, I was the object of much curiosity. Dolly and my other contemporaries wanted a detailed account of my experience; the older women were not quite sure what they wanted. They were too well bred to ask outright questions and puzzled as how to react to a girl of their own class who had been abducted. So they smiled politely, shook their heads at me, and said, "What is the world coming to?"

The younger men were as attentive as ever, unable to understand why I kept refusing their invitations to theater parties, to teas, and to Sunday afternoon rides. I still hoped to hear from Derry. I had retrieved his ring from the safe and wore it like a talisman. Someday, any day, there would be a letter.

One evening Papa casually informed me that he had run into Derry at the bank.

"Mr. Wakefield?" I asked, my ears reverbrating with shock.

"Says he's been back a week."

A whole week! I felt devastated. Seven days and he had not come to see me, written a note, or tried in any way to communicate! A week! Oh, Derry!

"He didn't have any luck," Papa said. "I knew he wouldn't. The mines are played out. Claims he's a pauper."

That was it then, that was why he had stayed away. He didn't want to come to me with empty hands. But no, I couldn't forgive him that easily. All the long weeks and months of waiting, the torment of disappointment each time I went to the Union Hotel, the mornings that dawned with his name on my lips—how could I sweep that away?

"I've invited Mr. Wakefield to have dinner with us tomorrow evening," Papa said.

"Oh?" Did I want to see him? Of course I did. I was not so much angry as hurt. "I'm sure he will have interesting stories to tell."

All that night I kept thinking of what I would say to Derry, how I would act. Cool, distant—and if he should have the opportunity to press me, I would tell him exactly how I felt.

But when he stood in the entryway, hat in hand, his face bronzed, his hair sun-bleached to a pale gold, his blue eyes apologetic, every recriminating word fled from my tongue.

"Papa will be down in a moment," I said calmly in a voice that belied the fluttering of my heart.

He took my hand and kissed it, his touch shooting quicksilver through my veins. "Carmella," he whispered, "I missed you so. If you only knew the letters I wrote and tore up. But I can't talk now."

I forgave him even before Papa descended the stairs and shook his hand. The time of waiting was but a moment, a ticking second gone and forgotten. Had I felt resentment, anger? Perhaps. But it didn't matter now. He was here, returned, the adoring look in his eyes telling me more than a thousand words that he still loved me.

"And what are you going to do now?" Papa asked Derry as we sat at supper.

"There isn't much I *can* do, sir," he answered ruefully. "A friend of mine who has just returned from the Sierra tells me they are panning a fair amount of gold in Trove's Gulch. He says that claims there can still be staked, but unfortunately I have not the means to finance another venture—at least for now."

"Just as well," Papa said, reaching for the gravy dish. "It's a poor gamble."

Derry winked at me and I threw him an appealing smile. But Papa was speaking again:

"If you are in need of employment in the meanwhile, I think I can be of some help. Mr. Abel of Kohler and Company is looking for a reliable, intelligent clerk. I'd be happy to put in a word for you."

"Why, thank you, Mr. Hastings. I would be most grateful."

Papa and Derry went on to talk of banking matters, the difficulty of shipping gold, and a newly proposed bond issue, dull subjects that held no interest for me. My one consuming preoccupation was how to contrive to be alone with Derry just long enough to set a time and place for us to meet.

When the meal was finished we moved into the parlor. The men smoked cigars; I poured coffee. Mrs. Tibbets, who had joined us for dinner, drank a cup, excused herself, and went up to bed. After a few minutes I left also, on the pretext of seeing to a fresh pot of coffee.

Once outside the parlor doors I sped upstairs, turned on the gaslight, and sitting down at my table quickly brought out paper and pen.

"Derry, my love, I must see you," I began.

But where? Dare we try the Portsmouth Hotel again? Some other place? Tomorrow was Thursday, Mrs. Tibbets's day to visit her aunt. She would be gone all afternoon.

"Can you come to the house at one-thirty?" I continued. "I'll watch for you and let you in. Please, Derry. I've missed you so! Tomorrow. I'll count on it."

I folded the page into a square small enough to fit into my palm. Then I hurried down the stairs, stuck my head in the kitchen door, and called, "Letty, could we have more coffee, please?"

An hour later when Derry took his leave I gave him my hand and pressed the note into his.

Mrs. Tibbets had been gone a half hour and the servants were having a late lunch in the kitchen, when I saw Derry riding up Gough Street on a gray horse, a hireling by the sorry look of it. Poor darling; but he sat that old nag with the ease and grace of a man accustomed to only the best of horseflesh.

I flew down the stairs on shoeless feet and opened the door. "Put your mount in the stable," I whispered. "No one's there at this hour."

I waited until he returned and then, taking him by the hand, with a silencing finger to my lips, drew him up the stairs. Once the door of my room was closed I turned and went into his arms. His mouth on mine was warm, life-giving, a draught of the sweetest wine.

When at last he released me, I looked up at him, his dancing eyes, the curve of his beautiful mouth.

"I love you, Derry. I thought when you didn't come . . ."

"How could I, darling? Such a failure—"

"Hush!" Straining against him I claimed his mouth, sealing it with a passionate kiss.

After a long while he lifted his head and began to undo my bodice. He paused suddenly and smiled.

"You're wearing my ring. Sweet, sweet darling."

"I told you I would."

"Brings back memories, doesn't it?" Derry fondled the ring, then pressed his lips to it.

"Derry . . ." My hands sought and found the buttons of his waistcoat. He leaned back, smiling into my eyes, as his fingers worked nimbly over hooks and fastenings.

I laughed, burying my face in his neck, when he picked me up, but I could as easily have wept. Shaken with emotion I clung to him, bringing his nakedness down over mine as he lowered me on the bed. His muscled arms, which had become like hardened steel on his mountain trek, enfolded and lifted me, thrusting me forward so that he might plunge his pulsating ardor into the very center of my being. We were one again, indivisible, joined together in a rite of celebration. And as he breathed my name over and over, whispering it in my ear, he carried me along on a tide of mounting tension. Even my heart seemed to stop and I held my breath as an indescribable slow heat rolled over me, bringing wave after wave of unbearable pleasure, lifting me to a tremendous peak of excitement. I hung on to his naked back with my fingernails until the world suddenly ripped apart as shudders of ecstasy thundered through every fiber of my body. A moment later Derry collapsed with a small cry.

We lay together, arms and legs tangled. Derry kissed me lightly on the cheek. My eyes, brimming with tears, looked into his.

"I don't deserve you," he said, tenderly pushing the damp hair from my forehead.

"Derry! I wish you wouldn't talk like that. Why—"

"Hush!" He smiled, placing a finger on my lips. "Any other woman in your place would have refused to see me. I didn't write. I tried, as I told you, but I couldn't, somehow the right words never seemed to come. I wanted to write about success and there wasn't any."

"It doesn't matter, darling."

He rolled away and lay by my side. He did not speak for a few moments but stared at the padded tester above us.

"What are you thinking of, darling?" I asked, leaning over and kissing his ear. "Disappointed because you did not find gold?"

"Very. I always seem to be too late. Everything I've ever tried. Too late. Someone has been there before me, found the treasure, the riches, whatever, and moved on." Bitterness tinged his voice.

"Derry, you mustn't feel that way. I know something wonderful is in store for you."

He turned and gave me an affectionate smile. "You're such a sweetheart. I love you for your marvelous optimism."

"Aren't you optimistic too?"

"Yes." He leaned over and pressed his lips to my throat. "When I'm with you, anything is possible."

"Derry . . . ?"

"Mmmmm?"

"If you took a job with Kohler, perhaps—well, Papa thinks very highly of them and he likes you. I know. I could tell by the way he talked to you the other day. Well, if . . ." Derry was looking at me, brows raised, but I rushed on. "If you had a job with a future, I am almost certain Papa would consent to our engagement."

Derry sank back on the pillows. "I hardly think so, Carmella. I know what those jobs pay—not that I would scorn one—I tell you I'm down to my last dollar. But I couldn't support a wife on meager wages; not a wife like you, Carmella."

"But I wouldn't care!"

"My dear, such nonsense. If you had to live in mean lodgings, wear shabby, mended clothes, and scrimp to make ends meet, love would soon fly out the window."

"But I was poor when I lived with Aunt Maude."

"And did you like it? Well, I didn't think so. No, Carmella, I want to give the woman I love pretty gowns, expensive earbobs and bangles. I want to see her glitter and shine when she walks. I want her smiling beauty to be a reflection of my ability to make her comfortable and happy. Why—darling, I couldn't even bring you a small gift the other night. Flowers, a box of candy—the sort of gift a suitor brings to a girl he intends courting."

He was that poor. How did he manage? Was he living on free tavern lunches, spending his nights in seedy cafés that never closed or down-at-the-heels hotel lobbies, using his last pennies to have his boots shined, his chin shaved, his horse hired? How selfish I was to think only of my own needs.

"Listen, sweetheart," he said earnestly, "perhaps it would be best if I stopped seeing you. If—"

"Oh, no, no!" I protested in horror, placing my hand over his mouth. "I couldn't. I would die, simply die. You mustn't even say that again. Promise!"

He moved, gathering me in his arms. "I would die too, darling. I was just testing you."

I felt him rising as he kissed my breasts, and my own body began to take on the slow fire that would in a few minutes, I knew, consume me in a passionate flame.

"Carmella—there's something—something I should have mentioned before."

"What is it, love?"

"I think we should be careful. What I mean is, you wouldn't want to get pregnant, would you?"

I could only stare at him. It had never occurred to me that I could. Looking back now, my naïveté seems laughable. I somehow believed that one did not think in terms of babies unless one were married. But now I suddenly realized how foolish that was. What difference would a few words spoken by a parson or a piece of legal parchment make?

"No—Derry," I stumbled, "not until we are husband and wife."

"Well, there are certain times during the month when a woman is fertile. Certain 'safe' periods when she is not. Just before her flow . . ."

I turned a deep crimson. I had no idea that men knew of such things, especially unmarried men. To discuss this most intimate and shameful "curse" even with another woman was simply not done. And to have Derry, heretofore the essence of tact and delicacy, speaking thus, discomfited me.

". . . and for a week or ten days after. Please don't blush, my darling. It's for your own good."

He was right. Why must I be such a booby? An unwanted pregnancy followed by a speedy, forced marriage would be a poor way to start our life together.

"I don't mean to blush, Derry." I looped my arms about his neck and drew him down. "And—and it's all right, now."

When he was ready to leave, I said, "Derry, will I see you again? Two weeks from next Thursday . . . ," turning a little pink. "It will be safe then too."

"Sweetheart, I would give my right arm to be with you, not just on Thursday but always. However—my circumstanced— not the most affluent—it's so embarrassing, I hate to speak of it."

"Darling, I understand. I do. You are short. Let me lend you some money. I have plenty."

"I should say not! I haven't sunk that low, where I'm ready to take money from a woman."

Nevertheless, while he was tying his cravat I managed to slip a twenty-dollar note into his coat pocket.

One afternoon as I was leaving Liebes, where I had bought a new bonnet, I paused in the doorway to rebutton my gloves. In front and a little to the side with her back to the building, stood a small golden-haired girl. She was holding a bunch of wilted wild flowers out to the passersby and crying, "A nickel—a nickel for my posies!"

For one wrenching moment I thought it was little Sarah, miraculously returned from the jungle. But then she turned, and I saw I was mistaken. She had a nose like a bird's beak and close-set eyes, a homely child, which made her all the more pitiful.

"I'll buy your posies," I offered, and searching in my reticule, gave her five dollars.

She refused to take it, saying her mum would accuse her of stealing, but I closed her hand over the bill. "It's little enough."

I accepted the flowers from her—not to do so would have acknowledged that she had been begging—and she ran off. I had seen a dozen or so such children in San Francisco, some singing for pennies below the verandah of the Bella Union, some peddling matches on Jackson Street, others frankly begging, holding out battered tin saucepans in their grimy hands. Were they orphans? I asked Papa. He did not know, but said there was a Benevolent Society that took care of widows and orphans, so if these children were without parents they had no need to solicit.

I thought of offering my services to the Benevolent Society. Perhaps it had something to do with a residue of guilt at not finding little Sarah, perhaps because the life I led—a round of parties, shopping, and gossip—sometimes palled. When I broached the subject to Papa, however, he judged it unwise.

"My heartfelt sympathies go out to these poor unfortunates," he had said, "but they are prone to carry diseases like typhus and the pox. I wouldn't want you exposed, Carmella. A generous monetary contribution would be just as welcome."

Ever since Sam Halstead (who had been tried without necessitating my appearance and now languished in prison) had abducated me, Papa had become very protective.

I was still standing in the doorway, the wilted flowers in my hand, when I noticed Miles Falconer crossing the street. I would have ducked back inside but he had already seen me.

"Why, good morning, Miss Hastings." A lift of his hat, a mocking smile that insinuated God knew what.

"Good morning."

His eyes went to my drooping bouquet. "I watched your generous gesture, but I daresay it was wasted."

"Why?"

"The child works for a gang master. I've seen her and her comrades pick pockets and snatch purses with a skill that would astound you."

His words had the effect of a wet rag thrown in my face. "Only someone of your suspicious nature would take note of such things, Mr. Falconer," I said tartly. "You are a cynic."

"Not at all—merely stating a truth."

"It doesn't change how I feel. If she's picking pockets to survive, then I feel all the more sorry for her."

His face softened. "Yes. I'm sure you do. Perhaps I should have kept my own counsel."

"It does help."

"Perhaps. By the by, I saw your friend, Derry Wakefield, last night."

"Yes, he has returned to San Francisco. He dined with us last Wednesday."

"Good. And is Papa looking with favor on our Mr. Wakefield?"

"Papa likes him. Derry—Mr. Wakefield is waiting before he declares his intentions."

"I should think so. He was losing quite heavily at cards last night."

"To you?"

"Not to me. I've given up gambling. It's a fool's pastime."

"You must watch yourself then," I said spitefully, "else you'll sprout wings and a halo."

He laughed. "I hardly believe so. I stop in now and again at the Bella Union to meet old friends and exchange news."

"Gossip, you mean. If Mr. Wakefield were winning you probably wouldn't bother to tell me."

"Probably."

"You don't like him."

"No."

"That is why I take everything you tell me about him with a grain of salt. Well, good day to you, Mr. Falconer."

I rode home thinking: I had the last word. For the second time since I have known Miles Falconer I had the last word.

But somehow the thought did not give me the satisfaction I might have expected.

CHAPTER

SEVENTEEN

DERRY CAME to the house the following Thursday and after that—with an occasional skipped week for "safe" purposes—many times more. Only once did we have a narrow squeak when Handy the butler knocked on the door to ask if anything was wrong. He had heard a curious thumping on the ceiling and wondered if I had hurt myself. No, I said, I was only practicing a new dance step. That seemed to satisfy him. If he suspected anything other than what I had told him, he gave no sign. Mrs. Tibbets, of course, believed I spent those afternoons reading.

Derry and I would have preferred arranging our trysts elsewhere, but his lodgings were out of the question and, since Miles had seen me going into the Portsmouth, hotels were too risky.

I hated to deceive Papa under his own roof, but my need to go on seeing Derry was stronger than my conscience. Derry was food and drink to me, bread and butter, cakes and ale: my sustenance. How I looked forward to his touch, the sound of his voice, the way he wrapped me in his arms, the feel of his skin next to mine, the way he kissed and fondled my breasts! Even thinking of it made my nipples go taut. It was wrong, it was sinful. But, ah, the sweet guilt of those Thursday afternoons! The thrilling wickedness! The stealthy hand-in-hand tiptoeing ascent of the stairs, the carefully closed door, the first stolen kisses, the hushed laughter, the whispered endearments. Illicit nakedness spurring passion took us across the carpet, tumbling us into bed, rolling us over and over locked in the embrace of a heated ardor that renewed itself with every meeting.

When we were together Derry preferred not to discuss his plans for the future. He did not want me to be disappointed, he said, to get my hopes up and have them dashed. (The job at Kohler and Company had gone to the relative of an officer at the bank.) However, he talked quite freely of the past. He would hold my head under his chin, stroking my arm, and reminisce.

He told me about his reason for leaving Virginia. It was over cards, as I had suspected, an unfounded accusation of holding an extra ace. He spoke of his boyhood, telling me incidents both funny and sad, drawing me into the intimate moments of his life, wondering as he did so.

"Isn't it odd?" he would say. "You're the first person I've ever told that to."

I in turn talked about my years with Aunt Maude, but not much else. I suppose I was like my father in many ways. There were some secrets—the truth of my marriage and how Miles had raped me at Aspinwall—that I could not bring myself to disclose.

And I kept those Thursday meetings, which had become the world to me, a secret from everyone. I was afraid, in a superstitious way, that if I said anything our trysts would suddenly cease. But they could not go on forever, even I knew that. I kept hoping that by some stroke of luck Derry would come into money and we could be married before an unforeseen circumstance separated us for good. But it was Derry himself who put an end to it.

"Just for the present," he said, kissing me. He had found a friend willing to stake him to another attempt to find gold. Calaveras, this time. Again rumors, nothing concrete, had induced him to take to the trail.

"I may not have another chance, Carmella. I am getting nowhere in the city."

We had just made love, not quite up to our usual passionate standard, and I had sensed Derry's preoccupation. My first thought was that he was growing tired of me. It helped some but not much to know this was not the case.

"Take me with you," I pleaded.

He laughed. "You can't mean it!"

"I do. Let me go. I'll make myself useful. Oh, please, Derry."

"Don't talk nonsense, Carmella. Your father would be after me with a horsewhip. Besides, the mining camps are no place for a woman."

"That's what Papa used to say about San Francisco."

"Well—he was right. God knows I'm going to miss you. I'll do my best to write this time. And Carmella love, you must promise to take care of yourself."

I had told him about Halstead and he had been horrified.

"I will."

"And one other thing. Don't fall in love with another man!"

"As if I could!"

He was gone six months before I heard from him, a brief note from someplace called Murderer's Gulch. He was on to something big, he said. He missed me. Love, Derry. I did not receive any sort of communication after that, and I carried the one short letter he had written in my bosom next to his ring until it fell into tatters.

I got over the more acute stage of missing Derry within a month or two, though I never quite lost the empty feeling inside.

Dolly, noting my wan appearance, said, "You look peaked, and so thin. Are you ill? Is something wrong?"

"No." I hadn't realized I looked that bad. "Just a little bored."

"What you need is a change. Some sea air. I've been think-ing of it myself. And God knows my papa could use a vacation. There's a lovely hotel at Seal Rock overlooking the ocean. The McAllisters and Fields always spend a season there and rec-ommend it highly. What do you think?"

"It might be fun," I said without enthusiasm. "But I doubt my father would care to go."

"I'll have no trouble convincing my papa, and I'm sure he can talk yours around too."

I don't know what Mr. Hobart said, but three days later

Papa announced that he had arranged to take a fortnight from his work and that we would spend it at the Seal Rock House.

So one Sunday, our trunks securely lashed to the carriage top and with Handy in the driver's seat, Papa, I, and Mrs. Tibbets set out for Seal Rock. Behind us were the Hobarts, their carriage similarly decked with luggage. We took a country road, little traveled, running between fields of yellow-blooming wild mustard. The weather was perfect as it can only be in late September after the foggy season has passed, a clear warm day with a cloudless blue sky and a soft breeze blowing in from the west. I began to look forward to our holiday, curious now about Seal Rock House.

To say it was a disappointment when it finally hove into view would be an understatement. Dolly, who had never seen the hotel, had painted it in such glowing colors that the actual sight of it was bound to be a surprise but it certainly shouldn't have been a shock. A rambling, weatherbeaten frame building with smudged windows, it rose in places to three stories, in others to two, each end extended by a wing, afterthoughts that clashed with the original design, the whole looking like a gray wooden hodgepodge sitting among the chaparral-dotted dunes.

The inside at first glance proved just as disheartening: furry sofas, cracked leather chairs, sandy floors, and the all-pervading odor of dampness and mold. However, our rooms faced the sea and we had an incomparable view of the Pacific, a deep scintillating blue melding with the distant horizon. And as Mrs. Tibbets noted, the linens were clean and the beds comfortable. Nor could the food, served in a large dining room in the left wing, be faulted. After supper that night I felt more optimistic, and settled in with the others prepared to make the most of my outing.

The men in our party amused themselves by fishing and swimming, although they complained of swift currents and cold water. We women had to content ourselves with wading, daring in itself, and done in a small cove out of sight from others.

I loved the beach, especially at ebb tide when wide expanses of hard-packed sand lay exposed to the glittering sun and the stiff-legged sandpipers poked for food with their long bills along the foaming fringe. I loved the smell of iodine in the wind, the convoluted bleached shells and spiraled coral ones we picked up on our walks, the coarse dune grass we wove and plaited into little baskets. But loving all that beauty only made me miss Derry the more.

Papa was having such a good time he extended our stay until the end of the second week. Shortly before we were to leave, Miles came to see him. He and Papa had some business matter to discuss and were closeted for a good part of the day. Later Miles joined us for supper and by happenstance sat next to me at the table. Dolly, seated on the other side, spent the whole meal flirting outrageously with him, trying to capture his attention. Her father did not seem to notice, but her mother looked very uncomfortable, throwing perturbed glances at Dolly from time to time.

When the cloth had been cleared for dessert, Miles turned to me and in a low conversational tone said, "I have some news concerning Sam Halstead that might be of interest to you."

"They're not letting him out of prison?"

"He managed to get out on his own. Escaped. But—"

Dolly, leaning across, interrupted. "What are you two whispering about? A secret?"

"No," I answered. "It's nothing, really." I had no wish to discuss Sam Halstead at a table full of hotel guests who were strangers to me.

It was not until the following afternoon that I had an opportunity to speak to Miles again. I had left the others to their siestas and gone to walk along the beach, armed with a large parasol against the midday sun, when I saw Miles approaching from the opposite direction. He was hatless, his dark hair blowing in the wind, his coat unbuttoned, his shirt opened at the throat. I could not help noting how closely he resembled the theatrical image of a swashbuckling pirate, with his powerful stride, wide shoulders, and narrow waist, and his scowling look of arrogant pride. However, when he saw me he actually smiled.

"Good afternoon, Carmella."

By now, according to his form of address, I could pretty

well gauge whether Miles intended to be pleasant or unpleasant. Today, since he used my Christian name, he meant to be pleasant.

We exchanged remarks on the continuing fine weather, and then I said. "You never finished telling me about Sam Halstead."

"True. I did say he escaped, didn't I? Well that lasted all of one day. They caught him that night at The Parrot on Jackson Street, reeling drunk squaring off with the barkeep. But I don't think we have to worry about him—not for a while. The police captain, a Mr. Lees, a friend of mine, finally agreed to have him shipped out. Legally. We gave him a choice—solitary confinement or the *Star of the East* bound for the Orient. He chose the *Star,* but with very little enthusiasm."

"And what if he comes back to San Francisco?"

"I will see to it, personally, that he leaves again."

Miles fell in beside me as I began my return stroll.

"Mr. Hobart says the criminal element is growing bolder," I said. "An acquaintance of his was robbed and murdered as he was leaving his shop last month. It's a pity people can't feel safe even in the better neighborhoods. The Vigilantes should never have been disbanded."

"They were criminals themselves, my dear. Anyone who puts himself above the law is breaking it. Pure and simple. And many of the men heading the Committee have pasts that do not bear looking into. Sam Brannan, for instance. He built his fortune on monies diverted from church tithes and property that had been entrusted to him."

"How dreadful! But if we can't rely upon these so-called *good* citizens, what's to be done?"

"A well-paid, highly trained police force would help. And politicians in public office who feel a responsibility toward the community, not toward lining their own pockets."

"We should have that now."

"Certainly. But unfortunately San Francisco burgeoned from village to city overnight. There wasn't time to build a solid community, especially with gold as its drawing card. The mines attracted a variety of ill-assorted scoundrels, many who fled from justice abroad and in our own country. Unscrupulous embezzlers, forgers, con men. Your father is one of the few businessmen I would trust unconditionally." ·

"Ah, but you are a skeptic by nature."

"Nonsense. I became that way through necessity. Once bitten, twice shy. I only wish your father was the same."

"I like him as he is. Besides, I would guess that he commands a great deal of respect. A rogue would give pause before he attempted to cheat him at business."

"Let us hope you are right."

But I wasn't. After we returned to Gough Street I learned that the reason Miles had come to Seal Rock was to warn Papa against buying shares from a man named Henry Minton. Papa had argued that the man had dealt with merchants, brokers, and banks for several years, and that his signature and reputation were above reproach.

Whether Minton saw a way to make a killing or whether he had been long prepared to bilk the public on a grand scale, no one could say. But he formed a bogus corporation and issued $300,000 worth of stock, promising to pay exhorbitant rates of interest. By the time his fraud was discovered, Minton had fled to Australia. Papa, and hundreds of others, were left with worthless paper. In addition to his own private purchase, Papa had made quite a few for his clients; and because he felt responsible, he paid them off from his own funds.

We were left with very little. Papa, of course, did not mention, let alone discuss, the financial debacle that had brought us to the edge of penury. A gentleman did not air his monetary difficulties at home. Papa simply said that he would sell the carriage because it had developed a squeak, and two of the horses (we had three—one a hunter, which he sometimes rode himself) because they appeared to have gall. It was when he asked me to defer ordering any new gowns for a month or two that I began to suspect something. From experience I knew it was useless to question Papa. He would never tell me. So I buttonholed Miles.

"I don't know why your father has such old-fashioned notions about shielding womenfolk from the facts of life," Miles said. "He can't possibly keep up appearances—your clothes, that house, Mrs. Tibbets. I offered him a loan, which he has refused. Another sign of stubbornness. But he will have to take it unless he begins to economize."

"I don't mind living in a smaller house," I said, "and we could certainly do without Mrs. Tibbets. As for gowns—I have enough. It won't be such a hardship."

He looked at me, a cynical expression in his eyes.

"You don't believe me. You think me a spoiled darling. Well, you're wrong. I would gladly sacrifice whatever Papa deemed necessary. I would work, too, if it came to it, without complaint."

"You've never worked. You've never had to. How would you know anything about it? To you, work is a romantic notion, something you saw at the theater or read about in a two-penny novel."

"How nasty you can become. How odious! And just when I was beginning to think you had changed for the better."

"Heaven forbid!"

"You—you are a . . ." Bit it was no use. Whatever name I called him would bounce off without the slightest effect.

Papa looked more and more harrassed, tired, worried. I longed to say, "Papa, it's all right, I understand." But, of course, I couldn't.

Then one night there was a change. Papa seemed almost cheerful as he sat down at the supper table, and rubbing his hands together said, "I have heard wonderful news, Carmella. Ah—is that terrapin in lemon sauce? Good."

For the past several weeks Papa could have been served a goat in aspic for all the notice he took of his food. Now he helped himself to a large portion while Mrs. Tibbets and I waited for the "wonderful news."

"Delicious," Papa said, wiping his lips on a napkin. "Yes, Carmella, the best news I have had come my way in a long time. Silver has been discovered at Gold Hill, just below Sun Mountain in the Washoe district of the Nevada territory. Miles and I have decided to try our luck. I think we have an excellent chance of doing well."

"I am sure of it, Papa. What a wonderful opportunity!"

"Indeed. It's an extraordinarily rich vein, situated where men have been digging gold for years, one of the largest silver lodes ever to be found. Great beds of it. A man by the name of Comstock, an old hand up there, thought for a long time that the silver ore was worthless, just got in the way of his search for the real thing. ''Blue stuff,' he called it, 'leavings.' Leavings at fifteen hundred dollars a ton!'' Papa smiled faintly at the irony of it.

"When do you plan to go, Papa?"

"We," Papa corrected. *"We* are going—you and Mrs. Tibbets too."

Leave San Francisco and miss Derry on his return? I couldn't. "But, Papa, you always said that a mining town is no place for a well-bred woman."

"True, true. However, I think the situation is different in Washoe today than it was in San Francisco of '49. I am given to understand there is a fairly comfortable little town, Virginia City, nearby. The main thing, Carmella, is that I shan't be running off and deserting you again."

"I don't see it that way at all."

"Perhaps not. But I'd feel better having you with me." He paused. "Would you please pass the bread, Carmella? Ah—thank you. Yes. Many of my old Hangtown comrades are planning to make tracks for Gold Hill too. Remember my speaking of Oswald Piper? He's going. In fact, he's writing to some of his friends who're now up at Calaveras—I believe Derry Wakefield is one of them..."

My ears pricked up. Calaveras!

"...giving them the good news. My dear, you aren't objecting?"

"Of course not, Papa." I felt sure Derry wouldn't want to miss out on a strike of such proportions. He'd come to Gold Hill and I would see him again, sooner than I had hoped perhaps.

"Good," Papa said. "We'll make preparations at once then. The Hobarts have offered to find the servants other positions. As to our belongings, the furniture"—he looked around—"I think I can arrange to sell what few pieces of our own we have acquired."

"And now, Mrs. Tibbets," Papa said, "we haven't heard from you. How do you feel about this move?"

Mrs. Tibbets had sat in stunned incomprehension ever since

Papa had announced his news. "W-well..." she said with fluttering indecision.

"You do not have to join us, if you have no wish to," Papa said.

I could almost hear the turning of wheels, the clank of levers, as Mrs. Tibbets set her apricot jam tart teas with the old aunt against the wild unknown of a mining town she had never seen. But she had little choice, after all, for positions as housekeepers were not that plentiful.

"I suppose, if I must," she began, and then realizing that this was not the answer Papa would have liked, added with a forced little smile, "I understand the mountain air is quite edifying."

So we set out three days later on our trek to Sun Mountain, each of us with a different expectation—Mrs. Tibbets's reluctant one to breathe edifying mountain air, Papa's to find silver at $1,500 a ton, and mine to see Derry again.

CHAPTER

EIGHTEEN

DOLLY AND I had parted with girlish tears, in-
numerable hugs, kisses, and promises to write. She envied me,
she said "all those handsome miners" and wished her own father
would take to the road as we had. "Everybody, just everybody
is going," she maintained. "They say it's '49 all over again."

It certainly seemed that way. The boat we caught from San
Francisco to Sacramento on the first stage of our journey was
loaded to the gunwales with prospectors bound for Washoe.
They were a mixed lot: physicians, sailors, lawyers, a sprin-
kling of clergymen, journalists, clerks, merchants, and gam-
blers, a few swaggering about with guns at their hips, individuals
with the arrogant, cocky look of born bullies. I saw only three
or four respectable-looking women, poke-bonneted wives
clinging to the arms of their husbands. The other females were
obviously prostitutes, a band of them herded by a madam with
a black moustache. The sight of the harlots and the bullies
distressed Mrs. Tibbets, but she soon found a friend, a Reverend Franklin, who gave a sympathetic ear to her complaints
and aggrieved sensibilities.

While Mrs. Tibbets and the amicable clergyman commis-
erated about the deplorable depths to which society had fallen,
the other passengers were consumed with a single topic—
silver. The air fairly crackled with eager anticipation. It was
like a fever. Many of these prospectors had left friends, fam-

ilies, and sweethearts behind, deserting businesses, farms, banks, shops, and foundries as if the Pied Piper himself had suddenly appeared tootling his irresistible, seductive notes at their doorsteps.

Papa seemed like a changed man. Not that he became garrulous—not even silver could do that—but he talked a good deal, more than I had ever heard him do. I have a feeling that Papa would have gone up to Nevada even if his brokerage firm had not failed. There was a streak in him that defied understanding, a romantic gambler's streak.

At Sacramento Papa sent our baggage on ahead by mule train; and on the following morning at dawn, Mrs. Tibbets and I boarded the Placerville stage. Papa and Miles, having purchased horses, were to ride beside us.

The morning was shrouded in a chill, pearly mist, and as the driver cracked his whip over the sleek rumps of the team, a shaft of golden sunlight broke through. An omen, I remember thinking happily, a sign of good things to come.

"Giddy yap!"

We were off, wrapped in our cloaks against the cold, packed tightly in with two other women and two men a Mr. Steward and Mrs. Tibbets's friend, the Reverend Franklin.

It wasn't long before we began the climb into the foothills. There autumn had tinged the deciduous trees with scarlet and gold, and they stood out among the dark green pines like tattered patchwork clowns, drifts of brown crumpled leaves at their feet. Tiny runnels of water trickled across the road to dribble into the river below us. In spring and winter the trickles would become gushing streams, making the road difficult if not impassable, but now, with comparative ease of travel, it was crowded with adventurers hurrying to Sun Mountain. We passed a few covered wagons, a coach, another stage. Many men, like Miles and Papa, rode horseback, some rode mules, but most went on foot. It was a good-natured caravan of bantering souls who hailed us with merry good-mornings. Redshirted miners plodded along with their packs—a blanket, a frying pan, a coffee pot, and a pick—lashed to their backs. Some trundled wheelbarrows or drew sleds piled high with their belongings and tools to dig the riches they were sure to find.

Soon the road became steeper. Still we managed to travel at a good clip through oddly named villages—Sportsman's Hall, Pete's, Dirty Miles—mining settlements of shanties and tents, the ubiquitous saloon cum whorehouse cum gambling hall, a cafe-hotel bordering a single unpaved street that sent clouds of dust under our wheels. We spent the first night at Berry's Flat, Miles and Papa putting up at Berry's Tavern. Mrs. Tibbets and I shared a narrow bed in a frame cottage that passed as a hostel.

After Berry's the road became tortuous, ascending in switchbacks, the oaks and ashes and digger pines giving way to the soaring sugar, ponderosa, and lodgepole, evergreens clinging to the sides of precipices and marching dark-needled and brown-coned up to a blue sky. When we reached the crest at Johnson's Pass, we paused to let the winded horses rest.

"Would you like to have a look at the view?" Papa asked.

Mrs. Tibbets declined, but the Reverend and I got out and walked to the edge of the chasm, gazing back on the lower valleys we had just left, the wooded hills, the streams and autumn meadows.

"Pretty country," Reverend Franklin remarked. "It's a wonder it still has such a tranquil appearance after so many of us has trampled across it."

Picking our way over the rubbled ground we moved to the other side to have a look at the eastern slope of the mountain and beyond it to the country that was our destination. There could not have been a greater contrast: at our backs, a rich Eden-like garden; ahead a stony desolation, a landscape of the moon with giant rocks and flinty outcroppings flung about by some distant, long-ago upheaval, a desert of stone and parched earth, folded and marked and striated with treeless valleys and long barren ridges. Though I strained my eyes, nowhere could I see a touch of green or a healthy flourishing plant, only the occasional tufts of coarse yellow grass, wormwood, and sagewood.

"There's Sun Mountain," Papa said.

Across the wasteland the mountain rose from the plain, solitary and awesome in its bleak majesty.

The Reverend sucked in his breath. "It's a long way still to go."

We put up that night in tents. It was bitterly cold and I lay muffled in my cape, listening to the howl of some animal in the trees below. After a while, unable to sleep, I got up and went outside. The fire was slowly dying and a few men were sleeping around it. I picked my way over their prone bodies, threw some nearby sticks on the embers, and sat down, toasting my hands, feet, and face as the hot flames shot up again.

"Can't sleep?"

It was Miles, wearing a greatcoat slung over his shoulders and brown breeches tucked into leather boots.

"The cold keeps me awake," I said.

He lowered himself next to me. "You're not worried about what you will find in Virginia City?"

"Not at all. I'm looking forward to our adventure. Do you think my father will be lucky?"

"I can't see how he could miss."

"And you?"

"I won't complain if I make a rich strike, but it really doesn't matter that much."

"Are you that wealthy?"

He smiled, his teeth gleaming white in the firelight. "What an impertinent question. Are you interested?"

"Not at all," I said huffily.

"But curious about me, isn't that right?"

"Well, I do wonder sometimes. Not often, but sometimes. I wonder, for instance, why you have never married."

"You think something is wrong because I haven't?" His voice held a faint amusement.

"No." I blushed, grateful that the shadows hid the color surging to my cheeks. I knew what he meant. My experience with Lyon had taught me much about sexual aberration.

"I haven't married, I suppose, because I haven't found a woman I think I could live with. They all seem rather—silly and . . ."

"Childish," I supplied.

"You might say that."

"As for the physical side of marriage, to put it delicately, I can have that without a wedding ring."

"One can buy anything, even love, I'm told."

"You mean whores. Not put delicately, eh? I wasn't thinking

of whores, Carmella. You would be surprised at the ladies who've offered themselves merely for an afternoon's amusement."

At once I thought of Dolly fluttering her eyelashes at Miles, bending over to talk to him at the table so that he could see her inviting white cleavage. Had he made love to Dolly? The thought annoyed me.

"I presume you never refuse?" I asked, my voice tingled with acid disdain.

"I wouldn't say never. Let us say I'm selective."

"Promiscuous is a better word for it."

He turned his firelit face toward me. "What I like about you, Carmella, is your unabashed pietistic attitude. The hypocrisy of it stuns me! When I think of how many afternoons you must have spent romping between the bed sheets with your lover, Derry—"

"How dare you!" I cried, raising my hand.

He grasped my wrist in steely fingers. "Hush! Do you want to wake everyone?"

I jerked my hand away.

"What I can't fathom," he went on with biting irony, "is how someone with a modicum of intelligence could fall in love with a man like Derry Wakefield."

"That's because you don't understand the first thing about love," I retorted. "It's the heart that's involved, feelings, something . . . Oh, how can I explain? Cold, cynical intelligence has nothing to do with it."

He stared at me for a long probing moment. "Perhaps you are right. Still, it does not alter the fact that Derry—despite his devasting charm—has little to offer. He's weak—"

"How can you say that when he took the same risks as you facing those cutthroats in the Mexican jungle?"

"*I* never considered it a risk, what with the support of four companions and shooting behind the protection of heavy foliage."

"Bravo!" I taunted. "Isn't it just like you to twist things to make you seem superior and the other fellow small. The truth is you don't like Derry," I went on with mounting anger. "But I don't much care. And I wouldn't care if everything you say or think about him were true. I love him. Can't you get it through that thick, iron skull of yours? *I love him!* He makes me feel like a woman—that I matter—not like you, who are always cutting me down."

He laughed. "There you go. The pot calling the kettle black. I'd say you're no mean novice yourself at 'cutting down.'"

I hated it when he laughed. "I don't know why I ever started this conversation with you. You're impossible!"

I got to my feet, stumbling over one of the sleepers. Too upset to return to my hard pallet in the tent, I stomped through the trees to the tongued hulk of the stage, leaning against its side, twisting my hands.

Miles followed me. "I suppose I should apologize."

"I don't want your apologies. You're a bully, not the brave man you pretend to be."

"You've never known a man," he said evenly, but in a tone that told me I had touched a nerve, and it sent a thrill of unaccountable triumph through me.

"Ha! So *you* believe."

He pulled me into his arms. "Shall I show you?" His face above mine was hard with anger.

"No—I don't . . . !"

His mouth came down on mine, covering it, stifling the protest in my throat. I beat at him, making incoherent sounds, but he held me fast, his strong, thin lips moving back and forth, bruising, hurtful, holding me so tightly I could feel the heat of his body through the cloth of my cape. I had the sensation of an electric virility surging from his veins, leaping into mine, a vitality that ran through my blood like a terrifying millstream. I couldn't fight. Uncontrollable tremors shook me and I clutched at the back of his coat. Of its own volition, my mouth opened and his tongue found mine, a feverish mingling that seared and burned. Mind, thought, reason receded in a turmoil of sensations. My hands slowly crept up his back past his straining shoulder blades and linked about his neck as if to hold fast, to prolong the whirling, tumultuous sweet darkness.

Suddenly he released me, pulling my arms away. For a moment I swayed in the dark, but he made no attempt to steady me, standing a little apart, breathing heavily.

"You vixen!" he accused bitterly. Then he turned and strode away.

I stood leaning against the stage, my hand pressed to my bruised mouth, wanting to cry. How could I have felt anything but revulsion, loathing, a desire to strike and to maim? This man was a thorn in my side, mocking, snide. My enemy, and I had actually—for a handful of moments—enjoyed his kisses. Hot tears of self-recrimination rolled down my cheeks. If I loved Derry, how could I allow myself to be moved by another man's touch? It shan't happen again, I promised myself, I won't *let* it happen.

The next morning we started the steep descent to the valley floor below. Because the road had become narrow, Papa and Miles rode behind the stage, a circumstance that made it easier for me to ignore Miles. I burned with shame when I thought of his kiss and was glad I didn't have to look at him. Out of sight, out of mind. As far as I was concerned, he could disappear altogether, drop into an abyss or drown in a river.

The going was tricky. The horses seemed unsure and each time a wheel hit a large rock, jouncing the springless stage, they whinnied and reared, threatening to bolt.

When we began the descent of a particularly precipitous grade that tipped the stage forward, Mrs. Tibbets grasped my arm, her nails digging into it, and the two other women closed their eyes. Suddenly the rumbling carriage, hitting some impediment, bounced high. We heard a shout as the driver tumbled from his seat, and the next moment the frightened horses, now unrestrained, began careening down the mountainside at a breakneck speed. Mrs. Tibbets screamed, then fainted dead away. The two women clung to one another, howling like dogs; Mr. Steward sat as if poleaxed, his eyes glazed with fright, and the Reverend turned a sickly green. We clattered and jolted, plummeting downward, the carriage swaying perilously from side to side. With nightmarish terror I saw the gray, stony ledges flying by. The thundering hooves, the crash of wheels, the whistling wind raised the hair on my scalp, clogging my throat with fear so that I could not find the voice to scream. With desperate fingers I tried to pry open a door, thinking to jump, little realizing in my horror-crazed state that it would most likely be fatal. The door, however, would not give. I was trapped within a moving, hurtling coffin. My dry lips tried to form a plea to God, but in my state of panic I couldn't even do that. I was dimly aware of a shadow streaking past and the sound of an echoing shot.

A few moments later the coach came to a screaming halt, throwing me and one of the women forward into the laps of the Reverend and Mr. Steward, and the comatose Mrs. Tibbets to the floor.

Papa poked his head in the window. "Are you all right, Carmella?"

Mr. Steward helped me back into my seat. "Yes—yes, I think so," I replied in a quavering voice.

The Reverend was trying to revive Mrs. Tibbets. He kept clucking over her, "Oh, dear, oh, dear!" The two women were weeping.

"I want—I want to get out," I said in that same unsteady voice. Papa's face swam before me.

"Do you feel faint?"

"No, no. Just some—air."

Papa helped me out and I leaned against him, my legs trembling, my whole body shaking. "It's all right now. Miles has the horses under control. It's all right."

"I thought—"

"Miles shot the lead horse, and the others stopped."

I looked up to where Miles, dismounted now and with the aid of two other men, was unharnessing the slumped corpse of the dead animal. A few feet beyond him, the road turned at a sharp angle, veering from the edge of an abyss. I buried my head in Papa's shoulder to blot out the sight.

Papa said, "Reverend, if you'll search in Mrs. Tibbets's reticule I'm sure you'll find some sal volatile." To me he said, "Would you like a sniff, Carmella?"

I shook my head. He led me to a rock and I sat down. "If I could have some water, Papa?"

He unstoppered his canteen and I drank the lukewarm water, taking large gulps of it. I began to hiccough.

"Brandy helps too," Papa said, handing me his flask.

The brandy went down smoothly, easing the tension in my chest.

Meanwhile a knot of men had gathered and were dragging the dead horse from the shafts.

"Close," I heard one say. "If you hadn't been such a good shot, Mr. Falconer, the whole shebang would've gone over the side."

At this point the coachman caught up with us, hobbling, painfully bruised, but not incapacitated. He shook Miles's hand and thanked him. "Never lost a coach yet," he said.

It took all my nerve and another draw at the flask before I could force myself to get inside the stage again. Mrs. Tibbets, however, surprised me. After she came out of her faint I expected her to refuse point-blank to go on. But, pale and shaken though she was, she expressed no such sentiment. Rather a look of rapt admiration lit her eyes as she thanked the Reverend effusively for his kind attention.

Love struck the unlikeliest people in the unlikeliest of places.

The following morning, after an unsuccessful attempt to replace the missing horse, we set out across the desert below Sun Mountain, as barren, hot, and depressing a spot as I would ever hope to see. Not a pine, not a twisted oak nor a single Joshua tree lifted its height from the burning landscape, not a patch of shade marred its bleak terrain.

We were all relieved when the country at last became hilly and the first willows appeared.

"Gold Canyon," Papa said as the carriage entered a narrow, rocky rift in the hills.

We climbed at a snail's pace, the wheels squeaking and protesting on the rough, slaty road. Presently, by leaning out of the window, I would see a sign stretched across the road. DEVIL'S GATE TOLL ROAD—50¢ PASS ON. The fee was paid and we moved under a wooden barrier, through a dusty, shantytown lying in the shadowed lap of the mountain.

The canyon became darker, deeper, overlooked by sheer granite walls. A cold fitful wind blew down from the heights, and though we fastened the isinglass curtains, we could feel its penetrating chill.

We reached Gold Hill late in the day, another cluster of wooden shanties and saloons. Someone pointed out Eilley Orrum's boardinghouse. "The only decent eatery in these parts," he said, which gave me a sinking premonition of what to expect.

Some ten miles farther we topped the divide and looked

over Virginia City itself. The premonition had hardly anticipated the actuality. No city, not even a town, but a vast mining
camp of tin-roofed shacks, of tents fashioned of canvas, old
blankets, and dirty woolen shirts, a helter-skelter ragtag sprawling slum settlement clung like a running sore to the side of the
mountain.

Papa dismounted and put his head in the coach window.
"Ladies," he said, addressing Mrs. Tibbets and me, "I'm afraid
Virginia City will be a bit of a disappointment."

Oh, Papa!

CHAPTER

NINETEEN

*O*NE DAY Virginia City would boast all the amenities of a refined city, several theaters, churches, newspapers, plush hotels, mansions with silver doorknobs, restaurants that served fine cuisine, and a glittering, jeweled society that gave balls and parties to equal any of those in San Francisco. But when we arrived, there was no hint of its future glory.

Since Papa (deeply apologetic because he had been so grossly misinformed) could not find satisfactory lodgings in Virginia City, he put Mrs. Tibbets and me up at Eilley Orrum's. As a rule she did not furnish accommodations, only meals, but consented to take us in. "Two decent ladies are as rare as hen's teeth," she said.

Papa and Miles had to seek shelter in the camp above, Papa promising to join me for supper whenever he could.

Mrs. Tibbets and I shared a bed that was clean, though narrow, and we were given wash water without having to ask for it. Mrs. Tibbets confided in me that she hoped to become Mrs. Franklin.

"Not right away," she said. "The Reverend is going to start his church first. Naturally that will take precedence. But he did say something about needing a helpmeet and I think he feels I would make a good one. I know I would. I haven't been so fond of a man since I married Mr. Tibbets."

"Are you willing to stay—up there?" I pointed with my chin in the direction of Virginia City.

"Oh, yes, if I have the Reverend Franklin."

It was hard to believe that Mrs. Tibbets, who was so attached to her little comforts, could look forward with such calm assurance to residing in a crude mining town. Perhaps she felt life with the Reverend, despite its drawbacks, offered better security than her tenuous position as a housekeeper. Or perhaps she was really in love. If so, I could understand her indifference to Virginia City's rawness. For I would certainly feel the same if I had Derry.

I began to look for him. I watched and waited, questioning everyone who came through the door. Eilley Orrum's at the crossroads, was the ideal place to conduct such an inquiry. Every evening she had a full house of men who either worked in the mines or were on their hopeful way up to the diggings. They would sit on rough benches at a long table, ten or twelve to a shift, while the Chinese cooks brought in platter after platter of potatoes, beans, beef, mutton, chicken, and biscuits. It was plain fare and costly, $8 a meal, since every bit of food had to be carried in from down below or carted across the mountains. The men paid it gladly.

I had been at Eilley's a week when it happened. Derry walked in the door one evening. Derry, bearded, in shabby clothes and mud caked boots—but Derry.

I was sitting in a small alcove, assisting Eilley with the collection of money, and for the first moment or two I didn't recognize him. Then he turned and our eyes met. I was out of my chair and flying across the room into his arms.

"Derry!"

The men gawked. My attitude toward them had been one of cold contempt, and seeing me dissolve into tears against Derry's chest stunned them. But only for an instant. A roar went up, the stamp of feet and applause, whistles, catcalls.

Derry, a little embarrassed, released me, still holding my hands, however. "Oh, darling!" I exclaimed. "It's too good to be true! I'm so happy!"

"I know, sweetheart," he said in a low voice, "but let's go outside where we can talk in private."

Amid the clamor of hoarse cheering, Derry led me out into

the autumnal cold and pulled me around the side of the building away from the fierce wind blowing down the mountainside. Taking me in his arms, he kissed me, his mouth on mine warm, hungry, passionate. Everything in me sang, my blood, my heart: *Derry! Derry!* He was with me at last, my body pressed to his long, lean one, the way I had dreamed it would be. I clung to him while the pulsing stars reeled overhead.

"Papa thought you and your friends from Calaveras might be coming to Sun Mountain," I said, eyes shining up at his shadowed face.

"I wrote to you," he said. "I told you I planned it. Didn't you get my letter?"

"No. It must have arrived after we left. Papa was in a hurry."

"It surprises me that he brought you with him."

"People told him that Virginia City was a decent town. He didn't want to leave me. Besides, he lost his money—he thinks I don't know about it, but I do—and he could not afford to keep the house."

Derry hugged me, enveloping me in his arms again. "I'm glad you're here whatever the reason."

We kissed again, Derry's mouth moving, nibbling my cheek, sliding down to my throat, his rough beard scratching my skin. "How good it is to hold you. You smell so sweet. Are you staying here at Eilley's?"

"Yes, she's letting Mrs. Tibbets and me have a room as a favor. Space is so limited. Papa had to find quarters uphill in a tent. Everyone there is crowded into bunkhouses, sleeping in shifts."

"I know, darling. Even the whores have no privacy."

"Derry!"

"Sorry, darling. I shouldn't have said that. I apolo—"

I closed his lips with a kiss.

After a long while he said, "We'd best be going inside."

"Yes. You must be hungry. How thoughtless of me—and I've asked nothing about you. You have traveled far?"

"Thirty miles today. And I *am* hungry. Hungry for you." He gave me a squeeze.

I took his hand. "Papa will be happy to find you have joined us."

"Carmella, are you sure? After he hears of our lover-like

greeting he may not be all that glad to see me."

"Well," I said, not caring, "he would have to know sooner or later. And now, since your prospects are as good as his, he might even be happy to have you as a son-in-law."

"I doubt it. If ever I was in a poor position to present myself as a suitor, I'm that now. Look at me! I have nothing. Please, Carmella, I love you, but you must understand. I want to do things right."

"But . . ." I sighed. "Oh, very well. We won't quibble about it, sweetheart, not now. Whatever you say."

When I saw Papa two nights later, he was far from happy about Derry. Apparently tongues had wagged in the interim. He had been given several versions of how Derry and I, alone, hand in hand, had disappeared outside for over an hour (a gossipy distortion of ten minutes that infuriated me) and had come back inside, Derry looking like the cat that swallowed the canary and I with my hair and clothes disheveled.

"You must remember, Carmella," Papa lectured, "that a woman has to work twice as hard convincing folk of her respectability in a place like this than at home."

"Papa," I said, controlling my temper with effort, "I did nothing I am ashamed of. Mr. Wakefield kissed me—true. But for the rest we talked. We are old friends and I—I love him."

There—it was out! I was glad.

"Papa, he loves me too, and he wants to marry me."

"Marry! It's the first I've heard of it. Why hasn't Wakefield asked me for your hand as a proper suitor should?"

"Because he's poor. He doesn't want to come to you as a beggar. He wants to make a rich strike first. Can't you see?"

"No. A man who compromises a woman's reputation as Wakefield did yesterday, has little respect for her, let alone love. I am very disappointed in him."

"It was as much my fault as his," I pleaded. "Please try to understand. It's been so long since we've seen each other and we couldn't say a word in here. All those rough men were looking at us, listening and jeering, thinking their dirty thoughts."

"I realize a conversation under such circumstances would be difficult, but I don't want you seeing him—or any man—

without Mrs. Tibbets in attendance. Do I make myself clear?"

There was nothing I could say, but "Yes, Papa."

"At any rate, I shall have a talk with Mr. Wakefield and have him promise that the incident will not be repeated."

"You're not going to forbid me to see him?"

"I'll think it over."

Derry did not appear at Eilley's for several days, and in the meanwhile I fretted, thinking Papa had scolded him, worried that he might have affronted Derry and turned him away.

"I'm not angry at you or your father," Derry said when I finally saw him again, "but your father did put it to me bluntly. He wanted to know what my intentions were."

We were sitting at one end of Eilley's dining room, Mrs. Tibbets and the Reverend Franklin close at hand. We spoke in low monotones.

"I didn't want him to press you, darling," I said, hoping nevertheless that Papa had, but tactfully.

Derry shrugged. "I told him I wasn't ready to take a wife, that I had the highest regard for you, but was in no position to consider matrimony."

"What did he say to that?"

"He agreed. But, Carmella, even aside from my financial situation, I have a feeling your father would not look too kindly on my suit."

"Why not?"

"I believe he would favor someone already rich, someone older, like Miles Falconer, for instance."

"Miles!" I exclaimed in disgust. "I hate him. He's mean, sarcastic, never has a good word to say to me."

"He's building a house."

"A house? In Virginia City? Whatever for?"

"Says he likes his comfort. And God knows he has the money to see to it. He's hired a dozen down-and-out miners, and put them to work. It's not a mansion, mind you, but it's a lot more than most can afford. Miles doesn't seem the least bit interested in staking a claim."

"He doesn't have to. But let's not discuss *him*."

Derry threw a glance at Mrs. Tibbets and the Reverend who

were deep in their own conversation, then hitched himself closer. "You're right. Miles doesn't interest me either. It's you I want to talk about."

I gave him a melting glance. He had trimmed his beard and cut his hair and somehow had acquired new boots and a coat. How handsome he looked: lean, taut, and bronzed.

"Carmella," he said, lowering his voice even more, and I had to lean forward to hear him. "We have so much catching up to do. I want to hear what's happened while I've been away, and . . . Look, I'm bunking with another fellow. He has a canvas tent just beyond Farrel's tavern at the end of the main street. He'll be gone all of tomorrow. We could have several hours together."

"It would be difficult to get away, Derry."

"Yes, of course. Forgive me, darling. I sound like a rake trying to seduce you, though it's not the case at all."

"I know, sweetheart."

"It's just—well, I can't come here too often. Your father . . . As it is, I've behaved like a cad."

"Don't say that—*please*. If we've done wrong, we've done it together. Only I don't want to look at it that way. I love you, Derry."

He found my hand under the table and squeezed it.

"Have you staked a claim?" I asked, after a small silence.

"Yes. But it will take special tools to work it, equipment I can't afford."

"Papa will be glad to advance you a loan, I'm sure of it."

"I'd rather not be in his debt, Carmella."

"You're too proud, darling."

"I'm a Wakefield," he said simply.

We fell into silence again, my hand in his. Mrs. Tibbets was telling the Reverend about her aunt on Russian Hill. From the kitchen came the high chattering sounds of the Chinese cooks.

"Derry," I said, "I could offer to do an errand for Eilley tomorrow, and so borrow her mule and cart."

"But—"

"No, wait. What harm is there in it? We needn't *do* anything. Just to see you, if only for a handful of minutes. I can't bear having to sit here hoping you might come, watching and waiting. The days are so unbearably *long*."

"I wouldn't want you to risk—"

"Let me worry about it, Derry."

He gave me a long, eloquent look. "Damn!" he swore under his breath. "If I could only kiss you."

That night before I went to bed, I asked Eilley if I could go into town in her place. "I'm housebound," I said. "I haven't been past the front yard since I got here. And if you gave me a list I could get whatever you needed. It would save you time."

Eilley was a Highland Scotswoman as canny as they come. "Now isn't that strange," she said, hands on broad hips. "You wanting suddenly to do my errands. Would it have anything to do with that young man you flung yourself at the other night?"

"No," I said. "Nothing to do with him at all. What gave you such an idea?"

"I'd have to be blind and deaf not to see what's going on right under my nose. No, thank you, Miss Hastings. I want no part in your ruin. Nothing stays a secret around here for long, and when your father finds out there'll be hell to pay."

"You are absolutely wrong about me." Resentment had sent a flare of color to my cheeks. How dare this woman stand in my way? "Mr. Wakefield and I are good friends. If you think—"

"I know what I see. Good friends," she snorted. "I could be crude, couldn't I, seeing the way he looks you up and down, undressing you with those baby-blue eyes of his. No, my dear, you'd best stay at home."

I would go anyway, I thought rebelliously. I would find a way if I had to walk.

Morning dawned feebly under a cover of thick gray clouds. By ten o'clock it had begun to rain, a cold torrential downpour that soon turned the road in front of the house to mud. Eilley gave up going to town. The cart and mule would never make it.

"Like as not, no one will show for supper," Eilley said. "When it rains here, it rains."

I fidgeted all that day, running to the window every few minutes, gazing up, scanning the sky to see if it gave any signs of brightening. But the rain continued to pour without a letup. I wanted to weep out of sheer frustration. It was almost as if Eilley herself had maneuvered the foul weather to block me. I knew Derry would understand, but I had counted so on being with him. Blast it!

About three in the afternoon a lone man leading a mule came splashing across the puddled yard and knocked at the door.

"'Tain't fit for man nor beast," he said, dripping water all over Eilley's newly scrubbed floor. "Washed away half a hundred tents up yonder. Flooded the whole damn town what warn't on the hills, flooded the mines too."

"Was anyone hurt?" I asked anxiously, thinking of Derry and Papa. (Was it in that order?)

"Not that I heard of. You got a bit o' whiskey, Eilley?"

No one else came. During the night the rain stopped, and when the sun rose in the morning the brown tide outside had receded. But the mud was still ankle-deep and Eilley decided to postpone her trip up the hill another day.

By eleven o'clock of the following morning, however, Eilley felt the road would be passable and set out for town alone, having ignored my hints to be taken along. I was debating whether to try and hitch a ride with a passerby when Reverend Franklin, hatless, looking distraught, and driving a mule-drawn cart careened into our yard.

"I'll fetch Mrs. Tibbets," I said, letting him in. "I believe she's in the kitchen."

"No," he said grimly, putting a hand on my arm. "It's you I want to see, Miss Hastings."

My hand flew to my throat. "Is something wrong?"

"I don't like to alarm you unduly, child. Perhaps it will turn out to be less than we think. The Lord in His mercy—"

"Reverend, please, what has happened?" I interrupted. Derry had drowned. The torrential rain filling and overflowing hundreds of dried-up riverbeds had swept down from the mountains and carried him away. Derry—I should have gone this morning, last night, yesterday . . .

"Your father," the Reverend was saying, "has had an accident."

For a moment I couldn't comprehend. "Papa?"

"Yes, your father—"

"Oh, no!" I exclaimed, stunned with a sense of horrible guilt as if I had made some sort of bargain with God, a trade-off, Derry for Papa. "Oh, no! How—what kind of accident?"

"A gunshot wound. Here—here, Miss Hastings, sit down, sit here. You look so white. Perhaps I'd best get Mrs. Tibbets. I wasn't thinking." He raised his voice: "Mrs. Tibbets!"

She came hurrying into the room with a swish of black petticoats. "Carmella," she said, looking at me. "Bad news?"

The Reverend answered for me. "Mr. Hastings has been shot. A claim-jumper from what I could gather."

"You poor child."

I stumbled up from the chair. "I—I can't sit here while he may be bleeding to death. I'll get my cloak."

"Are you sure you'll be all right?" Mrs. Tibbets asked.

I didn't answer but ran into the other room and snatched my cloak from the hook, throwing it about my shoulders, fixing the hood with nervous fingers.

Mrs. Tibbets said, "I'm going too. It's my place."

We started out, the three of us wedged together on the cart seat, the mule straining at the shafts against the pull of the mired yard.

"Men recover from wounds," the Reverend said, breaking a silence as we jolted our way uphill. "I pray Mr. Hastings does."

I said nothing, but sat rigid, hands clasped, trying to believe Papa had sustained something comparatively harmless like a shoulder wound, trying not to remember Lyon and the way he died, the look of the dueling pistol, the round black hole at the end of the muzzle.

"How much farther?" I asked for the third time.

"Almost there," the Reverend answered.

Papa had been taken to Miles's newly built house, a two-story frame building that smelled of fresh pine board and wood shavings. Because they had been afraid to carry him upstairs, he was lying on the sofa in the parlor, his face as white as the pillows under his head. The doctor, a young man with ginger sidewhiskers, explained to me in a hushed voice that he was unable to remove the bullet. "Too deep," he said, "a dangerous spot to probe." Not the shoulder wound I had anticipated but a chest wound. Papa had lost a great deal of blood, and the doctor thought it a wonder he was still alive.

I felt sick at heart and desperately guilty.

"Let me fix you a cup of tea," Mrs. Tibbets offered.

I sat down on a chair in the dining room where I could look past the opened double doors at Papa in the parlor. The chair, the only furnishing in the room, was a cane-bottomed one, hard and uncomfortable.

Miles suddenly appeared, or so it seemed, though he must have been present when I arrived.

"He won't die?" I asked, begging for reassurance.

"I can't say, Carmella. Let us pray not."

"How did it happen?"

"He got into a tussle with a claim-jumper. The man was staking out your father's ledge when we arrived this morning. Your father ordered him to leave. The man drew a gun. I shot him, but not before he had put a bullet in your father's chest. If it's any consolation, the other man is dead."

"No," I said, twisting my fingers, "no consolation. I only want Papa to live."

He woke half an hour later. The minute he opened his eyes I was at his side. He was lucid, he knew me, he even gave me a faint, ghostly smile.

"Papa—you are going to get well. The doctor said so."

"Did he?" He patted my hand. "Well, he's lying."

That statement, so blunt, so frank, and uncharacteristic of Papa frightened me more than anything else he could have said. Only a horrible, final truth would make him speak without his usual courteous tact.

"Oh, Papa, please—please don't. He wasn't lying. As soon as you are able—"

"Carmella, I'm not going to be 'able.' Don't cry. I don't want you to cry. I want you to be brave. My own brave little girl."

I struggled with my tears, clenching my fists so as not to

distress Papa. But I could do nothing about the hard lump in my throat.

"Are you hurting, Papa?" I wiped his brow with my handkerchief.

"A little. Have I been a bad father to you, Carmella?"

"Bad? Whatever gave you such a notion? You have been the best a daughter could have." I leaned over and kissed his forehead, so clammy, so cold to the touch. "I love you, Papa," I said from the heart, the tears threatening again.

"And I, you, child. You're so young, and this is a frightening world. If you had a husband to protect you, I would rest easy in my grave."

"Papa, please don't talk that way. I can't bear it."

"I want you to be safe, Carmella. Marry Miles. He'll see that you are. I know you don't love him, but he's a fine man."

"Oh, Papa, I can't! I can't marry Miles. It's Derry I love. It's Derry I love to distraction."

Papa closed his eyes as a spasm of pain crossed his face. "Would—would you ask the doctor for a little more of—of his medicine?"

I ran at once to fetch him. He gave Papa a spoonful. Papa lay back on the pillows, closing his eyes, and after a minute or so his blanched face took on a little color.

"Carmella—I—I haven't much time. Derry Wakefield . . . does"—he paused—"does not have . . . the financial security I had hoped, but"—another pause—"never mind . . . if it's him you want, send the Reverend to get him. I think Miles would know where Wakefield can be found."

The thought that I would be Derry's wife at last held no comfort for me. What a terrible price to pay!

During that hour when Reverend Franklin searched for Derry I sat by my father's side recalling my early childhood in New Orleans, the small gifts Papa would bring home stuffed in his pockets—ribbons, pralines, bonbons, and toys. Papa embracing me after our long separation: "Buy whatever you like, Carmella." Papa who found it hard to show affection, nevertheless giving it with a generous heart.

I watched as he slept, listening to his ragged breathing, and knew that once he was gone he would leave a void that no one could fill, not even Derry.

The Reverend came back alone. "Mr. Wakefield left early this morning," he said, puffing, his face red with exertion as if he had been running all the way.

My heart sank. "Where did he go?"

"No one could tell me for sure. But he packed everything in his knapsack and said he was headed for the Fraser River."

Papa woke, blinking his eyes. "Carmella . . . ?"

"I'm here, Papa." How to tell him? "Just a minute."

I took Reverend Franklin aside. "Is there any way we can catch Mr. Wakefield?"

"Not with a three-hour start. You're sure this young man wants to marry you?" he added.

"Oh, yes."

"Carmella . . . ?" Papa's voice was weak.

"Yes, Papa."

"Is he—is Wakefield here?"

"No, Papa, not yet."

Someone touched my arm and I looked up to see Miles. "Come in the other room, Carmella."

I got up and followed him into a little anteroom on the other side of the parlor, bare except for a small case of books. Miles shut the door.

"That man out there is breathing his last," Miles said, his voice harsh. "Are you going to let him die in peace or do you plan to remain characteristically selfish to the last?"

"Oh, Miles—please—please, not now."

"I don't want to marry you any more than you want to marry me. But I would cut off my right arm for Arthur Hastings, lay down my own life if need be. He was like a father to me when I needed one desperately. The least I—we—can do is stand in front of the preacher and have him say his words, marry us and give that man, who has given us both so much, a few moments of happiness before the end."

"I know, I know." I twisted my hands distractedly, shot through with remorse. He was right. I had no call to think of myself in this terrible hour.

"It will be a marriage in name only," Miles went on. "And afterwards, you can do as you like. If you wish a divorce, or better stll an annulment, I'll arrange it."

"Yes, Miles. We must hurry."

The doctor propped Papa up on the pillows. His eyes had a glazed look, but he knew what was happening, for his mouth twitched into a painful smile as he saw Reverend Franklin, Bible in hand, instructing Miles and me to stand before him, Mrs. Tibbets and the doctor behind.

"Dearly beloved, we are gathered here—to join in holy matrimony . . ."

It was my second marriage. Hard to believe, for it did not feel like a marriage at all. Certainly there was no joy to it, no excitement, not even the apprehension and nervous anticipation I had felt when Lyon and I stood in the parish priest's parlor. I did not look at Miles but kept my eyes on Papa, forcing a smile to my lips.

"The ring . . . ?" I heard the Reverend say. "Does the groom have a ring?"

Miles slipped his signet from his finger and placed it on mine. It felt heavy and cold.

"I now pronounce you man and wife."

Miles gave me a chaste peck for appearances. Mrs. Tibbets hugged me, and the doctor shook my hand. I knelt beside Papa and kissed his forehead.

"I am so relieved," he whispered.

He lingered for another day and night, suffering agonizing pain not even the doctor's opium-laced remedy could blur. He died on the morning of November 5th without knowing me.

CHAPTER

TWENTY

Two days after Papa's funeral I moved into Miles's house. I had quarreled with Mrs. Tibbets and found it awkward to share a room, let alone a bed, with her. Papa had hardly been cold in his grave when she wanted to know what he had left her in his will.

"My father had very little when he died," I told her.

Mrs. Tibbets refused to believe me. "Why the man was rich!" she insisted.

For a woman who hoped to be a minister's wife, for one who had always toadied so meekly, she had suddenly become brash and unpleasantly aggressive.

"He lost all his money before we came to Sun Mountain," I tried to explain.

"He must have put me down for something. After all my faithful service. *Something*."

"Faithful service? Why you ungrateful creature," I exclaimed angrily. "We housed and fed and clothed you and paid you a salary well above your worth. What is it you want, a pension? When Papa's mule is sold I'll give you the proceeds."

"He's got a silver mine, hasn't he?"

"It hasn't been worked. I have no idea if anything will be found on it."

"I'll take a share," she said, bold as brass.

"You'll do nothing of the sort."

I packed and had one of the boarders drive me up to Virginia City that very afternoon.

Miles was not there, but the door was unlocked and I walked in. Setting my bag down, I went upstairs. There were two bedrooms, only one had a bed. The other was unfurnished, its curtainless windowpanes smudged with putty.

Downstairs, there was the parlor, a dining room, the ante-room, which now had a desk in it, and the kitchen. A small house, but much snugger than Eilley's ramshackle building. I did not know how long I would stay, in fact had no plans, no idea where I would go. I missed Derry. I needed his love and his strength to help me through this bitter time. A note he had written telling me about his departure to the Fraser River had been delivered to me at Eilley's the day after my marriage. In it Derry promised to return to me soon. I had to believe that, because beyond Derry was chaos.

Miles arrived an hour later. If he was surprised to see me sitting on the sofa in his parlor he gave no sign. "I meant to ride down to Eilley's and discuss the sale of your father's effects."

"I—I couldn't stay. Mrs. Tibbets has become impossible. She insists that Papa left her something in his will."

"He did." Miles took a chair opposite me. "But unfortunately it's not a new will and what he had when he made it is gone. I've had an offer, a fair one, I think, for his rig and claim. Twenty-five hundred dollars. I suggest you accept it."

"Yes—perhaps you are right."

"I owe your father some money, which, of course, will now go to you. I can arrange for you to have it in a lump sum or in a monthly allowance."

"You owed my father?" I asked suspiciously. "How much?"

"Something like twelve thousand dollars."

"Twelve . . . ? You must think me a fool to believe that. You forget that you told me you offered to lend Papa money and he refused. Why should he refuse when you were in debt to him to the tune of twelve thousand dollars?"

"Very well, then. I wanted to make this painless. You have a stubborn pride which I would find touching in other circumstances. You must live somehow. And since Derry has flown the coop . . ."

"Please leave him out of this."

". . . and you have no means, I will support you until you find someone who is willing to marry—I said *marry*—you and do the same."

"And so I'm to be the recipient of your charity?"

"Not charity, my dear. As my wife you are entitled to support."

"I'd prefer not to take anything form you, Miles. It might make the annulment or divorce more difficult."

Something flickered in his eyes. Anger? Irritation? I couldn't tell. "It won't. No one need know. Come now, Carmella, you have no choice."

"I'll pay it back."

"Do as you like." He got to his feet. "Before I forget, there are some papers you should sign giving me power of attorney. It will make it simpler if I'm to conduct business for you."

He went to the desk in the anteroom and withdrew a sheaf of official-looking documents.

After I had put my signature to the indicated blanks, he said, "I suppose you want to return to San Francisco?"

"I'm not quite sure what I'll do."

"You could stay with the Hobarts. They would be happy to have you."

"Yes." I thought of Dolly, her warm, lively gaiety. Her friendship would help. But I hadn't recovered yet. I needed time to be alone, time to get used to the idea that Papa was dead.

"There's a coach leaving day after tomorrow. If you wish, I can get you on it."

He seemed anxious to be rid of me and I resented it. I wanted to make my own decisions, not to be shoved into a course of action I wasn't ready for. But if I refused, he might think I was reluctant to leave him and that was the last impression I wished to make.

"That would suit me fine."

"Very well. You can have the bedroom upstairs; I'll bunk on the sofa."

"I hate to inconvenience you," I said with frigid politeness.

"Not at all. It will only be for two nights."

But again the weather intervened. Sometime before dawn a storm suddenly howled down upon us, a raging blizzard, the first one of the season, throwing a mantle of white over the city and piling drifts past our ground-floor windows.

Miles, coming in from feeding his horse, said, "I don't think the stage will be leaving on schedule unless the weather clears. Ah, I see you've found the coffee pot."

I was in the kitchen, trying to get the woodstove started.

"There's coffee somewhere in the cupboard. Here." He brought down a sack. "I'll fetch the water."

We sat at a newly planed round kitchen table, drinking hot coffee and eating stale biscuits, a temporary truce between us.

After breakfast Miles shoveled a path to the road. Then, donning rawhide snowshoes, he went out to assess the situation in town.

It began to snow again soon after he left, light flakes falling gently, covering the path Miles had made. Very few people had ventured into the street, so I was surprised to see a figure muffled in a great cape turn in at the walk. There was something familiar about the gait, and when the man lifted his head I gasped. Then I was running down the stairs, flinging open the door, rushing out into the snow in a flurry of wind-whipped skirts.

"Derry!"

We embraced. He lifted and carried me into the house.

"Oh, Derry!" I kissed him again and again, quick, hungry little kisses on his cheeks, his eyes, his cold gloved hands.

He laughed. "Wait! Wait! Let me catch my breath."

"Yes," I said, "yes," unwinding the scarf from his throat, taking his damp, snowy hat. "Oh, Derry, where have you been?"

"Didn't you get my note? I couldn't stay here. Silver is not a pick-and-sieve operation, and right now that's all I can afford."

"You said you were on your way to the Fraser River."

"I was. But when I got to the other side of the Chollar the weather turned nasty. I realized I'd be in trouble if I didn't double back. I understand your father was shot."

"Yes, yes," I said. "Papa died three days ago."

"I'm sorry to hear that, Carmella, so sorry. A fine man, your father."

"And, Derry—he wanted me to marry before he died. He was willing to have you as my husband—and we sent the Reverend to look for you." Oh, why hadn't I waited? Five, six days. But Papa was dying. There hadn't been time.

"And so you became Mrs. Miles Falconer?" he asked, scanning my face. "Is that true?"

"Yes—only . . ."

"I thought you hated the man." A muscle twitched in his jaw.

"Yes, but . . ."

"Why did you consent to such a wedding? I don't want to share you, Carmella. I told you once before I'm jealous, possessive—a fault—but I can't help it. You're mine. You swore you loved me. I only left here to better myself."

"I know, darling. And I do love you, I do! But we married to please Papa before he died—I and Miles—it's in name only. We can get a divorce. That was the agreement."

"Divorces are not that easy to come by. A man has to desert his wife—I don't know for how many years—and commit adultery. The man, not the woman."

"Then an annulment. We haven't—we haven't consummated the marriage. Darling, please don't be angry."

I put my arms about his neck and he drew me close, his lips finding mine.

It was at that moment that Miles opened the door. Derry broke away; I straightened my bodice. I knew that guilt was written all over my face, and I hated myself for it. Why should I feel guilty?

"Tendering your condolences, Mr. Wakefield?" Miles asked jeeringly.

"You might say so," Derry answered shortly, ignoring Miles's jibing tone.

"A pity you were late," Miles said.

"Yes." Derry tied the scarf around his throat and retrieved his hat. "I must be going, Carmella. If there is anything I can do . . ."

"Derry—can't you stay for tea? A whiskey?"

"I'm afraid not. I have business in town."

Miles stood by without speaking, his face expressionless. Why didn't he leave Derry and me alone? Why didn't he have the decency to go into the other room?

"You must come for supper," I urged Derry. "I don't know when I can leave. I was supposed to take the stage for San Francisco. But the weather... Come next Sunday. Monday?"

Miles, stony and impassive, remained silent.

"I'll let you know, Carmella," Derry said. "Good-bye. Good-bye, Miles." They did not shake hands.

When he had closed the door behind him, I turned angrily to Miles. "You might have been more courteous. You were rude!"

"Is a husband generally anything but rude when he comes home to find his wife in the arms of another man?"

"Husband, wife! Oh, you make my blood boil! We are nothing of the kind."

"You are married to me. You bear my name, legally, I must remind you, whatever other circumstances might pertain. And while you are under my roof you will behave with the decency required of a married woman."

"Oh—you make me sick! What are you afraid of? Afraid people will talk? Will say you are cuckolded?"

"I am not going to have a snip like you coupling in my bed with a lily-livered weasel."

"Don't you dare call Derry a weasel!"

"He is a spineless—"

I hit him. It was a reflexive act, done without thought in lashing fury. He grabbed my wrist.

"I warned you once before not to do that!" His face had gone very white, the sting of my hand standing out in a red imprint on his cheek.

I tore his signet ring from my finger and hurled it at him. "I am not your wife! Never!" I pulled the ribbon with Derry's ring out from my collar. "Derry is the man I love. Derry—"

His stinging slap shocked me into speechlessness. But only for a moment.

"You beast! You...!"

He grabbed the ribbon and, twisting it about his hand, jerked it from my neck.

"We'll see whose wife you are—damn you!"

"Give that to me!"

He tossed the ring over his shoulder. I backed away, fear rising with a strange, prickly sensation along my arms.

"You're the one to speak of decency," I went on despite the frightening glitter in his eyes, "when you swear like a guttersnipe *and* consort with whores!"

He caught me just as I was turning to get away, pinning my arms to my sides with hurting hands.

"Do I?"

"Let me—"

He closed my mouth with a hot, brutal kiss, his lips savaging mine. For a moment I went limp; then, gathering strength, I gave him a violent push and broke away. Wheeling, grabbing my skirts, I started up the stairs, taking them as fast as I could, running up into the dark shadows, my breath coming in short, frightened gasps. I heard him following with his quick, heavy tread and I climbed even faster, stumbling on the top step, rushing into the bedroom, slamming the door shut. Before I could take hold of the key in the lock the door was flung open.

I retreated, going back inch by inch until I felt the bed against my thighs. He stood in the doorway watching me. Twilight had darkened the room, but I could see his angry face, feel the glare of his eyes. Outside, the wind rattled the windows, moaning and keening, driving a whirl of snow before it. In a short time drifts would be piled against the door, locking me in with this man in the lowering night. My heart pounded but I could not utter a word. Miles shrugged out of his coat and threw it aside. Then, motionless, he stood there across the room without speaking, his white shirt gleaming in the dusk, his very silence full of threat. I wanted to scream, but all I could do was wet my lips and whisper hoarsely, "Get out!"

He stepped over the threshold and slammed the door with a backward kick of his boot.

"If you think . . ." I began.

In two strides he crossed the floor and jerked me into his arms. "Does it matter what I think?"

Again his mouth was on mine, not gentle, not tender, but angry, demanding, full of a passion that shook him and sent a flame through my body. In the midst of a spinning darkness I felt his fingers undoing buttons and ribbons, felt his lips touching, pressing the cleft between my breasts. And I forgot Derry—his face slipped from my mind—I forgot everything but the wild wind howling outside and the man undressing me, running his large, strong hands over my nakedness, cupping my breasts, his fierce mouth ravaging the nipples. I dug my hands into the crisp thickness of his dark hair, pulling at him, tugging, but with less and less strength. He swung me into his arms and for a moment I felt a pang of sheer terror.

I must have said something, for he growled, "Be quiet!"

He was carrying me into a deeper darkness, into inky, frightening shadow, lowering me until I felt the bed against my back.

"Miles!"

But he was on me, his lips on mine, trailing fire along my throat, my breasts, nibbling at my stomach, my hips, rousing my skin to a thousand sensations.

"You mustn't—you promised!" But the words were so weak as to be mere whispers that died as he began to stroke the insides of my thighs. Something stirred in the back of my mind, some dim memory, a feeling that I shouldn't be here, that I should not be reveling in this erotic stroking. I twisted myself away, bringing my knees up so that I caught his chin.

He slammed me back on the mattress. "Stay put!"

I struggled but he held me fast, his knee nudging my legs apart. When he entered me I grasped his shoulders and tried to lift him away, tried and failed.

Then he was moving, slowly at first, so that every stroke sent a ripple of pleasure through my pliant, trembling body. As his pace quickened, my hips arched and again my mind plunged into a sweet forgetfulness. His lips were on mine, my face gripped between his hands as he moved, faster and faster, sweeping me up with him, in a tumbling, battering storm that frightened yet excited me. The sensation of rising tension, the wild, mad feeling that I was rushing to some soul-shattering fate tore gasp after gasp from my throat. Then suddenly my body exploded in a final burst, sending shock waves to the ends of my fingers, to the tips of my toes. Miles, a moment later, collapsed on me, holding me tightly as his body shuddered in climax. For a long moment we lay there, my heart beating under his, our breaths mingling.

He did not kiss me. He rolled away and lay by my side in

silence, Miles again. That such violent intimacy should leave us still estranged baffled me. I looked up at the shadowed ceiling and tears brimmed my eyes. It should have been Derry, I thought, not Miles. I hated myself for responding to this man's savagery, for allowing myself to be drawn into the vortex of his mindless passion. Yet something told me that he was not entirely to blame. If I had not taunted him, if I had not struck him, if I had accepted his dictum with grace (after all, he had been right about the impropriety of Derry's kissing me under his roof), then none of this would have happened. It was almost as if I had wanted Miles to take me by force.

That was preposterous. But wasn't it also my triumph, that I could get to this man whose iron control irked me, that I could crack his armor?

If it was a triumph, the conquest had turned to ashes. I felt emotionally drained, exhausted. If Miles would only say something—an apology, a word of kindness—anything to take away my feeling of bleak weariness.

But when he spoke, he said, "I can't promise it won't happen again. You seem as unable to curb your tongue as I my lust."

It was not what I wanted to hear. I did not want to share the blame.

"I should think that a man who considers himself superior would not find it necessary to act like a billy goat," I said tartly, "just because a woman throws a few cross words at him."

The bed shook as he rose on an elbow. "You wanted it to happen, damn you!"

He got up and I could hear him drawing on his clothes.

"Now that I am really your wife," I went on spitefully, "you can beat me if you wish. I daresay the law allows it here as elsewhere."

He slammed the door as he went out.

The blizzard had only been the start of a series of whirling snowfalls that lasted for four days. When the weather finally cleared, the passes had been effectively blocked, we were told, with drifts up to sixty feet. We were cut off from the rest of the world.

The population of Virginia City as a whole—and that included myself—had no idea how long a Washoe winter could be, nor how lacking we were in supplies to sustain us through it. Provisions dwindled at an alarming rate. Long before Christmas, sugar could not be had for love or money; flour, when it could be found, cost $80 a sack; barley, $100, beans $125. Miles had to feed his horse hay mixed with shavings. The beautiful animal lost its sleekness and became bloated and sluggish; its condition dismayed Miles more than his own discomfort.

He and I reached a state of truce. We had no choice. There was no way for me to leave now until the spring thaw, and we settled uneasily in together—two polite strangers in a small house marooned by an implacable winter of freezing snow.

Miles, unlike Papa, did not try to hide the unpleasant aspects of our situation from me. I appreciated his frankness and understood the necessity of using the flour, our precious supply of coffee, and diminishing sacks of beans with a sparing hand.

There were a few things Miles kept to himself, however, things I did not hear about until years later. We had no meat. The last Virginia City chicken had been killed, the last pig and goat butchered and eaten long months ago. Game, except for a few scattered jackrabbits and packs of elusive wolves, had disappeared. So I was surprised one evening when Miles returned with a packet of "salt meat." I managed to soak, pound, and bake it into some semblance of stew, and I must say it tasted good. When I asked Miles what it was, he said someone had killed a deer. But a deer in those parts would have been as rare as an elephant. In order to survive, the miners had taken to killing and salting down their mules.

I had never lived through a more desperate winter. Looking back, I can't say what tormented me the most, the perpetual, howling wind, the bitter cold, the gnawing hunger, or the isolation. Miles told me that we were better off than the men who lived in tents, huddling in their ragged blankets by smoking fires, subsisting on mule flesh mixed with snow and a little whiskey. Many had sickened and died. Some had started back to Carson, and of those only a very few made it.

I worried about Derry. He did not come to the house. I heard not a word from him, and while I understood his reluctance to provoke a quarrel between Miles and me, it was a torment not knowing where he was, if he was ill, if he was freezing or starving. Finally, unable to hold back, I asked Miles.

"Oh, he's surviving quite nicely. He's installed himself in one of our better sporting houses. Shall I give him your love?"

"Please don't trouble yourself on my account," I replied shortly, sorry I had given him the opportunity to bait me.

I saw Mrs. Tibbets only once. She came by to invite me to her wedding. "A small affair," she said, preening. "The Reverend wants only close friends."

She had quite forgotten our quarrel, her need for a "pension" canceled out by the Reverend's proposal and the prospect of a lifelong berth. I promised to attend, but a snowstorm on the appointed day made it impossible.

It snowed frequently, snow piling upon snow. I hardly went anywhere and there were many days when even Miles was forced to stay at home. He would pace up and down in the parlor, the only room that provided heat, the fire on the hearth sparingly fed by chips of wood left over from the building of the house and whatever Miles could gather. He had bought shares in the Ophir and Gould and Curry mines and with my consent had invested the money from my father's claim in mining stock also. He would talk about the mines, now closed for the winter, and he paced. And I would listen, not so much to what he said, but to the sound of his voice, a human voice. The Devil's own mutterings would have been welcome; it was that lonesome, that frightening to look out day after day on a world shrouded in desolate white where nothing moved, nothing stirred.

The nights were long and achingly cold. We slept apart but I had given up locking my door, for Miles showed no interest in me. Neither of us had a wish to quarrel now. Living day by day seemed to take all our energy. One night I had a fearful dream that the wolves, made bold with hunger, had come down from the mountain and surrounded the house. In my nightmare I stood at the window and watched in terror as the gray, bony-ribbed, yellow-fanged beasts circled silently. Suddenly several, gathering in a knot, made a leap for the door, clawing and scratching at it, whining and growling as they tried to get in.

One began to climb the wall toward my window. Transfixed with horror, I could only stare as it came closer and closer, finally reaching the ledge. When it pressed its dripping muzzle against the glass, baring its ugly teeth, I screamed. The sound awoke me.

I lay drenched in cold sweat, wrapped in the horror of my dream. The wind rattled the windowpanes and, still thinking of the wolf, I screamed again.

Miles burst into the room. "What in God's name is it?"

"Oh, Miles, there's a wolf...!" I pointed.

He went to the window, parted the curtains, and looked out. "There's nothing, Carmella. You've been dreaming."

My teeth were chattering. "Miles—I am so afraid."

He sat down on the bed and took me into his arms. "Silly goose, there's nothing to be afraid of."

I leaned my head against him, his hard muscled chest giving me a sense of comfort and safety.

"They can't get in, can they?"

"Of course not. Besides, most of the wolves have been killed off by the boys in town."

"I'm so cold."

"Here, let me warm you." He got into bed and I made no objection. I wanted to be held, soothed, reassured, told that nothing evil from the wintry landscape outside could reach me.

I must have dozed off in Miles's arms. Through the mists of sleep I had the sensation that he was kissing and stroking my hair. I opened my eyes.

"Miles..."

His breath was hot on my cheek. Pushing the tumbled hair from my forehead, he found my mouth and kissed me, softly, tenderly. This was a new Miles, one that I never suspected existed. Lazily I nestled closer, my head resting beneath his chin. He tilted my face up and kissed me on the mouth again, parting my lips with firm tenderness. I closed my eyes, drowsy with warmth and pleasure. His fingers parted my nightgown, pushing the sheer linen from my shoulders. Then lightly, without hurry, his lips trailed down to my breasts, the skin sensitive, exposed and suddenly burning to his touch. A familiar fire ignited in the pit of my stomach, gripping my loins. When his lips closed around a nipple I gasped at the sweet pang that shook me. His hand moved down and pulled my gown up past my hips. He was rousing me, stealing what was not his by right, bringing me to a desire with his lips, his exploring hands, and I was helpless to stop him. I made one weak attempt to push him away, but instead found my hands grasping his shoulders as he swung over me and brought his muscular body over mine. He parted my knees and when he entered me, filling, exciting me, I found my voice in one last protest.

"No . . . !"

But it was a murmur, a sound in my throat, and his mouth was on mine, his tongue probing, his loins moving, willing me to join in the dance that was as old as time. And I rose to it, followed him blindly, step by step, holding him, fitting myself to the rhythm of his hips, his driving buttocks, a dance that grew wilder and wilder, clutching at the taut muslces of his naked back, pressing into him to get the full measure of his every thrust, forgetting the cold and the hunger, forgetting everything but the need for the ultimate ecstatic release. It came with the suddenness of a detonation, a quivering shock that shattered my nerve ends.

In the silence that followed I lay quietly, the glow slowly fading from my body, wondering how I could experience such pleasure from a man I did not love. Nice women did not enjoy sex even with their husbands. If it had only been Derry.

I gave a deep, soulful sigh.

Miles's body next to mine went rigid. "Comparing me to your lover?" he asked sarcastically, uncannily divining my thoughts.

When I did not answer, he rose, leaning over me. "It's a pity you must make do with second best. Even whores have the decency to pretend a man pleases them."

"Are you calling me a whore?" I flared.

"If the shoe fits, wear it!" he retorted, getting out of bed.

When he had gone, I lay for a long time huddled under the blanket, wondering what I had done to deserve a winter at Washoe with Miles Falconer as punishment. Derry had never left my bed in a huff, hurling insults at me. He had made me happy, *happy!* A great longing for him seized me, and burying my face in the pillow, I wept.

* * *

In March the first mule train arrived, staggering up the pass from Devil's Gate laden with barrels, most of them, to everyone's keen disappointment, containing not food but rum, champagne, wine, and bar fixtures. However, a few days later another string of mules arrived and this time they brought flour, sugar, and beans. Men like moles began to emerge from their burrows, blinking in the wan sunlight. Along with supplies, we received our first news from San Francisco, papers full of happenings, reports of balls and theater openings, political appointments, court trials, and financial scandals. Abraham Lincoln had been elected president of the country and there was a long article on the growing quarrel between the North and South. Judge Terry, quoted by one reporter, had put out a call for all good Southerners to hold themselves in readiness for the coming crusade against the verminous Yankees.

For the citizens of Virginia City these events seemed light years away. Glad to be alive, thinking the worst was over, they began to haul out shovels, picks, and dredges, preparing to go back to work.

However, the Washoe winter was not quite done with us. A week before the first day of spring, a sudden thaw triggered a series of disastrous avalanches, sending tons of snow and rocks crashing and thundering down Sun Mountain, killing dozens who had built their shacks or struck their tents on the sunny side of the slope.

As always when castastrophe struck I feared for Derry; and one morning as I got ready to go out and make inquiries, Reverend Franklin knocked on the door. He had a message from Derry.

"Mr. Wakefield is all right," the Reverend assured me. "Fine. Wasn't anywhere near the avalanche. He asked me to tell you he's leaving Virginia City."

"Leaving? Where to?"

"He's been offered a partnership in a mine in Utah. He wanted to come and tender his farewell in person but was afraid it might cause—ah—difficulties. His love and best wishes go with you. And he promises when he sees you again—soon, he hopes—he will be a rich man."

"Thank you, Reverend Franklin."

Tears of disappointment burned my eyes and I turned away, fumbling with the lace edging at my wrists. Why did Derry feel it necessary to keep running off, chasing rainbows for an elusive pot of gold? Why couldn't he stay put? Why...?

But it was no use. I couldn't be angry. All the whys in the world wouldn't change the way I felt. Despite everything, I loved him—now more than ever. I loved him for the very reasons I condemned him: because he refused to be discouraged and wouldn't give up; because he continued to battle against odds; because he was Derry.

Someday he *would* find his gold. He would come back and take me in his arms and vow never to leave again. I had to believe that. Nothing made sense unless I did.

One evening Miles said, "Had enough of Virginia City?"

What a question!

We left two days later for San Francisco, our trunks perched atop a Wells Fargo stage.

Miles rented a house on Rincon Hill, one much larger than Papa's, with scrollworked balconies and a gabled roof. The inside was lavish with plush carpets, carved oak furniture, and great loops of blue velvet drapery. He hired a butler, a cook, maids, groomsmen, and gardeners. For the most part, they had little to do but sit in the kitchen eating, drinking, and talking. Dolly and I resumed our friendship. She was jealous—"green," as she put it—because I had managed to snare Miles.

"I didn't 'snare' him." I told her our marriage had been Papa's wish. "It's in name only," I lied, feeling I had to. I wanted Dolly to know that because I still loved Derry I had remained faithful to him.

"Soooo...Miles Falconer is more or less a bachelor, is he?"

"Not exactly," I replied a little sourly. "We both have promised to keep up appearances."

"Oh, appearances be hanged!"

Miles gave a stupendous Fourth of July ball, to which all of society was invited. His silver investments in Gould and Curry were paying off handsomely (even my meager one, he said, was showing a respectable return) and he was a very rich man now. The ball was the most opulent one that city, known for its ostentatious entertaining, had ever seen. Oysters, lobster in aspic, venison, freshly caught poached salmon, prime beef, capons, dozens of salads, peaches in brandy, whipped chocolate fancies were but a few of the dishes offered, laid out on damask-covered tables set with chased-gold cutlery and imported Bohemian crystal. Champagne and whiskey flowed like water. I was gowned in gentian-blue satin trimmed with insets of lace and banded with pearls, and on my sleekly coiffed head I wore a pearl and diamond tiara. Two orchestras played, spelling each other, so the dancing never stopped.

Throughout that evening Miles and I did not exchange more than a few words, though we stood side by side greeting our guests and later danced the first waltz together. We had nothing to say to each other. It had been like that ever since our return to San Francisco. He gave me a large weekly allowance, went his way, and I went mine. The night of the ball he mingled with our guests, moving through the throng, pausing to converse with one group of gentlemen and then with another, smiling at the ladies, seeing that the waiters carrying trays of champagne-filled glasses kept circulating, while I danced each dance, making silly talk and flirting with my partners. Sometime around midnight, during the supper, Miles disappeared for about an hour and I noticed that Dolly was gone also. In her daringly cut crimson gown she had followed Miles all evening with hungry eyes. When I thought of the numerous unused bedrooms above, I had to fight the angry urge to dash up the stairs, to open door after door until I found the two of them, and . . .

And what? I didn't love Miles. Why should I be jealous?

The ball had been a huge success, but somehow Miles was not cheered by his social triumph. It was as if he had felt entertaining his cohorts and friends a duty rather than a pleasure. He was bored and restless. Some nights, after I had gone up to bed, I could hear him pacing in the library below. The sound of his heavy tread upon the hardwood floor, going back and forth, back and forth, would float up to me as I lay there in the dark. And in the morning when I went down I would

find the air in the library thick with stale cigar smoke and cigar
butts overflowing the brass spitoon, ash powdering the floor.

What set Miles to walking so restlessly from wall to wall
every night? What gnawed at him? Our sham marriage? But
he did not seem to care any more than I did. Our situation, at
that time, was a convenience for both of us. I went on being
Miles's wife because there did not seem to be anything else I
could do. My father had died, and Derry was somewhere in
Utah. I had no place I wanted to go. I was comfortable, and
as a married woman I had a great deal more freedom than if I
were unattached. So I let the days and weeks and months drift,
thinking of Derry, yearning for him, hoping he would return
and claim me.

Derry did not return, but I got a letter from him (the next
best thing) postmarked Spanish Fork. He still loved me, he
said, and hoped I hadn't become fond of Miles and forgotten
him. As if I could!

> I and my partner are on to a good thing here. But we need
> machinery—and so are selling shares in what we have regis-
> tered as the Cat's Eye Mine. So far we've sold ten shares at
> $2,000 each and have five more investors who are on the brink.
> Once they decide, we should have enough to give us a start.
> Keep your fingers crossed, darling, I have a feeling this is it.

I shared that feeling. Derry was overdue for the lucky strike
he had sought for so long. I *knew* he couldn't fail now. The
Cat's Eye Mine. I liked the name. People looking for a way
to make their money grow might find it appealing too. I thought
perhaps even Miles would want to invest. It was true he didn't
like Derry, but Miles never let personal feelings intervene when
it came to business.

That evening I brought the matter up while we were at
supper.

"And where is this so-called Cat's Eye Mine?"

I ignored his sarcasm. "Spanish Fork, Utah," I answered,
plucking the place name from the postmark on Derry's letter.
"It's registered."

"I'm sure. Any two-bit claim can be registered."

"I wish you would at least *try* to discuss this reasonably," I said, resisting the urge to match his nastiness.

"All right. What was the yield in the sample take? Is the mine located near a good source of water? Do they plan to use dragline conveyors?"

He went on in that vein, asking me technical questions I couldn't possibly answer. I told him so.

"Why don't you write Derry? Or another investor. Or perhaps the place where the mine is registered can send you the information you want."

"I can write, yes," he said. "But I may as well tell you it will be a waste of time."

"Why? Because the mine is Derry's?"

"Precisely. Derry is a muddler, in miner's terms a washout. He hasn't the kind of tenacity needed for real prospecting. Instead of flitting from one location to another, attracted by glitter like a June bug, he ought to make a study of geology, plan his expeditions with forethought. Not him. He's too lazy, too thickheaded, too—"

"Stop! I don't want to hear another word. If you're not going to do anything but insult Derry, then we'll forget I ever mentioned the matter."

"Suits me."

Throwing down my napkin, I got up and stamped out of the room, slamming the door behind me.

The next morning I went down to Gould and Curry, the San Francisco offices of the silver mine in which Miles had invested our money. I intended to withdraw my shares, cash them in, and buy stock in the Cat's Eye.

Ushered into a small cubicle, I shook hands with a Mr. Bundy, a tall, very thin man with a fringe of white hair circling his bald head like a crown.

"I've done business with your husband, Mrs. Falconer. A pleasure to meet you. And how can I serve you?"

I told him what I wanted.

He looked puzzled. "Shares in your name? Let me see."

He withdrew a manila portfolio from a wooden file and thumbed through it while I waited.

"I'm sorry, Mrs. Falconer, but there are no Curry shares I can attribute to your ownership."

"Why I don't see how . . . Ah, perhaps they were purchased under my maiden name—Carmella Hastings."

Again he rummaged in the file, this time for a longer period, shaking his head, moving his lips soundlessly.

"No," he said finally. "There is nothing under that name either."

"Then I have no separate shares in Gould and Curry?" *But he said he had bought them!*

"No. Your husband, however, has a large account with us. Perhaps there's been some misunderstanding?"

He was looking at me with concern—and curiosity—as if he could see the sudden black void under my heart. "I'm sure that is it," I said firmly, gathering my gloves, pride forbidding me to shout the obvious: *I've been cheated!*

Once in my carriage I told the coachman to drive along the bay front, anywhere but home. I was seething. Miles had taken advantage of my ignorance and bilked me. There was no other way to look at it. Those papers he'd had me sign . . . ! I hadn't even read them. What's more when he had offered to repay my father's so-called loan he had known all along I would refuse. He had *banked* on it. His apparent indifference to money was a fraudulent pose. The amount involved must have been petty when compared to his own stockpile of assets, and yet the shrewd tradesman in him had turned my small inheritance into his own profit. The thief, the . . . ! Oh, God, when I thought of it!

My first impulse was to confront him. But I knew exactly what he would say. "Why do you want the money, Carmella?" Then he would go into a long tirade against Derry. My shares he would manage to explain away. Miles was very good at explaining away. He knew the details of my father's financial affairs were a mystery to me. I hadn't even seen my father's will and what Miles had told me I'd taken on trust. At this stage it would be futile to hire a lawyer to represent me. I had no *proof* of Miles's treachery.

What galled me was his show of generosity. I knew now that the jewels he had bought me were a sop to his conscience. As we clattered along East Street it occurred to me that I might sell a bauble or two and so raise the money. The more I thought of it, the more the idea appealed to me. Why not? The jewelry had been given to me, it was mine, and by disposing of various items I would be less guilty of deceit than Miles.

I said nothing to him, of course. If Miles missed the emerald ring and matching earrings I chose to part with I could always exhibit shock and dismay, pretending a sudden realization that my emeralds had either been lost or stolen. Or I could tell him the truth.

The next day I took my jewels to a pawnshop on Bush Street. I got far less than I hoped but enough to buy a share in Derry's mine, and I sent a bank draft to his address in Utah.

Two weeks later my draft enclosed in Derry's letter came back.

Darling,

I appreciate your vote of confidence, but am returning your bank order, not because our endeavor has failed, but because we are holding the mine's large-scale operations in suspension. As you know, there are rumors of war between the North and the South and if hostilities do break out I and my partner (who is also a Southerner) will return, he to North Carolina, I to Virginia. In the meanwhile, we will confine our activities to panning. Who knows, I might find a 50-carat nugget or two! I love you as ever.

Derry

I didn't redeem my ring and earrings but retained the draft and with it opened a bank account under my maiden name. I wanted to have cash in readiness should the Cat's Eye Mine solicit investors again.

Miles did not seem to notice the absence of the emeralds. I saw less and less of him. We rarely went out and his occasional appearances at home were marked by a preoccupied withdrawal. It was on one of the few evenings when he deemed to grace our table that I, after a prolonged and morose silence, asked, "Is something wrong?"

He gave me a long look. "Haven't you been reading the papers lately?"

"Not too closely."

"A superficial glance at the *Alta* would have told you that the news is mostly about an impending civil war. Seven Southern states have already left the Union."

"But what has that to do with us in California? We don't have slavery, and we are thousands of miles from the people who are for or against it."

"You forget I am a Virginian."

Derry's local patriotism did not surprise me, but Miles's did. "That's the first I've heard you mention it."

"I know. I am not one like Judge Terry and his Knights of Chivalry, or whatever damn fool thing they call themselves here, to flaunt my Southern antecedents, my ham and grits background. But there's something about being born and raised in a place that takes hold of you and never leaves. If the hotheads get us into this war, I'm afraid Virginia will lose everything. The South simply does not have the resources to fight a long war. Southerners have the courage, the will, and a lot of foolish notions about honor, but they lack everything else that could put them on the winning side. They have no cannon factories and only a scattering of iron foundries. The few cotten and woolen mills and tanneries could hardly clothe an army. Our transportation system, a must in any sort of military campaign, is woefully lacking too."

"And so you believe you will be able to talk them out of war?" I asked cynically.

"I can try. I would like to put my voice in with the others who are against secession and there happens to be a large contingent in Virginia who think as I do."

He did not say anything for a few minutes and I watched him drink his wine, his eyes remote as if seeing Virginia, picturing it in his mind. I wondered if all this talk of preventing war was not a mask for a sudden nostalgia, a longing to see his birthplace. Miles sentimental? That was hard to believe. But he was a strange, many-faceted man.

"Does that mean you want to go back?" I asked, adding, "*Can* you?"

"You mean that business about the duel." He had never spoken of it and I had never asked. "That happened so long ago—I hate to think of *how* long. My father's dead, has been for years. Yes. I can go back, have, in fact, more or less made up my mind to it. You can stay on here if you like. I'll provide for you, though I prefer having you come with me."

"Why?" I asked with sudden interest.

"Because I promised your father I'd look after you."

"I see." I wanted to ask if that included the assets my father had left, but thought better of it. If war did break out as Miles believed, then Derry would be returning to Virginia too. And I wanted to be there. It wouldn't help to argue with Miles at this stage. "I'll go. I have nothing to hold me in San Francisco."

"Very well," he said in a noncommittal voice, one that I had become accustomed to. But I did not care. His indifference suited me.

CHAPTER

TWENTY-ONE

WE CAME to Miles's home, Wildoak, in early August, arriving, as he said, at the worst time of the year when the heat rose in a shimmering haze from the Pamunkey River, wilting everything that drew breath. We had gone by way of the Isthmus, stopping at New Orleans for a few days, then on around the coast of Florida and up the Eastern seaboard to West Point. There Miles's brother, Harold, had met us. The only resemblance between the two men was in the eyes. Harold was older and showed it; his face was creased, his brow furrowed, his hair grayed. But what he lacked in youthful appearance he made up in warmth and friendliness, putting me at ease at once.

I was grateful for that. It had been a long, tedious journey and I'd dreaded meeting Miles's family, chiefly because of the circumstances of our marriage.

"We needn't tell them," Miles had said. "But if we are going to keep up a pretense we shall have to share a bedroom." In San Francisco we had slept in separate rooms. "It won't be too much of an ordeal, Carmella. I plan to do a great deal of visiting away from Wildoak, looking up old cronies, seeing how they feel about this secession business, and so I won't be underfoot."

Harold's wife and daughters were waiting for us on the white-pillared porch when we drew up in front of the large, red-brick house. Miles handed me down and I ascended the half dozen steps conscious of being assessed by eyes that were not nearly as friendly as Harold's.

He said, "Beth Ann, this is Carmella, your sister-in-law."

A small woman with light hair and colorless lashes embraced me, giving me a chill peck on the cheek. "Welcome to Wild-oak," she said, her voice drawling politely.

"And these are my daughters," Harold said with proud propriety. "Deirdre." She gave me a curtsey, a lovely girl, just going into adolescence, with Miles's hazel eyes and her own luxuriant auburn hair.

"Elizabeth, my number-two girl." Elizabeth, about ten, favored her father, but had her mother's cool eyes.

"And the baby, Lorry."

"Papa—it's Lorena!" she exclaimed. "And I'm not a baby, I'm eight." Lorena was a replica of her mother, with fine hair and bleached lashes.

"And now—shall we go in?" Harold invited.

It did not take me long to discover that Beth Ann was a snob. At supper that night she began a long rambling story of a ball she had attended the week before, mentioning that the William Randalls had been present. The name meant nothing to me. The Randalls, I later learned, were elite members of Tidewater society, and though Beth Ann had made it sound as though she and the Randalls were bosom friends, she had actually never met them until the ball. Not only did she try to impress me with her notable hobnobbing, but she interrogated me as to who I knew in San Francisco. Had I met the Ralstons, the Randolphs, the Hunters?

"Only casually," I answered.

"I would think your father had joined their circle, being from Virginia and all."

"Papa was not much for socializing."

"Hmmm." She observed me for a few moments. "I never met your mother, of course."

Her condescending tone told me she knew all about Angelica O'Neil.

That night I went up to bed resentful and angry, determined to speak to Miles about his sister-in-law. But he did not come in until the small hours of the morning, when he slipped quietly through the door and put himself to sleep on the chaise longue.

The Fairchilds, neighbors of the Falconers, called the next day. I was upstairs, lying down with a splitting headache, a vinegar-soaked rag pressed to my brow, when I heard their carriage in the drive. One of the Negro maids was sent to fetch me.

"Please give my excuses, Delia," I instructed. "Say that I am terribley sorry, but I'm not well."

Five minutes later Beth Ann came up to see for herself. "Couldn't you manage it? For half an hour or so? They're here especially to meet you."

"Perhaps they can return some other time. I'm really sorry."

"I can't tell them that. They might think I'm putting them off. It wouldn't look right."

It wouldn't look right. It doesn't seem proper. What will people think? I was to hear those phrases over and over again. They were the principles that guided Beth Ann's life. Everything she did, what she wore, ate, said, the parties she gave, the friends she did or did not invite, was molded by the opinion of others—that is, others she considered her peers or her superiors.

"I suppose I shouldn't disappoint them," I said, struggling painfully to my feet. "I'll be down in ten minutes."

They were all there in the parlor, Miles too, talking to a man who I presumed was Mr. Fairchild.

"Ah! Here's the bride," Beth Ann exclaimed with false cheer. "Carmella—Prudence Fairchild."

Prudence gave me a limp hand. She was an attractive young woman in her mid-twenties, I judged, with golden curls, violet eyes, and a creamy skin.

"How do you do?" she said in a voice lacking any hint of cordiality.

I was introduced to Mr. Fairchild, a thin, sober-faced man much older than his wife. We sat and spoke of the weather until tea was brought in. While we sipped and nibbled at dainty sandwiches, I was conscious of Prudence's eyes. She was curious, of course, watching me covertly behind her polite smile and small talk. I had expected the curiosity as a matter of course, the interest natives have in an outsider, especially when that outsider has married one of their own. But there was something here beyond curiosity, a chill superiority that joined Beth Ann's snobbishness in cutting me down and placing me on a level beneath them.

But if Prudence watched me, I watched her too. I missed nothing, not a nuance of speech, a look, a movement. I caught the hidden barb when she asked me so sweetly if I minded being motherless. I saw her fluttering her lashes at Miles, smiling coquettishly whenever he chanced to address her. I knew she disliked me and I longed to call her and Beth Ann hypocrites. But it would only cause a furor and I saw no point in distressing Harold who had been so kind.

I had never been one to eavesdrop, not out of any moral delicacy, but because quite frankly I was rarely interested enough in other people's affairs to do so. The next morning, however, in passing the library on the way out to the verandah, I heard Beth Ann behind the half-open door speak my name and I paused to listen.

"Everyone knows about Carmella," Beth Ann was saying tearfully. "*Everyone,* Harold. They know about her mother, about that scandalous marriage to the Bridewell boy and how he was murdered. And to have her in my house . . . !"

"Beth, she is my brother's wife. You did not object too strongly, if I remember correctly, when I told you they were coming."

"But that was because I thought no one knew her background. I told people she was a Hastings. Good lord, how was I to foresee that someone would reveal the sordid truth?"

"Who would spread such gossip?"

"It certainly wasn't me. I'd be the last one. I don't know who. Lavinia, Mother Hastings?"

Papa's sister-in-law and mother. I had written the Hastings informing them of Papa's death but had never received a reply.

"You know," Beth Ann went on, "the old man refuses to meet his granddaughter."

"Ignore him."

"It's easy for you to say. You men seem to enjoy the idea of having a scarlet woman's daughter in your midst."

"Beth!"

My cheeks flamed. I wanted to go in and claw Beth Ann's face until she bled. Damn her!

"Well, that's what she is! And we won't be invited to Prudence Fairchild's social next week, the birthday party she gives every year for Hubert."

"Why, of course, we will. Carmella is a well brought up young lady with perfect manners. Prudence is just a little late asking us."

"We are not going to be invited," she insisted, her voice catching on a sob. "The invitations have already gone out. We shan't be received by anybody."

Serves you right! I wanted to shout.

Swallowing my wrath, I hurried to the door, making no attempt to soften the sound of my heels on the parquet floor. Let them hear. I didn't care. I went down the steps and around the corner of the house, walking blindly in the morning sunshine, seeing nothing but a blur of green. I turned and walked toward the road. I did not know where I was going. It didn't matter. I felt miserable, forlorn and alone.

I hated Wildoak. I was sorry I had come. I wanted to get as far away as I could. I wanted to go on walking and walking to nowhere, because nowhere was all I had. I wished I had a home. It didn't make sense to be married twice and not have a place I could call my own. If Derry . . . But there was no use in thinking of Derry. Not now.

The road became more rutted and I stumbled, twisting my ankle. But I went on walking, hobbling a little, concentrating on the throb in my foot because it took my mind off the ache in my heart.

Presently I saw a man on horseback approaching and I paused, shading my eyes against the sun.

"Carmella!"

It was Miles. He had gone out early that morning to visit a man downriver and now, apparently, was returning. For once I was glad to see him. He might call me stupid, a goose, a fool, a child, he might be spiteful and full of mockery, he might even have taken my money, but he had never thrown my mother or my unfortunate first marriage in my face.

"What brings you out on foot?" he asked, swinging down from the saddle.

"I—I thought I'd take a walk," I said in a voice that shook despite my effort to make it sound casual.

"Without your bonnet in this blazing sun?" He tilted my chin and I closed my eyes against his inquiring gaze.

"What is it, Carmella?" he asked, his tone oddly gentle.

"It's—it's . . ." And I could not go on. The tears welled and the next thing I knew I was sobbing against Miles's chest while he patted my shoulder and stroked my hair.

"Can't you tell me?"

I shook my head mutely and went on crying. It was more than Beth Ann that had sent me into a storm of weeping. It was everything: my father's death, Derry not being here in Virginia as I had hoped, my loneliness, having hateful strangers around me. Everything!

"Something someone said?" Miles prodded.

"Beth Ann—"

"What about Beth Ann?"

"She—she says she won't be received now that I'm at Wildoak."

"What of it? Here, here, wipe your eyes." He took a handkerchief from his pocket and pressed it into my hand. "Now, you can't really mean that my papier-mâché sister-in-law has gotten to you? My God, Carmella, what's happened to your spunk, your spirit, the vinegar that runs in your veins?"

"Don't laugh, Miles. It isn't funny."

"I find it very amusing. You running away from gossips when you were once ready to take on Sam Halstead."

"I'm not running away!"

"Certainly looks like it to me. C'mon, I'll give you a leg up."

"Miles . . ."

"Coward!"

I raised my fist, and with a short laugh he lifted me in his arms and swung me into the saddle.

I don't know what happened but the invitation from the Fairchilds, delivered by a small black boy, arrived the following morning. Perhaps it was delayed as Harold said, or perhaps Prudence had second thoughts, for in excluding us at Wildoak she would have had to do without Miles's company too.

Her infatuation with Miles was so obvious a blind man could have seen it. I wondered if she and Miles had been childhood sweethearts, affianced perhaps, the engagement broken off when Miles left Wildoak at the invitation of his father. But I did not want to ask Miles; I did not want him to think that it made one iota of difference to me whether they had once been in love with each other or even if they still were.

The Fairchilds' social, a festive outdoor barbecue attended by planters and their families from up and down the river, did little to convince me I was welcome to county society. The women were either coldly polite or ignored me altogether; the men, with a few exceptions, eyed me with veiled or open prurient curiosity. I could not have felt more exposed if I had stepped from the Falconer buggy stark naked. Miles, of course, noticed nothing. He disappeared with a group of his contemporaries into the library the moment we arrived, I suppose to discuss the burning issues of the day.

Only one person showed a friendly interest in me. Ruth Harkness, an older woman with expressive gray eyes and salt and pepper hair drawn neatly under a chignon, had the graciousness and genuine courtesy of a true aristocrat. We had a lengthy conversation. She complimented me on my dress, lamenting the fact that the Pamunkey River fashions were behind the rest of the world.

"We're rural, you know," she said. "We've only just begun to hear of crinolines."

She asked me about the theater, opera, and concerts in San Francisco, knowledgeable questions which I was happy I could answer. But our conversation was cut short by Beth Ann, who claimed Mrs. Harkness was wanted by her husband. Before she left, however, she promised to call on me at Wildoak, a visit, I assured her, I looked forward to.

On the way home Miles asked me if I had enjoyed myself. I was on the point of spilling out my chagrin, of telling him how I had been snubbed, of how Ruth Harkness had been the only person who had deigned to be kind, when I thought better of it. He would simply be amused, passing my complaints off with some glib remark. I certainly wasn't going to make a habit of dissolving into tears whenever one of those haughty bitches insulted me.

"I found the food excellent," I replied, "but the company tedious."

On the nights Miles spent at Wildoak he sometimes slept on the chaise longue, sometimes in the bed with me. It was the sort of bed that could accommodate two people who were strangers, wide and long and large enough for a platoon, with downy pillows and a feather mattress that one sank into with a sigh. Miles always seemed to drop off the moment his head touched the pillow, but on the night of the Fairchild party he lay smoking a pipe, his teeth clenching and unclenching on it with a clicking sound.

"Can't sleep?" I asked after an hour or so of this, for I was a light sleeper and he kept waking me each time I dozed off.

"Am I disturbing you? Sorry."

"Secession still on your mind?" I asked after a pause.

"As a matter of fact, yes."

"Are you thinking that Virginia might leave the Union?"

"It's a possibility. Ever since John Brown's raid on Harper's Ferry, there's been a growing hatred for Yankee abolitionists. And those in our own state who are against slavery are beginning to be called traitors. The rhetoric on either side is getting more and more heated." He sighed and tapped his pipe into a dish on the side table. "God knows what the Yankees are fomenting in Washington, or what Jefferson Davis and his cohorts are devising in Montgomery. I shall hope for the best but be prepared for the worst."

"If there's a war, will you go?"

"I believe so." He turned to me in the dark. "I've not much to lose. Except my life. Tell me, would you be sorry?"

He had caught me off guard. Of course if he died I would be free again, and if Derry—

"It would save you the bother of a divorce," he said, as though reading my mind.

"I'm not that heartless, Miles."

"Oh?" He reached out and drew me across the bed sheets into his arms. "Show me."

"Miles, if . . ." I turned my head away, but he cupped the back of my skull in his hand and brought my chin around. His face was in shadow. I could see the whites of his eyes.

"Show me," he repeated in a whisper. His lips brushed mine.

"Please, Miles, I don't want to."

"Still thinking of Derry?" He let go of me. "I notice you aren't wearing his ring around your neck."

"I don't want to risk you grabbing it again. I have it tucked away in a safe place."

"Between the scented pages of his love letters, no doubt."

"Well, what of it?" I said irritably, partly because Derry's letters were hardly what one would call impassioned. "You have your women. Oh, don't think I haven't guessed. I can't imagine a man like you living a monk's life. You and Dolly in San Francisco, and perhaps you and Prudence have arranged something between you here. It would be easy enough."

I thought he smiled in the dark. It felt like it.

"Jealous?" he asked.

"I couldn't care less."

"Liar!" he accused. "You don't want me, but then you can't stand the idea of another woman having me either. Isn't that it?"

"If you are going to call me a liar there's no point to this conversation." I sat up and, reaching for my dressing gown, got out of bed.

"Running off?" he mocked.

"I'm not running. I'm going downstairs where I don't have to listen to you."

I threw the dressing down loosely across my shoulders and started for the door.

Quick as a cat he leaped out of bed and grabbed me, wheeling me around.

"You like it when I make love to you," he said angrily, a lock of dark hair falling over his forehead. "*Admit it!* You get just as much lewd, lustful enjoyment out of it as I do."

It was a gibe that hurt because it was true.

"Leave me be! You—you coarse, vile—"

He jerked me into his arms, crushing me to his chest, his lips claiming my half-open, protesting mouth in a kiss that went on until I felt the struggle drain from my body. Then as suddenly as he had embraced me, he let me go.

"You have no right," I gasped, touching my bruised mouth. "You have no right to treat me this way."

"Haven't I?" he asked, the muscles on his throat working as he tried to control his quickened breath.

"No."

He turned and walked to the mantel. My robe had fallen and I stooped to pick it up.

"Go on, run along," he dismissed, his back to me. "I've decided it isn't worth the effort."

"Good—I feel the same. I'd sooner bed with a gorilla."

"Thanks for the compliment." A match flared as he touched it to a candle and his shadow sprang to life on the far wall, the broad-shouldered torso looming in the dancing firefly light.

"Perhaps it would be best," he said, turning to me, "if we didn't keep up this husband and wife mockery in front of the others. There's no point to it."

He meant separate rooms. And though he was right—we did not get along—I was reluctant to agree. I could well imagine Beth Ann's eyes popping at the request, since, to her, it would be a confession of failure—mine. I would be to blame for having failed to please my husband, for being derelict in my role as dutiful wife. Another sign of poor breeding, she would tell Harold.

"I suppose you are right," I said, too proud to voice my true feelings. "But tell me, Miles, why you've continued to put up with the mockery, as you call it, at all."

"Your father—"

"My father is dead, Miles. Is there something else?" I was fishing. Why? Feminine vanity, perhaps.

He looked at me for a long moment before answering. "What could there be?" He paused. "I don't know. You remind me— but then you don't want to hear about that."

"Yes, yes, I do!" I replied, alert, curious. "I remind you of someone, a sweetheart, a mistress?"

"Never mind."

But I couldn't let it go. "Tell me, do I resemble her? The same hair, eyes? Did you want to marry her? Perhaps you did. Did you love her, take her to bed?"

"Hush!"

I had sunk a knife into his vitals and it gave me an odd, triumphant thrill. "Who was she, Miles?"

"It was long ago. She's dead—so what does it matter?"

A terrible suspicion, like a noxious weed, sprouted suddenly in my mind.

"Miles," I whispered, "was it my mother?"

A bitter smile twisted his lips. "Whatever gave you such a crazy idea?"

"Well, whoever it was, you loved her," I said. "Was it that courtesan in San Francisco? I wonder—"

"I don't give a damn what you wonder!" he flared. "Why are you persisting in this inane interrogation? Jealous?"

"Of course not!"

He gave a short, humorless laugh. "You never were a convincing actress, Carmella."

He moved away from the mantel.

"I'm not acting. It's the truth." I did not like the look that had suddenly come over his face.

"And I suppose I'm to believe that." He moved closer, his lustrous narrowed eyes flicking over my breasts.

Stepping back, I covered them with the dressing gown, clutching it to my chest like a shield.

"Miles . . ."

He kept coming closer, slowly, his shadow following him. I thought of the door behind me but couldn't bring myself to turn and make for it. Instead I continued to retreat, as though I were wading through water, until I felt the wainscotting against my spine.

He stood over me, his hands braced against the wall, looking down at me in a way that made my knees go weak.

"Miles—you wanted . . ."

He brushed my lips lightly with his mouth, then bending down kissed my breast, his hot breath searing me through the gown.

" . . . separate rooms."

His hands came down on my shoulders, a heavy weight that pinned me to the wall. He exuded an air of sexual masculinity that hypnotized and trapped me. The robe fell from my limp grasp.

"You are my Delilah," he murmured, his mouth hovering over mine. He kissed me, pressing his ridged manhood against my thighs, sending a violent bittersweet pain through my loins.

"Please...!"

His hands dropped, lifting my gown, slithering it above my hips. Before I could guess what he was about, he stooped and, lifting me slightly, entered me.

"Miles!" I exclaimed, my voice muffled against his hard shoulder.

"No...!" These things were done in bed, not here, not like this, not against... Oh, God!

But I couldn't question or think. He was possessing me with savage, relentless fury, a wildness that found me responding, and at the last mad plunge raising my legs, twining them about his shuddering hips.

When he let me go, I retrieved my dressing gown and fled without looking at him, my cheeks scarlet with shame.

Miles left the next day for Richmond and I did not see him for two weeks. Beth Ann went out on several occasions in the afternoons, but did not ask me to join her.

"Calls," she said; "routine visits that would only bore you."

But I knew she had been asked not to bring me.

It was on one of those afternoons that Miles returned. I was sitting alone on the verandah, fanning myself, trying in a desultory way to read a book.

He threw his reins to a small Negro boy, then mounted the stairs. "Hello, Carmella." For a moment I thought he was going to stoop to kiss me, but he merely stuffed his hands in his pockets and looked down at me. "Seems awfully quiet. Where is everybody?"

"Harold's down at the stable; the girls, I believe, are upstairs napping. And Beth Ann is out."

"Out?" He lifted a brow.

"Making calls, I presume. At least that's what she says."

"And why, pray tell, aren't you with her?"

"She says I would only be bored."

His face darkened. "How long has this been going on? Well, answer me!"

"This? By 'this' do you mean the snubs? Miles, I've told you about them before. But it only seemed to amuse you."

"It doesn't amuse me any longer. I might not give two pins for you at the county fair, but as long as you bear my name,

those bitches will receive you if I have to ram my fist down
every one of their lily-white throats."

"Miles, I don't want people to accept my company because
it's forced upon them."

"My dear, Carmella, what you want isn't the issue here.
It's what *I* want."

I never knew what Miles said to Beth Ann, but the next
time she went on her round of visits, she asked, then tearfully
begged, me to accompany her. "For the sake of peace in the
family," was the way she put it.

I went. I was received. Politely but without warmth.

CHAPTER

TWENTY-TWO

THE WAR that Miles had so long dreaded erupted on April 12, 1861, with a shot fired on Fort Sumter. To the last moment, Virginia's governor tried to prevent secession but when President Lincoln issued a call for 75,000 volunteers to bring the rebelling Southern states back into the Union, Virginia, unwilling to fight her neighbors, withdrew.

Miles was one of the first to volunteer. Feeling that a show of force by the South at the very beginning would discourage the North from launching a full-scale attack, he and a group of Pamunkey planters offered their services to Colonel Robert E. Lee, a former West Pointer who had come home to defend his native state. Lee was pessimistic about the length of hostilities. It was said he contemplated a long war.

But we, like everyone else, felt it would be over in several weeks, a month, perhaps two at the very most. And in the meanwhile the women busied themselves making up kits for their men, providing the small necessities that would lessen the harsh rigors of campaigning.

Since Wildoak was fairly central, the ladies brought their sewing machines, scissors, and needles to the house. Beth Ann cleared the large table in the dining room and there we cut, assembled, and stitched from morning until late afternoon in an atmosphere of gossipy excitement. One would have thought we were preparing our men for a costume ball rather than for battle. Beth Ann was in her glory: her house, she in charge. Silver urns of tea, Sevres china cups and saucers, and cut-glass serving plates holding frosted cakes stood by on a scrolled pedestal table for those of us who needed sustenance during our labors. My past was brushed aside, and for all intents and purposes I was taken into the circle. But I had the feeling that if I were to leave the room for a few minutes, heads would bend together and conversation, suddenly hushed and confidential, would turn to the subject of my past.

In this time of zeal for the Cause when old grudges were ostensibly forgotten, the Hastingses relented, paying a visit to Wildoak, and for the first time I met my father's people. My grandfather was a very old man. I was surprised at his feebleness, at the palsied, liver-spotted hands that reluctantly took mine in a limp handshake. He was very formal. He said, "How'd you do, Mrs. Falconer?" and spoke a few words; what they were I cannot remember, but I do recall that he never once acknowledged I was his son's daughter. He did not speak of Papa, did not ask about his death, nor pose a single question about his life since leaving home so many years earlier. Grandfather's wife—referred to as Mother—was ten years younger than he, a pale shadow who looked to her husband for approval before uttering the simplest banality.

His daughter-in-law, Lavinia, confided to me that, "Father hasn't been the same since he lost his youngest son (there had been three, Papa the oldest) to fever last summer."

I couldn't imagine what Grandfather had been like before the tragedy, but I doubted he had changed much. His willingness to come to Wildoak may have been a sign of his unbending, but to me—despite the tremors and rheumy eyes—he appeared to be the epitome of a cold, narrow-minded autocrat.

My uncle, James Hastings, Lavinia's husband, bore a faint resemblance to Papa, but one had to look for it. He had the florid complexion of a drinker, and indeed when he spoke to me I caught a whiff of spirits. During his visit—they stayed two days—I never saw him without a whiskey glass in his hand. Grandfather was too old to go to war, though he claimed he was ready, sword in hand, to kill every one of "them scurvy Yankees," but James informed us he would be joining Jeb

Stuart's cavalry, taking with him three thoroughbred mounts and his Negro valet.

It was strange to discover I had cousins, twin boys, who were away attending Washington Academy. According to Uncle James, they were clamoring to get out and enlist in Colonel Magruder's company.

"I've told them they could," Uncle James said.

The old man grumbled, "It's about time. How will they ever grow up to be men, if you keep them in school?"

In May the Confederate capital was moved to Richmond and our local troop of fighting men went off to become part of what later came to be known as the Army of Northern Virginia. I said good-bye to Miles with mixed feelings.

He had made love to me the night before, and unlike so many episodes of our lovemaking it had not been initiated in anger. When Miles took me in his arms I gave my body up to his kisses, his embrace, the sensuous mastery of hands that could evoke a thousand delights, while my mind and heart remained aloof. I'm sure Miles knew where my thoughts were, but he said nothing, not wanting to spend our last night in a quarrel. As it was, an exchange concerning my jewels raised my hackles.

"I'd nearly forgotten," he said. "Deirdre's birthday is coming up soon."

"Oh? I doubt I'll be able to get to the shops in Richmond. Perhaps I'll give her my pearl earbobs." I had brought only a portion of my trinkets, leaving the more expensive ones, like the diamond tiara, in a San Francisco vault.

"I think she'd like that," Miles said. "Speaking of jewels—when I checked the inventory before we left, your emeralds were missing."

"They should be," I said without a pause. "I sold them. I felt it would make up for the loss of my father's money."

"Indeed? You don't seem to have suffered from it." He stifled a yawn.

"I don't see how—"

"Let's leave it for now, Carmella. It doesn't do any good mourning over such matters." He yawned again. Then turning over on his side, he fell promptly asleep.

In the morning, as the family stood about tendering their good-byes, I kissed Miles with a proper show of wifely affection. I was relieved to see him go. I don't think I could have held my tongue for much longer. The nonchalant way he had dismissed the fact that I knew of his petty embezzlement was arrogance at its worst. I was not cruel enough to hope he'd meet a Yankee bullet, but I wished with all my heart it was Derry instead of Miles who would be coming home from the war to me.

We at Wildoak settled down to a fairly regular routine. Nothing much seemed to happen in those first months, as if to reaffirm our belief that it was to be a short—and possibly, we hoped—bloodless war. Then in May of 1862 we received word that New Orleans had fallen to Union forces and that General Butler was occupying the city. The news stunned me. Yankee bluejackets on Bourbon Street? I could hardly believe it. The ladies said what a pity, but their snide little remarks conveyed their belief that only a city of ne'er-do-wells and cowards could have gone under so quickly.

In July they forgot New Orleans altogether when we won the first battle at Manassas (or Bull Run, as some called it). The announcement brought wild jubilation, cheers and applause echoing up and down the river. "We've got the Yankees on the run!" Harold chortled. He gave a ball to which everyone in the county was invited, including those yeoman farmers who had sent sons or husbands to the war. The inclusion of the "peasantry," as Beth Ann termed them, annoyed her. But Harold brushed her objections aside and they came, a little shy, their hair damp from washings in the rain barrel, scraping their Sunday boots at the door.

Harold served champagne and whiskey with a lavish hand, nearly depleting the stock in his cellar, ordered a beef killed, chicken, turkeys, and ducks roasted, a pig slaughtered and barbecued. The planters' wives appeared in a swirl of bright crinolined gowns, their absent husbands supplemented by officers invited from Gaines Mill some nine miles away and by a band of visiting Zouaves in their tight-fitting red jackets.

I had just turned away from a young, tawny-haired cavalry officer who had asked me to "take a stroll on the verandah," when I heard a bustle at the door, a few giggles, and a high-pitched squeal.

"Oh, Derry! If you aren't the one!"

For a moment I couldn't move. Then I began to thread my way across the room, bumping into people, murmuring, "Pardon—pardon . . ." ignoring their stares. The distance from the punch bowl to the door seemed endless, a thousand miles strewn with obstacles. And I couldn't even see him! I gathered my hoops, pushing through a knot of ruddy-faced farmers who suddenly parted, and there he was, standing in the doorway speaking to Beth Ann.

I did not think my trembling knees could take me a step farther. He was in officer's uniform, gray coat with buff-colored collar and cuffs, his light blue trousered legs booted and spurred. He had grown a moustache, which made him look older, distinguished, even handsomer than I remembered.

He must have sensed my rapt gaze for he turned, and when our eyes met a slow smile spread across his face.

"Mrs. Falconer!"

The sound of his voice sent shivers up my spine. Only the weakness of my knees kept me from running to him, falling into his arms, making a spectacle of myself (and of Derry too). Thank God one of us had the presence of mind to behave as though we were old friends and nothing more.

"Mrs. Falconer—how nice to see you again." He came forward and took my hand, bending over it, kissing it lightly, his lips caressing my skin in the old thrilling way.

"And you," I muttered, conscious of Beth Ann's boiled blue eyes on me.

"It has been quite a while," Derry said. "Virginia City—or was it San Francisco?"

I couldn't breathe for the pounding of my heart and the constriction in my lungs. And yet I had to say something.

"You've come back then to join the Virginia Army?"

"I couldn't stay away," he said, a double meaning dancing in his eyes. "I have been attached to Jefferson Davis's personal service in Richmond, a sort of aide-de-camp, you might say. And I thought I'd run home for a short visit. When I heard of Harold's party—"

Beth Ann put a hand on his arm. "Mr. Wakefield, do come

and have some punch. Whiskey perhaps?"

"In a moment, thank you."

When Beth Ann moved on, Derry turned to me. "Darling! But you're a sight for my sore eyes." He reached out and squeezed my hand.

"Oh, Derry . . . I . . . !" It was all I could manage.

"Shall we dance?"

It was a waltz. The instant Derry put his arm about my waist the half dozen fiddles that had squeaked and missed tempo all evening became a thousand singing violins. Round and round and round we glided, the crystal chandelier a prismed galaxy of light, the faces, the brightly colored gowns, the uniforms, the paneled walls revolving on a wheel of joy.

"What happened to the Cat's Eye Mine?" I asked, as if it mattered, as if anything mattered except that I was in Derry's arms.

"It's still there." He laughed. "I doubt anyone will steal it. After we flushed out that first vein, we found very little gold. But I got enough to buy my uniform and a good horse."

He drew me closer, lowering his voice, so that his warm breath was in my ear. "Carmella, is it possible for us to be alone? There's so much I have to tell you."

"I'll try, love. I might get away for a few minutes."

"Not a few minutes, darling. Hours, a whole night would be too short. It's been such a long time. Perhaps when everyone is gone we could meet away from the house—out-of-doors."

"Everyone won't be gone, Derry. This party will last until dawn."

"But after midnight the diehards usually become whoozy with drink and fatigue. No one will notice if you slip out."

An officer from Gaines Mill was singing "Jeannie with the Light Brown Hair," giving that lovely romantic ballad the benefit of a heart-catching lyrical tenor. Through the opened door and windows came the heady scent of jasmine. How could I say no? Yet . . .

"You haven't stopped loving me?" Derry asked in a low voice.

"Never. I've never stopped loving you."

"When I got back to San Francisco I heard that you had left

with Miles. I must say it surprised me. I thought you wanted an annulment. You and Miles haven't—"

"Oh, no!" I lied, quickly banishing a flashing picture of Miles's naked torso.

"Come, my dear, do you expect me to believe that? A beautiful, passionate woman like you—and Miles no saint."

"But I don't love him."

"Then why didn't you leave him?"

I could feel his displeasure by the way his arm tightened around my waist.

"I was waiting for you, Derry. I thought—if I came to Virginia—oh, please, darling! I swear there has never been anyone in my heart but you."

His eyes searched my face. "You've been my lodestar, Carmella. If I thought—"

"You have no reason to."

"Then you'll come? Say about three o'clock? In the wood a half mile down the road."

The music ended and I moved away, unfolding my fan, fluttering it at my heated face. He was watching me, his blue eyes urgent.

"Yes, Derry," I murmured.

Around two o'clock most of the ladies who were staying the night had gone up to bed and the families who resided nearby had already departed. I was sharing my room that night with Prudence Fairchild who, to my dismay, was a little drunk and as talkative as a chattering bluejay.

"I see Derry Wakefield's back. You knew him in San Francisco, didn't you? Beth Ann said you had. He left here under a cloud, I tell you, in disgrace. Did you know? My dear, he got his mother's personal maid pregnant—could you believe, a Negro slave! Of course I know it's done all the time, but his mother's maid—I think you have to draw the line somewhere, don't you? Not only that but they say he—"

"Prue, dear, I am dreadfully tired." I stifled a loud yawn. I didn't believe a word she said. She was a horrible gossip. "Shall we get some rest?"

". . . and did you notice how Alice Dinwiddie carried on with every man who asked her to dance? With Chester gone, it's scandalous. I wouldn't be at all surprised if she made an assignation for tonight." She looked at me knowingly.

"I doubt it. Some women enjoy flirting, but when it comes to risking their marriages, that's a different story," I said lightly, meeting her eyes without flinching. "She does have those four boys and a girl."

"She misses Chester—no doubt of that. She misses him so much she wouldn't mind someone consoling her for his absence. If you get my meaning."

"Really, Prue, I don't think you are being fair." Oh, what an insufferable, hypocritical bitch! If Miles had asked her to go to bed, she'd have risked Heaven and earth to make it possible.

"I think we owe it to our husbands to be faithful," she asserted sanctimoniously. "I must say . . ."

Her voice went on and on. I turned over on my side and closed my eyes.

I hadn't meant to fall asleep, and when I awoke a stab of guilt ran through me. I struck a match and looked at the clock. Twenty past four! Already the sky was beginning to pale. I got into a riding skirt, blouse, and boots, quickly, silently, casting furtive glances at Prue asleep on the far side of the bed. A faint whistling snore came from her half-opened mouth.

I let myself out and tiptoed down the stairs. Swiftly, like a thief's shadow, I moved across the hall to the door and out into the warm predawn light.

I ran all the way, stumbling over rabbit warrens, the dewy grasses snatching at my skirts. But when I reached the wood, breathless and anxious, he wasn't there. He must have left, thinking I had changed my mind. My disappointment was so keen I wanted to weep.

Derry stopped in for a brief call later that day. A few of the guests, including Prudence Fairchild, were still with us and it was impossible to talk to Derry alone. However, we were able to exchange several hurried words on the verandah as he got ready to leave.

"I'm sorry . . . ," Derry began.

"It's all right. It wasn't your fault. I overslept, I'm ashamed to say."

"Overslept?" He looked surprised.

"I know it's a poor excuse. I—I couldn't help it. Wait—here's Alice."

Alice Dinwiddie, a tiny brunette with wide, black-fringed eyes, came up to us, smiling coyly at Derry. "What are you two conspiring about?"

"Conspiring?" Derry dimpled at her. "Hardly. I was just telling Mrs. Falconer that I must return to Richmond tomorrow morning."

"Tomorrow!" I exclaimed.

Why hadn't he told me sooner? He couldn't leave without our having had the opportunity to be alone. Last night lost and now . . . I felt as though I had been run through by his cavalry sword.

"Perhaps you can have supper with us this evening, Mr. Wakefield," I suggested hopefully.

"I should like nothing better, but I promised my family I would spend the evening with them. Thank you, nevertheless."

"Then we won't see you for a while?" I asked, ignoring Alice Dinwiddie's sudden show of interest.

"I might be able to manage a furlough in a few months, but I cannot bank on it."

I searched his face for some sign that his talk of imminent departure was only for Alice Dinwiddie's benefit. But there was nothing except his charming smile.

I couldn't let him leave not knowing when or if I'd see him again. There was a terrible war out there. If he were killed, I couldn't bear it! Seeing him again had revived all the yearning in my heart.

"Good-bye," he said, taking Alice Dinwiddie's hand, then mine.

"Write, won't you?" Alice Dinwiddie said.

But I couldn't utter a word.

I watched as he ran down the steps, took the reins from the Negro boy, and swung himself into the saddle. Something seemed to break apart in me: I didn't care that I was Mrs. Falconer, married to Miles; I didn't care about reputation, about gossip, about scandal, about what people would say. All that paled before the stark reality of Derry's departure. I was down the stairs before I realized it, running toward him.

"Derry!" He wheeled his horse about, a startled look on his face. "Derry, darling—I love you, I can't let you go! I can't live without you! I'll do anything. Take me to Richmond. I swear..." Shaking with emotion, I grabbed hold of his leg.

"Hush!" he ordered. "Everyone is looking. I can't abscond with a fellow officer's wife. President Davis... Why I'd be drummed out of the army. Please, Carmella, control yourself."

My hands dropped to my sides.

"That's better. Now, go back, compose yourself. Say that you—you ran out here to remind me to send word concerning your husband."

"But when can I see you again?"

"We are fighting a war, Carmella."

"I *hate* the war. I hate the Yankees for bringing it on us. I wish I could kill every one of them myself."

"So do we all. Good-bye, darling. I love you."

I stood in the driveway, hands clasped tightly together, as he galloped away, the echo of his "I love you" still in my ears. It should have lightened the desolation in my heart, but it didn't.

Harold left in October. Several of the other men who had stayed behind for the harvest and curing, as Harold had done, went with him, all of them still feeling that war's end was only a matter of time. Beth Ann took her husband's departure fairly well. The running of the plantation had been left in the hands of their overseer, Tom Morgan, a capable man, quiet, industrious, courteous. He had no wife, but lived alone in a small white cottage just beyond the rose garden. We at the house had very little to do with him. He was not of the planter class, and Harold's dealings with him had been solely on a business level. Morgan had never been invited to any of our social functions, not even for a Sunday supper, until the Bull Run ball. Perhaps it was this snub, coupled with the fact that he was only a second-generation Southerner, that made him unsympathetic to our cause.

We, however, had no knowledge of his feelings, no inkling of his resentment. One morning he failed to appear at the well on the back lot, the place where he gave the Negroes their daily instructions. Joseph, one of the older slaves, went to Morgan's house. When no one answered his knock, he stepped inside. No sign of Mr. Morgan, Joseph told us, but everything had been left as neat as a pin: the bed made, the dishes washed and set on their shelves. A note had been propped against a vinegar cruet on the round kitchen table, and Joseph brought it to Beth Ann.

She read it aloud:

"Dear Mrs. Falconer: I'm leaving. I don't give a hoot for the slaves, they can stay in bondage till judgment day for all I care, but I'm off to join the Rebs. You are all so bloody sure of yourselves, so high and mighty, can't see the handwriting on the wall. Well, I'm going to be the one to show you. Tom Morgan."

Beth Ann turned white as the paper fluttered from her fingers to the floor. "I never...," she whispered, aghast. "Well, I never!"

"Sit down," I said, pushing a chair under her knees. "I'll get you some brandy."

I ran to the sideboard, splashed some liquor into a glass, and brought it to her. She drank it with closed eyes, and a little color came back into her cheeks.

"What are we to do?" She looked at me, then at the children who stood watching her with trepidation.

"I don't expect the world's going to fall apart simply because Tom Morgan saw fit to desert us," I said.

"It's easy for you to talk. You don't know anything about the working of a plantation. It will go to rack and ruin without an overseer."

"Why? Joseph here, I'll wager, can see to the plowing or whatever. Am I right, Joseph?"

He grinned and shuffled his feet. "Dass right, Miss."

"But you don't understand," Beth Ann exclaimed impatiently. "We can't trust the darkies to work unless they have a white man to tell them what to do. They're a lazy lot."

I knew nothing of plantation darkies. My experience had been limited to house servants like our own Cecilie in New Orleans who had worked very hard and loyally indeed. It seemed to me, however, that the Wildoak slaves must have shown some industriousness, for they had done quite well by the Falconers over the years. The house, the lavish meals, Harold's fine horses attested to that.

"I doubt we'll be able to replace Morgan," I said. "Perhaps the Fairchilds or the Harknesses can lend us their overseer."

Beth Ann and I knew so little of how our neighbors managed their holdings that until we asked we did not realize that the Harknesses had never even had an overseer. Their plantation was comparatively small and Alex Harkness rode his own fields. Prudence Fairchild could not spare her man because, aside from the fact that he had much to do, he was suffering from a recurrent bout of fever.

It had to be Joseph then. But he had been under someone else's authority all his life and now it was difficult for him to make decisions on his own. He would come up to the house at least three times a day. Should he plow the right field or let it lie fallow? What about seed? What did we want him to do with the bushels of tomatoes rotting in the shed? Should he let the mules graze in the meadow with the cows?

These inquiries flustered Beth Ann. She swore she didn't know, had a headache, felt ill, would I please handle Joseph? It didn't do a bit of good to argue that I had lived nearly all my life in a city and the only tomatoes I was acquainted with were those on my dinner plate.

"Do your best, dear," Beth said as she fled upstairs, leaving me with Joseph.

I'm sure I made many errors, but at least I tried. Often I would compile a list of Joseph's inquiries and, taking the sulky, trot down to the Harknesses and consult with Ruth and Alex. I learned much from them, but more, they gave me the encouragement I so sorely needed.

"You're doing fine," they would say. "Just fine."

In November we received a letter from Miles, written at Leesburg according to the heading. It had been addressed to all of us, including Harold. Apparently Miles had not received my letter informing him that Harold had joined his regiment. He wrote in part:

The Confederacy has just won a decisive battle at Ball's Bluff, repelling a Federal advance. The Virginians, assisted by troops from Mississippi, have aquitted themselves splendidly in view of the Union's superiority. . . . But a Virginian has the advan-

tage of upbringing. We've had hunting rifles in our hands since
we could walk and rarely miss a target. Now we are hunting
men with the same zeal. But to me it is like shooting fish in
a barrel. Many of the Rebs are very young and never have been
under fire before. It is hard for me, looking at their white,
fearful faces, to think of them as a threat to anyone, let alone
Wildoak. . . .

"That's treasonous!" Beth Ann cried. "The Yankees not a
threat! Why, saying that is the same as giving aid and comfort
to the enemy."

"If he were really a traitor," I said wearily, "he wouldn't
be fighting at Leesburg."

It seemed odd for me to take up for Miles. But more and
more, Beth Ann got on my nerves. She complained constantly—the meals were ill cooked, the housemaid neglected
the cobwebbed corners, the butler was always gone when she
wanted him—nothing was done right. And yet it was I who
had to reprimand the servants, I who had to face them once a
day with Beth Ann's carping orders. She seemed incapable of
doing anything but getting up in the morning, dressing, and
sitting by the window with a half-knitted sweater in her lap.
It was not that she missed Harold all that much, but she needed
his presence, needed him to run the plantation and, I suspect,
the house too, needed him to lean on, to be there. And without
him she could not cope.

The situation worsened. One morning we awoke to find that
all the slaves had run off, except one elderly mammy and her
small granddaughter—all the house servants, the field slaves,
Joseph too.

Beth Ann went to pieces. Until I could get enough paregoric
in her to quiet her down she gave me more of a scare than the
news of the runaway help. I had never seen anyone carry on
with hysterics like that, laughing and crying and shrieking. The
two younger girls were terrified too. Deirdre helped me calm
them, while at the same time I administered to their mother,
a juggling feat that left my nerves raw.

I spent the night with Beth Ann and when she awoke in the
morning, drugged and dazed, asking for water, I was there to

give it to her. She came out of her fog long enough to grasp
my arm, digging her nails into the flesh.

"Carmella—you won't leave, will you? Promise, cross your
heart, promise to God that you won't."

"I'm not leaving. And it's foolish of you to get so upset."

"I'm frightened," she said, the whites of her eyes rolling
upward. "The darkies might be planning to murder us all in
our beds."

"Piffle!" I replied staunchly. "The darkies have run off because the Yankees are offering them the Promised Land, all
they can eat, and nothing to do. I'll bet my best gown on it."

"Oh, Carmella, I hope you're right. You're so brave." It
was the first compliment Beth Ann had ever paid me, and she
offered it only because she was scared silly. "I don't know
what I would do without you. Nothing ever seems to frighten
you."

But I *was* afraid—afraid of the house suddenly gone silent,
the quiet that lay over the lawns, the fields, the smokeless
cabins; afraid of the Yankees out there, only God knew where;
afraid of the responsibility Beth Ann had suddenly placed on
my shoulders, a burden I had no wish to carry.

CHAPTER

TWENTY-THREE

EARLY IN December, when the Army of Northern Virginia went into winter quarters, Miles and Harold came home on furlough.

Miles was strangely silent. He had grown a beard, which gave him a dark, fierce appearance. Crow's-feet creased the corners of his hazel eyes, narrowing them in a keen, alert gaze. But at odd moments of repose they became shadowed and haunted. He sat without speaking all through supper, answering questions put to him with a word or two, sometimes simply with a grunt.

Harold regaled us with amusing anecdotes of camp life, describing the scanty food poorly cooked by a darky chef who had never held a saucepan in his hands. But as the hour grew late and Harold's wineglass was refilled for the fourth or fifth time, he lost his inclination to make light of the situation.

"The Union ships have bottled us up!" he declared, his face flushed, his speech heavy. "Blockade's tight as a drum. Damn! Excuse me, ladies, but it angers me. If only England or France could get through to us. They're clamoring for our cotton and we need their guns."

"But, darling," Beth Ann, restored to her former self by Harold's presence, reminded, "you said the war would be over soon."

"Well, it won't be, I'm sorry to say. It may take years. What do you think, Miles?"

"I think we were damn fools ever to get mixed up in it." He lumbered up from the table and stamped out toward the parlor.

"What a dreadful thing to say!" Beth Ann exclaimed in outrage. "He's lost what little manners he had. And such—such blasphemy!" Beth Ann's patriotism had returned too.

A half hour later we joined Miles, who sat brooding over a brandy in the parlor. It was after twelve and I dreaded the thought of going up to bed. I did not know what to expect of this withdrawn, noncommittal Miles who looked as though he were still behind the lines, a rifle raised to his shoulder. Would he want to make love to me? Would he be angry if I refused? Would it be right to refuse a soldier, one's husband fighting the enemy? All these questions tumbled about in my mind as I watched him from beneath lowered lashes.

The dreaded moment drew closer when Beth Ann and Harold said good night, leaving Miles and me alone. We sat mute, an awkward silence stretching between us. I searched my mind for a polite question to put to him. But what? I already, more or less, knew how he was and that the war was a touchy subject with him. The clock on the mantel ticked loudly away as the wordless minutes passed. I was getting ready to make a comment on the weather as a last resort, when Miles spoke:

"I must say you look well despite the hardships Beth Ann has been describing to us. Very well."

"Thank you." I shifted my eyes from the sudden blaze in his.

There was another long pause. I was wondering if we would sit there all night, he watching me like a cat at a mouse hole, I tense and waiting, when he suddenly asked:

"Shall we retire, Mrs. Falconer?"

I rose. He lit a candle and doused the lamps. Making a low bow, he indicated I was to go on ahead.

The candle flame threw our gaunt and towering shadows on the wall as we mounted the staircase. My heart was beating far faster than the climb of a single flight warranted.

When we reached the door to our bedroom, Miles stepped

in front of me and opened it. I went past him without looking into his face. Chill air greeted us, and I hugged my arms for warmth. Miles moved to the mantel, touching the candles there with the lighted one in his hand. Next he bent and lit the heaped kindling on the hearth. Little tongues of orange licked and sputtered, then burst into flame.

Miles turned and stood in the flickering light, looking around for a few moments.

"There's nothing like flounced white curtains, the sight of a large, comfortable bed, and a pretty female to take the sour taste of war out of a man's mouth."

"Miles . . ."

"But you wouldn't know. How could you? Oh, I daresay it hasn't been easy here, but not being easy is a long way from Hell."

I didn't know what to say.

"Do I sound bitter?" he queried. "I don't mean to, and I certainly have no intention of evoking the slightest bit of pity. Pity is so close to contempt, and that is not what I am looking for tonight."

"Miles . . ."

He reached back and, picking up the candlestick, came closer to have a better look at my face.

"Do I detect a note of reluctance in your voice?" His tone was light, amused, but his eyes glinting with reflected candle-light burned with a fierceness that filled me with cold apprehension.

"I am tired," I murmured, lowering my eyes. "I thought perhaps . . ."

"Perhaps what? That I should sleep elsewhere? Find another bedmate? Look at me. *Look at me!*"

I raised my head.

"Could it be that Derry and you have come together some-how?" he asked. "I've heard he stopped at Wildoak on leave from his sinecure in Richmond. But how did you manage it?"

"I managed nothing," I retorted, stung by the taunting note in his voice.

"Certainly not for want of trying. Isn't that so?" When I tried to turn away, he grasped my arm. "Isn't that so?"

"What difference does it make? I never made a secret of my love for Derry. Not to you. You knew it from the first. Have you forgotten the circumstances of our marriage?"

He let go of me. "No. But it seems to me that in the meanwhile there have been times when you've responded to my efforts with a passion ill befitting a woman in love with someone else."

My face turned crimson. "You are crude to throw such things in my face! Besides, it isn't true."

"Isn't it?" He leaned close and a hot blob of candle wax fell on my hand.

"Oh!" I cried, brushing it off with my skirt. "Now see what you've done!"

"Sorry. But if I was careless, blame it on your distracting presence." He set the candle on a table. "I am not going to beg for what God and a preacher gave me as my right. Oh, yes, 'the circumstances of our marriage.' I've heard them often enough. You ought to have that phrase stamped on your bosom. Or stitch it like a motto on your lingerie and wear it as a chastity belt. But it matters little to me. Good night, my dear. I shall find room on the sofa downstairs. It will be more comfortable than a wife's cold back."

He started for the door, and the taste of victory was suddenly like ashes in my mouth. "Miles..."

He turned, one brow lifted. "Seconds thoughts?" and his voice had the familiar jeer.

"No," I said firmly. "Good night."

Miles and Harold together with their two body servants, Negro slaves they had taken with them when they left for the army, plowed one of the lower fields, planting it in winter wheat. Neither Harold nor Miles had ever soiled their hands with farm labor, their parents having brought them up to be gentlemen. Yet I think both of them rather enjoyed toiling behind the plow mules all day, for they would come in at noon, scraping their muddy boots on the verandah, joshing with one another, Harold laughing and Miles grinning, his somber mood temporarily put aside. The brothers were getting along much better than they had before they went away, and it seemed as though a new affection had grown up between them.

One afternoon the weather suddenly turned from warm sunshine to cold bluster, the wind driving huge slate-colored clouds across the treetops, banking them into towering shapes overhead. I watched from the bedroom window as lightning throbbed and pulsed, the blue-white jagged streaks drawing crashing peals of thunder.

Shivering, I pulled my wrapper together with one hand, fastening the windows with the other. I had just finished taking a bath, a troublesome luxury since I myself must heat the water and lug it up to the tin tub kept in our hall closet. But I considered the effort worth it. A lolling half hour in warm scented water somehow gave me the feeling that we were still living normal lives.

I lighted the lamp and was sitting down to read when it began to rain. The spattering drops against the windowpanes soon turned to a heavy thrumming. A minute later I heard shouts from below—the men, I guessed, running in from the fields. The door slammed, voices floated up, heavy footsteps mounted the stairs.

Miles burst into the room, breathless, drenched, dripping water, his muddy boots tracking the carpet.

"You might have taken those off downstairs," I said. "There's no one to clean up after you—except me."

"Won't soil your hands with an honest man's boots, eh?" he asked sarcastically, sinking into a chair and beginning to struggle with them.

"Oh, here—let me."

I went to the wardrobe and got the boot jack. As I knelt at his feet to help him, he said:

"To what do I owe this sudden turnabout, this unexpected transformation into good little wife?"

"Hush. You talk as if I had never done anything for you. A short memory you have. Don't you recall how I cooked all that horrible winter in Virginia City? You never do give me credit for anything. Let's have the other foot."

"I remember Virginia City quite well. We were cozy there, weren't we?"

"God in Heaven. Cozy! I hope never to be that cozy again. Keep your leg still, please. Did you or Harold get around to fixing the chicken pen? We can't afford to lose any now."

When he did not answer I looked up. He was staring down at me, or more precisely at my breasts. My wrapper had accidentally fallen open. I clutched it to me and rose, flushed and annoyed.

"Finish yourself."

I went to the fireplace and pretended to rearrange the candlesticks on the mantel. Miles said nothing and when I heard the other boot thump to the floor my nerves jumped. I wished he had remained downstairs or taken refuge from the rain in the stables.

I twisted my head. "Shall I go down and get you some whiskey?"

He was undressing, tossing jacket and shirt in a corner. It had grown darker in the room and the lamplight gleamed on his bared chest.

"Does my manly nudity frighten you?"

"Of course not!"

"I wonder."

He unbuckled his belt and I turned from him, going to the window, looking out at the wind-lashed trees. Miles did not speak again. With my back to him I could not guess what he was doing, and it bothered me. The mood in the room had suddenly become tense, fraught with dark expectancy. The thunder growled and muttered, crashing with an earsplitting ferocity overhead. Rain streamed down the window. Miles's presence behind me was like a sword poised over my head.

"I must go down to the kitchen to see about supper," I said, turning at last.

He was still standing in the middle of the room, his eyes meeting, holding mine.

"Do," he said.

He was daring me and a sudden strange excitement squeezed my lungs.

"Are you going to bar my way?" I asked, my voice a little breathy.

"Why don't you try me and see?"

When I did not reply, he said, "Do you make a habit of going about the house in your wrapper?"

"No, but . . ."

"No, but you are afraid to change into your gown in my presence, is that it?"

"I am not afraid," I said, lifting my chin.

"Then come here."

I moved.

"Closer."

I could feel his breath on my cheek. I watched him warily, ready to spring aside.

But his eyes were the only thing that moved, his eyes going over my face, traveling down to my breasts. I felt hot. I wanted to hit him, to strike out; I wanted him to . . .

He dragged me into his arms and gathered my lips in his in a hungry, savage kiss that touched the something in me that I hated and despised, something that rose from my loins with a stab of fire, that mad something that made my breasts, crushed against his bare chest, burn.

Around us the thunder growled. The wind tearing at the house rushed down the chimney and blew the lamp out. In the roiling, turbulent darkness, he lifted me and all I thought of was the unyielding arms, the hard chest, the powerful shoulders, and the strong neck I clung to. I didn't want to feel anything else. The raging storm had entered my blood as it had his. I didn't want to think, to ponder, to analyze. When he brought me down on the bed, my hands fluttered a moment before they began to tug at his trousers. He drew them off. I felt a rush of air as he lifted himself and then his hard lean body was over mine and he was kissing me and I thought: I must be depraved, nothing else would explain my grasping fingers reaching out to guide his pulsing erection inside me, nothing else explain the way I could move with him. And— oh, but what did it matter? The darkness concealed everything, made it possible for me to give myself to him with an abandon that grew wilder with the wind outside, a madness that possessed me in a mindless frenzy, urging me on to the final spasmodic shock of joy.

We kept Christmas that year at Wildoak, inviting the Harknesses, Alice Dinwiddie and her children, the Hastingses, the Wakefields (who did not come because of the bad roads, we

were told), and Prudence and her children. Everyone brought
an offering, a covered dish, a cake, a roast hen, a pudding,
for food that winter was not in abundant supply and we were
beginning to feel the pinch. A tree had been set up in the parlor
and the children decorated it with red apples and small white
candles. Deirdre bossed the others in a high imperious voice.
She was of an age now to put up her hair and lengthen her
skirts, of an age to have a "coming-out" party and beaux. But
there were no young men in the neighborhood; they had all
gone off to fight, and many would never return.

Deirdre loathed the war because it deprived her of the things
she had been promised when she grew up. At thirteen she had
watched the older girls feted at birthday galas and balls, watched
with envy the dashing bachelors who had courted and squired
them to hunts and barbecues. And now she was being cheated
of the fun. Many nights I would hear her sobbing behind her
closed door and I felt for her. It brought back memories of my
own self at fourteen, fifteen, when I ached with a longing I
could not define.

Yes, Deirdre hated the war and she didn't give a rap who
won as long as it was finished, done with, over. She hated the
younger children who got on her nerves, hated her mother, me,
the other women who shushed her and told her it was wrong
to think only of herself. When Miles and Harold left, she clung
to them in a way that embarrassed Miles and made him a little
short. But I think Harold understood, for he gently untangled
her arms from around his neck and with a smile promised to
bring a prospective beau to her on his next furlough. No one
asked when that might be. In the meanwhile, Harold felt sure
we would be safe at Wildoak.

"Even if the Yankees should use the river as a highway,"
he said, "they won't bother you. They're after bigger fish."

Despite Harold's assurances, Beth Ann wanted to quit Wildoak and go to Richmond where the Falconers had kin—the
Bainbridges. She did not like being left alone without men,
without servants, without protection.

"You will do better here," Harold insisted, "in your own
home. Why, compared to cousin Jane in Richmond, you are
eating like royalty."

When she went on pleading, her husband, patient as ever,

said, "Do be reasonable, Beth Ann. Even if I wanted to, I couldn't take the time to get you to Richmond. You must be a brave girl. I'm leaving Ned and Ben behind." They were the two body servants. "So you are in charge now. I know you can manage ably."

I sensed a struggle taking place in Beth Ann—the twitching mouth, the uncertain eyes, the struggle between what Harold and Miles would think and her own craven fear. The former won, at least temporarily, and as she kissed Harold she said, "I'll do my best, dear."

CHAPTER

TWENTY-FOUR

*I*T WAS *during the last week in June, I recall, that* we first heard the sound of guns. In the beginning we mistook the faint, sporadic rumbling for thunder but then realized it couldn't be, for the sun was shining brightly in a cloudless sky. A terrified Beth Ann, certain that the Yankees were trying to reach Wildoak, went into hysterics again, laughing and crying, clinging to me, begging me to save her, sobbing that we would all be raped and murdered.

I had to give her a double dose of our precious laudanum before I could get her upstairs and to bed. The younger girls began to sob too. Deirdre, vexed and impatient, slapped each of them soundly and when they would not stop, threatened them with a stick. I think it was her anger, combined with a streak of sheer mulishness, that made her so fearless.

"I don't give a hoot in Hades if the Yankees are coming," she said. "It's better than going on day after day waiting for something to happen."

"I wouldn't let your father hear you say that," I warned.

"He'd be glad! If it was over, Papa would be glad. He'd come home. He doesn't care two pins for states' rights or secession. He hates the whole thing."

"Nobody likes the war," I said.

"It's a rich man's quarrel fought by the poor."

"Who told you that?" I demanded. "I know you didn't think it up by yourself. Who?"

"Uncle Miles."

"Well, Uncle Miles talks a lot of nonsense he doesn't mean."

The guns sputtered and boomed all that first afternoon, but as darkness closed down they fell silent. About midmorning of the following day a two-wheeled, mule-drawn wagon with a large white cross painted on either of its canvas sides rattled up the drive. The man on the front seat was a stranger, a runty-looking Confederate soldier with a dirty red beard. Behind him from under the mud-spattered canvas came the sounds of moans and sobbing.

"Ma'am," the soldier said, removing his forage cap, "the name's Blake, Sergeant Blake. I got wounded here. The hospitals and houses at Mechanicsville is full up. Would you . . . ?"

"No!" Beth Ann exclaimed from over my shoulder before he could finish. "We can't take them in. We have no room."

"Of course there's room," I said, annoyed, for she had long since abdicated her position as manor lady. "Sergeant, please bring them round to the barn. I'll see what I can do in the way of blankets and pillows."

"I forbid it!" Beth Ann cried.

I ignored her and sent Elizabeth to fetch Ben and Ned from the fields.

"Deirdre . . . ?" She was standing next to me, watching with a sort of feverish excitement in her eyes. "Empty the linen press. I'll strip the beds."

The two darkies and the wagon were waiting as Deirdre and I, arms laden with bedding, hurried toward the barn.

"How many?" I asked the red-bearded sergeant.

"Eight."

I instructed Ned and Ben to make up eight pallets using cornshucks.

Suddenly someone shrieked from the cart, "For God's sake, kill me! Put me out of my misery!" in a voice that cut through me like a knife.

The darkies hesitated, then quickly disappeared inside.

"We got one walking wounded," the sergeant informed me, unperturbed, as if begging to be killed was so ordinary an occurrence it needed no comment. "Harry!"

A lanky leg appeared over the lip of the wagon and a tall young soldier with sprigs of blond hair tufting out from a stained red kerchief wound about his head climbed down. He grinned at Deirdre, who stood transfixed, staring at him.

"Come along," I ordered her crossly. "We've got work to do."

As quickly as we could, we covered the mounded corn-shucks with sheets, laying a blanket at the foot of each and a pillow at the head. I sent Ned to the well for two buckets of water.

Then the sergeant and the blond soldier began to carry the men in. They were a ragged, pitiful sight, their faces haggard, some wrapped in remnants of tattered carpet, others wearing coats of patched coarse blue kersey cloth. All were bloodied and filthy. These were the privates and corporals, former plow boys, butchers' assistants, factory hands, grocery clerks, common soldiers, whose uniforms even at the early stages of the war were hit and miss; not like the officers, who wore rich gray cassimere, plumed hats, and gleaming spurs attached to polished boots.

The sick went past me one by one. Two were wounded in the face and I had to turn my eyes away; one had a mangled arm, another lacerated legs. There was no doctor, no pharmaceutical supplies. The driver, who said he was the regimental cook, had been recruited for ambulance duty only the day before and was as ignorant as I of even the rudiments of medical knowledge. Those who developed gangrene or other complications would have to die.

The last to be taken from the wagon was a young lad hardly more than fifteen. He had been shot in the chest and the front of his butternut jacket was soaked in blood.

"Janet," he whispered, clutching my arm as he was carried over the threshold. "Janet."

His hoarse, whispery voice, so full of quivering pain, so pathetic and childish, calling on Janet, a woman—whether sister or sweetheart, I never knew—obviously dear to him, tore at my heart more than the shrieks of the man who'd implored God to kill him.

All we could do for these tormented souls was to wash and rebandage their wounds and try to make them comfortable with spoonfuls of laudanum (which Beth Ann had unsuccessfully tried to hide). Twice in the midst of tearing the clotted rags from a man's ugly, enpurpled, festering wound, I had to run outside where I became violently ill.

I had the old Negress, Mindy (the single slave who had not run away), add water to our evening meal, a jambalaya that had been working on the stove since morning, and that together with a half dozen loaves of bread served as supper for the men. Only four of them could eat, however, which they did with ravenous appetites, claiming it was the only decent food they had been able to get in months.

Toward evening the shrieking man's voice became stilled, expiring in a long drawn-out moan. Thank God, he's dead, I told myself, it's finished for him. I asked the sergeant why they had sent such badly wounded men over a bumpy road to uncertain care instead of those whose condition might have given them a chance of survival.

"They're all pretty bad, ma'am," he said laconically, a straw stem working between his jaws.

I had Ned and Ben bury the poor man while I said a few words over his grave, commending him to an afterworld that I felt certain would give him more peace than this.

After eating a hasty supper at the house, I lighted a lamp and returned to the barn. Coming in from the out-of-doors and the fragrant smell of night-blooming jasmine, I felt the stench of gangrene, ordure, and sweat hit me like a blow. Fireflies danced in the raftered darkness, and the tossing and twitching, the moans, the curses, the prayers, and the pleas for "Doctor!" "Mother!" "Water!" were like the mutterings and cries from Satan's own Hell. The butternut boy lay with one arm flung out, one hand on his chest. He reminded me of how Derry might have looked at fifteen. I sat down beside him and wiped his damp forehead with a cloth. He opened his eyes and a sweet smile suddenly transformed his flushed face.

"Janet, Janet . . . ?"

I took his hand. "I'm right here."

"I—I'm afraid, Janet. Promise you won't leave?"

"I promise. I shan't budge from your side, I swear."

I would like to say that he died tranquilly with a gentle, peaceful look on his face. But he did not. His dying took a long time. And he went in such pain that thinking of it years later made me shudder. As I sat beside him in his last throes, watching helplessly as he coughed and hacked and vomited blood and tried to catch his ragged breath, I began to hate

Yankees in a way I had never done before. It infuriated me that someone could have done this to an innocent boy, hardly more than a child; that the gaunt tyrant called Lincoln sitting in Washington, had decided the South must be taught a lesson, that he had ordered *them* to invade *us*, spilling *our* blood on *our* soil.

I released the boy's dead, stiffened hand from mine and closed his eyes.

Then I found the sergeant. "Are they still fighting at Mechanicsville?" We had heard the faint rattle of guns all that afternoon.

"I dunno, ma'am. Might be at Gaines Mill by now."

I went to bed but did not sleep, kept awake by a seething, boiling anger that—as I look back now—bordered on madness.

Rising at first light, I dressed swiftly and returned to the barn. The same moans and grunts, the shrill whistling breath of the dying greeted me. I shook the sergeant awake.

"There's a grave already dug," I said. "I want the boy buried, but first I want his uniform. Bury him in a blanket."

"His uniform, what fer?"

"I'm going to burn it," I lied.

I carried the clothes back to the house and put them on just as they were, bloodstained and dirty—the overlarge sacklike jacket, the torn breeches, the shoes of rough, untanned hide. Rummaging through Miles's wardrobe I found a slouch hat, which I pulled down over my brow. From the desk in the library I took the heavy pistol Miles had left us, "just in case," and thrust it in my belt under the coat. I emptied the leather box of shells and filled my pockets with them.

The sun was just breaking through the clouds, catching the crystal rainbow glint of the dewed lawn, when I slipped out of the house and down to the stable. The old mare, the only horse left after Harold had given a sleek half dozen to the Confederate Army, stood dozing in her stall. I saddled and mounted her, feeling a little odd to be sitting a horse astride instead of sidesaddle.

Crossing the river at the plank bridge, I took the road that led past the Hastings place to Mechanicsville, some seven miles away. I had no clear idea what I would do once I reached the battlefield, except that I wanted to kill a Yankee, a single Northern devil, one snag-toothed, bushy-bearded, hairy murderer—just one—to wipe out the memory of the gaping mouth, the rush of black blood, the dying of a boy who should have lived to manhood. And now that I was on my way, I burned for vengeance with a white-hot flame so violent it shook me.

The sound of guns, the rattle of musketry, and sporadic cannon bursts grew louder as I rode. The sun, slanting in long pale rays between the clouds, finally disappeared altogether and presently a fine rain began to fall.

After I passed the Hastings place and headed toward the Chickahominy River, the trees became scrubbier, the terrain underfoot damp and in some places swampy. Here the booming of cannon could be heard more distinctly. By this time I was wet through and my slouch hat dripped water, a drop at a time, splashing on my nose and chin. But Miles's pistol remained dry and its steely hardness next to my hip sustained my determination.

I had been riding perhaps an hour when two men supporting a third between them, a wounded soldier with head and eyes bandaged, came haltingly up the road. They were Confederates in tattered jackets, one wearing a pair of too-short Zouave pantaloons, another a swordless scabbard; all three had shoes torn to ribbons, which showed their grimy blackened toes. When they saw me they halted. Their bearded faces were streaked with dust and fatigue. The two who could see had a sly, wary look in their eyes.

"Where'd you get the horse?" the Zouave asked suspiciously. "Been out foraging while the rest of us is getting kilt?"

"No. I'm carrying a message for General Lee."

The two men holding up the third broke into braying laughter.

"You 'spect us to believe that, boy?" the Zouave asked. "You stole that damn horse. Now git down." He took hold of my bridle.

I noticed the butt of a revolver protruding from the belt of his pantaloons, but I was damned if I would give them the horse.

"Let go of me!" I said.

"Now, you wouldn't wanna get hurt, would you? A lad like

you and on our side, too. Leave us the horse without a fuss
and—"

I pulled out my gun and pressed it to the side of his head.
His companion was so astounded he did nothing but gape at
me, while the wounded man whined, "Whass goin' on?"

"Are you going to let me go?" I asked, flicking the hammer
back.

The Zouave stepped aside, and kicking my heels into the
mare's flanks I took off down the road. I had nearly reached
a bend and comparative safety, when the man in the Zouave
trousers apparently recovered his wits, for a ball went whistling
past my ear so close I could feel its acrid heat. Terror lifted
me from the saddle. Leaning forward, I whipped the mare's
sides with the end of a rein.

Once around the bend I kept on going, galloping, urging
the poor creature under me forward, faster and faster until I
realized her muzzle was frothing. I drew up and, peering through
the trees, saw a small cabin, a trapper's or farmer's, I guessed,
standing empty in the middle of a burned-over clearing, the
windows broken and the door ajar.

I rode across the ditch and dismounted. Removing the blanket from beneath the saddle, I rubbed the mare's heaving sides
down, then led her to the stream to drink. The rumbling guns
had become silent and a quiet hush pervaded the woods.

Not wanting to risk losing the mare in another encounter,
I led her up to the cabin and put her inside the single room
which was bare of furniture except for a rickety chair. Throwing
her an armful of grass, I shut the door and started off on foot
just as the guns spoke again.

The ground became spongier and I found myself slipping
and sliding, sometimes sinking up to my ankles in ooze. The
borrowed shoes with their rough insides rubbed my feet, but
as the noise of battle grew louder I forgot my blistering heels.

Then suddenly, at the next curve in the road, I came upon
a cannon emplacement. Four or five men were swarming around
the twelve-pounder, but no one took the slightest notice of me.
A man, a Confederate officer by the insignia on his forage cap,
shouted, "Load! Canister! Double!"

A young beardless soldier, his face blackened with burnt
powder, shoved a rammer into the mouth of the cannon.

"Ready! By piece! At will! *Firrrre!*"

The deafening sound shook the ground under my feet and I recoiled, stumbling back into the shelter of the trees. There I stood, ears ringing, heart banging, throat dry. When I saw them reloading the cannon, I hurried on, only to find another gun embankment and another. I kept going, followed by the shattering *boom! boom! boom!* and the lesser crackle of gunfire. I had to fight the urge to turn and flee back to the quiet woods, the cabin, and the mare. But I forced myself forward, the din of the unseen battle drowning out the sound of my own heavy heartbeat. Reaching an open space on a sandy rise, I sank to my knees and peered down over the top of a bush.

The valley below was pandemonium. Men were kneeling, shooting, running, falling; horses reared and plunged in panic and screaming pain, wagon wheels bounced and flew, a cannon and its crew suddenly went up in a fiery explosion. The yells of the battle-maddened soldiers, the shrieks of those hit, rose above the rackety-rack of gunfire and the boom of crashing artillery. In the thick haze of dust and smoke, flame-seared trees stripped of bark stood out like ghostly fingers offering no protection to our men, who I could now see under attack from a line of bluecoats on a bluff across the river.

I couldn't go down to that! My anger turned to a sickening, gorge-choking fear which anchored me to the spot.

Suddenly from behind, emitting a blood-curdling Rebel yell, a band of Confederates came charging through and carried me willy-nilly along with them like a leaf in a storm. I tried to brace myself against the onrush, but propelled by the mob I continued to be swept down the incline. Someone running beside me shouted, "Where's your rifle?"

"It's a mistake!" I yelled. "A mistake!" But he had gone on and no one heard.

When we reached a breastwork of stone, the men dropped to their knees, I along with them.

"They've crossed the river!"

On either side of me the men were firing. A bullet skinned the shoulder of my jacket. I felt its heat and smelled the singed cloth, and terror such as I had never known gripped me in heart-hammering panic.

"They're coming—fall back!"

Fall back? Who? Where? Those around me were turning, some scattering pell-mell, others still firing their guns, retreating step by step, seeking shelter behind overturned wagons, dead horses, and the bodies of their comrades. I tried to scramble to my feet, at least to crawl away, but I couldn't. I could do no more than cower behind the stones, hugging them, trembling from head to foot.

A momentary lull descended. I opened my eyes to see a blue-clad leg straddle the breastwork and, without giving myself time to think, pulled the pistol from my belt. It was a Yankee, and as he came over I shot point blank. With a white, frightened look on his face, he tottered for a moment before he tumbled forward, his rifle springing from his grasp, his canteen rattling over the rubbled stone as he hit the ground. He twitched and rolled on his back, his hand feeling for something in his jacket. I thought it was a hidden revolver or a knife perhaps. Watching him closely and still holding my own gun, I searched my pockets for another shell. But when the Yankee brought his hand out, it held a wallet. The next moment he flung his arm to the side and the wallet went sliding away, spilling its contents. After that he didn't move.

I waited while the crackling, booming sound of battle started up again. Then, after what seemed a long while, I slowly crawled over to where the Yankee lay.

I had shot him through the chest. His jacket had crimsoned and was now sopping with blood much like the boy in butternut. There was another more horrilbe and, to me, heart-wrenching similarity. This Yankee could not have been much older than the boy. Except for his brown hair, he could have been the other's brother—the smooth, beardless face, the young mouth, the staring blue eyes. For a moment I thought my mind had played a trick. I imagined that the butternut boy's ghost had invested itself with a Yankee uniform and that I had made a brutal error by killing him.

I put out a trembling, tentative hand and touched his cold fingers. He was real, not a ghost. The other was buried by now in the graveyard beneath the sycamores at Wildoak. This was a Yankee, the horned devil, the fiendish, bearded savage I had wanted to murder out of anger and vengeance.

I looked down and saw that a photograph had fallen from

his spilled wallet. I picked it up. A woman with hair parted in the middle and drawn back from a pretty face looked out at me with level eyes and the stiff smile so characteristic of posed photographs. Words written across the bottom said, "God bless you, Mother."

I slipped the photograph back into the wallet and, gathering the scattered papers together, hesitated a moment. Should I read them, see who this boy was, where he had come from? No. I couldn't. His face, the staring eyes, the innocent curve of the boyish throat had already begun to haunt me. I did not want to know his name.

Exhausted by emotion, I still sat there with the clamor of battle receding up the hill. There was no use telling myself that I had killed an enemy who could as easily have killed me. He had been frightened too. We were all frightened, it seemed, except the idiots who enjoyed the feverish atmosphere, the bloodletting, and the gore.

What was it all about? I had forgotten. Why were we slaughtering one another? From the back of my tired mind, I dragged out the stale slogans, the catchwords, the oft-used platitudes, "For honor! For glory!" Were the Yankees fed the same slogans, were they rallied to the colors by huzzahs for God and country? Had they too gone off pelted with flowers and singing the "Battle Cry for Freedom?"

The sounds of gunfire had diminished except for a few isolated bursts. The sun, streaked with clouds of gray and tattered shreds of scarlet, was sinking in the western sky. I got up, swaying on my feet like a drunk, and staggered toward the rise from whence I had descended, it seemed, a hundred years earlier. Along the way, the sprawled bodies of the wounded, the dead, and the dying lay in awkward, grotesque positions, outflung arms, contorted bodies. I tried not to look at them, tried not to hear the pitiful cries, the shrieks of the badly wounded, those begging for succor, those pleading for a quick and merciful death.

When I try to recall that short journey on foot back to the cabin, only flashes come back: the rumble of a hospital cart, a begrimed captain shouting, a cannon wheeled across the hill nearly running me down, a cavalryman weeping beside his dead horse.

It was dark when I reached the mare. I knew I could not ride to Wildoak that night, picking my way over an inky road, meeting up with God knew who or what. I decided to bed down in the cabin, for the first time that day making a sensible decision.

It was well past sunup when I turned into the Wildoak drive. To my astonishment, Beth Ann, Ruth Harkness, and Prudence were standing on the verandah, shading their eyes against the glare as I trotted wearily toward them.

"Is it you?" Ruth asked, peering at me. "Is it you, Carmella?"

I must have presented a shocking sight, dressed as a soldier, hatless, covered with dust, my front bloodied, my face sooty with battle smoke.

"Yes, it's me," I said in a dull, tired voice.

"Where in God's name have you been?" Beth Ann exclaimed. "And what are you doing in that getup?"

Somewhere in my tired mind I recalled Mrs. Tibbets once asking the same questions.

"If you wait, I'll explain—"

"Look at you, just look at you!" Beth Ann went on. "If you don't beat all! Don't you have any sense of decency?"

I stared at her, at Prudence whose face registered the same disapproval, women with their soft, petallike skins, cared-for hands, corset-encased bodies, women surrounded by comforts, downy beds, decent food, and until now servants at their beck and call, the same women (myself included) who had embroidered silk pillows for the husbands they had sent off to war.

Why hadn't we said no? Women were supposed to be the nurturers, the guardians of hearth and home. We should have done everything in our power to prevent the hell I had seen at Gaines Mill. And now Beth Ann was scolding me because I had no sense of decency.

I laughed; the irony of it struck me as painfully funny. I could not stop. I laughed and cried, gasping for breath, sitting there astride the mare with tears streaming down my cheeks, until Ruth hurried down the steps and pulled me from the saddle. She held me in her arms where I continued to weep as though I would never stop.

CHAPTER

TWENTY-FIVE

Two days had passed since my return from Gaines Mill. During much of that time I had slept, often waking from horrifying, bloody dreams to find Ruth Harkness bending over me. It was she who had led me up the stairs, my face swollen with weeping; she who had fed, bathed, and put me to bed. It was she who had told me over and over that I was safe, that everything would be all right.

But now Ruth and the others—Beth and Prudence—were talking about me.

I paused on the staircase, one hand on the bannister, and listened.

"Carmella . . . she . . ."

They were in the parlor, so sure of not being overheard they had not even troubled to close the door all the way.

I descended the rest of the stairs on silent, slippered feet.

"It's just one more indication of her lack of good breeding," Beth Ann was saying, "a sign of wantonness. A lady would never be caught in public wearing men's clothing. My God, when I think of it!"

My face turned hot. The mealy-mouthed hypocrite! Grasping the knob I flung the door open. They stared at me like guppies in a fish bowl.

"I don't like to eavesdrop—it's considered rude," I said

with a tightly stretched smile, enjoying their discomfort. "So I thought I would let you know I was here."

Ruth said, "But, my dear, should you be out of bed?"

"I am feeling much better and decided I'd come down for a cup of tea."

"I'll get it for you." Ruth plumped up a pillow on the sofa. "Sit here. And, Carmella, nothing was said. Really."

"Only that I was ill bred, rude, and wanton. Now *that* is a lovely word. Wanton."

A long pause. Ruth looked dismayed.

"Well! Well!" Beth Ann puffed herself up. "I for one am not going to take it back. You went off in a stolen uniform."

"He died," I said coldly. "That poor boy died and where were you, you loyal Southern gentlewoman?" I infused that phrase with the sort of jeering mockery I had learned so well from Miles. "Hiding in your room because you couldn't stand the sight of blood? Did you see to his burial, did you say a few words over him from that Bible you clasp so sanctimoniously to your bosom when you pray for your own safety?"

"Carmella . . . please." Ruth tried to smooth things over.

Prudence, however, came to Beth Ann's defense. "I can't see where you gained anything by dressing in a man's uniform, Carmella, and going off to the battle lines, putting yourself in a position where you were subject to crude language and violent behavior."

"Violent behavior! My God! Who cheered and hoorahed the men on to 'violent behavior'? You! Maybe it would have done you all good to see some of that 'violent behavior.'"

"We all suffer," Prudence said.

"You have no idea, not the slightest, of what suffering is." I was so angry I could have throttled her.

"Carmella . . ." Ruth came over and took my hands. "Carmella, sit down. Please listen. I know you are upset. I realize the injustice of it all was what made you put on that poor boy's uniform and go off to fight the enemy. I appreciate your feelings of outrage, of frustration, and even applaud your courage. But it's foolhardy courage, my dear. At best you might have gotten in the way of the campaign, at worst had yourself killed. I am afraid I must agree—at least partially—with Prudence. What was gained except your own bitter disillusionment and torment?

Emotions that serve no purpose. I don't condemn you for the masquerade, for the inappropriateness of donning a pair of trousers. That seems trivial. As for women cheering their husbands on, I doubt it would have made much difference if we had protested and wept. Women have no say in the conduct of politics. We cannot vote—or make war."

"But we have influence," I argued. "We are wives, mothers. We can try to dissuade our husbands, we can teach our sons to be peaceable, to refuse to fight."

"My dear, you are such a romantic. Do you think we live in that kind of a world? If your husband or son refused to fight, they would be branded cowards though it takes the utmost courage to stand up for one's moral principles in time of war. Don't you see?"

Suddenly I felt tired and helpless. Would I think less of Derry, of Miles, of Papa—were he alive—if any one of them had told me he would not join the others in battle? Perhaps. I did not know.

"You forget," Ruth went on, "that beneath the rhetoric and oratory there is a reason for taking up arms. We Virginians resent having other people—the Northerners in this instance—telling us how to live, trying to impose their notion of right and wrong on us. We are as free as they and are honor-bound to protect that freedom."

The sincerity in her voice defied contradiction. Her view made sense, and yet in the back of my mind uncertainties lingered.

Of the eight stretcher cases that had come to us from Mechanicsville, four had died. The others seemed to be recuperating slowly, healed by nature, as the sergeant said. Neither he nor the big, blond soldier with the head wound (also recovering nicely) nor any of our invalids seemed in a hurry to leave. Two were brothers, South Carolinians, who had lost their farm home in the early stages of the fighting. Two were privates from Hood's Texas Brigade, farm boys also, who felt an understandable reluctance to rejoin their company. I could not blame any of them for wanting to remain in the comparative security of Wildoak. But something happened that finally made their continued presence unwelcome.

I had sensed Deirdre's attraction to the tall blond soldier they called Harry Page from the first but in the mill of subsequent events had forgotten it. Now I began to notice that every evening after supper she went out, for a stroll she said, and came back an hour later with a pink glow to her cheeks that I assumed was due to the night air. She always took Elizabeth with her, so her absence and the pink glow did not arouse my suspicions until one evening when Elizabeth said she didn't feel like walking and Deirdre got quite angry.

"What's wrong with you?" she demanded of her sister. "Lazy? Tired? You *promised,* and now you're going back on your word. Liar!"

I thought her tirade a rather extreme reaction to a refusal to simply walk about the grounds in the dusk.

"I'll go with you," I offered, "if you need someone."

"I don't *need* someone," she retorted. "It's just that Elizabeth promised."

After some further badgering, Elizabeth got a shawl and departed with her sister. I helped Mindy clear the table and later, as was my habit, went and sat in the parlor. Beth Ann and I were knitting socks. We spoke of inconsequential things, a patching over of our last quarrel, which nevertheless had left a secret resentment smoldering in my breast.

I must have been frowning, for Beth Ann said, "Drop a stitch?"

"Yes, I believe so." There was no point airing my rancor.

As I continued to knit, my thoughts returned to Deirdre. She was up to something that made Elizabeth uncomfortable. What? It could be a dozen and one things, none of them good. Finally a sense of urgency brought me to my feet.

"Beth Ann," I said, thinking quickly of a handy excuse, "I must run out and tell Ned to kill a chicken for tomorrow's supper."

"But we've had chicken all this week."

"Sorry, there's nothing else until hog-butchering time."

The sun had set, leaving a faint lilac and pale lemon glow in the darkening sky. I walked quickly, keeping to the shadows. I went around the back toward the barn, its windows now alight, thinking Deirdre might be visiting the soldiers. But as I started across through the apple orchard, I caught a flash of a white

gown near the overseer's deserted cottage. Standing behind a
tree trunk, I peered through the dusk. Yes, it was Elizabeth,
sitting on the step, swishing at the tall grass with a stick. Deirdre
was nowhere in sight.

I moved quietly down the weed-choked lane at the rear of
the cottage, paused at the window, and listened.

"Oh, do stop that!" Deirdre commanded with a giggle.

Rising on tiptoe, I looked over the sill. It was dark inside
and I could barely make out the two figures on the bed. But a
flash of white limbs, the heaving breaths, the grunts and ecstatic
moans told me what those two were about as much as if they
had screamed it aloud.

I hurried around to the front past an astonished Elizabeth
and slammed the door open. The man jerked away from Deirdre
and sat up. She lifted herself on her elbows, surprise on her
face, feathery wisps stuck to her hair, her small, white breasts
gleaming in the dusk.

I couldn't speak. I was too stunned, too full of guilt for
having allowed this to happen. Wildoak, whether or not Beth
Ann sometimes refused to recognize it, had become my responsibility; Deirdre too.

The brawny, blond soldier was the first to open his mouth.

"Oh—oh! We're done for."

I found my tongue then. "That isn't the half of it. You
ungrateful wretch!" I looked for something to throw at him and
finding nothing, shouted, "Get out! Get out, you big booby,
and if I catch you within a half mile of Wildoak I'll have the
sergeant shoot you! Better still, I'll shoot you myself!"

He grabbed his trousers and shirt and scurried past me. Then
I turned to Deirdre. "You bitch, you whoring bitch!" It wasn't
the kind of language she was accustomed to, but she got my
meaning.

"I'm nothing of the sort," she flung back. "I'm in love with
Harry."

What she said, the way she said it, brought back a searing
memory: myself facing Miles with the same heated avowal,
and it angered me because she (though unconsciously) was
putting my love on a level with hers. What I felt for Derry was
sincere, a love that had lasted through the years, and Deirdre,
bedding with a common lout she hardly knew, demeaned it.

"Get up!" I ordered, striding over to the bed. "Get up!" And I slapped her across the mouth.

"Why—you—you . . . !" she spluttered.

I slapped her again. *"Aunt* Carmella is the name, not *'you.'* Get your clothes on!"

The next morning I told the sergeant and the others they would have to move on. I gave no explanations. I felt I owed them none. Whatever Deirdre had done, or might do in the future, I had to protect her reputation. Why I felt that way I cannot say. Perhaps plantation society had imbued me with a morality that had eluded me until now. Perhaps it was simply guilt at my own well-hidden hypocrisy. Or had the war wrought a subtle change in me?

I said nothing to Beth Ann, feeling she would never believe me. Her girls misbehave? The accusation would be taken as an insult.

Some six weeks later I came upon Deirdre at the back of the house in the throes of losing her breakfast. I held her brow and afterwards brought her a glass of water. She looked deathly pale.

"It was the eggs," she said.

"They were new laid," I pointed out, "the same as always. And you've never been sick before."

"Can't there be a first time?" she demanded angrily.

My eyes went over her breasts. "True. There's a first time for everything. You're pregnant."

Her face screwed up and she began to cry, something, until that moment, I had never imagined her capable of doing.

"You—you sent Harry away," she sobbed. "If you hadn't sent him away, we'd get married."

"Do you really think that boy would marry you? Why, even if he said yes, your mother would have a fit. He's nothing but poor white trash."

"I love him! And you sent him away. Now what am I to do?"

Yes, what? I pondered the alternatives.

Perhaps I could locate the dastard Harry Page. Marriage with white trash would be preferable to the scandal of giving birth to an illegitimate baby. But I hadn't the foggiest notion of where to look. The sergeant and his little band had long gone. Harry had been from somewhere in Georgia, but where I never learned, nor did I think he had ever troubled to tell us. If I could only find a husband to replace him. But who?

Then I thought of Ruth Harkness. She was acquainted with everyone for miles around, and if there was an eligible man in our county (or the next) she would probably know him. Though I hated to disturb her with our problems at Wildoak—Alex had left only a few days earlier to join the Army of Northern Virginia—I could think of no one else to turn to. But first I informed Beth Ann of the situation.

She went through all the predictable antics: the disbelief, the anger, the breaking down into stormy weeping, and the final disappearing act into the sanctuary of her room.

Ruth, on the other hand, received the news calmly when I called on her the following day. "I had a feeling that girl would get into trouble if she wasn't closely watched," she said.

I had gone over to Rose Hill directly after breakfast and was now sitting with Ruth in her dining room, sipping a cup of freshly brewed coffee.

"I did the best I could," I said.

"My dear." Her hand went swiftly to mine. "Of course you did. Don't you think I realize Beth Ann's incompetence to deal with matters? She's a weakling, and though she likes everyone to think otherwise we all know that it is you who are in charge at Wildoak. I have no fault to find with your management, nor do I blame you for Deirdre's fix. She's going through a phase in her life where she needs a strong hand, preferably her father's. His leaving affected her more than she shows."

"She claims she loves this Harry Page."

"Oh?" Ruth, toying with her coffee spoon, smiled wistfully. "Perhaps she does. Perhaps this boy gave her the reassurance she needed so badly. I imagine it was a pretty shattering experience to see her mother go to pieces. Then along came a man who offered her a broad shoulder—and one thing led to another. For all her outward toughness, Deirdre has a vulnerable heart. But...," Ruth sighed heavily, "that doesn't solve our problem, does it?"

"No." I poured more coffee from the blue Delft pot. "There are women in San Francisco who resort to potions," I said after a silence. "They say it works."

She gave me a sharp look. "How do you know of such things?"

"Talk. Gossip." I turned crimson as she continued to look at me. "Surely you don't think I've attempted anything like that?"

"No. But even if we could find such a 'potion,' I would be wary of using it. Women have died quite horribly from taking such things."

I wondered how *she* knew.

"A husband," I said, "would be the solution. Could you suggest someone?"

"I wish I could. All the suitable bachelors are away fighting. The only males left are the the the very young— hardly more than children—and the old."

"I think an older man might be a better choice, don't you?"

She smiled. "I wonder."

Her smile warmed me. I liked Ruth. I liked her good sense, her honesty, her strength. More than that I felt as I had never felt until that morning, that we had become true friends.

"Deirdre would have a fit," I observed.

"She doesn't have much choice, does she?" Ruth stared out of the window for a long moment. "He couldn't be too doddering. People would talk about that as much, or nearly as much, as her having a baby without benefit of clergy. Still . . . Ah! I think I've found him. Beasley Morse."

"The old Colonel?" I had met Beasley Morse twice, once when we had paid a call upon him at Alder House, and the second time when he had come to our Manassas celebration. He was an elderly bachelor, the last of a respected family, a sour curmudgeon with ruddy, lined cheeks and accusing blue eyes blazing out at the world from under white, beetling brows. He chewed tobacco and took snuff, sometimes simultaneously, which would set him to sneezing and spitting. Not attractive attributes for a prospective groom. A zealous advocate of Virginia's secession, he was angered when the army refused his services because he was lame in one leg and walked with a stick.

"Deirdre will never consent," I said.

"Deirdre's consent does not worry me half as much as Beasley Morse's."

"Do you think we ought to tell him the truth?"

"I don't see how we can avoid it."

We rode to Alder House that very afternoon. Situated in a small valley, it stood by a meandering stream that a hundred years earlier had been a swift, full-flooded tributary of the Pamunkey. The tributary had shrunk and the house itself had fallen into genteel decay. Around it the fields had gone wild, old Morse having long given up the pretext of farming. The weeds, vines, and overgrown bushes that pressed against broken windows, the loose roof tiles, and the lack of paint or whitewash gave no indication that the owner of Alder House was willing or could afford to keep it up. The entire aspect was dreary, to say the least, and for a moment I felt sorry for Deirdre.

Beasely Morse himself came to the door, wiping his mouth with a large and not too clean white handkerchief.

"Miss Ruth—Miss Carmella! Indeed a surprise. Come in."

He led us into a dusty, cobwebbed parlor whose corners were lost in murky gloom.

"Please." Morse indicated a dark, upholstered sofa that looked as though it had been gnawed by mice. Tentatively I lowered myself onto it.

"We haven't seen you for ages," Ruth said, giving him a sweet smile, "and thought we'd pay a call."

"Hmmmm." He remained standing, his eyes going from Ruth to me and back.

After a few strained moments of silence, Ruth said, "And how have you been keeping, Colonel?"

"You can see for yourself." Another silence.

Ruth remarked about the weather, the humidity, the lack of a really good rain, comparing this summer to Pamunkey summers of years gone by.

Beasley Morse made a few perfunctory grunts. He was plainly uncomfortable with visitors. The one time I had been there with Beth Ann he had been just as bristly and guarded and we had taken our leave after twenty minutes.

"Well—well." Morse cleared his throat as he removed a

large watch from his waistcoat pocket. "Four o'clock, ladies," he stated pointedly.

"Really, Colonel Morse," Ruth chided. "Just because you've reached a certain age does not excuse you from good manners."

"I'm not that old," he said, taking offense. "I'm sixty-two, a young sixty-two, and if it were not for this blasted leg I'd be long gone from here."

"I'm sure you would. I cannot think of a more patriotic man on the river."

Somewhat mollified, he sat stiffly down on the rush-bottomed rocker.

"Did you ever think of getting married, Mr. Morse?" Ruth asked.

HIs bushy brows rode up. "Several times, but the thought always passed quickly."

"Have you any objections to the marital state?"

"None whatsoever. I simply prefer living alone."

"Ah," sighed Ruth.

How is she going to do this, I wondered. He's such a stubborn goat.

"Have you come here to propose a match?" Beasley Morse asked after another long silence.

"Now that you've mentioned it, yes."

"Who'd you have in mind?"

"Deirdre Falconer."

His eyes popped. "But she's only a child!"

"Sixteen," Ruth said. "And she comes of good family. She wants to get married."

"To me?" he asked unbelievingly.

"I think so. Perhaps. You see—she is expecting a baby."

The old man's skin turned a blotchy red. His hand shook as he reached for the snuffbox in his pocket. He tried three times, then finally managed to work a pinch of the amber powder up his nose. We waited while his face went through a series of contortions, finally ending in a resounding sneeze.

"So," he sniffed loudly, "you want me to marry a girl that's—that's..." I could almost see his mind working around what he would really like to call Deirdre and what his upbringing as a gentleman forbade him to say. "...that's already been to the well?"

"It is unfortunate. She was seduced."

"A Yankee?" One eye cocked suspiciously.

"No, a Confederate, an officer." I marveled at the smooth way Ruth fibbed, and my estimation of her rose even higher. "I won't give his name. He was already married."

"I can't believe that of a Confederate. Why, the dastardly, low down...!" Again an innate rectitude prohibited him from giving full vent to his outrage. "A horsewhipping would be too good for him!"

"I agree. But it's over and done with. We must make sure that Deirdre's reputation, the honor of the family, is protected. And I could not think of anyone who could see it in that light but you."

Beasley Morse twisted in his chair. It was obvious that Ruth's compliment was one he would have been happy to forgo.

"I've always respected the Falconers," he said. "Harold—such an upright, decent sort—fighting for the Cause."

"Just so," Ruth agreed.

"But someone else's child."

"No one would know. Except for us—no five, including Beth Ann."

"That's the same as shouting it on the heights."

"I don't see why," Ruth said, piqued. "I think we can be trusted to keep our counsel."

"It's still someone else's child."

Ruth leaned forward. "Mr. Morse, no one would know it wasn't yours. I advise you to think of this match in a more favorable light. You will be getting a young, pretty bride, a gentlewoman. She is Harold's eldest, and if he does not have male issue—which seems unlikely at this point—then his daughter's husband stands to inherit."

The prospective son-in-law, some twenty years his would-be father-in-law's senior, fumbled for his snuffbox again.

"There's the war," Ruth reminded. "No one knows what will happen."

"I'll have to think about it."

"There isn't time."

"You are pressing me, Miss Ruth," he warned.

She sighed and leaned back on the sofa.

He turned to me. "And what do you make of all this folderol, Miss Carmella?"

"Something has to be done, and I think you are the man for it." His eyes seemed to brighten. And I went on in the same flattering vein. "We could have packed her off to Richmond. There are plenty of suitors there. But the Falconers and Morses have been neighbors for years. I don't think she could do better than right here."

Ruth flashed me an approving look.

"People will talk," Beasley Morse said, but I sensed he threw that in just to be difficult. I had a feeling he had already made up his mind.

"They'll talk even more if she has the baby," Ruth said. "We can pass the word along that Deirdre and her mother don't get along, that Deirdre had long admired you, and that when you proposed she accepted with alacrity."

"Not very flattering to me," Beasley Morse said.

"But more believable. To pretend that she's madly in love would not ring true, don't you think?"

"I don't know."

Again a long pause. Somewhere from the bowels of the house a clock began its brassy chime.

"It would be the honorable, the true Southern gentlemanly thing to do," Ruth said, in what I thought was a last-ditch try.

It worked. We left shaking his dry hand, agreeing that the wedding date should be set in two weeks' time.

Deirdre vowed she would kill herself first.

"He smells!" she cried. "He's a dirty old man and he smells like a goat!"

"You haven't any choice," I said. "It's either that or having the baby in disgrace."

"I'll have the baby in disgrace."

"Oh, no, you won't!" Ruth exclaimed. She had agreed to be present when I confronted Deirdre, and I was glad. Ruth, when she chose, could instill into her voice an iron quality that brooked no argument. "You either marry Beasley or you're going off to the Sisters of Mercy Convent in Maryland."

It was the first I had heard of such a convent, and I wondered if Ruth had invented it.

Nevertheless, whether real or imaginary, it had the desired effect.

Two weeks later Deirdre, tightly laced under her mother's wedding gown, married Beasley Morse in a brief ceremony in the parlor at Wildoak. Afterward the guests toasted the bridal couple with elderberry wine and partook of a simple supper, a far cry from the champagne and groaning board of past celebrations. When the meal was finished, Deirdre left on the arm of her elderly husband, her eyes flashing with black resentment. I didn't envy Beasley Morse. The inflexible, sour old man had met his match, and unless I missed my guess his peaceful, crotchety life at Alder House was over.

Deirdre had her baby in March, a healthy bawling boy she insisted on naming Page, after its shameless but unknowing father, Harry Page.

In May of the following year, somewhere around the 14th or 15th if I recall, Chester Dinwiddie, his arm in a sling, passed through on his way home on sick furlough. He had received a ball through the right shoulder at Chancellorsville where General Lee, in a series of brilliant maneuvers, had sent superior Union forces scurrying into retreat. That was the first news we had received in months concerning the progress of the war and, of course, we all thought, as we had so many times before, that the end was in sight. It would all be over soon. Chester forgot to mention that Stonewall Jackson had been fatally wounded, nor did he reveal that not long after Lee's aforementioned victory he had suffered the loss of ten thousand men at Sharpsburg. Chester claimed that morale was high, that the battle-seasoned troops had never believed more strongly in the Cause, omitting to add that the army had a deplorable shortage of food, medicine, clothing, and ammunition and that desertions were taking place at a fearful rate.

A fellow officer of Derry's enlightened us as to the grim realities of the Confederate situation. Derry, having been sent out as a courier on an official mission with a small band of mounted men, had taken a detour in order to spend the night at Wildoak.

As always, the sight of him after a long absence set my mind in a whirl, so that at the beginning I heard little of what was said. All I could do was feast my eyes on his face and every expression that crossed it.

At supper I went on watching him, listening to the cadence of his voice. Was he happy to see me? Did he still love me? I worried a little about my appearance. My gown was mended, somewhat shabby, and I guessed long out of fashion. I worried that I might not look as beautiful to him as he remembered, that compared to the society belles of Richmond I seemed countrified and dowdy. Were they still wearing crinolines, their hair in chignons?

It was not until one of the other officers, a little man with a pronounced tic, said something about bread riots in Richmond that I tore my gaze from Derry.

"Mobs of women with pistols and knives broke into the shops on Cary Street," he was saying. "Claimed they were hungry, wanted bread, just a loaf each. But then they began to loot the groceries, and next went on to smash into jewelry and millinery shops."

"In *Richmond?*" Beth Ann asked, aghast. "But why should they riot?"

"Because they had nothing of eat, I suppose," he replied dryly, his tic working rapidly.

Puzzled, too, I said, "But you look—" and stopped short.

The little man curled his lip. "We look well fed, is that what you mean?"

Derry clucked his tongue. "Oh, come now, let's not distress the ladies."

"Yes," Beth Ann agreed. "We don't want to get morbid."

Now that the subject had been broached, however, I felt impelled to pursue it. "Richmond is the capital of the Confederacy. I would imagine that there, of all places, we would have no problem with food."

"My dear Mrs. Falconer," the little man said, leaning forward, "I don't see how you could possibly come to such a conclusion. Don't you realize that the Southern ports are completely blockaded, that our railroad system has been bombarded

to fragments? Even if there were an abundance of foodstuffs—
which there is not—transport would be a problem."

"I had no idea it was that bad."

Derry smiled at me. "Of course you didn't," he said in-
dulgently, his eyes suddenly dancing with a look of love that
evoked passionate kisses and whispered endearments on fog-
shrouded afternoons. The bread riots of Richmond faded into
nothingness.

The men, told they could bivouac in the spare rooms upstairs, went off to bed. Derry lingered in the parlor, waiting
until a yawning Beth Ann excused herself. Alone at last, we
were strangely shy.

Derry cleared his throat. "Have you heard from Miles?"

"Not since February."

He rose and went to the fireplace. Leaning his arm on the
mantel, he stood looking down into the dead ashes.

I perched on the edge of the sofa, waiting, besieged by
earlier doubts—my hair, my gown, Richmond belles—while
the ticking clock grew louder in the awkward silence.

"Derry . . ."

He turned. "Sweetheart, my own sweetheart."

I was up off the sofa, flying across the room into his arms,
home, safe and loved, his mouth saying better than a thousand
words that he still loved me. He held me, his eyes poised above
mine, full of desire. I pulled his head down, claiming his
mouth, clinging to him as if I could keep him there forever.
His arms tightened about me and I could feel the thump of his
heart under the gray cloth of his uniform.

"Carmella." He laughed, taking me by the shoulders, then
pressing his lips to the throbbing at the base of my throat.
"You're as sweet and lovely as ever."

He sat down and drew me onto his knees. "I've missed you
so, darling. There isn't a day that goes by when I don't think
of you. Ah—Carmella." He kissed my hands, my face, my
lips. "Have you missed me?"

"Oh, yes, yes."

His hands went to the top of my basque.

"Wait . . ." I pushed away from him and got to my feet.

"What is it?"

I didn't know how to answer. A sudden feeling of impropriety had come over me.

"Not here?" Derry asked, taking hold of my hand. "Shall we go upstairs?"

I wanted him as much as he wanted me. I knew that. And there had been a time when I would not have hesitated, when I would have gone with him hand in hand into any dark room he chose, gone gladly, my heart tripping, my senses roused to aching need. But now—something held me back. Perhaps it was the thought of how I had chastised Deirdre and her lover, Harry Page, and the aftertaste of hypocrisy and guilt that made me hesitate.

"The walls have eyes," I said, feeling they actually did.

"Do they? Such a small matter didn't bother you once. Or have you grown fond of Miles?"

"Certainly not!" I answered stoutly. But it did pass through my mind that for some obscure reason I knew I could not enjoy Derry in the same bed where Miles had turned to me in the dark. "Darling, please believe me, I love only you."

He kissed me lightly on the cheek. "I believe you. I must. I don't want to think that things have changed between us."

"Oh, Derry, I want us to be all alone. The thought of the others here . . ." I waved my hand. "Please say you understand."

"I'm disappointed. I came to Wildoak especially . . . But I see your point. Never mind, dear—I understand. There will be other times. Good night." He kissed me long and lingeringly. "I'll see you in the morning."

But when I came down early, shortly after sunrise, he and his men had already gone.

CHAPTER

TWENTY-SIX

IN JULY, Miles came riding home to Wildoak with devastating news. Harold Falconer and my uncle, James Hastings, had been killed and Hubert Fairchild taken prisoner in a ferocious battle at a place called Gettysburg. It had been a disastrous defeat for the South. Miles himself had been narrowly missed by a ball that had lifted the hat from his head.

When told of Harold's death, Beth Ann broke down, but in a different and far more disturbing way. No hysterics, no crazy laughter or sobbing this time. Instead she went into silent, blank rigidity. We thought it would wear off, but she sat all of that first day and the next and the next, her eyes staring, her face expressionless. Not hearing, not seeing, she had withdrawn into an inner world where nothing or no one could reach her.

It frightened the girls, even Deirdre (who had been summoned with her husband and child from Alder House) and Deirdre did not frighten easily.

"Will she come out of it, Uncle Miles?" she asked.

"Yes, I think so. It will take time."

He himself looked like death. His skin had an unhealthy sallow look and the bruised circles under his eyes seemed to heighten his gaunt, hawk-nosed appearance. I could only guess at the horrors that were locked in his breast, for he refused to discuss the battle. But on the third night after he had drained the last of Harold's brandy and started on the elderberry wine, he seemed unable to contain his thoughts any longer.

We were sitting in the parlor with the doors and windows open to catch any errant breeze. It had been a hot day, and night had cooled the air only slightly. I was seated on the rocker close to the lamp, picking the hem out of one of Elizabeth's old dresses, too short for her now, when Miles suddenly said:

"The waste, the terrible waste!"

I looked over at him as he sat sprawled in his chair, a goblet between his large hands, frowning down at it with burning eyes.

"I agree," I said.

His head came up, one eyebrow lifted. "Do you? How could you possibly know?"

"Because . . ." I hadn't meant to tell him about my experience at Gaines Mill, but the jeering tone in Miles's voice prodded me. "We had some wounded soldiers here, as you probably know. One of them—he couldn't have been over fifteen—died and I put on his uniform and took the gun you left me and rode to Gaines Mill."

I went on to tell him what had happened, and a look of incredulity settled on his face.

When I had finished, he shook his head. "Carmella, Carmella, what a crazy thing to do." Yet his voice held nothing of the scolding condemnation I had come to expect. There was even a grudging admiration.

"Ruth felt the same, but in a way I'm not sorry I went. It made me see this war much more clearly."

"Yes," he said, sloshing more wine into his glass. "Though Gaines Mill, all of that Peninsula War, was child's play compared to this. I have never—never lived through such carnage."

He drank. I said nothing, watching him.

"They had the vantage point, you see, the Feds on the hill— on Cemetery Ridge—above us, firing down. The reinforcements we hoped for never came. I tell you that's the story of this war. One stupid blunder after another." He paused to sip at his wine, forgetting me, his eyes shadowed as he relived the past. "Water would have made a difference; a short rest and one long pull from a canteen while we were climbing up and up on that terrible hill might have saved us. The Colonel tried, but his order to stop and wait for the water buckets to reach us was countermanded and we had to keep moving. Moving while they raked us with solid shot! Men falling all around, their guts ripped out and their faces gone. And there was Pickett on his black horse urging us forward."

He drew in his breath. "The Feds charged when we were almost to the top. We were fighting hand to hand with bayonets. Can you imagine a rage that makes you want to kill a man you don't know, have never seen before, a perfect stranger? Maybe it wasn't rage; maybe it was fear. Kill or be killed." He took another drink. "They boxed us in—that's the long and short of it. The Colonel told us to try and save ourselves; 'Wait for the next barrage, then make a run for it.' I didn't run. To run was to be shot—front, back, side. I got down on my knees and crawled over ground puddled in blood. Harold was in front of me. . . ." His glass fell from slack fingers and he covered his eyes with a hand.

Filled with a compassion that made my throat ache, I put my sewing aside and went over to him, kneeling at his feet. "It's over, Miles," I said, my hand on his knee. "It's over."

He grasped my hand. "I wish to God it were." He lifted my hand and kissed the palm. We looked into each other's eyes and then he raised me, pulling me into his lap.

He began to kiss me, slowly at first, rather absently. Then he suddenly jerked me against his chest and his mouth bore down on mine, his tongue seeking the recesses of my mouth in a wildly passionate kiss. I felt my arms go up around his neck, felt his hands caressing me, moving with an erotic sureness up and down my back, stroking my arms and shoulders, exploring my breasts through the cloth of my gown. He began to unbutton it and then, suddenly impatient, seized the front in one hand and tore it open.

"Miles—my dress—I . . ."

"Hush!"

Then crushing me in his arms, he rose and carried me up the stairs. I had no thought of listening walls, no thought of the others in the house. I was only aware of the summer darkness, of Miles undressing me, of Miles kissing me, his hands and his mouth bringing a wild tumultuous oblivion that drew a curtain over the horrible war. That night we were not Miles and Carmella, but two desperate souls losing ourselves in one another, two passionate, almost frenzied lovers, draining each other, exploring with mouth and hands, moving with a tide that swept us into a different wondrous world of ecstasy.

But in the morning the real world returned. How quickly the aftermath of ecstasy recedes, how quickly the body and the mind take up the annoyances that seemingly disappear during the act of love.

At breakfast Miles said, "That child of Deirdre's—it's not Beasley's, is it?"

"No." I told him what happened. To my surprise he blamed me.

"Why should I be held to account for Deirdre?" I demanded. "I can't be everywhere. Beth Ann, as you see, is totally inept; she has shirked all her responsibility. Old Mindy can hardly crawl from her cot in the morning to fire the stove. I have to help with the laundry, the cooking, the cleaning. And now you feel I should have been Deirdre's nursemaid too."

"To hell with cooking and cleaning. Why didn't you let them slide? You, of all people, ought to know how a girl's head can be turned by a rogue."

"Are you implying Derry Wakefield is a rogue?"

"I'm not implying, I'm saying."

"It's untrue! Derry is a *proud* man. If his circumstances had been different we would have married long ago. And he loves me, a deep abiding love that still endures."

"Indeed?" He threw down his napkin, got up from the chair, and walked to the open window. Parting the billowing curtains he gazed out on the side lawn, studying it wordlessly.

His silent back irked me. "I suppose you think—"

He wheeled about. "Does it matter what I think? Does it? I'm told that Derry was here recently."

"Only overnight. He was on a secret mission; he came with four other officers."

"Overnight," Miles repeated mockingly. "I'm not in the least surprised."

A denial sprang to my lips but I bit it back. Why should I have to explain? He would never believe me in any case.

Miles and I did not part on very friendly terms. I tried to

tell myself that he was going back to the bloody, savage fighting, that his chances for coming out of the holocaust alive or even whole got slimmer and slimmer as time wore on. But whatever resolve I had made to forget our differences, what conciliatory words formed in my thoughts were stopped by his stony expression, his cold good-bye.

As he was turning his horse to ride away, Beth Ann came rushing down the stairs, shouting, "Wait! Miles—wait!" She looked demented, hair streaming, eyes bulging, her wrapper flapping about her legs.

He drew rein and dismounted. "What is it, Beth Ann?"

I went up to her and tried to take her arm. She jerked it away.

"I want to know," she said breathlessly, her hands clasping her heaving bosom, "Why you came home without Harold. Where is Harold?"

There was a stunned silence. Then Miles spoke, his voice gentle. "My dear, Harold was killed in battle."

She looked up at him, her mouth quivering. "If—if that's so, why didn't you bring his—his body back to Wildoak?"

"We could not remove our dead. We had no time. Harold is buried at Gettysburg."

"No, oh, no!" Her face crumpled and she dissolved into a storm of sobbing. Miles held her head against his shoulder where she continued to weep.

Finally Miles said, "She'll be all right now. Carmella, take her."

Beth Ann did not protest as I put my arm about her waist and drew her from Miles.

"Take care of her—of yourself," Miles said, swinging into the saddle.

"Miles—I . . ." But the hard look had returned to his eyes. "Good-bye."

After Miles left we received no news, only rumors we had no way of verifying. We heard that conditions in the army had deteriorated even further. Dispirited men, worried about their wives and children their unplowed fields, and the threat of famine that stalked their loved ones, took off for home. We had several stragglers stop at Wilkoak, bearded and dirty, their eyes dulled with fatigue. We asked no questions but gave them a meal, the first one they'd had in weeks, they said, and when they left stuffed their pockets with corn pone.

Many were silent; some talked freely. Vicksburg had surrendered. Port Hudson too. The hospitals were overflowing; there weren't enough cannon, enough doctors, enough anything, and profiteers in Richmond were making fortunes.

The summer dragged on. We at Wilkoak harvested our vegetables and shared them with our neightbors. Alice Dinwiddie had moved in with Prudence Fairchild. They were coping fairly well since most of the Fairchild darkies had remained on the plantation, unlike the Dinwiddie slaves who had run off as so many were doing all over the South. We still had our two, Ned and Ben. God knows what we would have done without them. But old Mindy became weaker and weaker, and one morning when I came down to the kitchen I found her dead, sprawled out on the bare wooden floor before the stove. Her grandchild sat on a chair bewildered as to why she could not rouse her mammy. I wanted to keep the little girl after we buried Mindy, but Ned and Ben said she'd be happier with them.

I did not realize how much of the work Mindy had done until she was gone, poor tired-out old soul. Elizabeth and Lorena had to take on a larger share of the workload, chopping and carrying wood, heating water for washing and laundry, scrubbing and wringing the large heavy sheets, tasks that had always been done for them. But surprisingly they did not complain. I wondered why until I realized they were frightened by their mother's odd behavior. Beth Ann had bad days when she would spend her time just staring out of the window; other times she would talk a blue streak, always about irrelevant matters, not about the war. She never mentioned Harold.

One humid September morning, Deirdre came galloping up the drive, her child on the saddle in front of her. I heard her shout, "Carmella!" and I came running out.

"Help me down," she said.

I took the child and she slipped from the saddle. My first thought was that marriage had made her sloppy. She was wearing an old faded gown and her uncombed hair streamed in tangled untidiness down her back.

But then she said, "Beasley is dead. An accident. He shot himself."

"He *what?*"

She seemed composed, despite her appearance. "He was cleaning his rifle this morning and it went off."

"Mother of God!" What should I do? Why did they always come to me?

"Shouldn't we—shouldn't we report to someone, some authority, a sheriff, a constable?" I asked.

"There aren't any. Hanover Court is the nearest. I don't even know if the Yankees have it or not, do you?"

"No," I said.

"It was an accident," she repeated. "We'll have to bury him."

I took Ben with us and we rode back to Alder House. Beasley lay face up on the library floor, a bloody, charred hole in his forehead. The stench of death filled the room and already the black flies had clustered about his face, buzzing in the silence. For a few moments the room seemed to sway around me as memories of Lyon, his eyes staring in death, crowded in. I had to clutch at the oak table to steady myself.

"I didn't move him," Deirdre said. "You can see what happened."

The rifle butt lay in the loose grasp of his curled fingers. His right hand held a crumpled oily cloth. I understood very little about guns, but I knew enough to realize that a man cleaning a gun that accidentally discharges is more likely to get his head blown off than to have a gaping dark hole in his forehead. Aside from that, in this part of the world, no male reached puberty without a thorough knowledge of hunting rifles. Beasley, a veteran of war, would hardly be careless enough to clean a loaded weapon.

All this added to a growing suspicion of foul play as Ben wrapped the man in a blanket and carried him out of the house.

"Shouldn't we try to get Reverend James to say a few words?" I asked. It seemed indecent to bury a member of the family— even if only by marriage—so hastily without some sort of funeral.

"Do *you* want to ride to Cross Hill and fetch him?" Deirdre said waspishly.

"I will if you want me to."

"It would take another day, back and forth. I don't see why it's necessary."

"All right."

No breeze stirred the trees that crowded against the windows. A band of hot sunlight had worked its way through the limp, still leaves and fanned out over the sofa, a chair. The room was like an oven. And the smell! Even with Beasley's body gone, it lingered. I wiped the sweat from my forehead with the edge of my sleeve.

"I suppose it's best to get him into the ground," I said.

Deirdre nodded.

"When did you find him?"

"Early this morning. I came down and there he was."

"You didn't hear the shot?"

"No," she said shortly.

"Did he make a habit of cleaning his gun in the library?"

"I don't know." She put her hands on his hips, her eyes narrowing. "Why are you asking me all this? I didn't kill him. Lord knows I hated him. I'm not going to weep because he's dead, but I *didn't* kill him!"

She was so emphatic I believed her.

"Have you a Bible?" I asked.

Her skirts rustled as she crossed the room and lifted one from the table.

"Is there any text you prefer?"

"None that I can think of."

I found Beasley's old cavalry flag and had Ben wrap it about him in lieu of a coffin.

While Ben shoveled the dirt, I recited, "I am the Resurrection and the Life, and whosoever...believeth in Me shall never..."

Deirdre packed her belongings and the few good things that Beasley owned into a small trunk. Then we climbed into the buggy and with Beasley's horse tied to the backboard trotted toward Wildoak.

In retrospect I sometimes think that Beasley's death was the beginning of the end. From that time on, things seemed to go from bad to much, much worse.

* * *

In the middle of September a small troop of emaciated Confederate cavalry men, covered with dust and riding rib-lean horses, jogged up from the river road. Behind them rattled a mule-drawn wagon. They had been sent out on a foraging mission by the Commissary Department with orders to confiscate foodstuffs and provender—stock, hay, fowl, salted meat, blankets—anything that could be of use to the army. Though the officer in charge was polite, offering to pay for what he took, he looked like the vulture he was, his hooded, reddened eyes darting this way and that as he mentally assessed the fields and cabins beyond the verandah.

"But, Lieutenant," I protested, "your money can't feed us here." Even if the Confederate bills had any value, it was impossible to buy food anywhere.

"I'm sorry, ma'am, but those were my orders. We can't fight the Yankees on empty bellies."

He was right—but so was I. If the whole idea of this war was to protect hearth and home, why were our own people stripping, if not destroying, us in the process?

While I stood there castigating myself for not having had the foresight to hide the cows and pigs, at the least, the lieutenant turned to his sergeant and started giving orders.

"Have two men scour the fields, two to the cabins, two to the stables..."

They apparently were not interested in our personal valuables, the silver and what few jewels we owned. But they seized everything that could be considered edible by either beast or man, leaving us with a pair of scrawny chickens, a rooster, one runty shoat, and a sack of wormy beans. Someone had overlooked a bushel of apple, and the yams were not ready to dig. That was it, that is what we would have to feed ourselves with that fall and the coming winter. The foragers had not even spared us coffee. In addition to cleaning out the storeroom, they had appropriated the mare and Beasley's horse, thus cutting us off completely from our neighbors.

A few days after the lieutenant and his scavengers had departed, Elizabeth came running down from her room.

"There's a fire on the other side of the river!" she cried excitedly. "Come see."

I hurried upstairs after her. The smoke rose in a thin grayish pillar above the treetops; and as I watched from the window the column widened, boiling out into a black greasy cloud tinged at the under edge with glimmering orange.

"Where can it be?" I muttered, perplexed.

"The Hastingses live in that direction."

"The Hastingses..." Yes, yes, of course. Grandfather, Mother, and the now-widowed Lavinia. It must be their house. But how? An accident? It did not seem likely. The foraging platoon? But why should they fire the house? Old man Hastings with his fervent patriotism would give them the shirt off his back if asked. It could only be the Yankees. But so close? Surely if they had been nearby the lieutenant would have warned us. Perhaps he had not wanted to raise an alarm. Worse, perhaps he had not known. That little band I had secretly reviled could have been ambushed, killed and now...

"If..." Fear splintered my voice and I waited, fighting it back. For the children's sake I must put on a show of calm. They were frightened enough. "If only we could help them."

Mingled with my fear was a feeling of utter helplessness. Without the horses we were unable to go to anyone's aid, unable to warn the people downriver, unable to do anything but wait.

My throat felt raw and my hands gripping the window ledge damp. "Elizabeth...," I ran my tongue over my lips, "Elizabeth, go downstairs and see to the mess of greens on the stove. You might have to add a little water."

"But, Aunt Carmella..." Her eyes were wide.

"Don't tell the others. We'll just make out as if nothing is amiss until... Well, we'll see. There's nothing to be afraid of. Go on, scoot now!"

When she left, I hurried down the hall to my room and got Miles's pistol from the drawer where I kept it now. The cool steel in my hands slowed my racing heart. Its blue-black glimmer gave me a sense of comfort, almost of power. We were not unarmed. Deirdre had Beasley's hunting rifle and old dueling pistol. There were knives in the kitchen, an axe in the smokehouse. We had two Negroes, strong as oxen, myself (Beth Ann I could not count), and Deirdre. Not many, but we had the vantage point; we could shoot down at anyone approaching, fire from behind the draperies, so that men coming up the drive would think the house sheltered a platoon. Together we might hold the Yankees off.

Elizabeth and I took turns all that day, watching from the upstairs window. Along about suppertime Elizabeth gave a shout that went through me like a knife.

"Someone's coming!"

I dashed up the stairs. By straining my ears I could hear horses' hooves. A moment later I saw the flash of a horse's rump through the riverbank trees. Picking up the gun, I steadied it on the sill.

"Get Deirdre," I said quietly, above the thrumming of my heart. "Tell her to bring the rifle; then have Lorena fetch Ned and Ben."

I stood there waiting, peering through the gathering dusk. Down below a door slammed and I heard the thud of feet on the stairs. Deirdre came into the room, the rifle carelessly tucked under one arm, the pistold hanging from the fingers of her right hand. Her eyes had a feverish glow to them.

"Yankees?"

"Maybe," I said.

The next moment a carriage came rumbling round the bend, a single lathered horse straining at the traces.

"Oh, for God's sake," Deirdre exclaimed. "The Hastingses."

After replacing the gun under a pillow I quickly descended the stairs. I came out on the verandah just as Lavinia was helping Mother Hastings down from the carriage. The inside of it was piled to the roof with mattresses, odd pieces of furniture, boxes and trunks.

Both women were white faced and trembling.

"Deirdre!" I called. I turned my head and saw her watching us from behind the parlor curtains. "Deirdre, come out here and give us a hand."

"Oh, Carmella . . . ," Lavinia began, her voice tearful.

"It's all right," I soothed; "don't talk now. Elizabeth, help me with Mother Hastings."

But she went limp before we could get her inside.

Lavinia and I carried her to the sofa. While Lavinia rubbed

her wrists I administered sal volatile and shortly her eyes fluttered open. She took one dazed look at us then burst into tears. Lavinia continued to sit by her mother-in-law's side, rubbing her thin, bony wrists, her head turned away. I knew she was crying too.

"Get the wine," I ordered. But it was Elizabeth, not Deirdre, who scurried off. Deirdre stood in the doorway. Her curiosity irritated me.

"Deirdre, please put some water on to heat," I ordered.

"Can't I hear what happened?"

"You will in good time. We'll want tea."

Elizabeth returned with the wine. Mother Hastings refused it, but Lavinia took a long draught. Then moving to a chair she sank down and closed her eyes. Mother Hastings went on weeping softly.

Soon Deirdre returned. Lavinia looked up and, sucking in her breath, said, "The Yankees."

I nodded. "I thought as much."

She bit her lip, her eyes filling with tears.

"What did they do?" Deirdre prompted.

"Deirdre!" I glared at her. "If you want to remain, I advise you to keep your mouth shut."

"It's all right," Lavinia said in a tired voice. "She wants to know. It would be better for me too, if I talked about it."

"You don't have to."

"No. I want to. You see—they came last evening. Papa was beside himself. He—I thought he'd have a stroke. We were at supper and didn't even hear them coming until the first one walked in the door, wearing a slouch hat and a two-day stubble on his chin- A dirty-looking bunch. I think they were deserters, renegades out on their own. Pape couldn't do anything. His gun—the only one he hadn't given to the army— was in the other room. It was the first thing they found. You know, the first thing. They stayed overnight."

"You mean," Deirdre said, unable to restrain herself, "they *slept* in the house? Did they—did they try anything indecent?"

"Deirdre!"

"Well, everyone knows how they go around raping women."

I half rose from my chair. "Deirdre, I told you . . . !"

"It's all right, Carmella," Lavinia said patiently. "To answer your question, Deirdre. They may have wanted to—to try, but they didn't get the chance. Mother, Papa, and I locked ourselves in the bedroom and spent the night together. We could hear them—all those long dark hours—ransacking the house, going through it, and in the morning they began to load their loot on their horses and in our carriage. Papa was furious. We had to hold him. He wanted to hurl himself out the window and down at them. They were still stuffing their saddlebags when—when the shots came. You can imagine our joy when we saw it was our own boys. The Yankees scattered in all directions. I think two—yes, two—got hit. The rest ran away. When it was over, we came downstairs and hugged the lieutenant. They were from the Commissary, a foraging party."

"Was the officer a tall man with a drooping moustache? Yes? They were here, too; took everything."

"We hadn't much, but you see we were so thankful and we were standing outside talking and chattering away about the Yankees when Papa said, ''I smell smoke.' One of the Yankee robbers must have sneaked back and set fire to the dining-room portieres. Out of spite, Carmella, sheer spite. We tried to put it out. Everyone helped, all of us running for buckets of water. The only darkies we had left were Jubal and Amos, and they helped too, but the fire spread so fast—and the smoke. We had to leave it. And we were standing in the drive—oh, it's too terrible to watch your house go up like that and not be able to do anything. Fire is so awful, so *savage*. Well, we were standing there when we suddenly noticed Papa tottering up the verandah steps. We yelled for him to come back, but he only turned his head and shouted, "Grannie!" I think—I think he was after her portrait. It hangs above the sideboard in the dining room—do you remember, Deirdre?"

"I can't exactly recall," she said.

"Papa's grannie had raised him, and the portrait was painted by Edward Peticolas, a famous artist. Papa didn't . . . The roof fell in and he—he never got out."

Tears welled in her eyes and rolled down her cheeks. "He wasn't liked by a lot of people, I know. But he—he was good to me."

I should have said, "He died a hero's death," but I couldn't see it that way no matter how I turned it around in my mind.

He had gone blindly into the house to save a picture, an asinine, sentimental gesture, which galled when I thought of his coldness and how he had never forgiven my father, much less said a single kind word to me.

Lavinia blew her nose and went on. "The lieutenant let us have the carriage and a horse. He said he'd come and fetch them later. We drove as fast as we could. I don't know how many of the Yankees got away."

We took turns watching all that night and for the next few days, but neither the Yankee deserters nor the Confederate foragers made an appearance.

CHAPTER

TWENTY-SEVEN

*W*INTER CLOSED *down on us with a chill rain* which soon turned to an icy, wind driven sleet, beating at the windows and rattling the panes. For some reason the foragers had left the stacked wood in the barn untouched, and a warm fire was one of the very few comforts we enjoyed during those bitter months.

Beth Ann and the younger girls complained loudly of hunger. We were all hungry, but I had known worse in Virginia City. Here at least we had fresh game from time to time— possum, rabbits, squirrels, birds, whatever Ben could trap, for we dared not use our small horde of bullets. In addition, we had apples, nuts, and greens that had survived the frost as well as the flour and lard Lavinia and Mother Hastings had brought in their crazily crammed carriage, foodstuffs that had somehow escaped the eyes of the foraging platoon. Not the best of diets, but it kept us alive.

Lavinia tried to be helpful, but I never in my life saw anyone so ignorant of the simplest household tasks. Like Beth Ann, she had always been waited upon. I doubt whether she had been in her own kitchen more than a half dozen times. She hadn't the vaguest idea of how to fire a stove, boil an egg, or make coffee. Unlike my sister-in-law, however, she seemed willing enough to learn, though she made a botch of every task I set her to.

313

* * *

It had been months since I had heard from Ruth Harkness. Worried, I drove to her place one cold, frosty December morning, chiding myself for not having gone sooner. When I came in sight of the house, the silence and the smokeless chimneys seemed ominous. The curtains in the house were drawn and as I approached, a bird flew out from under the verandah, sqawking as it flapped its wings.

I got down from the driver's seat, my throat tight with foreboding. Tying the horse to a post, I went up the wooden stairs. My footsteps made a hollow *tap-tap* sound, and when the wind howled around the corner in a sudden gust I shivered. I stood at the door and hesitated a moment before knocking. No one answered. When I tried the knob, I found the door was locked. I moved around to a side window and peered into the dining room through a gap in the draperies. Ruth sat sprawled in a chair, white faced, motionless, her head on her chest. That's all I could see.

I was certain she was dead.

Remorse rolled through me, a wave of sick regret. Why hadn't I come before now? A month, six weeks ago? Ever since Lavinia and Mother Hastings had arrived with the horse and carriage, I had had the means of transportation. Why hadn't I used them? I'd been busy; but busy with what? Ruth was my only friend and I had deserted her. The others for whom I ministered, cooked, washed, and served, didn't give a tinker's damn about me, but Ruth had cared. And I had neglected her.

I tried the window. It was locked, and in my frustration I rattled it, pounding on the wooden frame. Suddenly the curtains parted and Ruth, her face as shocked as mine must have been, looked out. We were to laugh about it later, but at that moment I felt sure that I was looking into the eyes of a ghost.

Then she smiled. "I'll open the door," she mouthed.

I nearly fainted with relief. A few moments later I fell into her arms, hugging and kissing her, and weeping. She shed a few tears herself. We all wept easily in those days.

Her two darkies, she told me, had slipped off immediately after the troop of foragers had gone through.

"You mean you've been here all alone?"

"Yes."

"For two months? Oh, Ruth, why didn't you come to Wildoak?"

"I didn't want to be a burden," she said.

"If that isn't the most ridiculous nonsense! A burden! What in God's name have you been living on? And don't lie, I can see it's not much."

"I had a full larder, really." Then she broke into a smile. "All right, not much."

"You're coming home with me."

Surprisingly, she didn't put up an argument. She was tough, though. I think she could have sat out the whole war alone if I hadn't come for her.

All during that winter and spring we saw no one. Ben beating the bushes for game met up with a darkie who told him the Confederates were holding their own. Whatever that meant we had no idea. Nothing was said about the loss of Little Rock or Chattanooga, two Rebel defeats we were to learn of much later. Nor did we have any inkling of where the Yankees might be now. We planted our garden in April, saw the trees blossom in the apple orchard, loosened our belts a bit when we slaughtered an old cow who had strayed into the copse of cottonwoods near the creek.

Toward the end of May we heard the sound of guns in the distance, just as we had two years earlier, and on June 1st they seemed to move south for they became louder.

"Cold Harbor, I'll wager," Ruth said grimly.

As the week progressed and the guns continued to sputter and boom, we all became jumpy and irritable. The heat did not help. We had gone from winter to summer with only the briefest of moderate intervals, and the sun that had been welcome in April became a curse in June. It was a sticky heat, a dripping humidity that made one move slowly and breathe shallowly. Only Beth Ann seemed cool, sitting in the shaded parlor calmly fanning herself with a palmetto leaf. Ruth laughingly said Beth Ann reminded her of one of those Eastern nabobs pictured in the illustrated *World Guide*. I failed to see the humor in it. Beth Ann had recovered enough of her senses to begin sniping at me again in that sweet, honey-smooth Carolinian drawl of hers.

"After all," she would say, "you are accustomed to a house without servants, aren't you?"

"I'm not lazy, if that's what you mean. And there's going to come a day soon enough at Wildoak where the lazy ones just won't eat."

"Well . . . ! I declare! I'll have you remember, Carmella, this is my house!"

"Is it? One would never know."

In tha past I had ignored Beth Ann's spiteful remarks, but the present jangled state of my nerves made me sensitive to irritation from any source. I noticed that Lavinia, now that the shock of her father-in-law's fiery death had receded and she had received reassuring letters from her boys who were at Cedar Creek, had taken to siding with Beth Ann and she was never around when I needed her; and Mother Hastings, when asked to set the table or sweep a floor began to cough pitifully.

Only Elizabeth and Ruth bore their share without complaint. Deirdre ranted and raved, but she never shirked. Whatever it was that festered inside gave her a restless energy that made her quick and efficient. She would have been a good companion during those trying days, but she kept everyone at arm's length, expecially Ruth and myself. Her forced marriage to Beasley Morse still rankled.

The faint, far-off sullen sound of cannon, like distant thunder, went on. It was worse when the guns fell silent, for then I would catch myself, whether at the stove or the table, in the hall or upstairs in my room, leaning forward, straining to listen. Had the Confederates won, pushed the Yankees back? Were our men, even now, in hot pursuit of a retreating blue army? Or . . . ? But I wouldn't linger on that.

After three days of silence I felt I would die if I didn't find out what was happening. I slipped out of the house, ran to the stable, and saddled the Hastingses' old nag. Ruth must have been watching me from an upstairs window, for when I galloped around to the drive I nearly ran into her as she stood in the way, arms outstretched.

"Oh, no, you don't! You're not going anywhere."

"You can't stop me!"

"I can and I will. Get off that horse." She put her hand on the bridle.

I was about to brush it away when it struck me that her hand was hardly more than skin and bone. I looked down at my friend, as if seeing her for the first time. How thin she had grown, how gaunt! She had never been a fleshy or large woman, but now she seemed hardly bigger than a child, one of those starved-looking waifs who haunted the back alleys of the Barbary Coast.

I slipped from the saddle and stood before her, feeling deflated, if not sheepish. "Ruth—I don't know what got into me. I'm terribly sorry."

She leaned up and kissed my cheek. "I understand, dear. Don't think I haven't felt like galloping off to Cold Harbor myself. But it's foolishness. Put the horse away and we'll have a cup of tea."

"Oh, Ruth!" I hugged her. She wasn't well, but she would never admit it.

That afternoon, Prudence Fairchild and Alice Dinwiddie came struggling up the drive, both atop a swaybacked plow horse that by all the laws of nature should have expired long ago. Prudence, in a shabby gown, thin and taut, nevertheless carried herself with a certain haughtiness and rode up to the verandah as if she had come mounted on a thoroughbred. In contrast, Alice looked bedraggled, her eyes round with fear, her shoulders slumped, her hair screwed into an untidy knot.

Prudence said, "We decided it was best to leave Fairchild. At least for a while."

We on the verandah, frozen and immobile, looked down on them like statues on a frieze. Only a catastrophe would pry Prudence away from Fairchild without boxes and trunks and her personal maid, even "for a while." We all were afraid to ask why she had come. It was Ruth who spoke first.

"Where are the children?"

"We sent them on to Richmond with Uncle Harvey and Aunt Betty when they passed through several weeks ago. Thank God for that. They didn't want to go, but our food supply was running low and—"

"We should have gone ourselves," Alice interrupted in a tearful voice.

"Oh, be quiet!" Prudence snapped. Then, turning to Ruth, she said, "If you'll hand me down, I would appreciate it."

We brought the two women into the house. It seemed as though I had relived this scene again and again, women arriving at the doorstep in distress, helping them into the house, the sal volatile ("Not needed, thank you," from Prudence), the bracing sip of wine, and the story of disaster.

They had been cleaned out by the foragers, just as we had. Whatever food they'd managed to save had gradually given out.

"Last evening," Prudence said, "the darkies came up to the house saying they were hungry, demanding their ration of beans and hog fat. As if we were holding it back! It was no use telling them we had nothing."

"No use," Alice repeated, her voice a little shrill. "They threatened to burn the house down if we didn't feed them."

"Imbeciles!" Prudence's eyes shone with indignation. "Jack-asses! Not a brain in their thick black skulls. And the Yankees want to free them."

Ruth said, "They were hungry."

Prudence bristled. "Are you taking up for niggers now?"

"No," she answered calmly. "Trying to understand."

"Oh, piffle!"

Beth Ann, her palmetto fan for once lying idle in her lap, ventured in a shaky voice, "Did they? Did they burn the house down?"

"Not yet," Prudence said. "At least it was still standing when we left."

Beth Ann's bloodless lips quivered. "Do you—do you suppose they'd be heading for Wildoak?"

"They might."

Beth Ann turned to me. "Carmella—I want Ben and Ned locked up!"

I stared at her. "You can't mean it. Why, we depend on them. They've served us loyally. We can't treat them like dogs."

"You're talking just like Ruth. I want them locked up! I don't trust anyone. The Rose Hill slaves were loyal too. I want them locked up!"

Deirdre exclaimed, "Mother! Be reasonable. Or at least—*try*."

Beth Ann's eyes filled with tears. "If your father were here you wouldn't speak to me like that."

"If Papa were here you'd be too ashamed to carry on like a—a coward."

There was a long, shocked silence, and then Ruth said, "It's no use our quarreling. We have to decide what to do."

"I say lock the slaves up," Beth Ann snuffled.

"That won't solve anything," Ruth said. "Food is our chief problem. Even if the garden should supply us with enough beans and corn to go around, it will be months before we can harvest them. Ben tells me the game has all but been hunted out. Then there is another consideration. I think you'll agree Wildoak is not the safe place we believed it to be. The war isn't over and we don't know where the next battle will be fought. We don't really know where the Yankees are now— marching up the river road for all we can guess."

"Oh, my God!" Beth Ann wailed.

Deirdre gave her a withering look. "Well, they aren't here yet."

"Nevertheless," Ruth said, "I think it would be best to refugee to Richmond."

I'd been expecting her to say that and was glad she had.

"I know it's not going to be easy," Ruth went on. "But we have the carriage and two horses. They aren't much, but I think they'll be able to haul a light load and carry two, perhaps three passengers."

Prudence sat up. "Two or three? What about the rest of us?"

"Why—we'll have to walk."

Beth Ann stuttered, "W-walk? I can't!"

And Prudence, "*I* won't."

"We can take turns," Ruth went on. "Mother Hastings, of course, will ride all the way."

Through a chorus of objections I spoke up, "And you, Ruth. You must also ride. You aren't well. Now, don't argue, I can see it."

Prudence snorted, "Piffle! I say piffle to all of you. One of those horses is mine. And I'll be a monkey's uncle if I'll walk and have somebody else have the benefit of my horse."

"Why you selfish . . . !" Deirdre began.

But Ruth, her cheeks flaming, held up her hand. "Hush! Hush, all of you! I can't believe it. I simply *can't* believe it! Where is all the gentility, the courtesy, the self-sacrifice, the *pride* we Southern women are supposed to possess? I've been listening to you squabbling like a gaggle of backwoods women at a peddler's cart and I can't believe it."

There was a momentary shamed silence; then Prudence said, "I don't fancy being likened to poor white trash."

"Then don't act like it. Act like a lady-born."

Prudence said, "A lady doesn't walk when she can ride."

"You are stubborn, aren't you?" Ruth said wearily.

Deirdre turned to Prudence and said, "If you won't walk, then you can stay behind."

"Please," Ruth begged. Her face had suddenly gone a ghastly white and she seemed on the verge of fainting.

I was angry now. "Can't you see how you are upsetting Ruth?"

I took her into the library and made her lie down on the leather sofa.

"I wish you'd tell me what's the matter," I said, fanning her strained, white face with a palmetto Beth Ann had left behind. "Don't try to cover it up. I know you aren't well."

"Does it show that much?" She smiled weakly. "I wish I knew. It's just a terrible fatigue I have to fight all the time. It scares me sometimes because I've always been full of energy and bounce."

"You need fattening up, decent food, red meat, hot yeasty bread spread with newly churned butter, thick rich cream and—"

"Oh, don't, Carmella—don't!" Ruth laughed. "You'll have me drooling in a minute."

"We can't get to Richmond soon enough. We ought to try and leave tomorrow, no later than the day after. What do you think?"

"I agree. We won't be able to take anything but a change of clothes and some food for the road. We'll just close up the house. I think Ben and Ned can fend by themselves much better than if they had us."

"Prudence—" I began.

"Oh, don't worry about Prudence. She'll come. She just enjoys acting up."

Once the decision had been made, everyone—except Prudence, who still carped—looked forward to leaving. One would think, from the talk and chatter, that we were going on an extended visit with rich relatives.

Deirdre and I baked corn pones all that afternoon, while Lavinia and the girls picked over the dried apples and made up a sack of them. We filled two large jugs and several empty wine bottles with water. Everything was packed that night in the carriage; Ben had oiled its wheels and joints and brought it around to the front door.

We were up before dawn. Deirdre and I went quickly through the house, locking and bolting the windows ("As if that will do any good," Deirdre said).

Richmond was some twenty-odd miles away if we took a roundabout route, little used and, we hoped, free of fighting. At the most, it should not be a journey of more than two days.

We gathered around the table for a hurried cup of boiled chickory root and then drew straws to decide who would start off riding in the carriage with Mother Hastings. Prudence let out a whoop when she discovered that she had drawn one of the short straws. Lavinia had the other. At least we would begin our travels in fairly good spirits. While I doused the fire in the kitchen stove, Deirdre and Alice washed up the cups and saucers.

I was taking one last look around when I heard Elizabeth shout from the front door, "Someone's coming!"

We all rushed out to the verandah. The man riding down under the leafy arch of trees wore a blue uniform, not like the cast-offs we had seen on the foragers and stragglers, but a trim military outfit with sparkling gilt braid, the collar standing up, white and spotless, the black leather belt and gilt eagle buckle, the silver sword and the black leather boots polished to a shine. Behind him rode two other men similarly attired. A platoon of cavalry brought up the rear.

Beth Ann gasped in horror.

But Deirdre watching, her eyes lighting up, said, "Well, I'll be damned, if it isn't the Yankees."

CHAPTER

TWENTY-EIGHT

*T*HE MOUNTED *officer in the lead halted, and rak-*ing his eyes over us, rested them on me.

"Morning, ma'am," he said, touching his wide-brimmed hat with a gloved hand. "Fixing to go somewhere?"

Captain? Major? Was Union insignia the same as Confederate?

"Yes, Major," I hazarded, my voice ringing oddly in my ears. "We were just about to leave for Richmond."

"Then I'm sorry to interrupt your plans. There will be some delay, I'm afraid."

Ruth stepped forward, her face parchment white. "Major— we . . ."

I caught her as she crumpled.

Lavinia exclaimed, "Quick, the smelling salts!"

The officer dismounted and lifted Ruth in his arms. "Devins!" he called over his shoulder. "See that no one moves until you've scouted the place for possible enemy."

"There isn't anyone here," I said venomously, "except us women and two Negro slaves."

"I'd like to take your word for it, ma'am. But I've been at this war too long to take *anyone's* word. Now—where do you want this woman?"

I led the way into the parlor. Beth Ann, as usual in times

of crisis, had disappeared upstairs. The major lowered Ruth onto the sofa and then—thank goodness—left us.

"Deirdre, get some water," I ordered. We had no more sal volatile, so I began rubbing Ruth's wrists. "Open a window. Someone open a window!"

It took me a little while to get Ruth back to consciousness. And when her eyes finally fluttered open she murmured faintly, "I'm sorry."

"It's all right, Ruth. Just lie still, don't try to talk. Everything is going to be all right. I think they'll let us leave. I'll talk the major into it."

Lavinia whispered, "What'll we do if he doesn't?"

Prudence sat down on a straight-backed chair. "They'll let us go, of course they will. Might even lend us a horse. I don't reckon I've seen such splendid animals since '61."

"Nor such good-looking men," Deirdre added.

There was an audible gasp, cries of "Deirdre—how could you? "Of all the . . . !" and "They're *Yankees!*"

"But they haven't got horns or devils' tails, have they?" Deirdre threw back. "I don't care if they are Yankees."

"A Yankee killed your father," Ruth pointed out.

"And how many Yankees did Papa kill? Oh, I'm not standing up for them, but it's so good to see men who are sound and whole, man without hacked limbs or bloodied heads. To see men shaved, and dressed in clean tailored clothes, not in ragtag strips of cloth and dirty bandages."

"My God!" Prudence exploded. "You ought to be shot as a Yankee sympathizer."

"You'd like that, wouldn't you?" Deirdre said spitefully.

Ruth tried to raise herself from the sofa. "Oh, please, *please!*"

"Hush!" I cried, exasperated. "You fools! We have to stick together, now more than ever. We can't go on fighting in this idiotic manner. You're only upsetting Ruth and giving comfort to the enemy. They're here! The *Yankees* are here!"

At this point Deirdre's little boy began to cry. She picked him up and, bouncing him in her arms, walked to the window and looked out.

Ruth tugged at my skirt. "Come closer. I don't want the others to hear." I bent over her. "Watch Deirdre. If she gets pregnant again, there's no one around to marry her."

"Yes. I've already thought of that. I'll do my best."

Suddenly the ringing of axes on wood echoed through the room. "They're cutting down the trees," Deirdre said, craning her neck as she leaned out of the window. "I can't see, but it sounds like it."

I went out of the room, followed by Deirdre, and down the hall to the passage that led to the kitchen. I paused at the window and drew in my breath. All across the back lawns tents were being set up, fires started, horses staked. The well pulley screeched. I heard the bluecoats laughing, and a far-off shout: "Nothin' here!"

They were searching for hidden food. We had none—no cows, livestock, poultry, or sacks of grain. They could, of course, loot the house. They could strip it of furniture, silver, heirlooms, spoons, lamps, and chairs, possessions that had been brought over in Colonial times or had come around the Horn across the world from the Orient. Why should I care? They weren't my things. I was only a Falconer by marriage, and a loveless, unorthodox marriage at that. Let the thieves have what they could find.

But Deirdre, whose mind must have been running parallel to mine, said, "I'd better hide the silver." And when I looked at her in surprise, she added, "It will be little Page's someday and I don't want him accusing me of giving his inheritance over to the Yankees."

"Go on, then, and while you're at it tuck the firearms in a safe place too. You'd better hurry. If I'm not mistaken that's the major riding up this way."

"Keep him busy," she said, brushing past me and heading for the dining room.

I went outside and stood on the stoop, watching as a cluster of men parted for him. He cantered up, reined in, and brought his hand to his wide-brimmed hat, but again did not remove it.

"You'll forgive me," I said coldly, "if I do not seem very hospitable."

"I understand."

"Are you staying for long?" I wanted to know.

"That depends. Perhaps. I'd like to come in and discuss it with you."

"And if I refuse?"

"I'm afraid you have no choice."

"In that case, perhaps you'd best speak with Mrs. Harkness."

"The lady who fainted? No, I prefer talking it over with you."

"Come around to the front door," I said. "I want to lock this one." It would give Deirdre a little more time.

I peeked in at the dining room, but she had already gone. When I opened the front door he was standing on the verandah, hat in hand, his back to me, looking down through the trees to the river, a man of medium height with broad shoulders.

"Come in, Major."

He followed as I led the way to the library. I motioned him to a chair and he waited as I sat down on a spindly-legged one.

Now for the first time I had a good look at him. His eyes were unusual, a brownish yellow with flecked irises. They betrayed nothing, neither friendliness nor hostility. He had a strong aquiline nose, a thin mouth, and a clean-shaven jaw. His hair was wavy, dark brown, worn short above the ears and long at the nape. Something about him reminded me of Miles, though there was not the slightest physical resemblance between the two.

"I am Major Ward Gamble of the Fourteenth Illinois Cavalry. And you?"

I hesitated. "This is hardly a social call, Major. Does it matter who I am?"

His eyes seemed to harden, though his voice remained courteously cool. "If you do not care to abide by the amenities, then I shan't press you."

I knew then why this man brought Miles to mind. It was his aura of power, his air of authority, and a strong sexuality that was tightly held in check. But whereas Miles had tempered these characteristics with mockery and a jeering humor, this man was deadly serious.

"Shall I go on?" he asked in an even, civil tone.

"Please do."

"My men have been instructed to refrain from vandalism and—"

"How can you say that," I interrupted, "when they are already chopping down our trees?"

"Not wantonly, ma'am. Vandalism is wanton. The wood is necessary for their cooking fires. They will take nothing they do not need. There will be no looting, nothing in the house will be touched except, I'm afraid, we will have to confiscate any firearms."

"There are no guns of any kind," I lied. "They've all been taken by our own men."

"Then you won't mind if I have the house searched?"

"I certainly do mind. I won't have your dirty-pawed soldiers going through our things. Why—the very idea!"

"Perhaps it would be more acceptable if *I* conducted the search?"

The inquiry itself, made in a courteous manner, nevertheless had a sinister ring to it. I was thinking of how I could refuse in a way that did not arouse his suspicion when he rose to his feet.

"Shall we start with this room?"

It seemed I had no choice. "As you like."

"I will do my best not to disturb anything with—as you put it so nicely—my dirty paws."

He went through every drawer in the sideboard, thoroughly, quickly, replacing each item exactly where it had been before he moved it. One part of my mind wondered where he had picked up such professionalism; the other wondered how I could get away from him long enough to make sure Deirdre had hidden the rifle and the two smaller guns.

The dining room was next. A blank circle surrounded by dust showed where the silver tea urn had been, and when the major opened the cutlery drawer the velvet slots were empty. He said nothing, but examined the cupboards, shelves, and drawers with the same meticulous care he had shown in the library.

The women were still in the parlor, Ruth on the sofa, the others sitting about on chairs. I tried to signal Deirdre, but apparently she thought I had the silver in mind, because she gave me a broad grin and rolled her eyes.

Ruth asked, "Major, may I inquire what you are looking for?"

"Certainly." He answered with smooth, icy politeness. "Firearms."

I saw Deirdre's body tense. While the major was examining the drawer of a side table with his back to her, she began to move stealthily toward the door.

"I wouldn't if I were you, ma'am," he said without turning his head. "Just stay where you are and there will be no unpleasantness."

"I wanted to go upstairs. My child—"

"I'm afraid you and your child will have to remain here," he said, going on to the taboret in the corner. "It won't be long."

I preceded him up the stairs, my mouth dry, my heart beating like a drum. He paused before Beth Ann's room.

"We can't go in," I said. "Mrs. Falconer is not well."

He gave me a long look. "Please," he said in a hard voice, "open the door."

It is so difficult to convey the kind of deadly presence that man had, the steely control. I wondered if anyone—or anything—had ever managed to ruffle his chilly poise, if anyone had ever jabbed him into anger. No. He was unlike Miles. Miles got angry, Miles had a boiling point, Miles became very human, very passionate. Not this man. Cold-blooded.

I opened the door. Beth Ann sat at the window, hands tightly clasped in her lap, her eyes bulging with terror.

"The major wants to search the room."

"He will have to get permission from Harold," she said.

I didn't explain or try to. I owed this man nothing.

"I'm sorry, ma'am, I'll make it as quick as possible."

Beth Ann's chin quivered; then her shoulders began to heave. Oh, God, I prayed, don't let her go to pieces now. I went over to her and put my hand on her shoulder.

"What will he do?" she asked in a hoarse whisper.

"Nothing, if you don't cross him."

"Oh, Carmella—he—he's going through my underthings," she quavered, her eyes brimming.

"Don't cry. If you cry," I said, squeezing her shoulder

tightly and using the magic words, "what will people think?"

He finished—as he had promised—quickly. Then went across the hall to Deirdre's room.

When he lifted the mattress the silver forks, knives, and spoons that Deirdre had bundled hastily into a towel, fell to the floor with a clank and clatter. Under the circumstances, the sight of the ill-concealed cutlery might have brought a wry smile or a light comment, but the major said nothing. Shoving the jumble of silverware aside with the tip of his boot he went on with his search.

He found the rifle at the back of the wardrobe, the dueling pistol stuffed inside a boot. He said not a word, but I noticed he now scrutinized the various cupboards and drawers with extra care.

My room was the last. I stood at the closed door, the major behind me, my heart congealed with dread, unable to lift my trembling hand to the knob. He leaned over my shoulder and with a sift, precise movement twisted it and pushed the door inward. The action took but a moment, yet his breath on my cheek triggered a shock that ran through me like streaked summer lightning.

I entered the room on legs of straw, resisting the urge to wheel about and slam the door in his face. Without looking at him, I crossed the carpet and unlatched the window, nudging it open. The sound of twittering birds outside, so natural, so normal, only heightened my feeling of unreality. I gazed down at the sycamore that overhung the verandah, as if its rustling leaves could reassure me.

"And this room—who does it belong to?" His voice was harsh.

I turned. He was standing near my bed, one hand on the counterpane.

"It is mine and my husband's. Surely, you don't—"

"But I do."

Our eyes met—there was a long pause. And suddenly I knew, I *knew*.

He wanted me. Desire—sheer naked desire.

I can't exactly say why I felt that way, for his expression of cool imperturbability had not changed. He did not look at me with lust, or even with interest. But I knew he wanted me, knew down to the very marrow of my bones, an instinctive knowledge as old as time.

He drew the covers back, inserting his hands between the sheets, moving them swiftly, going down to the foot, then back under the pillows. Suppressing a shudder, I turned to the window again, grasping the sill. I felt as though he were violating me. I couldn't watch. I heard his booted footsteps and the squeak of the armoire door. He was searching through my gowns, his hands brushing them aside, his fingers feeling the silk and taffeta. My heart was hammering against my ribs. I can't let him know how I feel, I thought, I can't let him know I'm afraid. But, oh, how I wished he would finish and leave. Having the major in my room was a worse ordeal than I had anticipated, not because of Miles's hidden pistol, but because of his presence so close to the bed where I had lain naked in a man's arms. And he was aware of it; he was aware of me. Was he imagining the two of us, myself and the unknown husband, in the act of love, warm moistness receiving hard thrusts, the cradled rhythm falling and rising, the small moans and whispers, the clinging kisses? How long had it been since the major had bedded a woman? But I mustn't think of that. Oh, hurry!

I heard him move a chair, lift a cushion, and I held my breath.

"Ah . . . !"

He had found the gun.

I waited for him to say something caustic, accusing, derogatory. When I could bear it no longer, I turned.

He was tucking the pistol into his belt. "You can't blame me for lying," I said.

"Not at all. I would have done the same."

He moved to the chest of drawers, pausing, the tips of his fingers on my two hairbrushes. He glanced at the bottles of scent, the box of rice powder, a packet of dried lavender. Then he raised his head, our eyes met in the mirror, and for an instant a naked flame seemed to leap from those black-pupiled yellow-brown eyes to mine. Then his gaze dropped downward as he drew the drawer out and began to riffle the contents. Chemisettes, corsets, pantalettes, stockings, handkerchiefs, all mine, all emitting a strong fragrance of lavender. It was more painful than when he had gone through my gowns.

"A Southern officer would never have the audacity to enter a woman's bedroom," I said, "let alone fumble through her belongings."

"A Southern officer would if it meant chancing a bullet in the back," he replied without looking at me.

"Now, you know, Major, I wouldn't shoot you." It was a silly remark, artificial and coquettish, one I regretted the moment I spoke.

His head swiveled about and his eyes, narrowing slightly, swept over me. "I believe you *would* shoot, given half the chance, ma'am."

I lifted my chin, darting him a glance of scorn.

He went on to the desk, a sewing table, its drawers crammed with odd bits of material, pattern pieces cut from old newspapers, needles, pins, and thread.

When he had finished he said, "The attic?"

"There is none. But we have a cellar for storing root vegetables. You may find a few of last year's dried carrots or beets there."

"I shall have a look nevertheless. If you will unlock it for me?"

"Certainly."

He held the door for me and we descended the stairs in silence. We went through the kitchen into glaring sunshine and breathless heat. I twisted the key in the large rusty cellar padlock and he lifted the double upswinging doors.

"Will you be needing my any further?" I asked.

"No. But I would like to speak to you when I'm done."

"Can't you say what you have to now?" I didn't want him inside the house again if I could help it.

"I'd prefer not."

"Very well. I shall wait for you in the library."

As I passed the parlor, the door cracked open and Lavinia peered out. "Are you alone?" she whispered cautiously.

"For the moment."

"Is he—are they—the Yankees going to stay?"

"I don't know."

"Will they—what will they do to us?"

She meant rape. It was written all over her pale, frightened face.

"I think if they had wanted to harm us they would have done so by now."

"That's what Ruth says, but how can we be sure?"

"We'll just have to hope for the best."

"It's not knowing... Can't you talk to him, Carmella? He seems to like you. Can't you talk to him and persuade him to allow us to leave?"

"Talking to him, having anything to do with him, is unpleasant. I've already been through the house with him and I tell you he makes my skin crawl."

From behind her Ruth called, "Carmella? Can you come in for a minute."

"Just one." I closed the door behind me. "The major is coming back. He found the rifle and pistols."

"Was he angry?" Ruth asked. She looked so ill.

"No. I don't believe he ever gets angry. Wait—I think I hear him."

"Carmella," Ruth said, her voice resolute, "don't promise him *anything*."

I didn't ask what she meant by that.

The major and I went into the library. Again he waited until I was seated. The house had begun to heat up. The last vestige of night coolness having evaporated, the air hung heavy with the odor of beeswax and the greens we had cooked for last night's supper. The major's brow, I noticed, was beaded with perspiration. So he sweats like the rest of us, I thought, rubbing clammy hands against the sides of my skirt.

"To answer your question as to how long we'll stay, ma'am, I can't say," he began without preamble. "And on the matter of your departing for Richmond, that's impossible."

"Why? Why is it impossible? Why can't you let us go? We aren't prisoners of war but refugees, a group of harmless women and a child."

"A group that can give a pretty accurate report to the Rebs; who we are, how many men are encamped here, how many horses, guns, and so on."

"If I give you my word of honor...?"

His look told me how much my word of honor was worth.

"We have nothing to eat," I said bitterly. "If we stay, you will have to feed us. Or perhaps you won't feed us. Perhaps you will find it more expedient to let us all starve."

"We are not monsters. Of course we will share our rations."

"Small thanks," I said acidly.

"I don't expect thanks. Ma'am, we shall get along without any difficulty if everyone obeys orders. We shall try not to disturb you. Myself and my two senior officers will set up our headquarters in the house."

"What?" I rose out of the chair. "How dare you move in! How dare you!"

"May I remind you," he said, leaning forward, "that you are in no position to protest? Do you realize how many plantation houses such as this have been burned since the start of the war?"

I sank down again. He was right. He would always be right. He was the enemy—the enemy in possession. I was—we were—at his mercy. Still, I could not meekly acquiesce without some show of opposition.

"Perhaps I cannot keep you out of the house," I said, "but I find the idea of you and your officers under the same roof as myself distasteful."

"Do you?" he said, and his eyes widened slightly, the black pupils dilating like a cat's. I felt something respond in me— an electric crosscurrent I did not want to acknowledge.

"You need not fear us, ma'am."

Had I shown fear? Could he read it, or worse, see that secret, unacknowledged something else, in my face?

"We do not have any designs on you women."

How tactfully put, I thought.

"Our men have been instructed to behave. But I would advise all of you ladies to stay close to the house."

"In other words, we are your prisoners."

"For your own good. My men are well-disciplined soldiers, but they *are* men."

"I see. Are you quite finished?"

"Almost. I take it for granted you would not care to eat at the same table with us?"

"Heavens no!"

"Very well, we shall arrange to eat in shifts. I'll see that a schedule is worked out. In that manner we won't have to spend time in each other's company."

Should I thank him? I knew he was behaving in a far more gentlemanly way than rumor had led me to expect. We had been treated to story after story of enemy ruthlessness, the pillaging and raping of defenseless women as the Yankee forces swept along, and this man and his company had acted with remarkable restraint thus far. But I could not thank him. I could not bring myself to do so.

We unpacked our provisions from the carriage, but nothing else. Our emaciated horses had been taken down to the camp. I wondered if they would be commandeered. We ate a late midday meal in silence, broken once by Deirdre's comment, "That must be their cook."

Through the window we could see a corporal hauling sacks of food to the kitchen. He poked his head into the dining room when we were nearly finished.

"Would you ladies like some real coffee?"

All of us stared at him incredulously. We hadn't had real coffee for over a year, nothing but ground-up okra seeds and bitter chickory.

Ruth said, rather stiffly, "No, thank you."

When he had gone back to the kitchen, Prudence turned on her. "Why not? Why can't we have one cup? I'd give my arm for a cup of *real* coffee."

Surprisingly it was Deirdre who answered, "Do you want to be obligated to them?"

Deirdre sometimes baffled me. When I had spoken to her about her apparent interest in the Yankee soldiers her jaw had hardened. "I may look at them, Aunt Carmella, even admire their big, broad shoulders, but you won't catch me letting a man use me—never again!"

After our meal, the kitchen corporal, as I came to identify him, handed me the schedule, We would have the use of the kitchen from eight to ten in the morning, from one to three in the afternoon, and from seven to nine in the evening. That seemed reasonable enough. It was the officers moving in that I minded. Two of them took the library; a captain, an older man with graying sidewhiskers; and the lieutenant, boyish with a round face and blue eyes. The major preferred the small room at the back of the house, sometimes used as a spare bedroom when we had an overflow of guests.

It was an awkward arrangement at best. Never for one moment were we able to forget that the Yankees were at Wildoak. Though we avoided them as much as possible, we could hear them at all hours of the day, their booted feet on the verandah, their masculine voices floating up the stairs from below. Despite bolted doors, I doubt any of us slept well at night.

I did not trust the major any more than he trusted me. His hard, cold, animal sexuality frightened me. Oh, if only we had left a day earlier, if only we had been on our way. But, Ruth pointed out, we could have easily met the Yankees head on and been dragged back to Wildoak, carriage and all.

Ruth needed a doctor, medicines, nourishing food, needed to be taken care of in a quiet, safe place. And as the days went on, I could see the need was becoming urgent. If she didn't have attention . . . but I refused to think of the "if." She *had* to get to Richmond.

One afternoon I left a note on the dining-room table addressed to the major, saying I would like to speak to him that evening. He came in as we were finishing our supper and said that the meeting was agreeable with him.

"Say, ten o'clock, ma'am."

When he left, they all looked at me questioningly. "What's this about?" Ruth asked.

"I'm going to try and persuade him to let us go."

"But you've already tried."

Prudence quickly broke in. "It doesn't hurt to try again. If you speak firmly, perhaps you can convince him."

There was a chorus of assenting voices.

"As if," I said, "I am in any special favor with the major."

"Oh, but you are," Deirdre averred, throwing me a meaningful look.

"Perhaps you'd better talk to him in my place," I suggested acidly.

"No offense meant, Auntie."

Ruth said, "Please—let's not argue. Carmella, I suppose there's no harm in speaking to him." But her voice sounded dubious.

I lingered after everyone else had gone up to bed, wishing I had some brandy. Just a small glass to give me Dutch courage. Miles had drunk the last of it—how long ago?—and the cut-glass decanter stood empty on the sideboard. Perhaps the Yankee officers had a bottle tucked away in the little cupboard under the long center drawer. That was where Harold always kept his supply of brandy. I pictured the bottle, squat and amber, nearly full, could almost smell the liquor, feel it as it burned my lips and slid down my throat in comforting warmth.

A small glass.

I was standing at the sideboard, my fingers on the brass pull, when I heard him enter. Like a child caught at the cookie jar, I whirled about, red in the face, hands thrust behind me. I hated myself for that rush of guilt, hated him for causing it.

"Good evening, Mrs. Falconer."

He had learned my name, another breach of etiquette to resent, like the riffling of my intimate garments upstairs, like coming into the dining room just now without knocking.

"Were you looking for the brandy, Mrs. Falconer?" Mockery tinged his voice, though neither his eyes nor his lips smiled. "I believe there is a bottle or two in the sideboard."

Horrid man!

"As a matter of fact I was hoping to find some," I said, holding my head high.

If he had expected an abject denial or some flustered excuse, he showed no sign.

"Allow me, then."

I sat down at the table while he got the brandy. The bottle clinked against the glasses as he poured.

"I respect a woman who admits to liking spirits," he said.

"I don't recall that I said anything about *liking*."

"Needing, then?"

"Yes." Why not tell this bully the truth? "I find dealing with the enemy repugnant."

"That bad, hmmmm?"

He gave me the glass. His hand, surprisingly warm, brushed mine, an accidental touch that conveyed an erotic, masculine vitality.

I ignored it. "I'll not waste your time, Major," I began, "but get to the point."

"By all means." He raised his glass, watching me over the rim. "The brandy is very good. French."

I sipped at mine, the warmth flowing through my chest, renewing my strength as I had imagined it would. I took another sip. Yes, better. Much.

"Major, we women would like to leave as soon as possible for Richmond."

"I believe I've already informed you that I cannot allow it."

"We must go. Mrs. Harkness is badly in need of medicine, of a doctor's care. Mrs. Falconer, my sister-in-law has had a mental breakdown, as you might have observed. She is not getting better. The situation here"—I waved my hand—"is far from beneficial."

"You seem to have the illusion that Richmond will offer a haven, Mrs. Falconer."

"I feel sure it will."

"Do you realize that Richmond is under siege?"

"Hasn't it been several times during this war? We've always managed to push you back."

"The Confederates may have had small victories, but they are only temporary. Your losses at places like the Wilderness, Spotsylvania, have been enormous. But that is not what will defeat you. It's lack of food, of clothing, of medicines, of replacements. Your army is hardly more than a threadbare starved cadre of men who are fighting on nothing but sheer spirit. I take my hat off to them for that. But sheer spirit will not win this war. You are losing through attrition if nothing else."

"Perhaps. But then I would be accepting your word for it, wouldn't I?"

He shrugged.

"Whatever the situation, it still does not alter our wish to be in Richmond."

"Impossible."

I took another sip of brandy. He sloshed his around in the glass, then polished it off with a single draught. He was, as always, in uniform, his heavy cavalry jacket buttoned to the high collar, though the evening was warm.

"Is there nothing that will change your mind?" I asked.

He seemed to hesitate for a brief moment. "There is nothing I can think of."

After a long pause I said, "If you would give it some further consideration, perhaps?"

His eyes flicked over my bodice, a glance like a lightning whiplash, and unaccountably I felt my nipples swell.

Damn him!

"Perhaps." He got up and went to the sideboard. "More brandy, Mrs. Falconer?"

"No, thank you."

He filled his glass, then turned, surveying me dispassionately, almost coldly. "You are a very attractive woman, Mrs. Falconer."

It was a statement of fact uttered in a detached voice. And yet his whole body seemed to shout words, feelings, desires that were far removed from our polite fencing. For a duel was going on between us, a duel of eyes, of hidden meanings, a duel of wills that neither of us would admit to.

"You compliment me, Major. I had no idea you noticed such mundane matters."

"I do, but not often."

He reached up and unfastened two of the gilt buttons at the top of his jacket. His forehead was damp, and I noticed a pulse beating in his throat.

"Then it is a double compliment, Major. You are human, after all."

"Did you doubt it?"

His gaze held me and I forced myself not to look away, my hands interlocking so tightly the nails dug into the skin.

He lifted the glass to his lips and drank, his yellow eyes watching.

"I didn't think . . . ," I began, pausing, wetting my lips. "I didn't think you had much use for any matter that did not touch on the military."

"A good soldier always considers his duty first and does his best according to circumstances."

"Circumstances," I repeated, picking up my brandy. I did not drink it but pressed the cool glass to the side of my neck. His eyes lingered on the glass, then went downward to my breasts. There was a flash of raw lust in them before he shifted his gaze to my face again.

"Perhaps we can compromise," he said, after a long, tense pause. "Perhaps we can reach an agreement."

I knew what he wanted. I would have been an idiot to have remained innocent or ignorant even if I had been so at the start. But I was not going to be the one to offer; I was not going to offer him *anything*.

"You say Mrs. Harkness is ill?"

"Yes. Seriously ill."

"It's a pity our own doctor was killed in the Wilderness. We have no medical man attached to us now." He set his brandy aside. "I might allow Mrs. Harkness to go on alone, escorted by one of our men."

"I'm afraid that will not do, Major. Mrs. Harkness would refuse. She is a very proud, stubborn lady. She would never leave without all of us."

"You are a hard bargainer, Mrs. Falconer."

"Oh? I had no idea I was bargaining."

"Did you not?"

He was parrying not only with me but with himself—duty versus desire—a contest that no one walking into the room at that moment could possibly guess. But I knew. The very air seemed charged with combat.

"No," I said. "I have nothing to bargain with."

He walked across the room, passing but not looking at me. Now, I thought, *now* he will say what he has wanted to say ever since the morning he searched my bedroom.

But when he spoke it was brief, unexpectedly final. "I hardly think we have anything more to discuss."

I rose. Was I relieved? Disappointed?

"Very well. Good night, Major."

I had reached the door when he suddenly called, "Mrs. Falconer..."

I turned.

"On the other hand..." There was a slight, almost imperceptible pause before he continued: "I believe I do have an offer which might interest you."

"Oh?"

He approached me, coming so close I could see the flecks of gold in his eyes, the faint blue shadow of his unshaven jaw, the curve of his thin mouth. He smelled of brandy, tobacco, and horseflesh, a male odor that evoked a fleeting image of unbridled lovemaking, of masculine kisses that ravaged and burned.

"What is it, Major?" My voice sounded unnatural, as though the air had been squeezed from my lungs.

"I will let all of you leave—no reservations—if you will spend a night with me."

He had said it! The major's capitulation gratified my feminine vanity, but the self-congratulation lasted only a matter of seconds, for I suddenly realized the full implication of his proposal. This was no flirtatious give and take; no fluttering fan, no moonlight, no honeysuckle perfume accompanied it. He was deadly serious—bald sex without embellishments. I would have to stand naked beforethe major. He would use me as he wished, and he was not a kind or gentle man.

Should I suddenly play the lady, order him from my presence, be indignant because he had insulted me? Hardly. At this point it would be preposterous. I had asked for it. Furthermore, hadn't I already considered this possibility as the only way to reach Richmond?

"May I—may I think it over?"

"Do that. If you should agree, you know where to find me. I think midnight would be a convenient time for us both."

There was no change in his voice or expression. It was as if he were arranging a meeting to discuss the state of the kitchen larder.

"Good night, Major."

He opened the door, and as I passed him I was again acutely aware of his rampant but leashed sexuality.

I could feel his eyes on me as I went slowly up the stairs, my thoughts in turmoil. Had I really won that duel? Why hadn't I told him no, "no!" loudly with righteous indignation? I paused at the landing. Then I heard the door downstairs click shut in the silence. I imagined him going back to his brandy, a faint smile of satisfaction curving his thin lips as he lifted the glass.

What had I done? Bargained with my body like a whore. Yes, like a whore. The shame of it! But wait—I hadn't agreed yet. I hadn't said yes. It wasn't too late. I could ignore the whole episode as if it had never happened.

But what about Ruth, wasting away hour by hour before my very eyes?

I couldn't. Ruth would never forgive me. But if I kept it a secret? How? She would know; she shared the same room with me. Everybody would know. I would be crucified—a Southern woman giving herself to a Yankee. They would say, "What could you expect from a prostitute's daughter?" And there was Miles, my husband, fighting for the Cause, risking his life day in day out, in danger of being killed by just such a man as the major. But, curiously, more than that, more than my being an outcast, more than the prospect of having stones thrown at me, would be the distressing knowledge that I had betrayed Derry. I loved Derry, and this man was Derry's enemy too.

They were all waiting up for me in my room—Prudence, Alice, Deirdre, Lavinia, Mother Hastings, even Beth Ann, gathered about Ruth who, pale and anxious, was propped up on the bed pillows.

"Well—what did he say?" Lavinia asked, her eyes fixed apprehensively on my face.

I did not answer but went to the water pitcher and poured myself a glass. The brandy had made me thirsty.

"Aren't you going to tell us?" Deirdre wanted to know. "Did he say, yes, no, maybe?"

"He said yes, he—"

A chorus of jubilant voices interrupted me.

"Wait! He said yes, under certain conditions."

"What conditions?" Ruth demanded harshly.

"I am to spend the night with him."

There was a small silence; then everyone began to talk at once.

"Be still!" Ruth cried above the hubbub. "Hush! Carmella, you refused, of course."

"Why should she?" Deirdre demanded.

"Hold your tongue! You ought to be whipped," Ruth said angrily.

"Don't upset yourself," I begged, going to the bed. Her thin chest was heaving with exertion and a dull red had stained her pale face.

"I'll try not to," she said, clasping her hands together. "Please, everyone—everyone leave. I want to talk to Carmella alone."

"Why?" Deirdre asked. "This affects me too."

"Leave!" Ruth said with a steely ring to her voice, one that must have cost her great effort.

When they had at last trailed reluctantly through the door, Ruth said, "You can give me some water too. I need it."

I sat down at her side while she drank. Then, setting the glass aside, she took my hand. "You told him no, of course."

"I said I would think it over."

"How could you?"

"We'll never get out of here any other way. The major says the Feds are winning, Ruth. I don't know whether to believe him or not. But I do know this; he wouldn't hesitate to burn Wildoak in a minute and leave us the charred ruins if he thought it would advance the Union cause. He's a ruthless man."

"And you are considering . . . ? Oh, Carmella."

"What would you suggest?"

"We'll stay, of course. There's no question about it. We'll stay."

The angry color had drained from her face. Her grip on my hand weakened and she lay back on the pillows closing her eyes. In the candlelight she looked like a corpse, and fear squeezed my heart. She couldn't die; I would not let her.

"Ruth—he might relent. He might think us a burden. If he did—do you think you would be up to the journey?"

"He won't relent," she said in a tired voice.

I made her as comfortable as I could. Then, undressing, I put on my nightgown and slipped into bed beside her. In the darkness I heard her shallow breathing.

I thought of the major downstairs. Was he waiting? Was he sitting in his austere room, smoking cigar after cigar, his eyes on the clock? Or pacing the floor perhaps, his blouse unbuttoned, his forehead damp, that pulse beating in his throat?

Ruth sighed in her sleep and turned over. Ruth, the kindest, most generous woman I had ever known. Worth the whole lot of them. And every day we waited here, she died a little more.

Trying not to wake her, I slipped out of bed and felt for my wrapper in the inky blackness. Belting it, I went to the door and carefully inched it open. A somnolence lay over the shadow-cloaked house, a breathing silence. I eased myself through the door and started down the hall, feeling my way carefully. My bare feet made no sound as I descended the staircase. I moved down the lower hall, my heart beating frantically. Beneath the door a band of threshold light glowed in the dark as if awaiting me.

CHAPTER

TWENTY-NINE

*W*HEN I *opened the door he rose from his chair.* The draft made the lamp wick dance, and in the flickering light I could not see the expression on his face clearly.

"So you came." He did not sound surprised.

"Yes." I shut the door behind me.

An awkward moment, two, three ticked by. He had removed his jacket, and the stark white of his shirt made a sharp contrast to the sun-bronzed tan of his face. My legs were trembling and I wanted desperately to sit down, but he did not offer me a chair. So I stood there, the closed door at my back, one hand resting on the skirt of my wrapper.

"I had given you up," he said. "It's after one."

My eyes went to the clock. "Oh? I hadn't noticed the time."

A half-smoked cigar lay in a dish, an empty glass beside it.

"Can I offer you some brandy?"

"No, thank you."

He took a step toward me, and another, and as he reached out to touch me, I grasped his wrist.

"Before we go on Major, I want your solemn promise, your word of honor as an officer and a gentleman, that you will allow all of us to leave. Tomorrow or the day after at the latest."

"You have my word. If you'd like it in writing..."

343

"No. That won't be necessary." By now I knew he was above tricking me. He had too much pride.

"Good," he said, with a slight nod of his head.

His eyes reflected the glimmer of lamplight, the centers black as night. I was reminded of the gun barrel pointed at me so long ago at Willowfoxe, the gun that had killed Lyon.

"You're not afraid of me, are you?"

"No," I lied.

He brushed my cheek with the back of his hand, let it fall to the neck of my wrapper. He parted the collar slowly, pushing it down past my shoulders. I was sure he could see my heart hammering beneath my nightgown. It had been stitched for me years ago by the seamstress in San Francisco just before Miles and I had left—a garment made of sheerest batiste, embroidered in pretty pink roses. The embroidery had since faded, the material turning even more transparent and fragile after so many washings. I thought: He'll tear it, he will rip it to shreds. But nothing like that happened. He undid the drawstring carefully and bent his head to touch his lips on the skin just below my neckline. His hair was thick and crisp, and I had an overwhelming urge to dig my hands in it, to pull at it. He lifted his head and stared at me for a few moments, then slowly began to undo the ribbon that bound my hair, letting it fall in a cascade past my shoulders.

"Lovely," he murmured and brought his mouth down on mine.

His lips were surprisingly warm, and his kiss, though possessive, soft.

His arms went around me. He pulled me closer and instinctively I tried to draw away. He murmured something that sounded like a protest in my ear. Then suddenly, as if a dam had burst, the long tamped down reserve broke, releasing a torrent of passion. His arms tightened, crushing me to his chest. He kissed me wildly, savagely, his mouth hurting, bruising, his tongue parting my lips, going inside as though he would swallow me whole. I arched my body away and tore my mouth from his.

"You are not—"

"But I am," he said. "You have been teasing me long enough."

He ripped the gown from my shoulders, exposing my naked breasts.

Still holding me by the shoulders, he examined me, his eyes drinking in my nakedness. Then he was kissing the white mounded flesh, his lips closing around a nipple, his tongue brushing, licking, sucking hungrily, his hands moving down my back, pressing my pelvis into his hard swollen manhood. Sliding quickly down on one knee, his lips trailed across my belly, his hands spread my legs apart, his fingers caressing the warm moistness between.

I tried to push him away, tried to suppress the little thrill of pleasure that began to work itself up my spine. Damn him! I would endure but not enjoy.

He rose to his feet, resting his mouth in the hollow of my throat. He was breathing hard.

I waited for him to speak, to commit himself, to say that he had desired me from the moment of our first meeting. But he remained silent. And there was something in that hard breathing silence that caused me to shiver again.

"Has it been a long while since you've had a woman?" I asked, breaking my resolve to converse as little as possible with him.

He looked at me, then spread his hand at the base of my throat, the fingers slightly curled as if he were about to strangle me.

I tried not to show fear, although goose pimples had sprouted on my arms.

Suddenly he swung me up, the robe and gown falling away. He carried me to the cot in the corner, lowering me onto the gray blanket. Kneeling beside me, he began to peel off his shirt. I turned my head, afraid to meet the fire burning in his eyes. I heard him undressing, the rustle of cloth, the thump of boots. He blew out the lamp, and the darkness closed around me like a black velvet glove. I bit my lip to keep from crying out. Gradually the darkness lightened and the window appeared like an oblong of gray. His body passed between it and my sight, blocking it out.

The cot squeaked as he lowered himself over me, supporting his weight on his hands. He was trembling. I could feel his arms shaking. Why? Was he afraid of letting go again? Or was he rattled by a strong emotion, one he was trying to repress?

My hands fluttered up to his bare chest, and he swept them aside. His weight came down on me as he buried his face in my hair, my breasts, his hands kneading my flanks.

His hard-muscled masculine body no longer trembled but covered mine with a powerful assurance. An animal heat emanated from him, one that enveloped me, infused me with a sudden leaping desire. I must not give in to it. I must not! This was a bargain, an arrangement. But he was a man, touching me in a dozen places that were weak and craving, arousing a hunger in me that brought a sob to my throat.

When he entered me I wanted to shout, "Stop!" though I did not want him to stop. He lifted my buttocks so that he could penetrate deeper, and each strong thrust filled me with pleasure I could not deny. I tried to imagine him in his uniform, the hated blue of the Yankee invader, but the picture blurred and all I was conscious of was my own body and the widening ripple of tense, delicious expectancy, the ripple drawing closer and closer until a dizzying whirlpool sucked me under for a moment before throwing me out into the blinding light.

He lay over me, his breath and mine mingling, and it seemed to me that this union was more intimate and therefore more shameful than our actual coupling.

I stirred and he rose. Still without a word, he covered me with a blanket and I heard him moving away. A moment later a match flared in the darkness and I could smell the acrid smoke of a cigar.

Would he let me go now? I did not want to think of going through it all again, to have him know that I hated him only in daylight, that in the dark of the night he could take me, make me submissive, arouse me, as if I were some army baggage, a camp follower that craved desire.

"Major . . . ?"

He must have guessed my thoughts, for he said, "We agreed you would stay the night. I shall keep my part of the bargain if you keep yours."

I didn't mean to fall asleep; but I must have, for the next thing I knew he was on the narrow cot with me once more, kissing me, caressing my breasts, stroking my thighs, his hands sliding sensuously over my skin, slowly drawing me into that erotic vortex again. I could not let it happen. I would not allow myself to become his partner in passion as I had done earlier.

"Please . . . ," I protested.

He paused.

"I'd rather do without the preliminaries."

He said nothing but his hand came up and grabbed the hair at the back of my skull. He jerked my face forward so that our mouths barely touched and held me there in a painful grasp. I could feel the angry heat of those yellow eyes. Then he was kissing me, his lips ravaging mine with burning, brutal hunger. Holding my arms tightly to my sides, he lifted himself and, bending his head, sunk his teeth into the tender, unprotected flesh of my shoulder.

A scream rose in my throat, a scream stifled by his smothering mouth. We lay like that, mouth to mouth, rigid, unmoving, his heart thundering against mine. Then he let go.

"Did you like that better, Mrs. Falconer?"

Tears rose to my eyes, but I did not speak.

Still lying side by side, he nudged my legs apart and brought one over his naked hip. When he entered me with an iron-hard thrust, I flinched and his arm under my waist crushed me to his chest. His movements were swift, strong, probing, a thunderous assault that bound me to him in passionate fury. I was glad he did it that way, glad to have it over with quickly, glad he did not take the pains to excite me. I wondered if he had ever loved a woman, if he was married, if he had left someone soft and feminine behind. But I would not ask.

When he finished he rose, and through the dimness I could see him putting on his clothes.

"You'd better go now," he said in a harsh voice. "It will be morning soon."

We left the following day. We had repacked the carriage, and Ben had brought the horses around. Having been fed by the Yankees, the two nags seemed a little perkier, though they were still a rather dreary pair. We were also better provisioned than we had been originally. The lieutenant who stood by to see us off did not swear us to secrecy, perhaps because he knew (as we did not) that whatever information we could give the Confederates hardly mattered.

I did not see the major.

No one, not Ruth, Deirdre, or Prudence, has asked my why the major had suddenly let us go. It was not mentioned, not discussed. And because it wasn't, I felt their disapproval all the more. The enormity of my transgression—adultery compounded by sleeping with the enemy—put me, at least for the moment, beyond the pale. Apparently no one cared that we might be cooling our heels at Wildoak indefinitely if it hadn't been for me. No one except Ruth. She squeezed my hand before we set out, saying, "I'm very angry."

It was an exhausting journey, but not as dangerous as we had anticipated. At that time—the middle of June 1864—both armies were engaged at Petersburg, a city south of Richmond, the Union forces laying siege to Lee's gray-clad defenders and hoping that victory would give them open access to the Confederate capital. Unware of these developments, we took the circuitous route we had decided upon when we first made our plans, while Ruth, who knew the back roads well, guided us from her seat inside the carriage.

Deirdre, the two girls, and I walked most of the way. We only rode in the carriage for short intervals—joining little Page, Mother Hastings, and Ruth—usually toward the end of the day when we were so exhausted we could barely take another step. Lavinia, Prudence, Alice, and Beth Ann rotated walking and riding, for a change not arguing with one another, though Beth Ann protested and crabbed constantly, threatening, at least twice a day, to faint. Prudence and Lavinia surprised me. They bore up remarkably well and kept urging us on, not to stop but to hurry. They were anxious to get to Richmond. We all were.

Only once did we have a fright. We met up with an old man on a mule, a codger with a weather-seamed face and a tobacco-stained white beard. He warned us that we were heading straight for a deserters' camp.

"Yankees and Rebs both," he said. "Skulkers. Desperate varmints. Take one looked at you ladies"— his eyes went over us—"and they'd skin you alive."

We made a long detour across a field past a dense copse of

pines, sweating as we dragged the horses through a marshy spot, fighting off midges and mosquitoes that swarmed in the millions, fearful that at any moment a bearded felon would pop out from behind a tree trunk. Night found us still far from a road, and the worst of it was that Ruth could not recognize a single familiar landmark.

"You mean we're lost?" Deirdre asked.

"Not yet," Ruth assured her.

"But we could be walking in circles!"

"Not if we keep the position of the sun in mind. Southwest is where we should be heading.

We decided to camp for the night and pulled the carriage into a deserted farmyard. The house itself had been gutted; and as a swirling mist rose from a nearby creek, its paneless windows and charred walls appeared ghostly. No one suggested we stay inside. Deirdre drew water from the well, the shriek of the winch echoing eerily through the gloom. We built a fire and huddled around it, listening to the croaking of frogs and the shrill clamor of katydids. For some reason, ever since our journey had started, Deirdre's Page had taken a great fancy to me. And as we sat nodding over our ration of stale pone and beef jerky, he climbed into my lap and fell asleep, his head on my breast. He had his father's tow hair and Deirdre's pert nose and fresh, rosy complexion, and as he lay in my arms, his lashes making faint crescents on his cheeks, I had the sudden inexplicable desire to weep. Would I ever hold a child of my own? Derry's and mine? That night Derry seemed more distant than the hidden stars.

The following morning, after leading the carriage across a field of wild rye, we came out upon the Mechanicsville road, which would take us into Richmond. We passed trenches crisscrossing the highway here and there, old trenches where battles had been fought, each side facing the other, sometimes only a few yards apart.

"Makes you wonder," Deirdre said, "which was Union and which Confederate."

More and more refugees were tramping the roads, all bound for the same haven as we. They walked singly, in pairs, some in straggling groups, a few riding mules, others trundling carts— women, children, and old men mostly. We passed a contingent of our own soldiers, and a sorry lot they seemed—barefooted or wearing tattered, makeshift boots, many with only the remnants of what once had been uniforms. They looked hungry, tired, hollow eyed.

"Are we winning the war?" Deirdre called cheerfully.

"Any day now!" a young lad who could not have been more than fourteen shouted back.

We crossed the Chickahominy on a pontoon bridge, Beth Ann, Alice, Lavinia, and Mother Hastings praying with closed eyes while Deirdre and I held the horses. The river ran swift and deep and a false step, an involuntary movement by one of the horses could send the carriage tumbling over.

It was late afternoon when we entered the city. I was too tired to notice anything but the occasional rude stare of a passerby. For the most part people ignored us. Ruth kept encouraging us, giving directions, "Turn here," ". . . take that street . . . ," her face lighting up as we drew nearer to journey's end.

I plodded on, leg muscles stiff, my thin, worn-out shoe soles feeling every cobble under them. My mind, my thoughts, my whole body was one palpitating desire for a bath and a cool place to lie down, a place where I could sleep for the rest of my life.

We deposited the Hastingses at the home of Mother Hastings' sister, a mild-looking little woman dressed in rusty black, whose face, it seemed to me, blanched at the sight of her unexpected guests. But she recovered quickly when she discovered that only two of us were to stay. Poor woman, she had already opened her arms to a score of relatives and I could hardly blame her for feeling dismayed.

Prudence and Alice had planned to put up at the home of Prudence's cousin Amy Caldwell on Marshall Street, where they both had sent their children some seven weeks earlier. But when we arrived there, we discovered the house had been taken over by officers and men from the Quartermaster. The Caldwells and the children had gone from Richmond, refugeeing north to relatives living in a remote part of the Carolinas, which they felt was safer than the city.

We found much the same situation at the home of Ruth's niece, the family having departed a month earlier, leaving the house in the care of strangers. After a hurried conference, we decided that all of us should go on to the Bainbridges.

I had never met the Bainbridges (Mrs. Bainbridge, Jane, was a second cousin to the Falconers), but in my early days at Wildoak Beth Ann had spoken often of them. Morton Bainbridge was an aristrocrat who could trace his lineage to wealthy English squirearchy, and Jane herself held a position of high regard in Richmond society. Beth Ann, in her snobbish way, had also hinted that these relatives were most particular about those they accepted into their circle. I did not look forward with enthusiasm—if I could have mustered any in my bone-weary body—to a meeting with them.

But contrary to my expectation, Jane Bainbridge welcomed me with open arms, saying how delighted she was to meet me at last and how happy she was that we had made the journey safely. It did not discomfit her in the least to have a band of women descend on her without notice, and she showed us to our rooms, apologizing because we would have to double up. Ruth and I shared a small bedroom, which had been partitioned off by a screen from a larger room. It was not until after I had put Ruth safely to bed and had that longed-for bath, donning freshly laundered underthings and a gown, a little tight under the arms, lent to me by Jane Bainbridge that I noticed our hostess was wearing black.

Of course, most of us were in mourning, but in the country where we could not buy the black bombazine to make up the proper widow's gown (or bereaved sister-in-law's, as in my case) nor find the dye to blacken an ordinary dress, we wore black armbands or aprons. I thought at first Jane might be mourning her husband, that Morton Bainbridge had died on the battlefield, but no, she excused his absence by saying he was drilling that night with the home militia.

We ate a marvelous supper. Actually, it was plain fare, but to us it was heavenly; succulent ham, roast kid, *real* butter, and a lovely flan.

"I'm afraid our supplies are dwindling," Jane said. "Until a few weeks ago we obtained our fresh foodstuffs from a farmer near Laurel. But the foragers cleaned him out and I was forced to look elsewhere. It *is* a problem."

We made no comment, although I'm sure each of us was
thinking at that moment of our own meager repasts at Wildoak.
But to give Jane credit, she did have many to feed, for in
addition to us her guests included Jane's elderly mother and
two female cousins, not to speak of the wounded soldiers she
had taken in and put up in the carriage house. To one and all
she showed unstinting generosity and never in the darkest days
to come did she begrudge sharing whatever she had.

After supper we retired to the parlor to listen to one of the
female cousins sing and play the piano.

Jane Bainbridge seated herself next to me and during a lull
leaned over and said, "My dear, I haven't had the chance to
offer my condolences."

I gave her a startled look. Could she be referring to Harold
Falconer?

"You haven't heard then?" she asked, surveying my puzzled
face. "Oh, my dear. Come with me to the library."

I rose, cold with apprehension, and followed her out across
a narrow hall to a book-lined room that smelled of leather and
cigars.

"I would have thought they sent you a telegram," she said,
opening a drawer.

"We have received no mail, telegrams, or letters for the last
year, Mrs. Bainbridge."

"Call me Jane, dear." She patted my hand absently, her
eyes suddenly filling with tears. Then she drew out a folded
page, torn from a newspaper.

It was the casualty list from the *Richmond Daily Dispatch*.
I held it in my hand but did not read it.

"My dear, please sit down. I—I don't know how to break
this. If you had a mother..." She hesitated, her cheeks col-
oring. "Or if your father were alive. And—and Ruth is too ill.
My dear, your husband, Miles, was killed at Drewry's Bluff."

I experienced a sudden surge of relief—not Derry!—before
guilt pushed it back.

"It is terrible, I know," Jane said, taking a handkerchief
from her sleeve and dabbing at her eyes. "He was such a
wonderful man. A bit of a scapegrace in his youth, but a true
Virginian. When he came back..." She paused, wiping her
eyes and blowing her nose. "When he came back and I saw

him in the uniform of our army, I knew what I had always predicted, that his fine blood would show someday. And now . . ."

She went on, speaking of Miles, so caught up in memory and regret she did not notice my silence. I should weep and grieve too, I thought, cry for a gallant husband killed on the battlefield, but I couldn't. I was too immobilized with shock. It was true that I had considered the possibility—so many dying every day—but I had never *really* believed that Miles, so strong and indomitable, could actually be killed. I saw him again as he had sat in the Wildoak parlor brooding over a brandy, saw the harsh lines of fatigue in his face, the shadow of past battles in his burning eyes. Miles . . . And now he was dead.

Something twisted in my heart. I don't know what. He and I had been at loggerheads since the day we first met, and yet we had known each other in my father's time, both of us had been close to him. We had lived as man and wife and there had been moments between us, an intimacy, an outreach of tenderness when he had soothed a hurt, comforted a fear, or chided me out of painful resentment. Recalling those moments brought a rush of tears to my eyes.

Jane Bainbridge blew her nose delicately. "My dear, it's too terrible—to hear this way. If you want to cry, please do. You needn't hold back."

She pressed her damp handkerchief into my hand and I stared at it as the tears came faster and faster. I wept for Miles, something I never would have believed possible, and yet in some obscure way perhaps I was weeping for myself as well.

Where Miles was buried no one could tell us, but we held a memorial service for him at St. Paul's. Ruth was too ill to attend. Jane's husband, Morton, had persuaded a doctor from the Chimborazo Hospital to come and look at her and he advised bed rest for an indefinite period.

The church was hot and crowded with people waiting their turn to hold their own funeral rites, row after row filled with black-gowned women and their pale-faced children, crying, bewildered, and afraid, bereaved fathers and mothers, sisters and sweethearts. The coffins draped with regimental standards were lined up under the windows along the walls. A high, sweet tenor voice sang:

> We shall meet but we shall miss him
> There will be one vacant chair:
> We shall linger to caress him,
> When we breathe our evening prayer.

Prudence, weeping uncontrollably and overcome with grief, had to leave midway through the service, leaning heavily on Alice Dinwiddie's arm.

"They were childhood sweethearts," Jane Bainbridge whispered in my ear.

A queer little pang jabbed at me. Prudence and Miles. Well, he ought to have married her in the first place. Perhaps she would have made him a better wife, certainly she wept more than I, sitting upright and tearless, muffled in black and hating every minute of it.

I came back to the house, my spirits dragging, feeling that if it hadn't been for Ruth I should have been far better off to remain at Wildoak. Miles's death continued to torment me with a sense of guilt, as if I had left some task of vital importance undone. But what? What words had been left unspoken? He had been such a hard, often harsh, man to deal with.

I felt worse at the reading of Miles's will.

The lawyer, a Mr. Gan, having preceded us from the church, was waiting in the library when we arrived. A thin, little, elderly man with a clipped beard and dark brown eyes, he requested that only family members be present. There were nine of us: the Bainbridges, Beth Ann and her three children, Lavinia, Mother Hastings, and myself. To each of these Miles gave bequests, very generous ones to Beth Ann and the girls, the latter to be kept in trust until they came of age. The bulk of his estate came to me. But there was more:

> My wife's separate holdings, purchased some six months after her father's death from assets bequeathed by Arthur Hastings to her, have been invested in real estate on Sansome and Green Streets. These interests are recorded under her maiden name and can be liquidated or held, whichever she chooses, through the offices of B. D. Boyd, 515 Broadway, San Francisco.

My first reaction was one of bewilderment. I didn't understand. Did that mean that Miles hadn't cheated me as I'd supposed? What other assets could Papa have left me but those that came from the sale of his effects?

Afterwards I took Mr. Gan aside and asked him to explain.

"As I understand it," he said, "Miles had originally invested your money along with his in Gould and Curry. But he was afraid silver mining was too risky a business—not for himself, he could afford a loss, but for you. He thought real estate was far more secure. He was right, you know. Gould and Curry went under in '63."

Oh Miles! I remembered when I had thrown the sale of my emeralds in his face, saying it made up for the loss of my father's money. How outraged I had been when he answered, "Indeed?" I realized now that he was thinking of Papa's San Francisco financial debacle, not the small legacy he had left me. I was glad I had never openly accused Miles of fraud. But I cringed with shame when I thought how often I had silently called him an embezzler.

After the reading of the will, Aunt Jane had ordered a light lunch to be served, and it was laid out on the dining-room table. But I excused myself. "I'm not hungry," I said.

I was hot, uncomfortable, and oppressed by self-reproach. I wanted nothing more than to remove my heavy black dress and my corset, which seemed to be cutting me in two. Starting up the stairs I met Ruth coming down, holding up the trailing skirts of a borrowed wrapper, looking lost in the long robe, like a child in grown-up clothes.

"Ruth! What are you doing out of bed?"

"It got so boring, Carmella. I thought I'd come down to the parlor for a bit."

"The others are having lunch. Would you like some?"

"No. I ate earlier. I do feel a lot better. Don't I look it?"

"Yes—of course."

We went into the parlor. "Leave the door open," Ruth said. "It's cooler that way. There now." She lowered herself onto the sofa. She paused, looking over at me. "How did the funeral go? Was it an ordeal?"

"Yes."

"They say it gets worse later on."

"He left everything to me," I said.

"That shouldn't have been a surprise."

"No." But I couldn't tell her how I had misjudged him.

We fell silent. I picked up a newspaper and began to fan my heated face. From the dining room we could hear the clatter of cutlery, the hum of voices. Suddenly Prudence's rose above the others.

"I tell you," she said indignantly, "she's a harlot. She sat all through that ceremony without even looking sad. But she can go to bed with a Yankee . . ."

I went hot, then cold.

Jane said, "Now, Prue, surely you must be exaggerating. Carmella does have an unfortunate background, but that is no reason for such an outrageous accusation."

"I tell you she went to bed with that Yankee. Ask Alice here."

There was a small silence. I did not look at Ruth. I heard someone murmur a few words I could not catch.

"Well, Jane?" Prudence asked loudly. "Do you believe me now?"

"I declare!" Jane answered, shock making her voice tremble. "And to think I embraced her, kissed her, felt sorry for her because of Miles. And he, leaving her all that wealth. While she—oh, God!"

Ruth struggled to her feet, her face flushed.

"Don't listen to them," I said. "Don't get involved. I really don't care. It doesn't matter."

"Maybe not to you. But it does to me. Give me your arm, Carmella."

"No." I didn't want to face those she-cats with unsheathed claws. I did not care if they all dropped dead. I wished I had never come to Richmond with them. "No."

She walked slowly, unsteadily across the carpet and out into the hall.

"Ruth—please . . ."

She made a negative gesture with her hand. I went out behind her, afraid she would fall. The dining-room doors were open.

"I'm glad she isn't here." Prue was speaking. "It simply galls me to sit at the same table with her."

Ruth cleared her throat and everyone looked up.

"My dear Prue," Ruth said in her old authoritative voice, fixing Prue with steely gray eyes, "you are lucky to be sitting at *any* table; and if it were not for Carmella, most likely you would be absent from this one."

Shock and embarrassment held them all immobile; Alice open-mouthed, Deirdre crumbling a crust of bread in her fingers, the younger girls and the cousins blinking their eyes.

Jane recovered first. "Ruth—you know you're not well enough to be downstairs."

"Thank God I am. Thank God I'm here and so able to right a wrong you are doing to this brave girl."

She had begun to tremble. "Ruth," I said, putting my hand on her elbow, "leave it. Come away."

"No," she said. "I won't. It has got to be said."

Jane rose to her feet. "Then sit down, my dear. You know this isn't doing you any good."

"Oh, but it is. There are things I have wanted to say for a long time."

I led her to a chair and she sank into it. "A little water, if you please."

A glass was poured. Prue said, "Now, Ruth, I know you are always taking up for Carmella, but you must admit what she did was unforgivable."

She. As if I were an inanimate object, part of the furniture, a chair, the sideboard, a lamp. She. Oh, how I *hated* her!

"Carmella is too kind to mention your shortcomings, Prudence," Ruth said, "but I'm not. You're a whiner, self-indulgent, vain, a snob, a disgrace to Southern womanhood. Oh, don't think I hadn't noticed you batting your eyes at Miles— God rest his soul. You're a fine one to speak of someone else's morals. But I won't go into that now. Carmella has made a sacrifice that you in your selfishness would never dream of making."

"I don't understand any of this," Jane said.

"Quite simply," Ruth explained, "the only way the Union major would allow us to leave was for Carmella to give herself to him."

Jane Bainbridge drew in her breath. "But no Southern woman would allow a sister to make such a sacrifice. No gentlewoman

would consent to having one of her own kind . . . She—she
would die first."

"Would she? Which one of you would have died first?"

Ruth looked around the table. Silence, an uneasy, fidgety
silence answered her.

"You see, Jane," Ruth went on, "they wanted to get away.
They wanted to get away and didn't care how it was accom-
plished."

"Is this true?" Jane asked. "is it? Prue, Alice, Beth Ann?"

Beth Ann wet her lips. "I—I didn't know anything about
it."

"Didn't you?" Ruth mocked. "What a brave woman you
are. So brave that every time an unpleasantness arose you
pretended shock and made for your room, locking yourself in.
Who was it that carried the household all those months, years,
in fact, ran what was left of the plantation, tended the girls,
saw that Deirdre was decently married? Carmella. All Carmella. I say she did what she thought was the only thing she
could do. Nine of us at Wildoak with God knows what hanging
over our heads. As far as I am concerned, Carmella showed
as much, if not more, courage than any soldier fighting for the
cause."

They all looked away. No one met Ruth's eyes or Jane's.
They gazed at their plates, their hands, fussing with their collars, twisting a fork, a napkin.

Jane squared her shoulders. "I had thought . . . But never
mind. Please come here, Carmella. Move over, Deirdre; let
Carmella sit next to me."

I felt like a schoolgirl given special privileges because I had
done well in grammar.

"First," Jane went on, "*I* want to apologize. I didn't know.
I am truly sorry, I can't tell you how sorry."

"Please, Jane, I—I'd rather not talk about it."

Somewhere in the back of my mind I wondered whether
I'd have done it if the major had been ugly and smelled badly.
If he hadn't been such a virile, compelling animal, would I
have walked down those dark stairs in bare feet, going to him,
giving myself up to his arms? But there was Ruth. I had to.
The decision would have been harder. And yet I didn't feel I
deserved Ruth's praise or Jane's contrition.

Jane continued, "I want each of you to apologize."

Prue said, "I can't."

"Oh, yes, you can. If you want to stay under my roof, if you want to be received in Richmond society, you will apologize, each and every one of you."

It was a distressing scene and I wished I could vanish into thin air. But there was no escape and I had to sit there in an agony of embarrassment while the women in turn murmured, "I'm sorry."

"Now," said Jane, "I want no word to go beyond this room. I want nothing said. We will forget what happened at Wildoak. I want you all to think of the war that we must win, all pull together. We must be friends."

But I knew I could never be friends with them—Deirdre perhaps; and Jane, in a cool distant way, because she was basically a kind and honorable person; and Ruth, who had become dearer to me than ever. But not the rest. They weren't sorry. Sorry! My foot! They had been blackmailed into apologies none of them meant. Their opinion of me hadn't changed.

Richmond was in a state of siege and its citizens were hungry. I don't know what sleight-of-hand Jane and Morton Bainbridge performed to bring food to our table; but from what I gathered, we suffered less than most of the population, which had swelled, according to the newspaper, to 100,000. With the Union tightening up the blockade at Charleston and Wilmington, another source of food had completely dried up. Inflation was rampant, prices doubled, thievery became common. No one dared leave a chicken unattended in the yard or a pie cooling on a sill. Only the free food depots prevented the poor from rioting again as they had done earlier in the war.

In the midst of all this privation a gay social life still existed. Ruth said it reminded her of stories she had read of the Black Death during the Middle Ages when people were dropping like flies while those who had not caught the plague made merry with dancing and wine.

We had been at the Bainbridges two weeks when Mrs. Stanard invited our household to a supper and dance. According to Jane, Mrs. Stanard was the crème de la crème of Richmond society rivaling Varena Davis (wife of the Confederate president, Jefferson Davis) in the list of notables she drew to her functions.

Since I was in mourning, it would not do for me to appear in public except in the old dress I had dyed black for Miles's memorial service. It was ugly, and for a while I thought of not going at all. But Ruth suggested I alter it a bit.

"Make a neckline of sorts," she said. "There's no law that says you have to wear the collar up to your ears."

I'm afraid I cut out more than Ruth had envisioned, for the curve of my breasts showed just above the décolletage. But she did not criticize me.

"Black suits you, Carmella, goes well with your white skin. It's a pity you don't have a string of jet beads."

What little I had brought to Wildoak in the way of jewelry had been buried together with Beth Ann's and Ruth's beneath one of the slave cabins, and we had not dared dig it up when we left. Ruth, I knew, had tactfully suggested the beads to cover some of my nakedness.

"Never mind," I said, "I shall wear a light shawl and no one will notice."

Mrs. Stanard's house was a blaze of lights when we arrived, excited, our differences momentarily forgotten at the prospect of attending a party, a *real* party at last.

"I won't know how to act," Deirdre said. She had refused to wear black, though she was a widow too. She said her husband had not died in the war, so why should she? Deirdre, of course, could carry it off. She was young and her antecedents, unlike mine, were above reproach.

I didn't care. I knew I looked attractive. It was good to forget the war for a few hours, good to be greeted by a smiling, beautifully gowned hostess, good to see men again, the gray and light blue uniforms not quite as spruce as they had once been, but the officers wearing them still handsome and gallant.

In the ballroom two fiddlers were tuning up near the piano and the Negro servants moving in and out among the guests were carrying trays of—could it be?

"Champagne!" Deirdre exploded. "Oh, *champagne!*"

How many eons, since I had drunk champagne? I closed my eyes as the bubbly nose-tickling liquid slid down my throat, warming my chest with a delicious sense of well-being.

"Oh, look!" Deirdre exclaimed. "Look who's coming in the door!"

I turned my head and saw a man at the entrance removing a plumed officer's hat.

"Carmella!"

There was only one man in the world who could pronounce my name in the exciting way. Derry!

CHAPTER

THIRTY

"*I* HAD no idea you were in Richmond," Derry said, bending over my hand.

"We've not been here long."

"I heard about Miles. I'm sorry. And this," he turned to Deirdre, "could this be Harold's little girl?"

"Not little at all." She smiled coquettishly up at him. "I'm a widow too."

"Are you? My condolences." His eyes moved swiftly over her and a surge of jealousy rushed through me, so strong it was frightening. I fought for control, telling myself, how ridiculous; of course Derry would admire a young girl. Men did. I had to accept that. It was me he loved.

When he turned back to me, all smiles, I saw I was right, and that foolish tide of green envy ebbed swiftly away.

"Have you had supper?" he asked.

"No."

"May I?" He gave me his arm. "And you Deirdre?"

But a young man in a gilt-buttoned coat was speaking to her and she said, "Thank you. I think I'd rather dance for now."

"How lovely you look," Derry said as we threaded our way through the crowd to the dining room. "You can't know how wonderful it is to see you again. I've missed you dreadfully. But then you must know. My letter—"

"We haven't received mail at Wildoak for ages, Derry."

"I wrote when I learned Miles was killed. I've been so worried about you. I was hoping you'd come to Richmond."

"We had to leave Wildoak; the Yankees took it over."

Small knots of guests, women in watered silks and lace-edged taffetas, men in uniform, were standing on either side of the table. It was buffet, and we helped ourselves to chicken salad, mousse, cold ham, roast beef, olives, jelly cake, and champagne. I hadn't seen food like that in years, and Derry's presence made every bite seem like a feast for the gods. He had a new air of authority about him, a self-assurance that went with his gray cassimere coat, the high, polished boots, and the tasseled scabbard at his side. My heart swelled when I compared him to the other men, for he was easily the best-looking officer in the room.

"I see you've been promoted to captain," I said. "Congratulations, darling. You look so *successful.*"

"Thank you, my dear. The pay *is* a little better, though I'm still a courier." He explained he was on President Davis's staff, one of several aides who acted as liaison between the president and General Lee in the field.

"Not the most dangerous job," he said. "I'm a glorified messenger boy."

"You belittle yourself, Derry. I'm sure what you do is of the utmost importance. I can't think of anything more perilous than carrying dispatches to and from the battlefield."

"It does have its moments, but let's not talk about that. Where are you staying?"

"With the Bainbridges."

"I shall call on you. Jane Bainbridge is no stranger to me, and neither is Beth Ann. I shall call on you and Beth Ann. Two bereaved ladies. Why not?"

"All right." I tried not to smile or to look happy, I didn't want talk to start up again. Not that I minded what people said; it was Ruth's good opinion I cared for. I did not want her to think that her faith in me had been ill founded.

"What I would really like," he said, lowering his voice, "is to see you alone. Is that possible?"

"I don't know."

"Don't you ever take a stroll?"

I thought quickly. "We—Prue, Alice, Deirdre, and Jane—will be working at Clopton General Hospital on Wednesday as volunteers. Perhaps I can get away early."

"How early? Three o'clock?"

"I—I think I can manage it."

"Clopton is on Franklin Street. Say we meet on the corner of Third and Franklin. All right?"

"Yes—I . . ."

He glanced up and the expression on his face suddenly changed.

I turned my head. Prudence was standing behind me.

"Mr. Wakefield, what a surprise-" she said in a light, taunting tone. "I had no idea you were in Richmond. Renewing old acquaintances with Mrs. Falconer?"

Derry gave her a gallant bow, taking her hand, kissing it. "My dear Mrs. Fairchild, I never have to renew my acquaintance with any of you lovely ladies. You are always fresh in my mind."

Mollified, smiling, tapping his arm playfully with her fan, she said, "You must call on us at the Bainbridges."

"How kind of you. Mrs. Falconer was just saying that perhaps it would not be proper—her husband and Beth Ann's—so soon . . ." His voice trailed off.

"I'm sure it will be perfectly all right."

"Then I shall be delighted."

Oh, what an actor he was, how beautifully he buttered her up! Was it any wonder I adored him?

On the way home that night, feeling giddy, drunk not only with champagne but with love, it suddenly occurred to me that I was no longer married. I was free, a widow, one with a considerable fortune. No sooner did the thought pass through my mind than the old guilt rose like an accusing shadow pointing a finger at me. How could I feel happy about my widowhood even if I had not loved Miles? How could I think of his money, with him buried in a battlefield grave?

It wasn't right. And yet no amount of self-castigation could alter the fact of his death, nor could a lifetime of culpable breast-beating bring him back. He was gone, I was unattached again, and Derry was still a bachelor. I only hoped that Miles, somewhere in the hereafter, would look down and forgive me.

When Wednesday morning came around, I deliberately pushed all guilty thoughts from my mind. Today I would be meeting with Derry! I remember getting out of bed, going to the window and parting the curtains for a look at the sky, and the little thrill of joy that stretched down to my toes when I saw the sun was shining. A day steeped in azure. Something good was going to happen to me, I knew it in my bones, something wonderful. I could put hardships and disappointment and all the niggling irritations of these past few years behind me now. Derry and I would be together. Perhaps he would ask me to marry him. If . . . But I must not be impatient.

He was waiting for me, seated in a smart-looking buggy drawn by a horse that was in considerably better condition than the pair that had brought us to Richmond. When he saw me, Derry swung himself down and helped me up beside him.

"Am I late?" I asked breathlessly.

"Not at all. Lovely." He leaned over and kissed me on the cheek.

"Derry! Suppose someone sees?"

"Let them." And he gave me another kiss.

"Perhaps we could take a ride in a more secluded neighborhood," I suggested. "Away from curious eyes."

"I have a better idea. But before I forget . . ." He reached into an inner pocket. "I have a letter for you."

"Me? How did *you* get it?"

"It came to Lavinia Hastings by mistake. I happened to see her at the post office this morning and she asked if I wouldn't drop it by the Bainbridges' house."

I glanced at the tattered and thumbprinted envelope, just barely able to make out the San Francisco postmark.

Probably Dolly, I thought. "I'll read it later," I said, tucking it into my reticule.

We started off, clattering through busy streets, past the Spotswood Hotel, and across Capitol Square. To all my questions about our destination Derry answered, "You'll see." But he did point out the sights: the smokestack of the Iron Works;

the capitol building with its rotunda; the house where President Davis and his wife, Varena, had taken up residence. We descended a hill to an avenue that ran close to the canal, a section of warehouses, mean shacks, and frame shanties. Jolting down an unpaved side street, we stopped before a small house, the brick fascade crumbling in places, clumsily patched with dabs of gray mortar in others.

I looked at Derry questioningly.

"Come along." He jumped down and held out his arms for me.

"Here, Derry?"

"Here. And I had a hard time getting it. Every other place is either crowded, taken, or public. I managed to bribe one of our officers to let us have it for a few hours."

"But Derry . . ."

"I know it's not the best, but how else could we be together."

"Yes, yes, of course. You're right."

Derry reached under the buggy seat and brought out a hamper. "Victuals, Carmella. And champagne. We'll have a picnic."

The run-down house with its neglected weed-choked yard and sagging step seemed hardly the spot for a picnic. But why should I carp? I was with Derry. Wasn't that enought?

Inside, the air hung heavy with a musty odor, the damp smell of rotting upholstery and mice. A threadbare carpet covered the floor, and pushed into one dark corner was a large bed with a soiled cover. Derry parted the curtains and opened a window.

"Phew! It will cool off presently. Meanwhile, my darling . . ."

I went into his arms, and his mouth took mine possessively in a long exploring kiss. Holding me, he pressed me closer with little squeezing hugs. I could feel his hard chest through the cloth of his uniform, and a sudden vision of Miles rose before me—a vision I quickly pushed down into the darkness of my mind.

"You aren't kissing me back," Derry murmured, his forehead resting on mine.

My arms went up around his neck and I pressed my lips to his, summoning a passion I somehow could not feel, clinging to him, trying to dispel the odd feeling that something was wrong. But how could it be? I still loved Derry, I told myself. *I still loved Derry.* I hadn't changed.

His tongue parted my lips, flicking inside, while one hand edged between us, unbuttoning my bodice.

"No—Derry." I pushed myself away. "No—wait."

He looked puzzled. It baffled me too. There had been moments in the past when his fingers touching a button at my throat, loosening a drawstring, parting my collar, would have sent a wild shiver up my spine. But now—I didn't feel that way at all. It was disconcerting. Perhaps I had seen too much suffering. Perhaps we had been separated too long. I must give it time, and after a while the old magic would come back.

"We need champagne, sweetheart," Derry said. "That's what we need. Coming from that awful hospital—how could I expect you to be loving at once?"

"Yes, champagne." Oh, Derry!

I laughed as he uncorked the bottle with a festive *pop!* and withdrew two glasses from the hamper.

"To love," he said, "to many happy hours!"

The champagne was warm, a little flat. Derry filled our glasses again.

"Let me make a toast," I begged. "To happiness in the years to come."

Did he frown? No, he was drinking, smiling over the rim of his flass.

"Feeling better?" He took the glass from me and set it down. "Lovely, lovely Carmella. If you knew the hours I've spent dreaming of this moment." His hand went to the buttons again. "I'm sorry about the bed. It's not the most comfortable, but we won't mind, will we, darling?"

How did he know about the bed? He had used it before? But I mustn't think of that.

"Wait," I said, taking hold of his hand. "I—Derry, I wanted to talk to you."

A tolerant smile edged his mouth. "About what, darling? How strangely you are behaving. Don't you love me anymore?"

"Oh, yes, yes! Of course I do. But, Derry, I was wondering—if . . ."

"So that's it, my darling." He hugged me, rocking me back and forth in his arms. "I haven't stopped loving you. Is that what's troubling you?"

"I'm not troubled, Derry. I thought..." I released myself and walked to the window sill, where he had set our glasses. I lifted mine for something to hold, not because I really wanted more champagne. But he took the gesture as a sign that I did and quickly poured a large dollop into my glass.

"Derry..." I swallowed and took the plunge. "Derry, I'm free now. I'm not married. I'm a widow."

"So you are. And a rich one, no doubt, unless Miles converted his money to Confederate bonds."

"I—I don't know. He never discussed finances with me. Derry, do you still want to marry me?"

"Still...? Carmella!" He held out his arms. "Must we talk of marriage now, must we be serious on this our first afternoon together in years?"

He was making me feel like a spoilsport, a nagging killjoy. But I *had* to know.

"Forgive me, Derry. I hate to be serious, and I realize it isn't proper for the woman to ask. But, oh, Derry, I can't help it! I've waited so long, so many years! And always there was some reason. My father, your lack of funds, my marriage—but now all those reasons are gone."

He sat down on the bed and crossed his legs. "I don't know what's come over you. You've changed. You're not the same. We had such wonderful times together. And now you are harping on marriage."

"I always thought..." A lump had mysteriously formed in my throat and I found it difficult to speak. "I always thought it was what you wanted too. And now you say 'harp.'"

"Why can't we go on as we were? Why can't we go on being happy with one another without such complications as marriage?"

I swallowed. "Is that what marriage means to you—complications?"

"It isn't because I don't love you, darling. I do. Don't you understand?"

I lifted the hamper from the chair and sat down. My legs

had suddenly gone weak. "No," I said.

"My dear Carmella, my lovely, lovely girl. I can't marry you."

"You—you mean—you mean you already have a wife?"

He laughed. "No—I'm still very much a bachelor, although I do intend to marry someday. But I'm a Wakefield. I come from a long line of aristocrats, and the girl I choose as wife will have the same background as myself. Can't you see it's impossible for me to marry the daughter of a whore?"

If he had struck me full across the face with the back of his hand I could not have been more stunned. The breath went out of my lungs, my throat clogged, and for a few black moments I thought I would strangle. I tried to speak, but the words refused to come. I kept staring at him through a mist of disbelief, not really seeing him, aware only of my pain.

"I would not have said that," Derry went on, "but nothing would satisfy you except the truth."

The truth. I had pressed him and he had told me the truth. Oh, if the pain would only go away! If I could be somewhere else, anywhere—at home, a dark, dark hole, a cave where I didn't have to think, to feel, to hurt.

"But you said—you told me in San Francisco, in Virginia City the reason you didn't ask Papa for my hand was because of your situation."

"That's true. And I may have played with the idea at one time. But now—coming back to Virginia, to my family, to my roots, the war—I realize I owe a responsibility to my heritage."

"What high-sounding words! If that were so, why didn't you tell me all this sooner?"

"I was afraid I'd lose you."

"Lose me? For what? You didn't want to marry me. You *never* wanted to marry me!" I stared at him, the bitter tears burning behind my eyes. "You didn't think of me as a wife— but as a mistress."

"Carmella, I swear, my one wish was to make you as happy as I could. I wanted to be able to give you—"

"I know, I know!" I interrupted vehemently. "Jewels and gowns. You wanted a woman who 'glittered when she walked.'

You wanted a toy. That's why you were so jealous of other men, of Miles. You didn't like the thought of sharing your toy with anyone else."

"Come now, Carmella, don't be so upset. You know the facts of life. A gentleman dosen't marry a girl whose mother—"

"Don't!" I cried, anger lifting me from the chair. "Don't use that word again. My mother had an—an unfortunate life. She was driven to it—you don't understand—if she were here now you would see what a lady she was."

"Part of your charm, Carmella, is your naïveté," Derry said. "That girlishness—if I may be so blunt—excites me. But, darling, let us face facts. Your mother was a—"

"Don't say it!"

He got up and poured himself more champgane, watching me over the rim of the glass as he drank. "You think she was unfortunate, that she was seduced, forced into a life of sin? Ah, yes. Or that she was poor, ignorant, and had no other choice? My dear, it's simply not true!"

"How do you know? People who have met her, Mrs. Halstead, Miles—"

"They were telling you little white lies. You can see for yourself. That letter I gave you—"

"You read my letter?"

"Yes. Lavinia asked me to. She had opened it, thinking it was for her, but couldn't make head or tails of it. She wondered if I thought it might be yours. It is. I suggest you read it."

"I don't feel up to—"

"Please read it, Carmella."

There were actually two letters. The first I unfolded was written on cheap paper, the handwriting crude and barely legible.

Dear Miss Hastings:
My wife Kate died sicks months ago. She diden leave me nothen but a few persenal belongens and a pack of your mamas letters. They aint worth nothen to me but I thot youd want them. All I ask is eckspenses—ship fare and such—one thosand dollars for the lot. Inclosed is a sampal, so you'll know I ain't fibben.

Sam. P.S. I'm followen the strate and narow now. The money will help a good citisen.

S. Halstead.

Still shaken by the revelation of Derry's true feelings, I saw Sam Halstead's letter only as an oddity, a thinly disguised plea for blackmail money.

But the second letter was quite different. The spidery script, now faded, had been set down on cream vellum, the sort of paper my father favored for his personal correspondence. The letterhead in bold black, said MRS. ARTHUR HASTINGS. The page trembled in my hand, and it was a moment or two before I could bring myself to read it.

Dear Kate:

I hope you and the girls are well. I am doing fine. Arthur is a sweet man, very generous and kind, and I'm not sorry I married him and I *do* love him despite what you all thought when I agreed to be his wife. But, oh, Katie! I am bored, so *bored!* I miss the chats with Tillie and Tina and Bess, the company, the parties we had. I never regret a moment I spent with you. I never regret a moment of that life. I knew when I chose it, that it would make me happy. You must write and tell me if Tillie ever got her Paris gown, if her friend, Mr. Tompkins . . .

I couldn't go on. It was as if the roof of the small shabby house in which I sat had suddenly begun to crack and crumble, the mortar already falling about me. *I knew when I chose it, that it would make me happy* . . . She had been happy as a prostitute—happy, happy, *happy!* Oh, dear God, why did he have to show me those letters? Why hadn't he burned them? Why did I have to know? Everything inside me, like the house, was disintegrating to dust. Only the skeleton under my skin kept me from sinking into boneless ash.

"What can you expect?" people had said; *"her mother was a whore."* And I had always excused her, telling myself she couldn't help it; that poor and defenseless, she had nowhere else to turn. I had led myself to believe she had been an unwilling victim. And I had woven this fantasy, never allowing myself to associate her with the sordidness I had seen on the

Barbary Coast or in New Orleans. A fairy tale, all untrue. She had enjoyed a life of sin.

"Well," Derry say saying, "do you see what I mean?"

For the first time in my life I really looked at him. He sat there, a small smile on his lips, complacent, smug, cruel. Had this man once had the power to move me, to make me tremble, to kindle desire, excitement, passion? The thought of Derry had sustained me through so many trials, lighted me through so many dark places. But the Derry I had loved was no more real than the mother I had pitied. They were both part of a romantic fabric I had woven out of whole cloth, flimsy material that had no substance, that disintegrated and disappeared in the cold, gusty wind of reality.

"It doesn't make any difference in the way I love you," Derry said.

The way he loved me — selfishly, childishly, as a possession like a good horse or a fine set of pistols. A love without honor.

"I never lied to you about that, Carmella."

And I had taken his avowals as having the same depth and strength as mine. Derry could never love anyone except himself. He was weak — Miles had tried to tell me, weak and a coward. His staff duties (and what strings had he pulled to get such a soft, safe position? a messenger boy, he himself called it) allowed him to live in comparative comfort. It kept him and his horse sleek while others starved, kept him from fighting, from the real danger, from the ugly, bloody mess of combat. How could I ever have loved him?

And yet I must have sensed something awry, perhaps long ago. Why else had I defended him so vehemently to Miles? And the last time Derry came to Wildoak, my reluctance to bed him, I now saw, had been more than a fear of being found out. Why hadn't I seen through him sooner? Why had it taken so many years? Because I wanted to cling to my sentimental notions of love. I had lived through poverty and distress, had seen the lurid life of the cribs and the savagery of battle, and still part of me had refused to grow up.

But I grew up in that room. Oh, yes, I grew up, and it was a swift, shocking, heartbreaking growth. I looked around at the dusty cobwebbed corners, the gray balls of lint under the bed, the smoke-blackened fireplace, the dirty, limp curtains at the flyspecked windows. It was all so sordid, so painful, I wanted to weep.

"I don't love you, Derry." And saying it was not as difficult as I thought it might be.

"Come now, Carmella. Why should it change things? You liked me well enough once; I made you happy, didn't I?" He got to his feet and came forward, lifting me from the chair.

"No," I said, turning my face away from his lips. "Let me go."

"I shan't force you," he said after a moment. "There are plenty of attractive girls I can have. There's a shortage of able-bodied men, if you get my meaning."

"I want to go home," I said.

"All right." He picked up the glasses and put them back into the hamper.

"I prefer going on my own," I said.

"You can't. I may be a bit of a cad, but I can't let you do that in this neighborhood."

"What difference does it make? My mother was a whore."

"Carmella . . ."

I tied the strings of my bonnet firmly under my chin. "Goodbye, Derry."

It was a long walk back to the Bainbridges, but I made it, I hardly knew how, for once away from Derry I had to fight tears every step of the way.

CHAPTER

THIRTY-ONE

DAY AFTER day we could hear the tramping of feet, soldiers marching through the city on their way to strengthen General Beauregard's twenty-five-mile line to the south. For Petersburg was still under fire. A city of strategic importance, the center of Lee's supply (five railroads and a network of highways ran into it), its loss would not only be an irreparable blow, but would give the Union Army access to Richmond.

We tried not to think of a Yankee breakthrough as we tightened our belts and waited through the hot days of June and July. Few people gave parties now, and those who did were criticized. Jane refused to accept any invitations. She said it was a disgrace to make merry in times of such tribulation.

Her husband claimed the war could not last much longer no matter how bravely and willingly the Southerners fought. Grant's Union Army outnumbered ours two-to-one; and for every man the Yankee general lost, another sprang up to replace him. We had used all our reserves. There simply were no more. Men were deserting by the hundreds, and those still fighting were worn thin by lack of food and rest.

Petersburg held, but on September 2nd Atlanta fell, and later Winchester was taken by Sheridan, who went on to devastate the rich Shenandoah Valley. There was talk of supplies in South Carolina that could not reach us because speculators had bribed the railroad to hold them back. Some of these swindlers, the *Dispatch* hinted, were men close to President Davis. When I read that I thought of Derry with shame and disgust. I had not seen him since the morning I had walked away from the shabby house near the canal, and he'd made no attempt to call.

As September drew to a close and autumn woodsmoke threaded the purple dusks, I had other things besides the war and Derry to think of.

Ruth was dying. Dr. Gordon had finally diagnosed her illness as pernicious anemia, a disease that destroyed the red blood cells and invariably killed its victims. There was no cure. How stark those simple words sounded when the doctor first spoke them. No cure. He had not embellished, had offered no kind words, no hope, no sympathy. I suppose he had seen too much horrible suffering to feel sorry for a middle-aged woman who, unlike his wounded, would die comforted by friends in a decent bed with clean linen.

Ruth took the news stoically enough, but I knew how depressed she must feel. However, when her husband came home in October her spirits lifted considerably. Alex Harkness, unaware that we had left the plantations on the Pamunkey until he returned there to empty houses, had been invalided out of the army. He had lost his right leg at Lynchburg, and when I saw him hopping up the stairs, his empty trouser leg pinned to the knee, maneuvering the crutch under his armpit a little clumsily, tears came to my eyes. But Major Harkness had the same iron will as his wife, and he made it clear he wanted no pity.

"I'm alive and grateful for that," he said. "And Ruth," he added with determination, "is going to get well."

We all prayed that she would, hoped that the doctor was wrong. But as day passed into day it was obvious that she was sinking. I went about, my throat aching with grief. I couldn't believe it was happening. Ruth had been the mother I had never known, the friend I'd never had. She had grace and understanding and warmth; she redeemed the cruelties of the human race. The world would lose one of its few decent human beings, a lady. It wasn't *right*. It didn't make sense!

I sat for long hours by her bedside. When she was awake I read old copies of *Harper's Weekly* to her, the same articles over and over, for we hadn't received a new magazine in three years and the papers were too full of the war.

One morning she said to me, "You were never happy with Miles, were you?"

I was sitting on a low pouf next to her bed, and when she said that she looked directly into my eyes. I was so taken aback I could not lie.

"No. I—we were married at my father's request. And I believed at the time—believed all along—that I loved another man."

"And you still do?"

"No—oh, no. That's past. It's over. I found—I found he was—unworthy." Unworthy! Oh, God, if it had only been as simple as that; the years of hope, of dreams wiped away. Unworthy.

"Do you think if Miles had lived you might have come to love him?"

I looked down at my hands. "I have thought of it—yes."

I had thought of it with bitterness, regret, and not a little guilt. I had taunted him, mocked him, just as he had taunted and mocked me, but he had given me far more than I had ever given him. He had saved my life, literally, on more than one occasion. He had looked after my financial interests, making a point to guard them against risk though I, in my blindness, had chosen to believe otherwise. He had warned me about Derry, but I would not listen. And he had tried to protect me from the unflattering truth about my mother, as my father and even Kate Hempstead had done. They had let me have my little illusions. Whereas Derry . . .

"My dear child." Ruth's dry hand crept over the covers to touch mine. "Please forgive me for bringing it up. I should have realized talking about Miles would be painful."

"It's—it's all right."

Now he was dead, and I would never have the chance to say, "I'm sorry. Forgive me."

"Cry, go ahead. I shan't mind."

"No. There's too much to cry about. Once I start, I'll flood us both out."

"Oh, me! It hurts to laugh, but isn't it the truth?"

"Shall I continue reading? Here's an interesting bit on polishing brass."

No one wanted to talk about defeat, yet the erosion of the South went on apace. On September 29th, news reached us that Fort Harrison, an earthwork rampart southeast of Richmond, had capitulated to the Yankees, putting the capital in grave danger. The governor called on every able-bodied man in the city to shoulder arms, civilians from fifteen to sixty, whether government workers, shopkeepers, or laborers. If they would not come willingly, he gave orders to have them arrested and impressed. The stores were closed, the public offices and foundries shut down. The tocsin rang night and day, a mournful, frightening sound. Alex Harkness oiled his Colt and stumped down to the recruiting office, determined to do his share. "Doesn't take two legs to shoot a Yankee," he maintained.

The expected invasion did not come and the old men, young boys, and civilian shirkers trooped back to take up the business of keeping Richmond in some kind of functioning order again. Prices rose to outrageous heights—bacon $20 a pound, flour $1,000 a barrel! Food was not only dear but scarce, as was clothing. We turned hems, patched and mended, put cardboard in the soles of our slippers. It was a miserable winter, cold with sleet and rain.

Four days before Christmas the Union Army occupied Savannah. Alice Dinwiddie had a sister living there and she went about the house, pale and frightened, whispering that her sister would never live through it. One morning a small boy came to the door with a note from Lavinia. Her mother-in-law had died quietly in her sleep.

All through that bitter, sleet-driven winter Ruth hung on. We managed to ignore the gloom by discussing light topics; dress patterns, hair fashions, the crossstitch, recipes that called for fewer ingredients, eggless cakes, bread made with ground, parched corn, meatless loaves.

In January peace feelers were sent out, but still no one spoke of defeat, at least not openly. The South wanted a cessation of hostilities and thought it could set its own terms. It was a vain hope. Conditions worsened with each passing hour. Winter gave way to spring, and on April 1st the Battle of Five Forks ended in a decisive victory for the North. On April 2nd, President Jefferson Davis ordered the evacuation of Richmond.

It was a Sunday, I recall, a lovely day with blue skies and warm sunshine when Mr. Bainbridge, looking agitated, came home from a council meeting with the news that Davis and his cabinet had already boarded trains for Danville.

"People are leaving by every means available," he said. "I can manage to get passes on one of the last trains."

"But where would it take us?" Jane asked. "Ruth can't be moved. And I have no wish to leave my home."

"The mayor is trying to organize a committee that will arrange for surrender. Perhaps it won't be as bad as we imagine, only a peaceful transfer."

Everyone was gathered in the parlor, and I remember looking around at the white faces.

Jane turned to us. "If there are any among you who wish to leave, Mr. Bainbridge can see to it that you do."

Beth Ann, her two younger daughters, and the female cousins decided at once to accept Morton Bainbridge's offer. They hurriedly got a few things together and sat in the parlor while he went off to make arrangements. We could hear the guns booming to the south, but no one knew what they meant. Occasionally a carriage would rumble by, people would shout.

Beth Ann wrung her hands; one of the cousins sobbed. They were sure the Yankees had already arrived, that it was too late, that the conquering army would massacre us all, or worse.

Noon arrived. I took some chicken broth up to Ruth. She insisted I not stay on her account. "Go with them," she urged. "Alex and I can do very well. No one will harm two old invalids like ourselves."

But I wouldn't think of it. "It seems we've had this argument before. You know very well I shan't leave."

Around five o'clock, when Mr. Bainbridge had not returned, Jane could no longer conceal her anxiety. Alex Harkness went out to look for him.

"Something's happened," Beth Ann said. "I know something's happened."

"Oh, be quiet!" I commanded. "You aren't helping things by whining."

She broke into tears.

Deirdre, who had been sitting on a chair calmly turning the pages of a magazine, lifted her head. "I'll try to find out why he's so late."

Jane bristled. "No you won't! Two gone is enough." Then after a long silence, "Shall we have some supper?"

No one was hungry.

Finally at ten o'clock that night both men arrived, rather frazzled and breathless. "I had to do some wangling," Mr. Bainbridge said. "Everyone in Richmond is at the bureau clamoring to get on that train. It's supposed to be the last one. We had better head for it right away, though I don't suppose it will leave for hours. Come along now. Beth Ann, get hold of yourself."

He and Alex helped the women into the carriage and they started off. I stood at the door, listening to the sound of the wheels growing fainter with an empty feeling inside.

Jane said, "We ought to eat," perhaps for the third time.

We had a hastily put together meal of bread spread with sorghum-sugared gooseberry jam and watery tea. Even that we ate listlessly, with one ear cocked to the sounds of distant booming and the rackety passage of wheels on the cobbles outside. In the midst of the meal, Alice rose trembling from her chair.

"I'm going," she announced. "I can't stay. I've changed my mind."

"It's too late," Jane snapped. "You had your chance and it's too late now."

I had never heard Jane speak in such a manner. She had always been courteous, calm, and self-possessed. To have her suddenly turn waspish added to our uneasiness.

Alice, her cheeks scarlet, repeated, "I'm going! You can't stop me. It isn't too late. Mr. Bainbridge said the train wouldn't be leaving for hours."

"The carriage isn't here," Jane said. "And there's no way of getting to the depot."

"I'll walk, if I have to. I'll walk all by myself! You can't keep me here! You can't!"

Her shrill voice so filled with fear grated on my ears. "I'll take you," I offered. Anything to shut her up, to have her out of the house.

"You must be mad," Jane said. "The streets aren't safe."

"The streets are full of people too busy trying to save their own skins to pay attention to us," I said. "Come on, Alice. It's a long way."

We had no difficulty until we turned the corner of Franklin Street, and then it was like plunging into a roaring river. The clamor of fumbling wheels, shouting voices, screams, curses, whinnying horses, and crying children was deafening. A tide of people poured past us, riding in carriages, barouches, wagons, and carts, some on foot dragging belongings in sacks or barrows, some carrying their youngsters on their shoulders, all frantic, all terrified, all wanting to get out, *out* before the Yankees arrived. Alice and I, arms linked, pushed our way through, buffeted and shoved, our feet trod upon.

"Shall we turn back?" I yelled above the tumult.

She shook her head. Her face had the damp, pale, perspiring look of panic. Sirens wailed, church bells rang, people sobbed. Houses we passed were shuttered and bolted. Jane had been right. We were mad.

We were a block from the depot when the long, piercing wail of a locomotive reached our ears. "God—they're going; they're going without me!" Alice cried. She broke away from me and ran, pushing, elbowing frantically through the crowd.

"Wait—Alice, wait!" I dashed after her, caught her by the shoulder and dragged her to the edge of the passing throng into the shelter of a shop doorway.

"Do you want to get killed?" I shouted. "If you fall you'll be trampled to death by this stampede."

"Let go!" she sobbed. "They're leaving without me!"

I hit her, a slap that rattled her teeth. "Shut up!" I yelled, furious at her, at myself, at my own fear and the stupidity that had allowed me to leave the comparative safety of the Bainbridge house.

We stood there, cowering in the doorway as the people continued to flow by. Now above their heads I saw a horseman approaching, a Confederate cavalryman, and behind him a small mounted troop. The crowd pressing against each other parted. Someone shouted, "General! General Early!" As he rode under a flaring lamp I saw his face set in grim lines, the eyes shadowed and hollowed.

So this was the famous Early who together with his riders had threatened Washington, D.C., frightening the Union government, the tough, driving Southerner who had tried vainly to stem Sheridan's tide in the Shenandoah. His men followed in as tight a regimental formation as the width of the street and the crowd would allow. The band winnowed by death and four years of attrition, lean, exhausted, their uniforms faded and shabby, still rode, even in the face of coming defeat, with a certain élan, a military smartness, their heads held high. Watching them, I felt my throat constrict. No one, not even the most rabid antiwar spectator, could watch those brave, dauntless men without feeling a swell of pride.

After they had gone, Alice and I moved again toward the depot carried along by the throng, Alice gripping my arm in a bruising hold. Suddenly a deafening explosion, followed by three more, froze us in our tracks.

I grabbed a soldier who was hurrying past. "What is it?"

"The gunboats in the James River! Ours. The army's been ordered to destroy them. They're blowing up the last bridge too!"

Another thundering, crashing explosion shook the cobbles under our feet and the horizon lit up with flames.

"Fire! Fire!" Shouts went up all around.

A pall of smoke spread quickly above the flames. Ashes and hot cinders fell, one catching my skirt, scorching the cloth before I rubbed it out.

"We can't stay here, Alice. We have to try to get back.-'

I couldn't budge her. She held to me, the whites of her eyes enormous. I slapped her again. She tore away from me and ran shrieking into the mob. I followed at her heels, but a stalled cart with a rearing horse separated us. When I dashed around it, I couldn't find her. She had disappeared. Vanished. The blood-red sky and twisting smoke continued to light up as bursting shells detonated with a deafening and terrifying din.

"Alice! Alice . . . !"

I buttonholed one person after another, shouting above the

noise, asking if he or she had seen a small brunet woman in a dark green gown. But I might as well have been yelling in Chinese, for people were too caught up in their own fear to notice anything or anyone else. I myself wanted to run blindly away from this horror, away from this inferno, but how could I explain about Alice? Oh, damn her! Damn her!

Without quite knowing how, for I had thought I was still going in the direction of the depot, I came out on Capitol Square. Across it, on the far side, rose a wall of roaring, crackling fire, a flaming barricade blocking out the horizon. To my right, on the capitol grounds, a host of people had gathered, entire families who had fled their homes bringing with them what belongings they had managed to carry. One woman, her dress half burned, her hair scorched, kept screaming endlessly while another tried to calm her. Mingled with the odor of fire and ashes was the strong smell of whiskey. It puzzled me until I saw a darkie leaning down and drinking from the gutter. Others, poor whites, shabby-coated men and bare-legged harlots, were scooping and dipping with bottles, cups, ladles and their hands.

Later I learned that the City Council, afraid the liquor shops would be sacked by an unruly mob, had rolled the whiskey barrels to the curbstone, broken the lids, with axes, then emptied the contents into the gutter. But this ploy did not stop the drunkenness or the looting. Men, women, and even children, both black and white, hurried along toting boxes, pictures, feathered hats, footstools, and bolts of cloth, rushing across the square with their booty, some staggering with the effects of the whiskey, others staggering under the weight of their loads.

Main, Cary, and Canal Streets were all ablaze. It was futile to go on looking for Alice in this pandemonium. Perhaps she was already headed back to the Bainbridges on her own. At any rate I couldn't stay. I ran on, the uproar, the noise, the horrible din following me on to the side streets, the choking smoke so thick in places I could scarcely see a few feet ahead. My ears rang with the painful banging of my heart; my lungs, constricted by my corset stays, screamed for air.

The sky was beginning to lighten into dawn as I turned a corner—Grace Street at last. And there—yes, it was all right, the Bainbridge house still stood, its window panes lit up with garish light from the distant fire. I stumbled the last few steps down the block, and when I reached the front of the house I paused, hanging on to the hitching post, head bent, listening to the rasp of my breath as it tore through me.

"Carmella . . . ?"

I looked up. There framed in the doorway was Miles.

I knew then that I had died back there in the holocaust, that I had caught fire and burned to death and now I was in some limbo, perhaps Hell itself and that the ghost of Miles Falconer had stepped forward to greet me. This was retribution, vengeance, my payment for all past sins.

"Carmellaaaah . . . !"

But the voice seemed to be fading away, and the swirling darkness around me stilled it altogether.

CHAPTER

THIRTY-TWO

*M*ILES WAS *flesh and blood, real, not a ghost.*

The report claiming he had died at Spotsylvania had been false. Taken captive there along with dozens of other Confederates, Miles had been sent to the notorious Federal prison at Fort Delaware. Six months later he and several companions escaped. The others had been run down and shot, but Miles got away. Intending to rejoin his regiment, he began to travel southward, but exhaustion and illness soon overtook him and he spent more than a month—he could not be sure how long—nurtured by a farm woman and her elderly mother in return for a promise to help them with the spring plowing when he recovered. He received no news and had no idea of how the war was progressing. Then, one day not long after he had fulfilled his commitment to the two women, he managed to obtain a newspaper and from it learned of the siege of Petersburg.

"But as you can see I was too late," he concluded wryly. "And here I am."

His entire story had taken only a few minutes to relate, the bare bones of an ordeal delivered in a succinct, almost dry manner. Perhaps he might have gone into greater detail later with Alex Harkness and Mr. Bainbridge, but to us sitting there in the parlor after I had come out of my faint, he refused to say more, turning our questions away with phrases like, "I'm sure that would be of no interest to you."

He looked older, careworn. And hearing his terse story, watching him, I felt an overwhelming tenderness, which he quickly squelched by remarking:

"And you, Carmella. I see you haven't gotten over rushing pell-mell into things. What on God's earth—even given Alice's hysteria—made you dash out on a night when decent folk stay inside?"

In former days I would have flung a biting retort at him, something wounding and spiteful. But too many things had happened since then. I was not the same Carmella. She was gone, and though his remark hurt, I could not summon the old anger to retaliate. Besides, he was right. I'd had no business offering to take Alice to the depot. Any my guilt was compounded a thousand times some hours later when Miles, Alex Harkness, and Mr. Bainbridge, who had gone in search of her, returned bearing Alice's dead body. She had been trampled to death.

One would think that a point could be reached beyond which tragedy could no longer move one. Not so. I had never liked Alice. She had been weak, a complainer, a clinging vine. But she had never willfully harmed anyone, and to have died such a horrible death seemed cruelly unjust. I did not grieve for her, but I felt a terrible remorse which plunged me into despondency.

Late in the afternoon Mr. Bainbridge came back with the news that the Yankees had marched into Richmond several hours earlier and the Federal troops led by General Weitzel were quickly restoring order. The conquerors, he told us, had behaved in exemplary fashion, even helping to put out the fires. The ashes were still smoldering and a large portion of the city, from the river up to Capitol Square had been burned to the ground.

"The only building left near the square is the Custom House," he said morosely.

That night Miles and I shared the bedroom that Beth Ann and her two younger daughters had vacated. I felt exceedingly shy when at last I found myself alone with him, as if I were a bride on a wedding night. He didn't look at me. He unbuttoned his ragged shirt slowly—he had long since lost his tunic and had come to Richmond in farmer's homespun—peering at himself in the mirror.

"Don't look like much, do I"

"Oh, Miles—of course you do!"

His brows went up. "I wish you wouldn't try to placate me. I look like hell and you know it."

"All right. Does it disturb your vanity to look like hell?"

His lips twisted into a smile. "That's better. I hate feminine coyness. Does it disturb my vanity? No, not at all. It was just a passing remark."

He shrugged out of his shirt. There was a horrible scar on his back, ridged and angry.

"Oh, Miles . . . !" I began, then caught myself, for he was scowling at me.

I sat down on the bed, suddenly not knowing what to say or do. I suppose I should have undressed. There was a screen in the corner and I looked at it, thinking I could go behind it and get into my nightgown there. Most wives undressed behind a screen. But I had never done so. Such false modesty was alien to me; Miles knew it, and I was certain he would laugh.

Miles felt in the pocket of his shirt and drew out a cigar. He sniffed at it, bit off the end. "A Yankee colonel gave it to me this afternoon. Out of the goodness of his heart. 'No hard feelings,'" he mimicked sardonically. "A Yankee."

I slipped off my shoes and running my hands up under my skirt carefully peeled off my stockings. Miles lit his cigar, leaned back on the chair, and began to puff at it, watching the smoke rings rise lazily toward the ceiling.

Why, I thought, he doesn't even know I'm here; I might as well be in Timbuktu. I got up and went to the chest and pulled out a clean nightgown from the drawer. I had taken a scalding bath earlier, but now wished I could take another. I moved to the dresser and toyed with a bottle of scent, a comb.

"Why don't you quit fussing?" Miles suddenly asked.

"I'm not fussing."

I turned down the bed and plumped up the pillows.

"My cigar's gone out," he said. He searched in his trouser pockets. "No matches, blast it!"

"There are some in the parlor," I said.

He put the cigar down and went out. Quick as a rabbit I

got out of my clothes and into my nightgown. I scrambled into bed, pulling the covers up to my chin. Should I feign sleep? No, it was too soon for that. As I lay there, I looked over at the table where Miles had left his cigar. A thin curling thread of smoke rose from it. But why would he pretend that it had gone out? Could it be that he sensed my shyness and had made the excuse to leave the room so I could undress withoug embarrassment? I turned the thought over in my mind and dismissed it as being unlike Miles.

He came back shortly. "Well," he said, picking up the ciagr, "made a trip downstairs for nothing."

Several minutes later he blew out the lamp. I heard the rustle of his trousers as he dropped them, and my heart began to beat loudly in a silly, schoolgirlish manner. The bedsprings creaked.

"Miles . . . ?"

He turned to me in the dark.

"Miles—I—I'm glad they didn't kill you."

A silence. Then, "What a pretty little speech. I wonder if you mean it."

His curtness fired the old anger, a single flare that died quickly. I wasn't mad, I couldn't be. He had every right to mistrust me.

"Miles . . ."

"Don't." He pressed fingers to my lips. "Don't talk—not now, not tonight."

He drew me into his arms and held me. Despite the warmth of the night and the covers, his body was cold. And so thin, so painfully thin. I drew my hand slowly down his back, feeling his shoulder blades, tenderly touching the ugly scar, then going lower to the taut buttocks. Suddenly his grip tightened. I could feel his heart pounding under my crushed, flattened breasts. He rolled me over and penetrated me, his skin no longer cold but emanating a feral heat. His thrusts were quick, deep, urgent, and toward the last frenzied. Before I could become aroused he was through. His weight lay sprawled over me, perspiring and damp. Breathing heavily, he mumbled something I could not catch. Then he shifted back to his own pillow. A minute later he was sound asleep.

It had all happened so fast. Not a single word of endearment, not a single kiss, a single caress. It wasn't right. I wanted more. I felt cheated, used, put upon. It didn't help to remind myself that this man had lived too long in places too terrible to speak of, had endured God knew what torture and despair, had been deprived of humanity, of civility, of the comforts of a woman's body. It did not help at all. *I* wanted to be loved. More importantly—and this came with a sudden astonishing illumination—I wanted to be loved by Miles.

Why? How could this be?

Because, I told myself, looking up into the darkness, because I loved him. I loved Miles. He had always been there, behind Derry's false, cheery front, there in the shadows, protective, a rock, strong, never dissembling. He had always been present but I'd never seen him and until this moment had never realized I loved him. How strange—and how futile. For Miles still considered me a wayward, spoiled child. I was not his idea of a real woman.

But I loved him. It was not the same breathless, "Oh, Derry!" love, but something deeper, quieter, a feeling that I had come home to something wonderful after a long and hazardous journey. Home to safe, strong, and protecting arms, home to a lover, a virile man who could be tender and passionate.

Yes, I loved him and the knowledge made me both happy and miserable, for he did not love me. Could he care in time? Ever? I did not know. Was it hopeless? Perhaps not. I had an advantage; I was his wife. Or was it a disadvantage: Except for a bout in bed now and then, did he ever think of me? He had said nothing about missing me, nothing of how he had thought or dreamed of me during those long nights away. He had not even embraced or kissed me, as most husbands did when returning from war. Of course I had fainted, but still . . .

I went on in this vein, my thoughts seesawing between hope and despair until I finally fell asleep.

The next day I told Miles about the letters.

"Sam Halstead again," Miles said grimly. "The rogue keeps coming back like a bad penny."

We had remained in the dining room over cups of tea while the others adjourned to the parlor. We could hear their voices as they received guests who had attended Alice's funeral. Miles got up and closed the door.

"It was sent over a year ago," I went on, as he seated himself. "To Lavinia Hastings by mistake. Then Derry..." I hesitated.

"Derry what?" he prompted.

"Derry delivered it."

"Here?"

"Well—not exactly. But it's not what you think," I added hastily.

He threw me a look of scorn.

"Believe me, Miles." Why had I been so foolish as to bring Derry's name into this? "I swear. As a matter of fact we quarreled—"

"Spare me, Carmella. I don't want to hear about it. Let's simply discuss the matter at hand. Have you the letters?"

"No, I tore them up. I was so disturbed."

"I don't think Sam Halstead can harm you, at any rate, not from a distance."

"It wasn't Halstead. My mother..." I wrung my hands as if to assuage the painful memory of her spidery script and its damning revelation. "Oh, Miles! My mother was *happy* on St. John Street. Why did you tell me she was 'pure of heart'? Why did you let me believe she was a lady?"

He moved his teacup aside. "Carmella, because she was happy as a—a courtesan doesn't mean she could not have been a lady."

"Miles! You're splitting hairs. You know it!"

"All right," he sighed. "I said what I did because I saw no reason to disillusion you."

"Then tell me—what was she *really* like?"

"I told you I knew her only briefly."

"Was she silly? Childish? Shallow?" I persisted.

"Carmella..." He got up from his chair and went to the sideboard, where he stood for a few moments as if searching for something. Then he turned. "Carmella—what's the use of all this? She's dead, poor soul. If she had lived, perhaps she would have made a wonderful mother, happier in her role than she could have possibly been on St. John Street."

"Perhaps," I echoed bitterly.

"Look at it this way. Do you remember Mrs. Porter and her little girl, Sarah? She refused to leave that lonely stretch of land, but stayed on to search for her daughter, probably forfeiting her life in the process. In a sense your mother did the same. She died giving birth to you."

"My mother had no choice."

"If she had had one, how can you be sure she would not have made it in your favor?"

"I—don't know."

His eyes held mine and I read compassion in them. A sudden hope, a wish to make things right between us, prompted me to say:

"Miles—about Derry. It's—I'm through with him."

The soft light in his gaze went out like a pinched candle flame. "Are you?"

Did he believe me? Was he going to make it difficult?

"Yes, I—"

Jane Bainbridge, opening the door, interrupted me. "The Carys are here," she said, "and are asking for you."

After that I seemed unable to find the courage to meet Miles's skeptical eyes and explain about Derry. Time, I promised myself, would mellow Miles. I must give him time to heal the wounds of war, and the right moment for explanations would come of itself.

General Robert E. Lee surrendered at Appomattox on April 10th, ending the long war that had torn the country asunder and devastated Virginia. But we at the Bainbridge house had a more personal tragedy to contend with. Ruth had taken a turn for the worse and was sinking rapidly.

She had held on for so long, had made such a gallant fight, I had come to believe—as we all had—that she simply would not die. And when Alex Harkness stumped down the stairs early on that April morning with a worried look, saying, "I must fetch the doctor," I still could not bring myself to face the seriousness of the situation.

"I'll sit by her," I offered.

I crossed the room and sat down beside her, afraid to speak, afraid my voice would betray me. She was suffering and I ought to be glad that it would soon be over, but I couldn't be glad. I was too selfish, too concerned with my own distress. Like those self-indulgent diehards who, even at Richmond's last gasp, even as Lee was withdrawing his dwindling army and making his last stand at Sayler's Creek below Appomattox, had urged him to go on fighting, I wanted Ruth to go on living.

"Ruth . . . ?"

Her eyes focused vaguely on me.

"It's Carmella."

A small struggle seemed to be taking place behind those soft, hazy eyes. She frowned, and then, "Ahhh, Carmella." Her voice was like the faint whispering of dry cornstalks.

"It's me, Ruth dear." I took her hand, as weightless as an autumn leaf. "I'm here. Is there anything you want?"

"No."

Don't go! I wanted to beg. *Please, please—I couldn't bear it!*

"Carmella . . ."

"Don't talk if it hurts, darling."

She closed her eyes and was silent for a long moment. Her lids fluttered open. "Carmella—you—you shouldn't—you shouldn't have gone to bed with that Yankee. For—me. It wasn't right."

"Oh, Ruth!"

"You are not to blame—you—are brave, brave—all my fault."

"Ruth, please . . ." I was mortally afraid of breaking down, of sobbing wildly. I wanted so desperately to weep, but I knew it would distress her.

"Carmella—there is something—you—Miles . . ."

Her eyes closed and I could see her lips moving as she struggled for words.

"Don't talk now. Please, darling, try to rest."

I sat there holding her hand, and soon I noticed that the small pulse at the base of her throat was still, that the covers no longer rose and fell with the movement of her chest.

She was dead.

"No, no, *no*, not yet!" I whispered. I hadn't told her I loved her, I hadn't told her that she had been the only true friend I'd ever had. I hadn't told her—oh, so many things.

I was still sitting beside her, dry eyed, holding her hand,

when Alex Harkness and Dr. Gordon arrived.

"She—she's gone?" Alex asked, his voice breaking.

I nodded mutely, my throat tight.

He fell to his knees beside her and burying his face in her chest began to sob, his shoulders heaving convulsively, his hands slutching the bedclothes. I had never seen a man cry, and it tore me apart. The tears I had not allowed myself to shed earlier filled my eyes and coursed down my cheeks, and with a choking gasp I fled from the room.

We buried her in Hollywood Cemetery, where we had laid Alice to rest the week before. A half dozen funerals were taking place at the same time, for war's end had not healed the wounded in the hospitals nor put food in the mouths of the starving, and many died daily. It was a depressing sight; black crepe and wreathed coffins and weeping mourners all, like myself, consumed with grief.

Prudence, who had been staying with Lavinia since before the fall of Richmond, attended the last rites and afterward, together with Lavinia, came on to the Bainbridges for a simple repast. Though pretending to grieve for Ruth, Prudence could not hide her joy at seeing Miles. She embraced him, wept a little. Under the circumstances such behavior did not seem forward or out of place. We all embraced one another; we all wept. But I knew how Prudence felt about Miles, and as she gazed at him with tear-lashed eyes, smiling sadly with a helpless, "Oh, me!" look, I felt like grabbing a pickle fork from the supper table and stabbing her with it. I was ashamed of my jealousy, but not ashamed enough to feel differently. Prudence stuck to Miles's side like a limpet, and he did not seem to mind. I wondered if he was telling her the things he had not told me. I wondered if he was confiding in her. As Jane chatted with me, my ears were primed for a stray remark between those two. But all I heard was Prudence saying, "I would be so grateful if you would help me. Now that Hubert is gone . . ."

Yes, Hubert had died in a Yankee prison, and now she was a widow, an appealing, attractive (to give the bitch her due) widow, looking for a new husband, a new father for her children. She would be a compliant wife, dutiful, disciplined, eventempered, the way Southern women had been taught to behave toward their spouses. She would never lose her temper with him (as she did with me), never throw things or strike him (as I had done with him). Perhaps that was what Miles wanted in a woman these days. After the turmoil of the last four years, he might welcome domestic peace and tranquillity.

The more I thought of it, the more miserable I became. If Miles asked for a divorce I was honor-bound to give it to him.

Instead, he said to me one afternoon, "Carmella, you and I should sort out our differences and come to some conclusion about our situation. But my first priority is getting my brother's family settled. I must return to Wildoak and see what has to be done. I could use your help, but if you prefer staying on in Richmond—"

"No, not at all," I interrupted hurriedly. "I will be happy to do whatever I can."

It was the first time Miles had ever remotely suggested that I could be of use to him, and it cheered me. But not much. I knew what he meant by "our situation."

In August, Deirdre, little Page, Miles, and I went back to Wildoak. The house was still standing, but vandals and looters had left the inside a shambles. The fields had gone to wild; the orchard, woods, and fences reduced to splintered stumps and sawdust. Beth Ann came up from Danville only to collect whatever personal belongings she could salvage. She and the two girls were going on to South Carolina to join her kinfolk. She didn't want Wildoak. She asked Miles to sell it.

"My dear Beth Ann," he said, "do you realize how little land is going for now? You forget that Virginia bore the brunt of this war; the countryside is in ruins. On the other hand, if you wait a few years—"

"I don't want to wait. I want to sell it now. I want to go home."

Deirdre spoke up. "You can't sell it. I refuse to go to South Carolina. Besides, Wildoak will be Page's someday."

"Wildoak is mine now,-' Beth Ann retorted, flushing. "Your father left it to me. If I want to sell it, I will."

Deirdre's eyes blazed. "You can't sell my son's inheritance. I won't let you!"

"Why, you impertinent—"

Miles interrupted. "Stop! For God's sake! Let's look at this thing sensibly. Deirdre, even if your mother, out of the kindness of her heart, gave you Wildoak, what could you do with it? You have no money—or very little. I don't suppose old Beasley left you much. Do you realize what it would take to repair the damage, to make the house livable, to say nothing of clearing the fields, putting in a crop? What would you live on, how would you eat?"

"I don't know," she said. "But I'd find a way."

"Brave talk won't buy seed."

"It's a rotten shame to see Wildoak go out of the family. Mama doesn't care, but I do!"

Miles looked at her, a glint of admiration in his eyes. I had to admire her myself. How could such a gritty female to be the offspring of a powder puff like Beth Ann?

"Tell you what," Miles said. "I'll buy it. I'll give you a good price, Beth Ann. In that way the plantation will remain in Falconer hands, and if Page, when he comes of age, wants it, then perhaps we can work something out. I've always had a mind to try my hand at being a planter."

It was an undertaking that absorbed Miles all through the winter and into the spring. He hired all of Wildoak's former slaves who had wandered back, paid them decent wages rather than taking them on as sharecroppers as other planters who were impoverished and without funds had been forced to do. Miles had the cabins and sheds rebuilt; then he had the fields plowed and planted, some in tobacco, some in peanuts and truck vegetables, for according to his theory a one-crop farming operation was a bad gamble.

The house was my domain. Miles wanted it completely refurbished. He sent for catalogues, and Deirdre and I spent days going over them, chooseing new beds, bureaus, sofas, tables, chairs, and draperies.

"What this must be costing Uncle Miles," Deirdre said one afternoon as we debated over several carpets. "Is he so wealthy?"

"I don't honestly know. But he did say that except for the loss of some silver stock, the money he left in San Francisco grew more than he had anticipated."

(I had to blush even now when I thought of how I had once suspected him of defrauding me. Thank goodness I had told no one.)

"It must be wonderful to spend what you like without a care for the expense," Deirdre said with unabashed envy.

During the past few months Deirdre and I had become friends. It hadn't happened overnight, but gradually, little Page having been the first link between us. Seeing how the child she loved so fiercely had cottoned to me (and I to him), Deirdre could not help but look at me in a new and more favorable light. Soon the last of her bitterness faded and there were moments when we came close to real intimacy.

One evening as we were leafing through a new catalogue, she stopped at the pictured display of canes and snuffboxes.

"Reminds me of Beasley," she said. "How I hated that awful snuff—his yellow-stained fingers, the way he would sneeze."

"It wasn't a happy time for you, was it?"

She shook her head. "You see," she went on after a moment, her eyes suddenly misting over, "whatever you and Ruth thought, I really did love Harry Page. And that made it so much harder."

"But we couldn't let you have the baby without a husband."

"I realize that now. My child has a name, and truly, Carmella," she put her hand over mine, "I understand you did the best you could."

She looked back at the catalogue, hesitated for a moment, and turned the page. "I still think of Harry. I know you won't believe this, but he was *kind*—and he made me laugh—he said he wanted to marry me, but . . . He didn't fight very hard when you sent him away, did he?"

"No. Perhaps if he had known about the baby, he would have behaved differently. But then he knew he wasn't liked at Wildoak. He might have felt that *you* would never marry him."

"Oh, well," she sighed. "But I *am* grateful to him for little Page."

Ruth—may God bless her memory—had been right about Deirdre. Beneath the tough and sometimes contentious exterior, the girl had a vulnerable heart. Deirdre once told me that the only way to survive disaster was to shake a fist at it. Perhaps she was right.

In the meanwhile, we busied ourselves with choices and decisions. Should we have a rococo Bohemian suite, or would the Empire sofa look better in the parlor? And what about an étagère, some chinoiserie?

Miles also allowed us to order whatever clothes struck our fancy, and we did—although God knew there was no place to wear the gowns that came weeks later wrapped in crackling paper and nested in wooden crates. The grand houses that had not been burned lay empty for the most part. But we wore our new dresses just the same, using any excuse, even if it was only a drummer selling farm implements who sat down with us to supper.

Miles approved of our taste. Apparently he had lost the need to mock and jeer at me, for he became kind and unerringly polite. Sometimes, in a perverse way, I wished he would suddenly flare up in the old passionate anger instead of presenting this cool fascade of courteous indifference. It was so out of character I felt as though I was living with a stranger. On rare occasions I would catch him watching me, an anticipatory look in his eyes as if expecting me to speak. And I tried—I tried. But somehow a shutter would come down and I would feel helpless and baffled before it. What was Miles thinking? Was he waiting, in gentlemanly fashion, for me to bring up the question of divorce? But I could never ask. I was afraid.

Only once did he really get angry with me, and on that night he was drunk. He had just come home from a four-day stay in Richmond, where he had conferred with brokers about the coming tobacco crop. I had already gone to bed and was deep in sleep when the sound of a striking match and the clinking of the glass lamp's chimney as it was lifted woke me.

"What time is it?" I asked sleepily, blinking in the light.

"One o'clock."

He reeked of brandy fumes and his tone had the curt edge of someone who has drunk overmuch and is determined not to show it.

"You rode back in the dark?" I asked.

"There's a full moon." A short pause. "I had several unpleasant things on my mind, I felt I ought to air."

I pushed myself up on an elbow. "What do you mean?" I asked, my mouth suddenly gone dry.

"It seems your hardships during the war were not quite as grim as you made out."

"I—don't know what you are talking about."

"Don't you?" He moved toward me, his shadow, huge and

grotesque, following him on the walls and the ceiling. "Can't you guess?" He leaned down and grasping the front of my nightgown pulled me up to where my face was within inches of his. "Perhaps I can refresh your memory. I am talking about the Yankee who shared my bed. Was it this one?"

I went cold. "Who told you?" I whispered.

He didn't answer. But I could feel rage in the way his arm shook as he clutched me.

"Prudence," I said. He let go of me. "I might have known it. She hates me so, she's jealous, she wants you. And she told you, conveniently forgetting, I suppose, the circumstances."

"I know the circumstances. I am well aware of your—er—ah, *sacrifice.*"

"But you don't believe it was a sacrifice."

He stood over me, his eyes slightly bloodshot, staring at me, and a small chill crept up my spine.

"Jane Bainbridge claimed it was," he said finally. "But that's not the point." He leaned down again and brought me up by the armpits. "Tell me," he said in a low, fierce voice, his alcoholic breath hot on my turned-away cheek. "Did you enjoy it?"

My hand flew up and caught him across the face in a resounding slap. I saw his eyes go black, and then he crushed me against his chest, his mouth coming down on mine in a hard, bruising kiss. No, not a kiss; this was more like a blow than a kiss. I struggled to free myself, but he held me so tightly I could do no more than squirm impotently.

When he finally released me, I was so furious I hit him again.

Then he was on top of me, tearing the gown from my body with angry hands, burying his face in my breasts as he sank his teeth into the tender flesh above the nipple. I bit my lip to keep from screaming, raking my nails down the bunched muscles of his back.

He lifted his head and gripped my chin, looking down into my eyes as if he could dissect me. Then he kissed me again, a hurting, violent kiss, savagely ravishing my bruised and swollen lips. I had wanted this, hadn't I? Hadn't I wished for his polite indifference to turn to passion? But not this brutal, animal assault.

When he parted my legs with a swift jab of his knee, a sob escaped my throat. He must have heard it, for he paused, leaning over me, his arms trembling. Then he moved away, falling heavily on the pillow by my side. He said nothing, but I could hear his hard breathing slowly return to normal. I wanted him, but in love, not in anger. And it seemed to my lying there in the dark that it would never be possible, that Miles would never respond to my yearning. He had married and taken care of me because he loved my father, not me. I was a convenience to him occasionally, an object of his wrath at other times. It was hopeless. The tears brimmed and ran hotly down my cheeks.

"You're crying," he said into the dark.

I shook my head. "No," I said, a weak tremulous no.

Silently he turned toward me, taking me in his arms. And though I tried not to, I found myself sobbing against his bare chest.

He didn't say he was sorry, he didn't say anything, just held me, gently stroking my hair, and his gentleness made me cry all the more. Gradually my weeping abated until I lay wet-faced quietly against him. He kissed the top of my head, lifting my face, wiping the tears away with the edge of the bed sheet.

"Poor child—I do take after you."

It was kindly, but I did not want to be his child. I wanted to be his woman. Yet somehow I could not tell him. And when he began to make love to me, to kiss and stroke me, this time with practiced hands and mouth to give me pleasure, my flesh responded to his and I soon could say nothing at all. He took me twice that night and it seemed to me that although he was no longer angry or drunk and the sexual desire was there—he was a man after all—his feelings toward me were mainly those of compassion.

And my pride, like his, resented it. I did not want him to feel sorry for me.

CHAPTER

THIRTY-THREE

*S*HORTLY AFTER this episode I noticed that Miles had grown restless. Having recently hired an overseer—a manager as they were now called—a Mr. Lester, highly recommended for his agricultural proficiency, Miles left the running of Wildoak in his capable hands. But his restlessness did not seem to stem from boredom. He had something of grave import on his mind. I had seen the same signs—pacing the library floor far into the night, trails of cigar ash on the carpet, the preoccupied air—before he had arrived at the decision to return to Virginia. What was he pondering now? Marriage—divorce? If so, he said nothing and I formed the odd notion that if I didn't mention the matter it would go away. I hoped that in time Miles would sense how my feelings toward him had changed, and perhaps—oh, a long hopeful perhaps—his would change too. And there were moments in bed when—ah, but they passed without bringing us any closer.

He made frequent trips to Richmond now, for business reasons, he said—but I wondered. Prudence and the children (who had rejoined her) were in Richmond, living with the Carys. Miles casually spoke of trying to find a buyer for her property. Of course he and Prudence would be seeing one another under those circumstances.

I tried not to let it bother me, but the thought of Prudence fluttering her eyelids at Miles, and of him smiling down at her, gnawed at me. In my fantasies I would see the two of them with their heads together, speaking in low tones, and later his lips on hers, his arms holding her, and the picture would drive me into despair. One August evening when he announced that he would be leaving for Richmond the following day I asked him to take me. He seemed surprised by my request.

"Do you really want to go? It's hot, more so in the city than it is here."

His attempt to put me off seemed to confirm my suspicions. "I should like to go in any case, Miles. That is, if you don't mind?"

He shrugged. "Why should I?"

But he was right. Richmond was steaming and I had been there only a few hours when I began to feel out of sorts. We were staying with the Bainbridges, and Jane, delighted to have me, began at once to plan the week, filling it with social engagements, a dinner in our honor, a musicale, and a shopping expedition.

"A good many of the commercial establishments have been rebuilt," she said on the second day of our visit. "Quite attractive. Very modern. Perhaps the old ones should have burned down long ago. You'll see what I mean this afternoon."

I hated to spoil her pleasure by pleading a headache and queasy stomach, so I went along with her. Soon I felt much worse, my nausea, my tight stays, and the heat combining to make me long to lie down in some cool spot. Determined to see the ordeal through, I said nothing.

"The milliner," Jane said as the carriage stopped in front of a bay-windowed store. "Elaine's has the smartest hats!"

I hardly got my foot inside when everything turned black.

The next thing I knew I was lying on a sofa in the back room and Jane was fanning my face.

"Why didn't you say you were ill?"

"It's just something I ate," I said. "I'm sorry. I didn't mean to faint."

"You look very green about the gills. You'd better rest where you are for a spell. How long have you been feeling this way?"

"Only since—since yesterday."

"You haven't—you don't think you might be"—she lowered her voice—"expecting a child?"

"No, no, I don't think so."

"When did you last . . . ? You know."

We woman never spoke aloud of our intimate monthly functions. I creased my brow trying to remember. "Why, I believe it must have been—I really can't say. Yes, I can. Five or six weeks ago," I said with some surprise.

She nodded. "I'm taking you to see Dr. Gordon."

I was pregnant. The doctor confirmed it. The news had a strange effect on me. I alternated between a sort of pleased wonder and fear—wonder because the idea was not at all repugnant to me, fear because I did not know how Miles would react. Would he be happy? Or would he feel trapped? Trapped, I thought. His restless discontent these past weeks had been obvious.

As Jane and I clattered through the streets back to the Bainbridge house, I swore her to secrecy. "You must not tell a soul. I'll let Miles know in my own good time."

"Of course, my dear. It is always best when a husband hears such happy tidings from his own wife."

I fully intended to tell Miles, but somehow—once more—the right moment never came. He was busy in Richmond and preoccupied on the ride back to Wildoak.

Once at home we never seemed to be alone long enough for me to speak to him. In the evenings he would stay late over his papers in the library, a bottle of brandy and a smoking cigar at his elbow. I would lie awake upstairs for hours, waiting for his step on the stair, rehearsing over and over again how I would break the news. When he finally came in, I was either asleep or struck mute by his cold silence.

A week after we had returned from Richmond we had visitors, the Carys, Lavinia, and the elderly lawyer Mr. Gan (the same one who had read Miles's will), whom Lavinia had known as a girl and recently married. The group also included Derry Wakefield. They were traveling to West Point to attend Lavinia's son's wedding and put up at our house for the night. I was always glad to have people stop at Wildoak. It gave us a chance to be hospitable and relieved the strained silences that had grown longer at the supper table. But I would have been happier if Derry had not come.

He looked well, dashingly handsome as usual, dressed in the height of fashion, a high-necked waistcoat of silk serge and a jacket with a black velvet collar.

He smiled frequently at me during the meal, addressing me as "my dear Mrs. Falconer." But his smile, his voice, and his warm glances did not raise a single heartbeat or instill a single regret. I could look at him coolly now, without passion or longing, and I wondered how someone so obviously shallow could have ever filled me with such ardor.

After supper the men remained in the dining room drinking brandy and smoking cigars and we women adjourned to the parlor. A half hour later Lavinia, pleading the need for an early start in the morning, went up to bed. Elaine Cary followed her a few minutes later, and Deirdre, yawning loudly, said she guessed she'd go to bed too. I was dousing the lamps when the door opened on silent, oiled hinges.

Derry stood on the threshold. "Carmella . . . ? Are you alone?"

"Yes. What is it?" I asked sharply.

He closed the door, clicking it shut with careful hands, then turned and came toward me.

"I was hoping I would have the chance to speak to you alone. Carmella—what a fool I was to let you go."

He held out his arms, but I ignored them. "I have nothing to say to you, Derry. It's all been said. Now, if you'll get out of my way."

"You can't dismiss me so lightly—not after what we've been to one another. I'm sorry I behaved so badly that last afternoon. I've tried to forget you, but I can't. You're the only woman who has ever mattered. Say you'll forgive me. You can't just stop loving me . . ."

"Oh, but I can. I did."

"I don't believe it! Carmella . . ."

He reached for me and before I could elude his grasp he pulled me into his arms. Then, as suddenly, he let go, his eyes staring in surprise over my shoulder. Turning I saw Miles standing in the doorway.

"A pretty scene," he said mockingly. "I suppose as the offended husband I should give the ritual slap on the cheek and challenge you to a duel, Mr. Wakefield. But I feel we would be grossly mismatched. I fight men, not boys."

"Miles—let me explain," I pleaded.

"I see no reason to," he said shortly, and turning on his heel left.

Miles did not come to bed that night; and after the guests left the next day, he had his horse saddled and rode off. It was evening before he returned.

The two of us sat down to supper without Deirdre. She and Page were visiting our new neighbors at the Harkness place. For the first time in weeks Miles and I were alone.

"About yesterday . . ." I began, breaking a long silence. He was sitting at the head of the table, I, at—what seemed ten miles distant—the foot. "Derry forced his attentions on me after I told him—"

"I'm sure you did, Carmella. It doesn't matter."

"Oh, but it *does* matter! You see—"

The butler interrupted, asking if he could clear the cloth for dessert.

"Yes, please do," Miles said. "Bring the brandy, if you will. Forget the dessert. Unless . . . ?" His eyes questioned me.

"Brandy will be fine."

"You're looking rather under the weather these days," he commented. "I meant to mention it. Beastly hot. Oh, thank you, Mason. We'll be all right. I'll call if we need you."

He turned back to me. "You were saying . . . ?"

I had been poised on the brink, ready to tell him about the child, but the words suddenly died on my tongue. "Yesterday—when Derry . . ."

"Yes. Well perhaps what I have to say will have some bearing on the subject."

He poured the brandy and came down to my end of the table, giving me the glass. Then he sat down next to me.

"Wildoak has begun to pall. Perhaps you've already noticed. I'm not much of a farmer. It was intriguing when I started; it was a dare. The place was practically a wilderness and I felt I owed it to the family—to Harold—to get the plantation back on its feet. It's on the way now. Lester is a good man. And someday when Page gets older he might want to take over. But it's not for me. I've grown out of it. I'm basically a city man." He sipped at his brandy.

I held my glass, not touching it, feeling cold and frightened.

"I'm going back to San Francisco. I belong there, not here. I'll get Lavinia Hastings and her new husband to move in with Deirdre. I think she will be all right."

"Yes, I think so." I had expected this, Miles wanting a change. Why then did I feel as though the bottom had dropped out of the world?

"When I came back from the war, I thought you and I might . . . But I realize now it couldn't work. I know you haven't been happy with me, Carmella. Ever since our marriage— not the most ideal, was it?—I have felt you chafing at the bit."

Oh, but I haven't been, I longed to say, to shout, but something in his manner, something in his eyes stopped me.

"As you can see, I am making a choice," he went on. "I give you yours. Do you wish to return to San Francisco with me or would you prefer staying on in Richmond?"

"Miles, I thought—"

"In San Francisco I can let you go. It will be easier there to arrange for a divorce, which I know you've wanted from the start. Your investments are paying well, and I of course shall supplement them, so you need not have any concern on that score."

"But Miles . . ." I fought against the tightness in my throat. "Miles—"

"I'll do it so that no scandal attatches to your name. Desertion and adultery on my part, I believe, are reasonable grounds. I think I can manage that without difficulty. Then, at least, you will be free, my dear, free to marry Derry."

"No!" I cried, stung. "Oh, no! Not Derry!"

He leaned back in his chair and surveyed me coolly. "I must say that surprises me. You don't want Derry? I know you once said something about 'it' being over, but when I say you two last night . . . Well, well! Will wonders never cease? You mean that all-consuming passion, that deathless love I could never understand—"

"Don't jeer, Miles! For God's sake don't jeer!"

Damn him! He didn't care. He would never care. He wanted to be rid of me. Perhaps it was he who wanted to marry again. Yes, yes, that was it—the restlessness, the frequent visits to Richmond. He would divorce me in San Francisco, then send for Prudence.

"All right, I shan't rub it in. But you do want the divorce, don't you? You are still young, very attractive—if not Derry, I imagine you could have your pick of suitors. Am I right?"

"Certainly," I said, lifting my glass with false nonchalance. I would die now rather than let him think I wanted him. I couldn't, I wouldn't tell him about the child. No, let him believe I was as eager to get out of the marriage as he. "It will be lovely going to balls and parties, being courted by handsome young men once more."

An odd look, one I could not define, flitted across his face, before it smoothed out into its usual imperturbable lines.

"Good. I shall proceed at once to arrange for our transportation. You are probably aware that the building of a transcontinental railroad is under way—the Union Pacific going west to meet with the Central Pacific from California somewhere in Utah. I'd like us to take the Union line to the last railhead and from there we can finish our journey by overland coach. Does that suit you?"

"Anything that is fairly comfortable and won't take too long."

"In that much of a hurry, eh? Then you won't mind getting ready, say, in ten days?"

"That suits me admirably."

It was a tiresome journey, for we were constantly changing trains and putting up overnight at hotels along the way, unpacking and packing, trudging out in the morning to yet another depot, another train. By the time we reached Grand Island, Nebraska, I was feeling out of sorts, my general malaise compounded by a cold I had caught while touring the Union Pacific roundhouses in Omaha on a wet day. I was worried about the baby. It had already made its presence known by a tiny fluttering rap on the side of my stomach, and I prayed no harm would come to it. More and more, that small bit of life took hold of my heart—the wonder that I would soon have a little one of my own to love and care for helping me face each bitter day. I understood Deirdre's fierce protectiveness. Whatever else happened, the child must come through this ordeal safely. It was mine and I wanted it with a will that pitted me against the despair that threatened to drag me down.

The railhead was now a few miles beyond Fort Kearney, our next and last stop. From there we would take the coach on its long jolting ride over the Rockies, a crossing I looked forward to with apprehension. Fortunately, we were delayed at Grand Island for a few days—some trouble with the Cheyennes, who had massacred a train crew and torn up a length of track—and I had the opportunity to rest. The hotel in which we stayed had surprisingly comfortable and clean accommodations for a town that had grown up around the hurly-burly of a railroad in the making.

My cough, however, hung on, and Miles, having met a physician in the lounge one morning, insisted I see him.

"I don't understand why you're so concerned," I said irritably.

"If you came down with pneumonia in the middle of the Wyoming wilds, I wouldn't know what to do. Best to scotch anything like that now."

The doctor, a thin, anxious young man, gave me an examination that I thought was a little lengthy for the minor ailment involved. Afterwards he said he would prescribe a cough medicine, and that I was not to worry. Then he went out to the anteroom and I heard him repeat the same to Miles.

"I think she will be all right," he said. "The cough is nothing. But I would consider twice before taking her on the stagecoach, although some women in her condition manage tolerably well."

"What condition?" Miles said.

"Why, Mr. Falconer, I am sure you are aware that your wife is expecting?"

There was a short silence, then Miles said, "Of course. I thought perhaps you meant the cough."

"Not at all."

They moved away still talking.

Suddenly I wished I had a drink. Brandy, even whiskey, something bracing, for I didn't know how I was going to face Miles. Would he be angry, abusive, jeering? Certainly he would not welcome the news, for it would put a hitch in his plans. Oh, damn that meddling doctor!

The outer door closed and I strained my ears to hear, then breathed a sigh of relief, thinking that Miles had gone out with the doctor. But a moment later I saw his shadow in the doorway and my hands turned cold.

He came in. "Why didn't you tell me?"

I tried to read his face, but I could see nothing except perhaps irritation.

"I didn't see why I should."

He didn't accuse me. He didn't ask or even suggest that the child might not be his, but why should he? Except for his brief visit to Wildoak, I hadn't seen Derry since the end of the war, and he knew there had been no other man I had the slightest interest in.

"This baby," I went on, "will make no difference in our plans, if that's what worries you."

"Do I look worried?" he asked lightly, lifting a brow. "Are you?"

"No," I lied. "I—I shall give it up for adoption."

The words rang hollowly in my ears. Give it up? The thought made me shudder. I would kill myself first. This child would be all I would have of Miles. Perhaps it would look like him, dark with bold hazel eyes, a boy growing up tall, prideful, and handsome. Or a girl with fine sculptured features and Deirdre Falconer's poise.

"I take it you don't want it, then?"

"Yes."

He shrugged. "Do you feel up to finishing the trip?"

"Why not?"

"You might lose it."

"Then that would solve everything, wouldn't it?"

The cruelty of those false words struck me with a superstitious chill. Oh, why didn't he leave me alone so I could crawl under the covers and sob my heart out as I so desperately wanted to do?

"Suit yourself." He started for the door. "By the way," he said over his shoulder. "I may be late this evening, so don't wait up for me."

He did not return until the early morning, and when he did he bedded down in a chair in the anteroom. At nine o'clock I got up and dressed and yet he slept, his legs sprawled across the carpet, his chin resting on his chest. He looked haggard though he did not smell of whiskey. I went down to the dining hall for breakfast, taking a long, leisurely one, hoping he would be up and gone from our room by the time I finished. Finally I was the only guest left at the tables, and when the waiters hovering on the edge near the kitchen threw me impatient glances I rose and went upstairs.

Cracking the door open I peered in. Miles was still there, awake, sitting with his face in his hands. As I stood watching him, he lifted his head and I drew in my breath. Rarely had I seen a sadder, more dispirited countenance. It was not like Miles. I had known him calm, angry, cool, mocking, indifferent, tired, even exhausted, but I had not seen him this unhappy since the dark days of the war. His shoulders sagged; he looked wretched, his eyes shadowed with a deep melancholy. Perhaps he had received bad news, an investment gone sour. No. That might distress him, but nothing financial would make Miles grieve. Perhaps he had been thinking of past battles, recalling Harold's death, or that of a comrade who had been close to him.

I wanted to reach out and touch him, to brush the hair from his brow, to erase that look from his eyes. I loved him, no matter how he felt about me, and it broke my heart to see him so miserable.

I opened the door. He looked up and as he did so a mask descended, wooden and without expression. But I was not going to be fooled by that mask again. Something was troubling him. What difference did it make if I humbled myself? My prickly vanity suddenly seemed pretentious and hollow.

"Miles, there's something wrong. What is it?"

"What a notion! Nothing is wrong."

Of course he wouldn't tell me.

I hesitated, my courage faltering. Then I noticed that his hands on the arms of the chair were balled into white-knuckled fists as if he were fighting for control.

"Miles . . ." I sank to my knees before him. "I have a confession to make."

His eyes widened slightly but he said nothing.

"I—I lied to you."

He did not ask why or what.

Swallowing, I went on: "I want the child—our child. I

shan't give it away, I—I never meant to. I've wanted it from the first moment I knew. But—but I couldn't tell you—you see, when you talked about divorce—I couldn't tell you. I was afraid you might feel trapped. No, Miles, wait—let me finish before I lose my nerve. There's more. I—I love you. I think I must have loved you a long time without realizing it. Derry— oh, God, when I think of it—such a silly fancy. I realized that two years ago. I saw he was—well, nothing. So you see . . ."

My eyes fell before his, now burning with a scorching light.

"Don't be angry, Miles," I whispered. "If you still want a divorce, I won't stand in your way."

He did not speak. Not a word. And his silence filled my breast with a sense of heavy failure. Perhaps I had made a mistake in telling him. Confession is supposed to be good for the soul, but I didn't feel any better, only worse. He didn't want me. With my talk of love I had succeeded only in complicating matters for him. I was a burden to him—for Miles, despite my calling him a cad and a brute, had a strong sense of honor. He would never abandon me, but keep and care for me even though I should be a millstone around his neck.

"I've never been a good wife to you," I went on, still not able to look him in the eye. "And I can't blame you for wanting the marriage ended."

"Carmella—"

"No, Miles." I lifted my head. "I would rather die than have us go on living together, with you tolerating me out of pity. Leave me that much pride. It would be—"

"Stop!" he said suddenly with a frown.

"Miles, I . . ."

Reaching down he lifted me onto his lap.

"Miles . . ."

"Hush! You always did talk too much." He tucked a stray strand of hair behind my ear. Then his arms went around me and he kissed me long and lingeringly, a lovely, beautiful, tender kiss that astonished and delighted me.

"Miles . . . ," I tried once more, my eyes moist with burning tears.

He put his finger to my lips. "Hush! Why do you insist on putting words in my mouth? What do you know about me? I never wanted the damn divorce. I thought you did. I thought

you stayed with me out of a sense of duty—my sufferings
during the war and all that sort of rot. I thought you were pining
to be free, to go off with Derry."

"I told you and I meant it, that Derry—"

"We won't speak his name. Never, ever again. But tell me
again, say it."

"I love you, I love you," I repeated, a happy sob catching
in my throat. "And—you . . . ?"

He hugged me tightly. "I think I've loved you ever since
that day I looked up from Kate Halstead's piano and saw you
standing there with her beside the red portieres. Remember?"

"Oh, Miles, why didn't you ever say so? Why didn't you
tell me?"

He drew me close, kissing me again, resting my head under
his chin, stroking my hair as he spoke. "You looked so like
your mother it took my breath away. I had formed a schoolboy's
secret desire for her years earlier. I was only eighteen—and
there you were bringing it all back. I felt so ashamed when I
found out you were Arthur's girl—you were so young. And
after Aspinwall—how I hated myself! I vowed to keep you at
a distance."

"So that's why you were always so caustic. In self-defense,
you once told me."

He laughed. "Yes, my darling. I had to fight so hard against
my feelings. But my attempt to put a curb on them fell completely apart on that hill in Mexico. Do you recall when I picked
you up from the ground and wrapped my coat about your
shoulders? You didn't weep, you didn't go into hysterics or
swoon like every other woman I've known might have done.
You just looked at me out of those dark blue velvety eyes and
in them I saw a girl of strength and courage, a woman a man
would be proud to love."

"Why didn't you tell me then?"

"Because by that time there was a certain gentleman—
whose name we decided not to mention—in your life. And
you could see no one but him. I was so jealous I could have
killed him. Whenever I thought I had come to a point where
I might let you know how I felt, you would say something
about him, how much you loved him. It angered me so, and
I suppose I took it out on you. It was insane but—"

I pressed my fingers to his mouth. "Please, darling, it was all my fault. What a fool I've been!"

"No more than I."

I looked into his eyes for one long moment, and then we both laughed.

We stayed the winter in Grand Island. Our daughter was born there, the first Falconer in more than a century to see the light of day outside Virginia, a girl we named Sabrina.

"Are you sorry it's not a boy?" I asked, as we stood together looking down at her fast asleep in her wicker basket.

"How can I be sorry when she's so beautiful?" Miles said, putting his arm about my waist, drawing me close. "Let us have no regrets, Mrs. Falconer. There will be time enough for boys."

And his kiss told me it would be so.